THE
VOICE

THE VOICE

A Novel of the New World Order

Michael Youssef

Thomas Nelson Publishers
Nashville

Published in Nashville, Tennessee, by Thomas Nelson, Inc., and
distributed in Canada by Lawson Falle, Ltd., Cambridge, Ontario.

Library of Congress Cataloging-in-Publication Data

Youssef, Michael.
   [Mastermind]
   The voice : a novel of the new world order / Michael Youssef.
     p.   cm.
   Originally published: Mastermind. c1989.
   ISBN 0-8407-3354-2 (pbk.)
   I. Title.
PS3575.065M3   1991
813'.54—dc20   91–26653
                                        CIP

Printed in the United States of America

1 2 3 4 5 6 7 — 96 95 94 93 92 91

To the congregation of the Church of the Apostles,
Atlanta, Georgia, faithful and true.

O·N·E

The Voice spoke again.

Tremors of fear, excitement, and confusion coursed through P. K. Sari's body as he listened to the instructions. As an Indian, he grew up believing in spirits and the spirit world, but this was a new experience. For almost a year this strange Voice had been speaking, guiding his activities, taking more and more control. For the past six days, The Voice had scarcely stopped speaking during Sari's every moment awake. Only in sleep did he find peace.

At times the East Indian tried not to listen; he hummed or chanted, but such diversions made no difference. The Voice persisted, coming from inside his head. Yet Sari knew the source was not from within himself. "I do not know what to do," he said aloud. "I do not know how you came into my head, and you leave me most thoroughly confused."

"You have not chosen me," The Voice said, "but I have chosen you. And because I have chosen you, I will also lead you."

"Yes, yes . . . let it be so," Sari said, weariness evident in his tone. "I can no longer fight you. I shall go mad if I do not listen."

"Do not be afraid. I shall reward you for obedience. Happy are those who obey me!"

The Indian dropped to his knees, no longer choosing to struggle against the power of The Voice.

P. K. Sari, a member of the Brahman or priestly caste, would not have been noticed in a crowd of Westerners; typical of those of Aryan descent, he had a small frame, light-brown skin, a thin nose, and straight black hair. Only a decidedly nervous twitch in his lower lip distinguished him. "This is insane," he muttered. "Quite insane. Who will believe me?"

"I believe you," said The Voice. "Now you must believe me."

If only he had someone to confide in, someone he could trust. But who? And each time he asked himself the question, Sari received the same answer: no one.

Before he reached the age of fifteen, Sari had moved away from the practices of the Hindu religion of his ancestors, making him a virtual outcast in his own city. Later, although he had done well in business, especially since The Voice had come into his life, everyone continued to shun personal involvement with him. Further, since his return to India ten years earlier, when he made known his contempt for the religious ways of his people, they had disliked him. When he publicly ate meat and demanded that his wife Nazmin prepare it, his ostracism was complete. In the past ten years no one had spoken kindly to him—no one except the foreigners.

Ah, the foreigners, he thought. *If only one of them would come back. I could ask them for answers to these troublesome questions, especially the beautiful woman. They could explain about The Voice that gives me no rest. They would help me. But they are not here.*

Sari stared at the decreasing light around him. Earlier a light rain had fallen, just enough to add a polish to the clean streets of Khasim. Now the yellow light faded, being replaced by a gray-green shadow that spread coldly over the ground. Soon the trees would rest in the darkness, only their pointing crowns still lit by the setting sun. The beauty of the evening depressed Sari even more.

He had never felt alone before, not until the foreign couple stayed at his hotel. True, many good things had happened since that event, but among the results was his increased sense of isolation.

He did not even know their names. Many times he wished he had insisted that they leave a forwarding address. Ordinarily he would have examined their passports, but from the moment he first saw them they had captivated him. And now, more than a year later, P. K. Sari felt as if he were still under their spell. Three days they had stayed and then left, taking the road to Bombay. They had changed his life, but they had never communicated with him again.

How very strange, he mumbled to himself many times over the ensuing months. *How very, very strange.*

It was morning in Atlanta and David Morgan awakened, but he lay quietly, allowing the events of the night to come back into focus. A strange dream had disturbed him, and afterward, for more than an hour, he had lain in bed, his eyes open, staring at the dark, trying to comprehend the meaning of the dream. Before dawn he relaxed and slept, only to have the same dream a second time.

Finally, sitting up in bed, David Morgan watched his lovely wife approach him with a steaming cup of coffee. She kissed his forehead and handed him the cup.

Katherine Morgan's pale face was thin and quiet, accented by the curve of high cheekbones. Deep shadows ringed her wide-set blue eyes. Even her thick black hair, normally lustrous, looked dull today. "You seemed to have such a disturbed night, I decided to let you sleep a little longer," she said. "Are you all right?"

He nodded, accepted the coffee, and sipped absently, his mind still focusing on the events of the night. Caught up in his own world, David didn't notice his wife's troubled features.

"Something wrong?" she asked. "Coffee too hot?"

"Not that," David said. "A dream. A strange kind of dream. I had the same dream twice."

Sitting on the edge of the bed, Katherine reached out and touched her husband's arm. Her fingers were like her limbs, long and slim, but they were delicately tapered, and the nails were shaped and lacquered to a glossy pink. "Want to tell me about it?"

"Hmm," he said, "you sound like a shrink now."

"Maybe, but do you want to tell me?"

"Yes . . . I need to tell somebody . . ." David began to summarize his troublesome dream to his concerned wife:

> *Two figures were talking. One of them glowed—like the brightness when you stare at the sun on a bright day. The one enclosed in light said to the other, "Can I do anything without first telling My prophets? Shall I not tell My servant before I make this happen?"*
>
> *The second figure said, "You promised that in the last days You would pour out Your Spirit upon all flesh. You promised visions and dreams, signs and wonders."*
>
> *"Then it is time," the first voice said. "And I shall tell My prophets. I shall tell My prophets who will listen."*

David finished telling the dream, then sipped his coffee again. "Twice I had the same dream. What do you suppose it means?"

Katherine looked away; she did not want David to see her tear-filled eyes. "I think you know, dear."

The year was 1997. After years of preparation, The Voice was putting the Master Plan into action.

T·W·O

"We're so fortunate to have you on this program," Annella Maxwell said to the famous actor Levis Cothran. "For ten years you haven't made a film, and yet you're as popular today as when you retired."

The studio audience at CBS interrupted with applause. A voice from the rear of the auditorium shouted, "He's more popular now!"

Levis Cothran flashed a smile that began slowly and spread across his face as he stared into Annella's deep-blue eyes. "I'm here only because you asked me," he said. "You treat people with integrity. You make your guests feel like individuals that you care about, and you don't trot them out here to be gawked at and ridiculed as hype for the program."

Annella Maxwell, long used to such compliments, had learned to flush with an embarrassment that made her audience believe she had never heard such high praise before.

"But you're not just an actor," Annella said. "You made only eighteen films in your career—all of them classics and among the top moneymakers in Hollywood history. Then you dropped out of the movie scene. Tell me, will you,

Levis Cothran, and our listening audience, what have you been doing for all these years?"

The slender but muscular blond actor stretched his lanky frame, and the camera zoomed in for a closeup. His dress was casual but immaculate—chino slacks with an open-neck blue shirt and buttery-leather boots. Strikingly handsome aristocratic features completed the image of the ultimate matinee idol. Behind the amiable expression, few people sensed a sharper, cruel look.

"I decided there had to be something more in life—and I went out to find it."

"Something more than fame and riches?" Annella said and laughed. "I'm told that unofficially and conservatively you're worth well over five hundred million dollars. According to a recent Gallup Poll, you place number two on name-recognition, coming in behind only the President of the United States. And you wanted something more?" The widened eyes and confused expression reflected the incredulity of her vast audience.

When the camera switched to frequent closeups of Annella, the television audience saw that her skin was flawless with a touch of natural color in her cheeks to give them life. Dark lashes framed her large eyes. The chin, nose, cheek, and brow were all so well constructed, a cosmetic expert's magic hand might have shaped her face. Her lips knew how to smile, and she did that often. But of all her features, her eyes, of a blue so deep that no one had ever described them accurately, especially demanded the attention of the viewer. She always classified her eyes as blue, but one admirer called them deep-violet. One of her enemies referred to them as gravestone blue.

Annella's simple rust-colored dress, sleeveless to show the slender tanned arms and to call attention to the pearls at her neck and on her ears, her smooth hair perfectly in place, made her the epitome of the fashion world. And Annella Maxwell knew her assets well.

"You see, Annella," Levis was saying, "money can't buy inner peace. Fame is wonderful but just not enough, at least not for me. I still had to go to bed like any other human being in the world. And every morning when I woke up, my face stared back at me in the mirror. I didn't like who I was, the way I lived, the things I did to others. Until one day . . ."

"Yes . . .?"

"One day I found the answer," he said. "It was the simplest answer of all—I only had to believe it—to reach out and receive it because it was there all the time, waiting for me."

"The Annella Maxwell Show" had won its hostess an Emmy Award for three consecutive years. She had begun her syndicated show with forty-nine independent stations, competing against luminaries such as Geraldo Rivera, Phil Donahue, and Oprah Winfrey. By the fifth month of her show, Annella Maxwell had garnered the highest ratings any talk show had ever achieved in the history of television—a thirty point rating and a forty-two percent share of the listening audience.

Since then she had continued to add more stations and greater audiences until Annella Maxwell became the doyenne of daytime talk-show hosts. CBS decided to pit reruns of her show against Johnny Carson, and to the amazement of the TV pundits she outscored him. Someone had finally dethroned the aging king of the nighttime shows.

America was no strange land to P. K. Sari. During his years of studies in the United Kingdom, taking his doctoral degree in history at Oxford University, he had traveled many times to large American cities.

"But what shall I do when I reach America?" he kept asking The Voice. "I do not know anyone there. Not a single person."

"I shall give you a name," The Voice said. "Annella Maxwell."

The name had a familiar ring, but Sari could not recall where he had heard of her before. She was an American, of that he was sure. And a well-known personality, he was certain. *Who is this Annella Maxwell?*

"Why do you ponder?" The Voice asked. "Have I failed you yet? Be at peace. My plan for your life is just beginning."

P. K. Sari's plane landed at Frankfurt, West Germany. The Air India flight attendant announced in English, Hindi, and German that the plane would be on the ground approximately forty-five minutes before they would reboard. Sari left a card to reserve his first-class seat and got off the plane to stretch his legs by walking through the airport concourse.

As he moved down the passageway, he approached a stand that sold Swiss and English candies. Having acquired a weakness for Cadbury chocolates during his student days, he paused to purchase a large bar to eat on the plane.

"Excuse me, Mr. Sari," said a heavily accented voice behind him. "We really must hurry, you know."

Startled, Sari turned around. Before him stood a uniformed man, a person he had never seen before. "I . . . What do you want?"

"This way, please . . ." The man smiled, but the authority in his voice made it clear that he expected no argument. He led the Indian through the International Flight section, and waved to a similarly dressed officer at the immigration booth. Sari followed, wondering where he was going, staring at the people around him.

"Fear not," The Voice said.

Slowly P. K. Sari relaxed. He did not understand, but he now had the assurance that whatever happened, it would be all right.

At the door of an unmarked office, the officer said, "I hope you enjoy your stay in West Germany. Your luggage is being cared for." Touching the brim of his hat, he opened

the door, bowed his head slightly, and turned away from
Sari.

P. K. Sari walked inside, staring as if he had entered the
drawing room of an American mansion. The room was furnished in chocolate and gold, with a white pile carpet domi-
nating the space. Sari knew that the decoration must have
cost a great deal of money. His eyes strayed from corner to
corner of the room, and he paused when he recognized a
Monet on one wall and, without verifying it, knew instinctively it was original. In the far corner, he fingered the
embroidered bellpull that dangled from the corniced ceiling
with its hand-painted panels of German pastoral scenes.

Sari became aware of the scent of roses from the smoke
crystal bowl on a walnut coffee table in front of a low couch
made of creme-and-gold material. He sat down on a high-
backed armchair of dark chocolate velvet; next to it was a
Carrara marble table. He then became aware of the portable
bar with its crystal decanters and silver ice bowl.

Sari snorted. It was the kind of room that only those
who had great wealth would furnish, those who cared nothing about anyone's opinion or their tastes. Not the kind of
place he would enjoy, he admitted, though the opulence did
impress him.

*But what is this kind of place doing in the middle of the
Frankfurt Airport?*

From a side door another man entered noisily. "Welcome to Frankfurt, Mr. Sari. I trust you have had a pleasant
flight," he said, speaking in precise English, although he
betrayed his Germanic background with his gutturals and his
inversion of the v and w.

"Who are you? What am I doing here?"

"I have been instructed to assist you," the man said as
he extended his hand. "Here is your new passport, with visas
already intact for the countries you will visit. I hope you will
find everything completely to your satisfaction." He bowed
slightly and then pointed to the wet bar. "If you desire anything further, please ring. You do so by pulling the bellcord
over—"

"Yes, I know."

"Someone will come immediately to serve you." The man exited as quietly as he came.

Sari inspected the plain envelope in his hand before he opened it. The Indian passport, complete with his photograph, named him as N. K. Patel, a solicitor from Bombay. He opened the letter attached to the passport. It read:

> This letter is to ensure you that everything is working according to my Plan. It is time for you to put aside all questions. From this moment on, you must listen carefully to The Voice and obey without hesitation.
>
> When you have finished reading this letter, tear it into pieces and leave it on the counter. You will now leave the Frankfurt Airport. Wait at the taxi stand, and you will receive your next instructions.

P. K. Sari did as instructed, although awed at the circumstances and wondering what he had gotten into. As soon as he walked outside, a driver pulled his taxi to the front of the line and motioned toward Sari. The Indian ignored him.

"A taxi, sir?" the man called out.

The Indian took two steps forward, and then heard a voice from his right.

"Ah, Mr. Patel! I have been waiting for you."

Sari whirled around and stared.

"If you would now be so good as to follow me, sir."

A uniformed driver led the Indian to a Lincoln Continental bearing diplomatic plates. "This way, please." He opened the rear door for his passenger before going around the driver's side.

Once they left the airport, the driver made no attempt at conversation. Afraid of making a mistake by saying the wrong thing, Sari sat in silence. Thirty minutes later, the car turned into the Kaiserplatz and stopped in front of the Hotel Frankfurter Hof. Although he had never been there before, Sari saw immediately that he had been taken to a luxurious cosmopolitan hotel.

As the doorman greeted him in German and opened the large door for him to enter, Sari heard the faint notes of a piano playing a piece that he recognized as Brahms.

The driver handed an aging bellhop a room key and a gratuity. "This is for you, sir," he said as he handed a note to Sari. "You are checked in. Proceed immediately to Room 666." He turned and left.

Sari walked behind the bellhop across the expansive lobby to the roomy elevator. Once they reached the sixth floor, Sari followed the bellhop, aware of the thick carpets in the corridor and how nicely they muffled outside noise. He paused once to admire a tapestry hung on the wall. Sari recognized the style immediately. *Well-made—early nineteenth century.* Once inside his spacious room, Sari opened the folded slip of paper and read the single sentence: "Call me as soon as you reach your room," followed by the number. It was signed, Hanse Wensela.

Sari dialed the phone. The voice that answered, a pleasant baritone with a lilting ring to it, said without introducing himself, "Ah, yes, Mr. Patel. Now it is time for us to meet and to compare information. I shall meet you in your hotel in one hour. Be there."

T·H·R·E·E

H anse Wensela, the second son in a wealthy European industrial family, had begun a path of rebellion from the time he learned to walk. Old money, spirited away and saved by his grandfather before the Nazi regime, had combined with larger sums accumulated by cooperative business ventures with the Third Reich.

The vast estate would have been divided equally between the two sons had it not been for the accidental death of Hanse's older brother. Rumors still persisted in dark corners of Europe that the brother's death had been no accident; other, stronger whispers hinted that Hanse had murdered his brother to gain the entire family fortune. As sole heir of the Wensela possession, on his twenty-first birthday the young man had continued to extend his empire. Now, at age fifty-three, Hanse no longer rebelled. Now he set the rules.

Although he was what some would call corpulent, Wensela walked with a grace that belied his girth. His legs seemed short because of his lengthy torso; he stood at exactly six feet. Not completely bald, having once had fine, golden-fair hair to match his eyebrows and lashes, he now had only a slight fuzz of thinned-out pinfeathers.

Wensela opened the door of P. K. Sari's room without knocking. The thin Indian lay on the bed, staring at the ceiling, feeling at peace and yet anxious to be on his mission—whatever it was. His reverie broken, Sari turned. As the two men focused on each other, Sari could see weary bitterness in the German's blue eyes, the face of a man who had experienced the world and its inhabitants too well and didn't care for what he had found.

Wensela attempted to smile by moving his facial muscles, but the hardness of his blue eyes denied any warmth his countenance projected. "Don't get up," Hanse Wensela said. He pulled up a chair and sat down across from the Indian.

In a split second Wensela had assessed the man, but then he practiced this often enough. Immediately reservations formed in his mind about Sari, wondering about the tenacity of such a man. Would he cave in when difficulties arose? Would he fail when most needed? No matter, he decided, The Voice had selected Sari Patel. He acquiesced to that decision.

"You are wondering about many things," Wensela said. "The Voice has instructed me to explain it all. Within definite limits, however." He leaned forward. "Do you have any questions?"

"I have nothing but questions," the man answered. He sat up on the bed. "To begin with, you're Hanse Wensela?"

"I am."

"Yes, you have given me a name, but who are you? What do you want with me? Why are you here?"

"Perhaps if I tell you a few facts about myself, you will understand. A year ago—that is, this past February—everything began to fall into place. Before that—" He paused and, getting up from the chair, walked over to the bar. "I like to drink something when I speak. Would you care to join me?"

Sari shook his head. "I wish only to hear what you have to say."

The heavy-set man poured himself a glass of schnapps, took two sips, and returned to his chair. "First, I shall tell you about myself. Although I was never conventionally religious—do you understand what I mean? . . ."

"Yes, but of course," said the Indian.

". . . I had a faint interest in traditional religion—meaning the Christian faith. But I saw little to recommend it to me. You know how it goes: Blessed are the poor. I frankly wanted a religion that would allow me to accumulate more wealth." For the second time in the few minutes they were together, Hanse Wensela tried to smile, but even he knew he had not pulled it off.

"I tired of traditional religion years ago, " he said. "Then, through the unwanted but undeniable influence of two Americans, my life changed. They disrupted everything, causing me to reexamine ideas I had ignored. And then . . . and then, Mr. Sari Patel, I heard from The Voice. Previously I had known vaguely about new developments in parapsychology and the esoteric sciences. I had done some studying of astrological signs, witchcraft in a variety of forms, but all with little interest."

"Yes, it is the same with me," Sari said.

"One day," Wensela said in a tone that showed he disliked the interruption, "I purchased a Ouija board. In time I could actually use it to receive instructions on business decisions." He took a longer sip of his schnapps. "Now you must understand that using such an object and depending on it for guidance was repugnant to me. Can you understand that?"

Sari nodded, wishing the man would get to the point. "That is only background. You understand?"

"Yes, yes—"

"On February 6 of last year, quite late in the afternoon, a Mercedes pulled up in front of my office here in Frankfurt. I have offices in twelve major European cities and seldom stay in West Germany. Only an emergency meeting brought me here." Hanse Wensela knew he was drawing out the details, but when he had a captive audience like P. K. Sari he wanted to hold the floor for as long as possible.

"I scarcely remember the man—and he's not important in what I wish to tell you. But the woman, ah, she was beautiful—the most beautiful creature I have ever seen. She had hair of an indescribable color—blonde, and yet as the rays of the sun touched it, it glowed with the redness of a ruby. And her eyes—"

"Blue. Deep, dark blue—"

"Yes," Hanse said, surprised. "Like the finest sapphire I've ever touched." Wensela closed his eyes, remembering the woman and the soft fragrance of her perfume that reminded him of oriental palaces. "The couple stayed less than five hours, and we walked outside together. When they got inside the Mercedes, the lady rolled down the window and handed me a parcel wrapped in brown paper."

"It was books," Sari said, his voice filled with excitement. "Six books."

Again surprised, Wensela said, "True. However, I didn't know the contents at the time. I returned to my office. It was almost as though something dragged me there. Once inside, however, I did not leave for four days and during that time—"

"Yes! Yes!" Sari said. "I know. You read the books again and again, starting with one entitled *Yours in the Earth*. Is that not correct?"

"Why—why, yes," Wensela said, "but let me tell you what happened next. That night I had a dream in which a shadowy figure appeared and instructed me to fly to Bonn—"

"And you returned with a great deal of money, did you not?"

"Yes—"

"And in American dollars?"

"How did you know?" Wensela asked.

"It is the same with me. I went from my town of Khasim to Bombay, but it is otherwise quite the same story."

"Since then," Wensela said, "The Voice has continued to speak to me, to guide my decisions. I have accumulated a vast amount of wealth." He did not mention that along with his inheritance, he would conservatively be listed as one of the ten most wealthy people in the world—that is, if those who compiled such reports knew of all his possessions.

"So have I," said Sari. "An amazing amount of money. For almost three months The Voice told me how I might double my investment *each day* and sometimes even quadruple."

For more than an hour the two men talked, and to their amazement their experiences ran parallel courses.

"When did you say this happened?" asked Sari. "The coming of the beautiful woman."

"February 6, 1996."

"No, that cannot be," Sari said. "It was that very day that *I* saw the beautiful woman and the man and received the books. Could she have reached both of us in one day?"

"Yes, but of course," said Wensela. "The aerospace planes travel rapidly. They could have traveled to Bombay in two, three hours. But you know, the strangest part is that I have never seen them since."

"Nor have I," said Sari. "And I must tell you that I am a little frightened by what has happened."

"Fear? Has The Voice not said he would never leave you? Has he not promised riches and everything you want?"

"Yes . . ."

"Then what troubles you?"

"It is—oh, perhaps my words will sound foolish to you."

"I don't understand."

"It is as if I am not who I am any longer. My body is the same, but . . . but I am different. I feel as if someone else lives inside me and has been slowly taking control of me, making my decisions, allowing me fewer and fewer choices. In the Hindu religion this is not totally unknown, you must understand. I personally know people who have spirit guides, inner voices that speak, so they say."

"But you don't believe them?"

"I have not believed them before. Although Indian, I long ago threw off all of my religious teaching."

"Which is just one reason why The Voice has chosen you. You have left yourself open to this influence."

"But surely this must be more than the Hindu faith—"

"Ah, far, far more as you shall soon discover."

"But you see," Sari said, "I have no wish to be a man of religion. I hate the concept of God! I utterly detest such things!"

Hanse leaned back, and this time he emitted a genuine smile. "I assure you, The Voice most definitely does not wish you to become religious."

"Then what must I do?"

"Give yourself totally to The Voice. Once you fully let go, the doubts, the fears, the hesitation will leave. The Voice wants to take complete control of you, Mr. Sari. And because you are holding back, you are thwarting *the Master Plan*.

"What master plan?"

"I can't say. First, I do not know any details. Second and more important, much more important, as long as you are reluctant to surrender yourself totally to The Voice, I have no more to say to you."

Sari got off the bed and knelt beside the man. "Please help me. It was this fear of having my mind polluted with religious nonsense that troubled me. I have also been fearful of going insane because of this fighting inside my head. Now that I have heard you speak, and know what The Voice has already done for me, I can never have peace until I fully give in to The Voice. Please help me."

"That's easy enough." Hanse laid his hands on the Indian's head. "I now offer you as a total sacrifice. I offer your body, mind, and spirit to The Voice—to the Great One whose name we have yet to learn."

P. K. Sari fell backward, and a wave of blackness overcame him. He could not move, and yet he did not want to resist. In his trancelike state, Sari heard The Voice speak to him. "Yield yourself to me. Yield so that I may take full control of your life. Do not be afraid ever again."

"Yes . . . Yes," P. K. Sari said. As he uttered those two words, the fighting ceased. He would never doubt again. The Voice had totally assumed control of his life.

"And so we can travel together," Wensela said. "We leave for New York where we shall meet others."

P. K. Sari did not ask who the others were. The Voice had given him the same message. He was ready to obey this command. He was ready to obey every command.

F·O·U·R

At the moment the two men prepared to leave the room, the telephone rang. Sari picked up the receiver, and before he could speak a voice said, "At the Lufthansa counter you will receive two first-class tickets." The other person hung up.

As instructed and without question, the two men went directly to the Lufthansa counter and handed the woman their false passports. Wensela said, "You have tickets for us."

"They are right here," she said. "If you will wait in the lounge, we shall call you when we are ready to board. It should be in less than an hour."

As they entered through the glass door, they saw a broad-shouldered man with a ruddy complexion who sat in an overstuffed chair. He smiled at them, cocked his head, and waved. His teeth showed very white, and they were all the whiter against his deeply tanned skin. People hardly noticed the color of his eyes, as if the other features of his face overshadowed their light brown. The man had a determined jaw, and although he smiled often as he talked, it often startled most people when they figured out that he was no fool.

As soon as the two men had handed the attendant their pass to the lounge, the stranger was in front of them, extending his hand. In a broad Australian accent he said, "Ga' day . . . I've been waiting almost an hour for you chaps."

"And who are you?" Wensela asked.

"Your companion to New York. Maison Quayle's the name, obedience is the game. Right?"

"And you are going to New York with us?" P. K. Sari asked, trying to hide his surprise.

"Of course I am, didn't you know?" he said and winked. "I got the same message you blokes received. Early on the morning of February 6 of last year."

Sari smiled. "No longer must I find anything surprising."

"And we are to meet Annella Maxwell," Maison Quayle said. "Been looking forward to seeing her with me own eyes for some time. A nice piece of female flesh, if you ask me."

"You know who she is?" Wensela said.

"I thought everybody, except those in the outback, knew of Annella Maxwell. Don't you blokes watch the telly?"

"No time," said Wensela.

"No interest," said Sari.

"Well, you boys have a treat waiting for you. A rare treat."

"Yes, of that I am certain," Sari said. "Something quite special."

"Oh, very, very special," Maison Quayle said as he pointed for the men to sit down. "The circle is half completed now. And once it is completed—"

"Circle half completed?" asked Wensela. "I don't think I understand."

"Perhaps not yet," Quayle said. He signaled a waiter. "Another brew for me and something for my friends."

After the three men were served, Wensela leaned forward. "You apparently know more about the future than we do. Is there anything you can tell us?"

"Just this. As you may know, you're both especially honored." He paused for his generous smile to take effect before he added, "There are six of us, carefully chosen from around the world. We shall all become part of the Mastermind."

"What is that?" Wensela asked. "And what do you mean by part of?"

"You got me there, mates," he said. "But not to worry and never to hurry. The Voice has said that we'll be involved in the greatest experience the world has ever known."

"I believe you," Wensela said. "It's just that I find it a bit difficult to grasp."

"It's beyond your wildest imagination, gents," he said. "Beyond anything you could believe in. Don't try to see, just let it be."

"And this woman—this Annella Maxwell—she's involved as well?"

"Involved? She's the key."

The interview with Levis Cothran was Annella Maxwell's highest rated program ever. Independent stations who had previously declined to carry her show begged for the opportunity to air the interview. As a direct result of that single program, Annella's daily program was now carried by all U.S. cities with a population over one hundred thousand. Two of the cable networks now carried her program twice weekly as "The Annella Special." The beautiful hostess now aired on more channels than any single program in television history.

During his second appearance the following day, Levis Cothran told the story of his life-change. "I discovered God," he said, his face relaxed and tanned.

"A religious conversion?" his hostess asked. "We've heard all about that before, haven't we?"

"Not just a relgious conversion. God. You know, the inventor of the cosmos. I found God—and you know where

God lives?" He leaned forward, and his voice exuded a tone of confidentiality. "Right here inside of me. Inside every single individual in the world really, but most of us don't know it. I didn't know it for a long time. That's why I'm back on Annella's program. I'm here to tell you this secret."

"Levis, tell us!" squealed Annella.

"Quite simple. You see, I am God, you are God, each of us is God—if we'll only accept that truth and believe it."

"Come now," Annella said, "we've also heard that before."

"You heard it before, but you never saw it demonstrated before. Here, I'll show you what I mean." Levis Cothran stood up and walked off the platform and down the aisle. He paused in front of a man sitting in a wheelchair. "What's wrong with you, sir?"

"What's wrong? You got all day to listen?" he asked and hastily added, "First, I'm diabetic. I have a congenital heart blockage. Then there's this rheumatic condition that began in my knees twenty years ago. Got so crippled and pain-filled I couldn't walk, and now . . . now I can't even stand on 'em. Yesterday the doctor told me that I've got cancer of the prostate. You want to hear more?"

"You can be healed, sir. Right now. It doesn't matter whether you have one illness or ten!" Without waiting for a response, Levis Cothran bent over, his face only inches from that of the old man. "I appeal to the god inside of you, Be healed! Heal yourself! I command you in the name of Master Mind of the Universe!"

A flicker of life replaced the deadness in the man's eyes, and he stared at the actor's face. "I—I feel something touching my knees . . . something light . . . burning . . ." He pushed Cothran away and pulled himself out of his wheelchair. "Look! Look! I can do it! My legs are straight and normal again. I can walk! And I got no pain—not anyplace!"

"Of course you can walk! You can dance if you want!" Levis said. "You can do anything you want. God lives inside you, and that gives you all the power and health you need for right now and all you'll need forever more!"

The man ran up one aisle and down the other, jumped, did a dozen pushups. The studio audience went wild with excitement.

"Truly remarkable," Annella said after the furor calmed down. "But, Levis, we've seen healing evangelists before—"

"Yes, but you are missing the point. I did not heal that man. I have no special power. Did you hear me pray to some god out there someplace in the universe to come down and do this? No! I appealed to the god within the man. That's the untapped source of all power. In each of us. Any of us—all of us—can heal ourselves. We can receive wisdom, guidance—whatever we need. It's all from the cosmos that resides in each of us."

Annella turned to the audience. "I know this man who has just been healed. His name is Daryl Prebble. I've known Mr. Prebble for at least four years. I personally asked him to come because I wanted to find out for myself if this kind of thing works."

"Do you still doubt?" Levis asked.

"I'm a skeptic—like most of my audience out there." She nodded to them to respond, and clapping broke out.

"Then I'll have to show you something else." He turned to the audience. "I want a volunteer. Somebody I don't know."

"Here's a guest!" a deep voice from the rear called out. "She's from Alaska and only came to New York today. First time out of the state."

"Come down here," Levis said as he waited for the woman to come forward. He asked her to tell the audience her name and to affirm that they had never met before. The woman said, "But I did see one of your movies."

"Guess that doesn't disqualify you," Levis said and, turning to the audience, asked, "does it?"

"If it did, nobody could come up there!" shouted an elderly woman.

"Okay, now here's what I want you to do. I want you to write down your birthday, then your favorite color, and one other word—a word that you're sure I'll never figure out." Levis called for someone in the audience to give the woman a sheet of paper and a pen. Several people volunteered and thrust the items into her hands. She wrote the information down, folded the paper, and held it behind her back.

"You were born on May 13—and you don't want me to tell the year, do you?"

"Please, no!" She covered her face in embarrassment.

"Your favorite color is orange."

"Right! I—I can't believe you'd guess that."

"I didn't guess," he said. "And the secret word is—" Levis Cothran started laughing. "It's the name of a character called Devil Dan I played in my third movie, *The Devil Did It*. Now, how's that?"

"One hundred percent!" She grabbed Levis Cothran and kissed his lips.

For the next half-hour, Levis Cothran answered an array of questions from the audience, giving out Social Security numbers, street addresses, and other minor bits of information. He told one woman, "You want to know where your husband has hidden five thousand dollars. You won't believe it, but he's sewn it inside the mattress—on his side!"

As Levis Cothran finished the program with Annella Maxwell, he said, "I don't want to leave without telling you how this great discovery came about."

"We've run out of time," Annella Maxwell said, "but, Levis, if you'll come back on Monday . . .?"

"I'll be here," he promised.

David Morgan lay on his back in bed, eyes wide open, trying to make up his mind. To ignore what he had seen on Annella Maxwell's program might be the wiser course of action. So much trash appeared on the talk shows anyway.

He had never taken a public stand before, never felt the need to do so. However, something about both Annella Maxwell and Levis Cothran troubled him, a feeling he couldn't identify and yet something that wouldn't let him push them out of his thoughts. Morgan heard himself say aloud, "Something evil." *Yes,* he thought, *that's it . . . a sinister feeling as if I faced Satan himself.* At that instant, a phrase popped into his mind and refused to leave: "With all power and with pretended signs and wonders . . ." A Biblical phrase he was sure. But what did it mean? Where in the Bible?

Finally, unable to sleep or to push the odd phrase from his consciousness, David Morgan got out of bed and went into the den. Picking up a concordance, he found what he was looking for—2 Thessalonians 2:9, 10:

> . . . the activity of Satan will be with all
> power and with pretended signs and won-
> ders, and with all wicked deception for
> those who are to perish, because they
> refused to love the truth and so be saved.

Is this God speaking to me? he wondered. He didn't want to accept any of this experience as a message coming to him from God. To accept this, he knew, meant he would have to respond. And how would he respond? Well, what could he do?

He stopped pacing the floor and stared out the window. As he watched, long streaks of yellow light split the gray sky. Day was breaking, and the birds instantly came awake and began chattering. The buffer of southern pines behind his property was a mass of black-pointed shapes with golden highlights. In the distance he heard the backfire of a truck. The city of Atlanta had started a new day. And David Morgan had not yet slept.

Moving away from the window, he asked again, "God, what can I do? I'm only a parish minister. And of a small church at that. I'm only one man."

As David Morgan spoke the words aloud, he paused to listen, hoping that some inner guidance would come. To his own amazement, from inside his own head he heard a voice so distinct, so powerful he had no doubts of its origin. In hearing the voice, he heard an answer he didn't want to hear.

"Abraham had no one by his side. King David was one man. Paul stood alone. Who honored Jeremiah? Daniel? When have people ever listened to My prophets?"

"Your prophets?" Rev. David Morgan asked aloud. "Are you putting me in that same category, God?" As he asked, he remembered the twice-given dream of the night before.

"Did you not offer your life to Me?"

"Of course, and I meant it. And I want to serve You—"

"Do you? Do you?"

David Morgan dropped to the floor and knelt beside his easy chair. Tears flowed and he finally cried out, "God, forgive me for my lack of faith, for being afraid—"

"I ask only that you heed My words. Am I not the giver of faith? Of gifts? Am I not the one who fits the caller to the calling? I have need of you in My service. I have called you to speak before great multitudes. And those who can hear, will hear Me speak through you."

"How do I know I'm not imagining this?"

"Because the last hours are upon the earth. And as the minutes tick away, I shall show Myself in extraordinary ways. I shall speak to you and to other open hearts, and you will quake with amazement."

David Morgan dropped his head to the floor and lay prostrate. Between sobs he quietly asked God to forgive him. A sense of peace followed, slowly creeping through his body as if it flowed through his bloodstream. He could feel a renewing energy empowering him, racing through his legs and arms, his head, his chest and abdomen.

"God, I'm just a pastor of a small congregation in a big city. So many talented preachers here in Atlanta could do better. They're gifted, sensitive . . . why me?"

"It is Mine to call, yours to obey."

F·I·V·E

The Indian, the European, and the Australian boarded the Lufthansa 927 aero-jet, headed for New York with an estimated travel time of two hours and twenty-three minutes. The flight attendant served each of them a drink before takeoff. Only then did Maison Quayle notice the dark-skinned man sitting next to the window. He was smiling at the Australian.

"Ga' day," Maison Quayle said as he picked up his drink.

"I am pleased to make your acquaintance," the man said in a thickly accented British-English. "My name is Amwago Zolo, the son of Odera—"

"If you'll excuse me, I've got my mates here to chew with—"

"But, I, too, am one of your mates, Mr. Maison Quayle. Are you not aware of that?"

"You are?" asked P. K. Sari as he leaned toward the man.

"Yes, Mr. Sari and Mr. Wensela—or if you prefer, Mr. Patel and Mr. Waldvogel, the names you are using on this flight."

"Then you are number four?" asked Wensela.

"Of my number I am unaware," the African said indifferently. "Although because I can count in English, I obviously am the fourth individual. However, I am here because The Voice instructed—"

"And you heard from the voice on February 6, 1996, didn't you?" Sari said.

"Ah, but of course. That is the day all six of us heard. Were you not aware of that?"

"We have only discovered this," Sari said. "It is most unusual, is it not?"

"We shall yet see many, many unusual things," Amwago Zolo said. "So The Voice has told me."

"Well, mate," Quayle said, resting his head on the back of the seat, "perhaps you'd like to tell us about yourself. What brought you into this little venture?"

"The Voice."

"We know that much. But tell the story, feel the glory. The three of us have told our little tale once, but we don't mind telling it again. An all-right kind of way to help partners get better acquainted, wouldn't you say?"

"Why should I object? I am quite pleased that The Voice has seen my fitness to become an emissary to the world."

P. K. Sari stared at the African as he heard the last statement. "To the world?"

"Why else would we all come together at this time?" Amwago Zolo said and then, dismissing the question, added softly, "For quite a long time I have known this was to come. I did not know when."

From across the aisle, P. K. Sari and Hanse Wensela leaned forward, straining to catch every word from the African. As Amwago Zolo spoke, his voice took on a singsongy lilt, typical of the way members of his tribe spoke their own dialect, which made it more difficult for each of the others to understand without full concentration. Yet no one thought to stop him or ask him to repeat.

Without betraying it, Quayle took an instant dislike to

this man with the tightly clipped kinky hair. Even the African's appearance put Quayle off. He was a tall, gangly skeleton of a man with (by African standards) a light-brown complexion, a thin mouth, and black agate eyes with no humor in them, even when he smiled. He was arrogant, peremptory, and devoid of social graces. Yet at the same time, Quayle quietly assessed him as having no more morals than he himself possessed.

Zolo, the son of a tribal chief in East Africa, had shown uncanny gifts in childhood. For example, he told his new companions, at age six four of his playmates had teased him because he was taller than they and extremely thin. Amwago stopped playing, closed his eyes, and pronounced a curse of pain, naming each child individually. Without exception each child awakened in the night with a high fever alternating with chills. Each boy complained of intense pains in his arms and legs. By morning each one recovered only to fall victim again at night. For six nights the boys endured the pain, fever, and chills. On the seventh morning the four children came together, pleading with Zolo to forgive them.

"You must pay for your mistakes," Amwago said. "Come back with a gift."

One brought sugar cane from his father's field, another a boiled chicken, the third a large can of shelled peanuts; the fourth handed him a silver-plated knife that Queen Victoria had given to his grandfather.

The fevers and chills ceased, but the abilities of Amwago Zolo had only begun. At school the teachers who displeased Amwago came down with strange viruses or encountered unusual accidents on their way to class.

"You are a devil!" Omore Haraka, his English teacher, said as he pointed to the boy. "A true son of Satan."

"You are perceptive, *japunj* (teacher)." Amwago nodded. "Most perceptive."

Had Amwago not been the brightest student in the entire school, and had he not won several prizes for achievement, Mr. Haraka, who also functioned as headmaster, would have permanently expelled the boy from school. Upon completion of the compulsory secondary school examinations, Zolo earned an "O" (Outstanding) in each area, giving him a choice of scholarships. He chose Cambridge and then Stanford University in America for his doctoral program. He earned a Ph.D., but it meant nothing to him. More pleasing, Zolo had inherited the role of tribal witch doctor, a position that fitted his talents well.

Amwago Zolo's great pride came from an uncanny transaction made when he was thirty-one years old in 1995. "Buy a portion of land that I will show you," commanded a spirit named Jodeko.

No one could have been more amazed than Amwago Zolo when he actually saw the portion of land on the Tanzania-Kenya border—rocky, unfit for raising anything but *muhogo* (cassava), a crop that requires little rain.

"I have no money," Amwago told Jodeko. "How can I buy?"

"Are you not my servant? I shall provide for you in every way," Jodeko responded.

Three days later Amwago Zolo received a registered letter with a check for four thousand East African pounds (at that time worth six thousand American dollars). "You need not know the donor," Jodeko said. "I have sent this money for my special use."

Obediently Zolo visited the chief of the location and, after bribing him with twenty pounds, purchased an area one hundred and forty hectares long by ninety-five wide. Ownership of the land included water and mineral rights.

"Water rights?" laughed the seller. "We have no water. We have less than ten millimeters of rain touch this ground in one full year." He laughed again at this foolish man. "I hope you enjoy your water rights."

After registering the transaction, Amwago Zolo had eight hundred pounds left.

"You have done well," Jodeko said. "Better than I had expected. You may keep the eight hundred pounds. You will soon realize that it is such a small amount."

"Small amount?" Amwago asked in amazement, and then added, "I do not doubt you."

"That is why my master will take you to many places and will extol your name throughout the earth."

"Your master is—?"

"You will learn when it is time," Jodeko answered.

Amwago Zolo did nothing to the land and allowed neighbors to graze their goats on the limited amount of grass that covered the surface. Six months later, a group of mineralogists, who represented a cartel of Dutch investors, surveyed a large portion of land, including Zolo's property.

Within a month after the survey, a Dutchman visited Amwago Zolo's home. Zolo sat in a simple flowing robe, animal-skin sandals on his feet.

After introducing himself, the man spoke in slow, precise English and said, "I like your land. I would like to buy it."

"That is possible," Zolo said. "For what purpose?" Before him on a table he had placed a gourd, filled with an amber liquid. He stirred gently and stared at the contents.

"I am working on a plan to irrigate the land. Since Lake Victoria is less than thirty kilometers away, I think I could do that and then begin to farm."

"I see," Zolo said. He did not look at the man. "And how much are you prepared to pay me for this worthless land?"

"I am willing to be generous. Quite generous. Let us say two thousand pounds, British sterling."

Zolo continued to stir in silence. Then he stopped and from a pocket he pulled out a dried leaf, shaped much like a bay leaf, and crumbled it over the liquid as he continued to mix.

After a lengthy silence the Dutchman asked, "If you wish to think about it, I could return tomorrow."

"Oh, I wish you to return tomorrow, but not because I need to consider this matter." Amwago poured the liquid into two glasses and handed one to the stranger.

"What is this?"

"A drink," Zolo said. "It tastes much like chocolate, but it is my own mixture. You will like it." Amwago took a long drink.

The Dutchman, unsure of the sanitary conditions, smiled and imitated the witch doctor. To his amazement it was quite tasty, and he said so.

"But of course," Amwago Zolo answered. "Now, as to your so-called business proposition . . . I do not wish any further insults. You will return, bringing with you a certified check for a first installment of one hundred thousand American dollars."

"That's preposterous!"

"Please," Amwago Zolo said. "Your firm will make annual payments to an account in Zurich which you will open for me." The witch doctor leaned forward, his dark eyes staring intently at the Dutchman. "The selling price is not negotiable. I want a total of one billion dollars."

The man opened his mouth to speak, thought better of it, and shook his head slowly.

"You think because I am an African witch doctor that I am an ignorant man? Why do you think I purchased the land? Do you want me to give away the diamonds? By now you have completed your survey and your assaying, have you not?"

"Yes—"

"And you wish to know how I received this knowledge? I am a witch doctor. This is the kind of information that comes to me through the spirits. But then, you are a learned, rational European and do not believe in such superstition. So it will do no good to discuss the source of my information."

"How *did* you know about the diamonds?" the man asked. "Mineralogists have been over this same land at least five times in the past thirty years."

"It was not the time for them to find the treasure," Amwago Zolo said, starting to lose his patience. "Do you think this field's output will equal that of the Kimberly Mines?"

"No, but we believe there is a fortune to be taken from under your land—several fortunes."

"Consult your executives. My price is reasonable. And if you delay more than a fortnight, I shall also demand a small percentage of the annual profits."

Eight days later the Dutchman returned with a certified check, a contract, and a small packet containing information on a Zurich bank account with the appropriate papers to sign.

When Amwago Zolo finishied his account to his new coworkers, he said, "And then, of course, on February 6 last, the beautiful woman came to me with a parcel of books."

"Yes," Sari said, "you are one of us."

But who are we? Maison Quayle still wondered.

S·I·X

"**S**o you see," Amwago Zolo said to his three companions, "I am now an immensely wealthy man. As I understand, each of us has accumulated vast sums of money within the past year. And we have only begun; our income will grow beyond all our dreams."

"Why is that?" Quayle asked, not mentioning that his personal income had, by dishonest means, reached one million dollars recently.

"Because," answered Sari, "when The Voice makes everything plain to us, we will be spending vast sums of money."

"How do you know that?"

Sari smiled. "The Voice has already told me that."

"All of us are wealthy, are we not?" Zolo said. "You have no need to hide the amount of your wealth from me, nor do I care of your value. Each of us has become affluent, if that is not too simple a word, and we have done it because The Voice has guided us."

No daytime program in the history of television had received so much publicity prior to the third appearance of Levis Cothran. Pundits of the industry tried to account for the interest in this one show. Religion on talk shows was nothing new; celebrities appeared every day. None of them had any way of knowing that making Annella Maxwell's program a commercial blockbuster had been meticulously planned and enacted by the same source that directed the other members of Mastermind to New York.

"It could be just another yak-yak show," said Bobby Hawkins somewhat skeptically.

"Not with the appeal of Levis Cothran," said the balding Sam Lesser, president of ABC, who never wasted unnecessary words.

"Aw, come on," Hawkins, his youthful-looking assistant, said. "The man hasn't been around for a decade."

"Part of mystique!" Lesser said as he slammed his hand on his desk. "Male counterpart to Garbo: remain in obscurity, while the legend builds. More bankable now."

"But that still doesn't account for—"

"You listening? He claims to be god!"

"Well, not exactly," Hawkins replied. "He says all of us are gods."

"You miss the point! People want to hear this—fulfill their fantasies. Gives secrets of power and money."

"I know I'm going to watch—" Bobby blurted out. "I mean—" Although twenty years separated the two men in age, Hawkins had a short, rotund body, a thick neck, and a round face similar to his boss's. They had worked together for nine years. Some said that the longer the two functioned together, they more they began to look like twins. Lesser's enunciation carried the slightest Slavic inflection at times, while Hawkins's voice reflected his Midwestern upbringing. Otherwise, many confused one man's voice on the telephone for the other. And both men liked it that way.

Sam Lesser growled and swore under his breath. "More than that. Almost—" He paused and stared into space as he gathered his thoughts.

Sam Lesser was his Americanized name. His parents had come from Yugoslavia in what had once been known as Serbia. They had often told him tales of witches, wizards, and people who could control the mind and will of others. *Odd,* Lesser thought, *that I should think about those stories now. Yet that's what makes me wonder. Is it possible that some . . . some wizard-type figure is orchestrating this? If they were alive, my parents would have accepted that explanation without question.*

The executive pounded the desk, a way to clear his thoughts. "Whole country hypnotized," he said. For forty years he had cultivated the use of clipped sentences, gaining the notice of others for his economy of words. It had become such an ingrained habit that Sam Lesser now found it impossible to speak differently.

"I've been hearing people all over ABC say they're planning to have their VCR tape the show, even though it's going to play again tonight."

"We're losers?" Lesser asked. "We get Cothran?"

"No chance," Bobby Hawkins said, long used to Lesser's verbal shorthand form of speaking. "We've already tried to lure him to ABC. Before he appeared, CBS locked him into an exclusive. Can you believe that? For the next nine months he can't make appearances on any other network."

"Plan B," Sam Lesser said as he leaned back.

"And what's Plan B?" his assistant asked, knowing that Lesser had probably worked this out hours earlier.

"Make our celebrity. Castigate Cothran."

"Hmm," Hawkins said, "I like that. We build up our counter-Cothran personality. In the process we might even uncover dirt well-hidden beneath obscure rocks." He paused and asked, "It's a fine idea, but who do we get?"

"Atlanta preacher. Straight-laced. Good speaker."

"You don't want someone well-known? Atlanta?" Hawkins said as he shook his head slowly. "I don't know. If he's an unknown . . ."

"Won't remain unknown. Create him."

"Hmm," Bobby said, considering the idea. He knew it

could work. With Sam Lesser's forceful personality and personal commitment behind a project, it had to succeed. Lesser knew how to make things happen. "Maybe . . ."

"1948. Graham."

Hawkins's eyes lit up. Yes, he remembered—not personally, but those in the business knew the story of unknown Billy Graham. Hawkins's radio-tycoon father told him that the newspaper magnate William Randolph Hearst liked a little-known youth evangelist named Billy Graham and sent out a memo to all his papers to "puff Graham." Until his recent retirement, Graham had been the world's best-known preacher for forty years.

"Hmmm," Bobby said, "if we push this man . . . who is he?"

"David Morgan. Lutheran."

"You nuts? A Baptist maybe. Possibly get away with a Presbyterian—"

"Thinks like Baptist! Clerical garb."

"Sure, with robes he already stands apart in a crowd. But would he be conservative enough for Peoria and Little Rock?"

"Yes."

"Then," Hawkins said, "he must also be a man who thinks for himself, who'll speak out against the ills and evils—"

"Yes."

"Educated?" Hawkins asked.

"Yes."

"Heavy breather?"

"No," Lesser said and smiled, amused that occasionally Hawkins got caught up in the word-economy game. He knew exactly what Hawkins meant, asking if the man was one who shouted, who, when preaching, breathed from the lungs rather than the diaphragm. Those types would get their momentum going, run out of air, take a quick gulp, and end virtually every phrase with "and ah" tacked on at the end, making it difficult for many people to concentrate on the message.

"Bright. Forceful," Lesser added.

"Becomes our creation," Hawkins said. "Crusader of the century, huh?"

"Exactly," said Lesser.

Bobby tapped his chin, a sure sign that he was thinking carefully. From under hooded eyes he said quietly, "Let's go for it."

That afternoon Sam Lesser sent a two-word message to the head of every ABC affiliate: "Puff Morgan."

"And who's Morgan?" asked Jaimie Dennis, the station manager at Atlanta's White Columns, the local affiliate of ABC.

"You'll find out," his secretary said. "I'm willing to bet that Peter Jennings will have a feature story on the man tonight."

Dennis was glad he didn't take the bet; he would have lost.

"In an interview today, the Rev. David Morgan, pastor of St. Luke's Lutheran Church in Atlanta, spoke about the recent Annella Maxwell program in which Levis Cothran appeared."

The camera cut to David Morgan standing in front of St. Luke's Lutheran Church. A reporter thrust a microphone into his face. "Would you give your reaction to the Levis Cothran declaration, 'I am God, you are God'?"

David blinked. "My response? Cothran is at least confused."

"If more than confused?"

"Then I'd have to say he's a tool of Satan. He may not know it, but he is doing lying wonders and signs to lead people astray."

"What about his declaration that he's god?"

"If he is God, how did he create himself?"

"I don't know the answer, Mr. Morgan. But tell me, do you think the healing and all of the information he pulled out was fake?"

"I do! Perhaps not intentionally done by Mr. Cothran. You see, the Bible speaks about lying and deceitful spirits. The Devil often duplicates the miraculous. Satan, another name of the Devil, will try any trick to turn people away from the true God."

"Surely, Mr. Morgan, you're not trying to talk like somebody from the ancient days who saw evil spirits everywhere he turned!"

"I wouldn't phrase it that way, but . . . yes, I believe in evil spirits. They're smarter and more sophisticated than we'd like to think. Their role is to deceive us."

"And do you think Levis Cothran is out to deceive people?"

"Possibly. Or else he is self-deceived. It comes out about the same."

"And what makes you think you're not self-deceived?"

"Only one thing." Morgan smiled. "I have a Bible, and I read it every day. That's the one safeguard I have against error and deception." He held up his hand. "Let me tell you something else. In the last century, the evangelist D. L. Moody said, 'God's Word will keep you from sin or sin will keep you from God's Word.' I'm echoing the words of Mr. Moody. Unless we turn to the Bible, God's Book of truth, we're open to all sorts of errors, deceptions, and tricks of the Devil."

The camera cut to the reporter, who told the audience that he was standing in front of St. Luke's Lutheran Church and gave a quick biographical sketch of Morgan.

"Some have called him the one sane voice for God," the reporter said. "Others have called him a good but misguided man. I suspect we'll be hearing more about and from Rev. David Morgan in the days ahead." He then gave his name, and anchorman Peter Jennings's face again flashed across the screen.

While Americans were watching the interview with David Morgan, a limo driver escorted four men to his car at JFK. "I have been sent to drive you to Manhattan," the driver said as he led them from customs to curbside. A second man was sitting inside the car, engine running, waiting. As soon as he saw the four men, he jumped out of the vehicle and opened two doors on the left side. The escort opened the doors on the right.

Before the escort closed the door, he pointed out the bar and glasses and explained how to bring the television out from its recessed area. "My instructions are that you are to turn on the set once I have joined the driver. A videocassette is ready for your viewing."

He bowed and closed the door. Seconds later the car moved ahead. Quayle leaned forward, pushed a button to bring the set up, and then turned on the TV. Instantly Annella Maxwell's face appeared. "Good evening, my brothers. You are on your way to my apartment where I await you. Your luggage is coming in a separate vehicle, and The Voice has provided each of you with new clothing which is already in your own apartments in this same building. You may be interested to know that we shall occupy the top six of the fifteen stories." Pictures of the luxury apartment appeared, with a doorman waving a greeting.

"Once you have moved in, you must let me know if there is anything you want to make you comfortable. Or," and she winked, "anyone."

"That is the one," Sari said. "The woman who brought me the books."

"Same woman who visited me," Hanse Wensela said. "There could not possibly be two women in the world as beautiful as Annella Maxwell."

"Well, mates," Quayle said, "she is the one who personally delivered the books to all of us. Didn't you know that?"

"While a surprise," Zolo said, not attempting to hide his contempt, "it requires little intelligence to arrive at such a conclusion."

"Good to have you along," Quayle said. "You have such brilliant insights."

"Gentlemen," Sari said, "I believe it is better if we remember we are being summoned to work together."

Neither man answered. Zolo, along with Wensela and Sari, turned his attention back to the set. Maison Quayle listened to the video but, sitting next to the door, stared at the passing neighborhoods. With little effort he dismissed Zolo from his mind. A day would come when he would have a chance to get even with Zolo. And for a man like Quayle, "get even" meant "destroy."

Quyale concentrated on the view outside the vehicle. He knew already that he liked New York, so different from Paris and Vienna, the only European cities he had previously visited. Cities of the Middle East were so different, they might have existed on a different planet. Immediately Quayle knew that New York City had a beauty peculiar to itself with its glacial buildings that towered through the clouds.

When the next set of images appeared on the screen, several seconds lapsed before P. K. Sari recognized the town of Khasim. Black billows of smoke rose from the eastern side of the city. He sat emotionless as the cameras focused in and the voiceover said, "At midafternoon an explosion rocked the town of Khasim, a suburb of Bombay, India." The clipped Englishwoman's voice explained that defective wiring had shorted, causing a fire in one home which spread over an area of ten kilometers, totally destroying eight buildings and gutting or badly mutilating at least ten more. "The blaze began in the home of P. K. Sari, a wealthy businessman. Although his body has not been yet found, rescue workers have dragged out the remains of his wife and three children . . ."

"What do you say to that?" Zolo asked.

"What is to be, will be," Sari said, now understanding why he had been given a false name for traveling. He smiled and said aloud, "The Voice's cleverness continues to amaze me. Only one month ago I transferred all my holdings into a limited partnership—at The Voice's direction. Under my new name I am the senior partner and will, obviously, receive insurance. You see, I owned every one of those buildings."

"Wish I'd thought of a proper scheme like that," Quayle said.

"But I suspect you have your own methods," Wensela said.

"Perhaps you are right," Quayle said. His mind focused momentarily on his four former wives, all now dead, all from wealthy backgrounds and each of whom made him sole beneficiary of her estate. In neither case had any question of foul play been mentioned. Truly The Voice knew how to arrange things well.

Thirty-seven minutes later the limo stopped in front of the apartment on Park Avenue South, and the doorman opened the two curbside doors. The man who had met them at JFK escorted them to the elevator inside. As soon as the four men were in the elevator, he pushed the button for the penthouse and stepped back, allowing the door to close.

At the penthouse, Annella Maxwell, dressed in a red silk couture cocktail dress, met the four men at the door. She smiled brightly. "I wonder if any of you expected to see me again?"

"Not here, that's for sure," Quayle said. "But then, I wouldn't mind meeting you anyplace."

The smile disappeared from her face and in her coldest tone she said, "Quayle, you and I will work together. Please remember that. We will be nothing more than coworkers."

"And if I should want more than that?"

"I'll leave explanations to The Voice." She turned her back on Maison Quayle and linked arms with Zolo and Wensela. She walked across the parquet floor and through a narrow hallway. The apartment, surprisingly spacious, was furnished with modern decor. On the linen-covered walls hung samples of the more extreme modern artists which, with the Swedish furniture, gave the room a sense of intimacy and warmth.

The first of three guest rooms had been done in natural-colored hide. The second was fitted to look like a ship's cabin and the third like a sheik's harem.

"This way," she said, and led them into a large room decorated in empire blue. From the center hung a magnificent crystal chandelier. Six Louis Philippe chairs, the only furniture, formed a circle in the center of the room.

Their eyes paused at the chairs. "I only count five of us," Quayle said. "Who's to be the sixth?"

"He comes from a different direction." Peering at her diamond-studded Rolex, Annella said, "He will arrive within the next five minutes."

As if she had commanded, the doorbell rang. "The last one has arrived. The circle is complete."

"And now?" asked Quayle.

"And now the plan begins."

Quayle started to ask, What plan?, but thought better of it. Instead he went over, turned one of the chairs around, and sat down. He was willing to wait.

S·E·V·E·N

Without waiting for anyone to answer the doorbell, a slim man of medium height walked into the apartment while the others stared at him. He bowed his head slightly, keeping his body erect as a smirk appeared on his face. "My name is Sami Yatawazy. I believe you have been awaiting my arrival."

Yatawazy's features and complexion resembled that of the stereotypical Jew with his black curly hair and heavy eyebrows. His large, hook nose and olive complexion, along with his accent, immediately gave him away as a Middle-Easterner.

"I'm Annella Maxwell," said the hostess, extending her hand as she moved toward him. "We have been waiting for you."

Ignoring her, Yatawazy moved past her and scrutinized each of the others.

Although the newcomer wore a suit, Maison Quayle was picturing him wearing flowing robes and turban. "We know your name. What's your game?" He stayed in his chair, not bothering to get up.

"I have come at the behest of The Voice. I did not come for games." Yatawazy's eyes quickly scanned the man with the ruddy complexion. "I am seeing you for the first time, and already I do not like you."

"Before we go any further," Annella said, "we're not here to be friends or to like each other. We are here because we have been chosen."

"I am aware of my being chosen," said Yatawazy, "but I have many questions about all of you—or at least some of you. Wensela I recognize. And I am aware of your 'work,' shall we say, Zolo?"

"I am, of course, flattered that a man of your reputation would know of an ignorant African."

"But a clever, ignorant African." Yatawazy said the words softly and without inflection, but the fire blazed in Zolo's eyes at the intended insult.

Annella pointed to the six Louis Philippe chairs. "If you will each sit down, we'll learn the reason we are here."

Maison Quayle turned his chair around so it faced the center of the circle. The others sat down. They had all read the books and knew what to do without direction. After closing their eyes, the six relaxed and waited. The only sound inside the room came from P. K. Sari as he began to chant sotto voce, his voice moving between only three notes. Slowly his chanting rose to a crescendo as if determined to fill the room until the walls burst. Then slowly the tone softened and the volume decreased. When he stopped, the six of them remained in silence.

Annella Maxwell's head snapped backward and her body jerked in contorted spasms, then relaxed again. "I welcome you, my special servants," said a heavy basso voice through the body of Annella Maxwell. "I am Mastermind."

"For many years I have been shaping a Plan for the total control of Planet Earth. I have many servants, in all corners of the globe; but I have been waiting for the right moment, the right combination of individuals. *You* are the instruments I need to accomplish my purposes."

Mastermind promised them vast rewards for their

labors, reminding them that he had already been behind their continued rise to wealth, ensuring that all their transactions had been profitable and making certain that they had not been arrested or interrogated.

"But I think I have barely escaped the law," said Sari.

"You must not allow that to trouble you," Mastermind answered. "Did you not promise to serve me totally?"

"Yes . . . oh, yes, Mastermind."

"Then you may rest assured that I will provide for you, keeping you from danger . . . all of you."

"Thank you, blessed Mastermind."

"Because my Plan cannot fail—must not fail—I have selected you from all the human creatures in the entire world. Thousands are ready to assist you with their talents, their resources and money. They await your direction. If you follow, you shall truly inherit the Earth, and each of you shall reign over millions."

"Sounds like a great plan, and I'm certainly your man," said Maison Quayle.

"You are *one* of six," said Mastermind. "And since you have spoken, Maison Quayle, I shall explain your life first. I have chosen the six of you because you are individuals without morals, without conscience, without pity for your victims. Each of you desires wealth, prestige, power—ah, most of all power. You are, as my one great Enemy would likely say, totally profligate and without scruples. You are exactly the kind of servants I need.

"Now, because you are going to work together, you must also know each other. You need not learn to like each other because that is beyond you. However, my Plan cannot go into effect, nor can your usefulness be shown until I strip you naked in front of each other. There will, from this moment on, be no secrets from each other about your past, your nefarious talents, or your quality of life. Is that clear?"

"Y' mean you're going to tell all?" Quayle asked.

"Precisely."

Quayle shrugged. "If you've got the facts, tell them my acts."

"Yes, Mr. Quayle. To some—especially women—you are an attractive man." Mastermind mentioned the name of Dora, Quayle's first wife. She was a widow, left with a hefty fortune by her first husband, and then she married Quayle. One year after their wedding, a thief broke into their home, apparently thinking the house was empty because Quayle was away on business. Interrupted while stealing jewelry, the thief struck Dora repeatedly with a bronze candlestick.

"Your second marriage was no less tragic," Mastermind said. "And to give you credit, you did not use the same method a second time."

"Nor a third," said Quayle.

"All in all, you have married and cleverly done away with four women in seven years. Only this time—"

"This time the police have suspicions."

"Exactly," said Mastermind. "That was insurance to ascertain your arrival. You are not to worry, because once you begin your committed service to me, you will be exonerated. I have already arranged for the apprehension of your fourth wife's murderer. Her lover, you see, has been persuaded to confess that when she tried to break off their alliance, in a rage he killed her. I do hope, Mr. Quayle, your masculinity won't suffer from this information. Part of it is true—your wife's unfaithfulness."

"You set me free, and I will agree."

"And now, let us turn to Sami Yatawazy from Iran. You have special talent, Mr. Yatawazy. No one in the world today can manipulate currency quite as cleverly. May I speak on?"

"Oh, by all means, Mastermind. I wish them to know of my expertise."

Yatawazy, explained Mastermind, had begun in Teheran as a petty money lender, gradually gaining more influential clients. In 1992 he had convinced the government of Iran to erect public housing for the indigent. Through a series of currency changeovers in no less than seven hands, each one slightly greased with the oil of profit, Yatawazy had provided such housing. Yatawazy then walked away with ten million pounds in British sterling.

"Mr. Yatawazy has the unique ability to make people pay, but because of the gains they receive, they are unaware of the real cost. At least they do not realize it until far into the future."

Mastermind also pointed out that Yatawazy had found it convenient to eliminate his competition and had, over his ten-year rise from 1987 until the present, been responsible for the deaths of twenty-three men and four women.

"Worthless garbage," Yatawazy muttered.

"If you will excuse my bluntness," said Hanse Wensela, "I am not certain that I belong among this—this rabble. I have never murdered, I have never—"

"Ah, but you are one of them," Mastermind said, "And you should be proud of your membership. And as for murder, it is true that you have not directly killed anyone. Aside from those you paid others to eliminate, I point out that in two instances you raided noble corporations, deposed their leaders, and destroyed the company after withdrawing all the funds. As a result, both of those heads took their own lives."

"Right bright," said Quayle.

"Annella Maxwell," said Mastermind, "went to Hollywood twenty-nine years ago at age fourteen, but she looked older. She already knew more about the seduction of men than most women could possibly learn in a lifetime. Did you ever have a failure, my dear?"

"None," said Annella, speaking in her own voice. "You taught me well."

"As beautiful as Annella is, you must remember that Hollywood has no dearth of such types. Annella broke into films fairly easily, moving into featured roles by the end of her ninth film at the end of her second year."

"She came from far, but turned into a star."

"Quayle," said Zolo, "your poetry does not please me."

"Your reaction," he said, "brings no retraction."

Mastermind interrupted to tell of Annella's meteoric rise to starring roles and then her venture into a television series. Eighteen months before she began her own show, a producer with whom she had lived at an early point in her career approached her with the idea of a daily talk show, bringing on celebrity guests who were willing to share their secrets. Only one thing prevented the project from happening: Annella had not counted on the competition of Rebekka Steele.

Rebekka Steele had come into the entertainment industry through inherited money, beauty, and far more talent than Annella Maxwell. To solidify her power, she married the Number Two man at CBS and kept an affair going with his assistant. To everyone at CBS in 1996 and early 1997, the saying behind the scenes was, "Whatever Rebekka wants, Rebekka already has."

And Rebekka Steele wanted her own talk show. The idea came to her, she said, in the middle of the night. More accurately, it came to her in the middle of a cocktail party when she overheard Annella speaking of her plans.

When CBS announced a Rebekka Steele show for the 1996 fall lineup, Annella telephoned her. "Congratulations. You may know I wanted that show, but I'll have to admit that nobody could do a better job."

Pleased at the acquiescence of her only serious rival, Rebekka Steele relaxed. She had feared retaliation from Annella because of unsubstantiated gossip that Annella never allowed herself to lose anything she truly wanted.

Four days later Rebekka Steele received a bottle of champagne from Saint Pierre de Montmarte winery at Chartres. The company made exactly one hundred bottles annually of what they called their Golden Blend, selling or giving it to only the most important people in the world. The President of the United States, enjoying his second term in office, had repeatedly been denied a bottle. In fifteen years, only four people in the entertainment industry had received a bottle of the Montmarte Golden Blend.

Rebekka Steele did not know that the bottle had come to her through Annella Maxwell, who had charmed and bedded the second-born son of the winery's owner. Upon receipt of the bottle, Annella injected the wine with ant-and-roach powder by the use of a hypodermic needle and then sent it to Rebekka by messenger.

Rebekka Steele, pleased and flattered at the gift which she assumed came directly from Montmarte, chose to celebrate alone—as Annella knew she would. After drinking, the woman suffered from severe abdominal pains for three hours before she died. Some people whispered that she had tried to use the telephone, but it did not work, although no one could substantiate the rumor. The bottle was mysteriously emptied, washed, and partially refilled with an inferior wine by the time the medical examiner arrived. "Heart attack," he said, and no one questioned him.

Six weeks later, CBS announced the beginning of "The Annella Maxwell Show."

"Quite accurate," Annella said, "but the others don't realize that I relied on you quite early, Mastermind. You have been a wonderful influence on my life."

"And we have yet to speak to Zolo and Sari," Mastermind said. The Voice told of the deeds of the last two, particularly emphasizing the witchcraft Zolo used against those who opposed him. Sari had become an expert of industrial sabotage, with the ability to make the incidents appear purely as accidents. No suspicion had befallen him.

"But I can never return to India," Sari said.

"Ah, but you underestimate me," Mastermind answered. "They have now found a body, close enough to your own skeletal size that they will accept the dead man as you. You can return under your assumed name of Patel or—"

"You give me a choice?"

"If you do my will, I will arrange for the authorities to see that you left India two days before the accident, that the man's body they found was involved in immoral practices with your wife."

"Yes," Sari said, "please make that so."

"Then it is done," said Mastermind, "because I value you—my true servant."

"I am your servant until my death," said the Indian.

"Yes, I know."

The buildup of David Morgan had begun. While a few voices derided his comments, most of the letters and telephone calls complimented him on his earnestness, his integrity, or his courage. As he finished reading the handful of messages after his evening's telecast, Morgan left the studios with a buoyancy he had not felt for a long time.

"People are responding," he said aloud to himself. St. Luke's Lutheran Church had immediately felt the impact of his messages by its continued growth. Before the telecasts, one hundred and fifty on a Sunday morning made up a good crowd. Now, only weeks after his national exposure, six hundred people filled the church, forcing David Morgan to have two morning worship services. The attendance continued to build, and he instituted a Sunday afternoon service at 2:00.

After another few weeks, so many were worshiping at all three services that many individuals had to stand along the walls. Next the church added closed-circuit television sets with giant screens which they placed in the Fellowship Hall. No one complained about inconvenience.

Eighteen families moved from Sandusky, Ohio, relocating in the Atlanta area to "hear the true gospel preached without apology and without error," said their leader.

Another ten families moved from Southern California to be near "a sensible practical proclamation of God's Word."

As the pastor of St. Luke's Church scurried from one activity to another, he discovered energy he had never known before. "It's wonderful to be a pastor in a time like this," he said to his wife, "speaking to people so hungry they almost drag the words from your mouth."

"Don't get caught up in numbers, darling," Katherine said as she squeezed his hand. "You were a fine preacher and a dedicated Christian before all this growth happened. That's what counts with me."

Morgan kissed the tip of her nose. "Thanks, and I hope I'll always remember that."

"I hope so too," said Katherine as she looked away so he wouldn't see the tears forming in her eyes.

As David Morgan prepared for his private devotional time the next morning, his mind began to wander. Instead of concentrating on his Bible reading, he kept thinking about Steve Grubman.

Whatever finally happened to Steve? he wondered. They had been such good friends in college. Both of them, fairly young in the Christian faith, eagerly wanted to serve Jesus Christ.

David could see his old friend now as he had been nearly twenty years ago. He had what David called a reliable face with intelligence that showed in the green eyes and alert brow, strength in the mouth, a firm jaw line, and a body kept in good condition.

David had observed only one weakness in his friend: the man admitted no weakness. "With Jesus Christ, I can do anything!" Steve declared often. Such statements—which Steve Grubman really believed—bothered David. Although Steve always gave credit to God for his talents, David often wondered if his friend thought himself infallible.

Steve didn't finish college because he began to preach at a local church, soon becoming the pastor. Within a year he had built the membership from a mere thirty people to seven hundred. A charisma clung to Steve Grubman in the same way that some men come across as handsome or athletic. Few paid much attention to his physical features, but they constantly talked about his zeal, his ability to communicate, his intensity that stirred them up.

From the local church on Atlanta's south side, Steve moved into evangelistic-teaching services, traveling across Georgia, then the Southeast, and finally covering the entire United States. His weekly television program made his name known to millions, both believers and nonbelievers. Around 1990 he established the Retreat-for-Advance Center near Conyers, Georgia. Soon a community grew up around the two hundred hectares of land, thousands of people wanting to become part of Grubman's ministry and to live near him.

Then the sad news blared out on every television station: Steve Grubman's alleged involvement with a prostitute, questions about the use of money designated for specific projects, and accusations that he was addicted to cocaine.

David Morgan phoned Steve as soon as he heard the news. "I'm sorry about all of this. But I'm your friend and—"

"Aren't you going to ask if it's true?" Steve said, a hardness in his voice that David had never heard before.

"I'm your friend regardless."

"It's true, David. That's what's so terrible. Not the addiction, but the rest of it. And more than that."

"Again, I'm sorry—"

"Sure!" Steve slammed down the telephone.

They had never seen each other again. David had tried repeated telephone calls and letters, and even went to his house once. Steve would not talk to him.

"How the mighty are fallen," David Morgan said as he wondered why he had been thinking about Steve Grubman this morning.

E·I·G·H·T

"**E**ach of you is already wealthy," Mastermind said. "But it is not enough. Money will never be enough, but I understand. I shall continue to add to your treasures, giving you everything you desire."

The six of them had been meeting regularly, setting the stage for Mastermind's great Plan to unfold. From all parts of the world, they now knew the names of key cooperative-agents, or as they called them, co-ags. These people were fully submissive to the will of Mastermind, though not yet aware of the spirit's identity. They knew only that they had given themselves to pleasure and profit and that an underground system had begun, calling occasionally upon their services. They had already received rewards and anticipated greater luxuries ahead.

Yatawazy had become especially busy, preparing for a new wave of prosperity for the Western nations. Sari had set up industrial accidents in fifteen key cities, destroying leaders who would not function as co-ags in places where Mastermind would need assistance. As soon as one such leader died, another co-ag moved in to fill the vacancy.

"Before we go into our first operation," Mastermind said, "I am ready to inform you of your rewards. To each of you, I give a palace—totally modern with conveniences many have not yet known or dreamed of—and your own fleet of aero-ships, which are already replacing jets in commercial aviation. You can now fly to anywhere in the world within seven hours."

"I'd like a grand castle if it's not too much hassle!"

"Quayle, I can bear with you," Mastermind said, "only because of your *other* talents."

"But y' see, Mastermind," Quayle said, "you took me the way I was, see. I have made my way because I've questioned authority and laughed at it. That's who I am. You don't want me to change now, do you?"

"I should like very much for you to change," said Sari, "but perhaps that is impossible. You do tire me and tax my patience."

"But I keep you honest," Quayle said, "in a way of speaking. Or maybe I should say honestly dishonest."

"And, my servants," Mastermind interrupted, "you may not only have your beautiful homes, but you may locate wherever you like in the world."

"I am *persona non grata*," said Amwago Zolo, "in my own land. Otherwise I should very much like to have a magnificent home overlooking the Rift Valley in Kenya."

"It is already being built for you," said Mastermind. "By the time you fly from here, your home will be ready."

"But is that not impossible? The President of Kenya knows that I have taken millions of East African pounds from the country, been responsible for the death of the Minister for Culture who opposed me, and—"

"You may rest," Mastermind said. "I have already begun to clear your name. By noon today here in New York, President Nyakwana will receive a registered letter from you. In this letter you will name the four men in his cabinet who have worked against the country, attempting to overthrow the government and place the nation under the thumb of the Soviet Union."

"How did you manage—?"

"Oh, it is true," Mastermind said. He named the four men.

"Impossible," Zolo said. "I know those men. They are staunch Christians, men of impeccable—"

"Silence! When I declare it is true, it is true! Never forget that."

"Y' mean, Mastermind, that you make it true because you call it that way?" asked Maison Quayle. "I like your style!"

"I make my own truth," said Mastermind. "And from this day on, Kenya will honor you, Zolo, for your courage in denouncing these traitors. The envelope in the hands of President Nyakwana bears evidence that no one can contradict. He also has the names of witnesses who will swear that they were coerced into joining with the traitors. When you return, Zolo, you will go back in triumph—a national hero!"

"Yeah, I kind of like your truth, Mastermind," Quayle said. "And you're going to do the same for each of us?"

"I have already done so. When you go to your apartments, each of you will find a large envelope with plans of your palace. If you do not like anything—any feature at all—you have only to contact the person whose name appears on the bottom of the white sheet, and she will make changes for you."

"Anything?" asked Quayle.

"Anything. I reward my servants well."

Mastermind explained that each would receive honors from their national governments and the highest respect. "My co-ags are at work, as I am always at work," Mastermind said. "And I have reserved the best for those who remain loyal to me."

"You are our master, for now and always," said Sari.

"You only will we serve," said Zolo.

"You got me—all of me," Quayle said.

The others affirmed their allegiance to Mastermind as well.

"One more thing before we put my plan into action. It

concerns your children. There are only four. Annella has a daughter, Wensela a son, and Quayle has twin sons."

"Woodrow and Ferdinand," said Quayle.

"I know them well. Each of them has, to some degree, followed their parents. It is my desire for you to bring them to the meetings of Mastermind. They will not be allowed to sit in the circle of six, they will not be allowed to speak, but I shall grant them to be privy to our proceedings."

Without giving Quayle a chance to interrupt again, Mastermind said, "We are ready for our first attack. Not only is it first, but it is our primary target. We are going against the Christian leaders throughout the world."

"Christian leaders?" asked Quayle. "Why not the Muslims? They're more fierce. Or Hindus or—"

"Because, Mr. Quayle, first, Christians are the only ones who have any inkling of my ultimate purpose. Second, Christians have the potential to defeat my truth. They will not win, of course, but they could. If we ignored them—as you yourself would choose to do—they could rise up against us."

"But I question this also," said Wensela. "Unless you speak of a caliber of Christian I haven't met—"

"You are right to question," Mastermind said. "This time, however, they are not our targets because of what they have done or what they will do. It is their *potential*. They have access to a power—a great power—that operates only if they call upon it. That is how we can win. We shall lull them into passivity."

"Ah, yes," said Yatawazy, "now I understand why you are preparing for prosperity to come to the West—"

"Where they are strongest—or at least where they are more in number. Most of them are now asleep, and we shall make certain that they do not awaken."

"Give me the Plan—I'm your man," Quayle said.

"First, you will attack the leaders of the churches. I have already selected the major voices in Christianity. Across the world we have seventy-nine. My co-ags are handling the lesser leaders."

"We kill them? Is that what you wish?" Sari said.

"No. We destroy their credibility, we ruin their reputations. Then we hold them up to be the buffoons of the world. A few may die, but that is not important," said Mastermind.

"How do we discredit?" asked Wensela. "Manufacture evidence against them?"

"No," said Mastermind. "We may—and shall—use such methods, but not as our primary forms of attack. No, we first build them up."

"Ah, the farther to the top, the greater the plop!" said Quayle.

"That is one way of expressing it," Mastermind said. "You will study these leaders. They are human, which means they have weaknesses—as each one of you has. You will exploit their vulnerable spot."

"We have to feel for the Achilles' heel—"

"Quayle, silence. I wish to make a principle of life clear to you. Those who know they are weak are the most difficult to trap. We must assist them to become oblivious to their vulnerability. You will enjoy this part of your work. For some they secretly yearn for power, others for possessions, or sex—"

"Like those of us in this room," Quayle said. "Oops, sorry."

"Yes, like all of you. These Christians are as weak as anyone else. Some frailties will appear obvious. For others, scrutinize their strengths. Where people are the most powerful, they are also the most impotent."

"You mean like that fellow . . . the preacher . . . uh, Grubman?" asked Quayle.

"Yes, my co-ags set him up and brought him to prostration. That is the method we will use. And have you not all used this yourselves?"

"Of course," said Annella. "I appeal to a man's pride, to what he values most about himself before I conquer him."

"And, Quayle, you are immensely successful with females for precisely the same reason. The difference lies in your motive. Annella calculates logically, systematically; you, however, work by intuition."

"Where do we start?" asked Zolo. "I am quite desirous to complete my assignments and to be ensconced as a ruler."

"We have already begun to prepare the important targets. Mr. Sari will work with co-ags this week to take care of Bishop Saboo of India. He is a man of immense greed and can be eliminated without great difficulty."

As Mastermind presented the names and assignments of the six, he saved the names Morgan, Wheatley, McFarland, and Staats for last. "Not because they are stronger and not because they are already important. These four men have a level of commitment to their—let us say to their cause—so that we must move more carefully. The wrong approach at any point, and they may yet defeat us."

"Morgan I've heard of," said Annella, "but not the others."

"You will hear, my dear," said Mastermind. "You have heard of Morgan because we are already in the upbuilding stage. You will soon know the others because you will play roles in their downfall, working primarily through your co-ags."

Woodrow and Ferdinand Quayle were identical twins and had operated as one individual since infancy. While they had learned to emulate their father—and had done extremely well at accumulating their own wealth—they had become as ambitious and as ruthless as Maison Quayle.

The sons, twenty-nine years old, had never known their mother because Maison Quayle had never married her and had taken the boys away from her within weeks of their birth. As their father, he had seen to their education by himself.

While the sons did not realize it, their father had no paternal feelings toward them. They were his creation, his work of making two men totally amoral and above the law.

He taught them most of the lessons he knew, and learned some from them; but always he watched them carefully. Maison Quayle recognized one danger from Woodrow and Ferdinand: they would destroy him if he stood in their way.

They respected Maison Quayle, admired his cunning and achievements, while secretly plotting for the day when they would do away with him and take over his growing empire of money and power. Maison Quayle had long anticipated this attitude and was determined to be ready for them when the day came.

John Alvin Wade IV, a tenth-generation Presbyterian and a sixth-generation preacher, had accepted the call to minister to Zaire in 1989, following the example of his father and grandfather. Being a capable man, he soon earned the respect of his fellow missionaries and the devotion of the nationals. In 1993 when the Zairian government asked all missionaries and foreign residents to leave, John Alvin Wade IV did a courageous thing: He became a citizen of Zaire. Already the recipient of enough money so he had no financial worries, Wade devoted himself to the needs of the people of his new nation.

Soon the Presbyterians, Methodists, and United Churches of Christ merged and elected Dr. Wade as First Shepherd. At first he was reluctant to accept such a post, but the Christians (none of them co-ags) persuaded him to accept. Despite his title, he still spent many hours each day helping the needy. Often he worked with hammer and saw alongside others to construct homes. Daily their leader distributed food after six weeks of severe rains destroyed the crops of 1996.

Mastermind would have paid little attention to John Alvin Wade IV if he had remained simply a do-gooder. But in late August, Wade became aware of changes within Africa. Prosperity had seeped in along with westernization (which had been present for half a century). But something about this wave of prosperity was different.

He observed the change in converts as they slowly pulled back from their dedication to Jesus Christ. Indifference set in and then, as their wealth increased, dislike for the church and what it stood for. "Opium for their minds, bread for their stomachs, and they empty their pockets for the church," said one former Presbyterian elder who refused to allow his children to attend worship services.

And then Dr. Wade unintentionally overheard a conversation between two co-ags when he visited a large *shamba* in northern Zaire where they raised a bountiful supply of sweet potatoes. He had negotiated for the entire crop and their transportation to Zaire City (formerly Paulis). Afterwards, Wade remained in the manager's office, writing notes in his small notebook, a lifetime habit.

Outside the door, two men were speaking in Lingala, a dialect Wade knew well. One explained to the other what they must do to discredit the pastor of a nearby church. From the way he talked, Wade realized they were going to bring a woman into his home while the man's wife was gone. Then the woman would accuse him of impropriety. Their scheme involved not just one pastor, but those all over the province. From this conversation, Wade realized that the underhanded dealings extended throughout Zaire, and he wondered if it might even extend beyond his country.

After the two men left, Wade drove to the home of the pastor and explained what was going to transpire. The pastor wisely called in headmen (as they called them) to spend the night with him. Wade sent messages to all of the pastors in the province, and not one of them was ruined by the evil design.

This might have been the end of Wade's involvement except for two pieces of news: First, his sister, a missionary in Bolivia, wrote to him, sad because of the terrible revelations that had come to light about their leading pastors. Second, he read an article in the *Presbyterian Survey* about similar stories concerning missionaries in Asia.

"A conspiracy is taking place around the world," he announced to the pastors and church leaders he called to their Shepherd headquarters in Bantu (the former Brazzaville). "Satan is raising up his cohorts, men and women determined to discredit God's people, to destroy confidence in Christian leaders, and to topple the evangelistic thrust of our work."

"Surely you are mistaken," said one leader, a recently converted co-ag.

"I think you have had too much beer," railed a second.

Despite their attempts to silence him, Dr. Wade denounced the planned attacks and told them of his experience in overhearing the Satanic plot. "We must rise up against all the tools and machinations of the Devil."

His actions came to the direct attention of Amwago Zolo. "I can handle this quite easily," he said to himself.

Dr. Wade, a widower, employed Fibi, a local resident, to cook and clean his house. She simply added ground glass to his food for three days until he started bleeding internally. Wade's doctor, also a co-ag, prescribed a medication to remove the pain. For two weeks the missionary had no further trouble with the bleeding and pain and decided to stop using the medicine. That evening he had more broken glass in his food, and he started taking the medicine again.

Within three weeks, Dr. Wade was addicted to the new medicine, made from a combination of hemp and three types of African grasses. When his doctor informed the Shepherd that no more medicine was available, that this had been an experimental drug from the Centers for Disease Control in Atlanta, and that it had been pulled from the market, Wade began going through withdrawal symptoms.

The doctor suggested a small amount of wine. "You know, a little wine for your stomach's sake, as St. Paul recommended for Timothy." Although a lifetime teetotaler, in desperation the learned missionary began to drink a little wine.

He did not know that Fibi was continuing to add bits of glass—small amounts, only enough to cause pain, never enough to arouse suspicion. His amounts of wine increased, and within two months Dr. Wade was consuming six liters of wine a day.

At this point, co-ags started a campaign to discredit him, and finally the Prime Minister of the Republic of Zaire found him passed out drunk on a Sunday morning. The next day Dr. Wade's citizenship was revoked, and he was asked to leave the country.

Readmitted to America, John Alvin Wade IV went to a drug addiction center, where he received no lasting help during the first two weeks. In the middle of his third week, an intern found his body hanging from the tower of the hospital chapel. No one suspected that he had been murdered; everyone knew his recent history too well.

"Well done, well done, good and faithful servant," Mastermind told Zolo. "You have shown your competence. Total victory is within sight for all of us!"

N·I·N·E

"A new voice for conservative evangelicals," cited *Newsweek* magazine as it profiled a reluctant David Morgan.

> . . . an immensely talented but modest man, David Morgan is attracting local attention, but has become a national figure in conservative religious circles.

> . . . Morgan's preaching carries conviction. His listeners sit as if they have never heard such messages before. Each service is filled with people, while most of the other churches in Metro Atlanta are half-empty.

"How do you account for this?" the reporter had asked.

David Morgan had shaken his head. "Only the grace of God," he said. "I haven't any idea why God has picked me or allowed me to attract these people. But I do know that as long as they come, they'll hear the message of God's love for them in Jesus Christ."

Morgan had responded sincerely. It had been months since God had first spoken to him in his dreams. And while he believed the promises of God, he still had difficulty understanding how it came about that these people flocked to services, some arriving as much as an hour early to get a place to sit.

David Morgan was suddenly the person to know. Invitations flowed in to speak at public gatherings, pray at the Braves' games, function as chaplain to the Atlanta Hawks. The mayor joined St. Luke's Church, and so did the CEOs of many corporations. The new governor was a member of Morgan's Lutheran church.

"You know, darling," Katherine said to her husband as they ate a quiet dinner together one evening, "it would be so easy to lose sight of what you're trying to do."

"What do you mean?" he asked.

"Oh, I was thinking about all the important people coming to St. Luke's."

"How I praise the Lord for them. Just think, they are the power-people of the city. They influence thousands."

"That's what I mean," Katherine said. She reached across the candlelit table and took his hand in hers. "These powerful people could easily turn your head, making you concentrate on the wrong things."

"I'm committed to Jesus Christ." A defensiveness crept into his voice.

"I know," she said and withdrew her hand. Katherine sipped her water, wanting to talk to him, wanting to say more, but she knew it would do no good.

"God has put me in a special place right now," he said. David told her of the opportunity he had to pray with the governor, and the following week he would be able to speak with a number of state legislators. Suddenly he paused, and a quizzical look spread across his face. "Something wrong?"

"I guess I was thinking of the common folks," she said, "the people who helped to build St. Luke's . . . Solid, middle-class people who don't seem quite so important any more."

David stared at her, his eyes narrowing, and then he said softly, "I love you. Without you around, I'm not sure I could ever keep my priorities right."

For the first time in days Katherine genuinely smiled. David understood. For now he would overcome this particular temptation anyway.

The fifteen-member Parish Council of St. Luke's met on a Tuesday evening. A buoyant mood filled the men as they heard the treasurer's report. St. Luke's Church was now giving more than nine thousand dollars a week to benevolent causes.

"When you demanded that fifty percent of our funds go outside the church to help the needy," Bob Kilgore said, "I didn't like it."

"You thought we'd go under, didn't you?" David asked.

"Well, at the time we were barely meeting our expenses."

"But we can never outgive a generous God," said Grayford Hart, who had supported David's proposal from the beginning.

"And now I have something I want to propose," said Kilgore, a lean man with deeply tanned skin. "We need more space."

"We need a bigger building!" said Tom Grundy.

David Morgan had been resisting the efforts to erect a mammoth structure. "We're attracting thousands of people, but how long will it continue?"

"Now who's speaking with little faith?" taunted Kilgore.

"I just don't know," Morgan said. "I don't feel right about spending close to two million dollars just for a building we use a few hours each week."

"But how else can we meet the needs of people?" Kilgore said, his voice rising. "I'm tired of coming an hour early just to get a place to sit!"

"Ah, come on," Hart said, "you pay one of your employees to come early and save four places for your family."

"Okay, but that only makes my point!"

For over an hour they tried to convince David Morgan that they needed a large tract of land and a bigger church. A month earlier they had enlarged their present building by extending both sides fifty feet and the front another seventy-five feet. They were at capacity now. Any further additions and they would use up their parking space—already cramped, with people parking on both sides of the narrow street, despite signs prohibiting it.

"Well, gentlemen," Grayford Hart said, "I've been sitting here for three-quarters of an hour listening to you push for a new building and hearing all the reasons, excuses, and reservations from our rector. So, I've taken the decision out of your hands."

"You've done what?" Kilgore said.

"I purchased a tract of land three, nearly four times as large as our present site. I hired an architect to draw up plans. The construction began yesterday. I have already hired enough men to run three shifts for sixty days." He paused and stared at the others as if to say, "Now fight that one."

At age sixty, Gayford Hart appeared ten years younger with blond hair barely streaked with gray. In his soft voice he continued, "Exactly two months from today, David, I intend to escort you into our new building—a building that will seat ten thousand people."

"Wait a minute," David said. "We need to discuss this—"

"Nope," said Hart. "This is my gift to God. Would you despise my offering and turn it down?"

David stood, his eyes unexpectedly filled with tears. "My brothers, I have no desire for bigness. I never asked God to make me a big-name preacher. But I bow in submission to the will of God. If this is what you brothers want—"

"I'm all for it," Kilgore said. "And I so move."

"I second it," said Grundy. "And, Gray, if you need any money, come to me. This new building won't have to cost the congregation one cent."

"Thank you, God," David said and called the group to a time of prayer together.

After they had prayed for half an hour, Walt Hiller said, "I have one more item I'd like to talk about before we dismiss."

David Morgan gave him the floor. At age twenty-four, Walt Hiller was the youngest person on the Council. He was a man of uncommon spiritual insight and had often been a challenge to David.

"I would like to see us change the style of worship here," he said. "And before you get uptight, let me tell you what I have in mind. David keeps telling us that we are living in the last days on the Earth . . . that Jesus Christ is going to come back soon and that we need to prepare ourselves for this. One thing we can do is to make changes in our style of worship."

"What did you have in mind?" Kilgore asked, already sensing he would not like the proposal.

"A no-frills church," Hiller shot back. "From this point on, unless something adds to the growth of the people, enables us to mature, or brings people to Jesus Christ, we eliminate it."

"Such as?"

"Such as a lengthy time for an offering. Why an offering at all? We can teach people to be responsible to give on their own. We can install small boxes at the end of each pew, and people can put their money in. That's one thing."

"And before anyone reminds us that we've never done it this way before," said Joe Strenk, "that might be good enough reason to make a change."

Morgan smiled as he listened to Joe Strenk, the newest member of the Council and a man who thought for himself.

"I'm behind our pastor," Joe Strenk persisted. "I'm also behind anything that will reach more people with the gospel."

"You know, I think I like the idea of no time spent for collecting money," Grundy said. "We have a printed bulletin, and it'll contain all the information about our financial needs."

"Also, I want to eliminate the formal choir," said Walt Hiller. "I'd like to see more spontaneity, more opportunity for people in the congregation to sing or to speak."

"We'd have chaos!" thundered Kilgore.

"We might have the Holy Spirit working because we'd be seeking guidance," Hiller said.

"I think we need to talk this over," Grundy said. "I have never heard of a Lutheran church without a choir!"

"If we're nearing the end of time, and if it's important to get the Word of God to as many as possible," Hiller said, "then I'd like to suggest that we rearrange our worship services so that preaching is the center."

"But it already is the center!" Kilgore said.

"Perhaps that is what we intend," Grundy said, "but we're not living in normal times."

"I want more preaching and teaching," said Walt Hiller.

"I do too," added Joe Strenk, "providing our pastor does it." He faced Morgan. "I'll tell you what brought my family and me to St. Luke's and what keeps us here. You preach to my heart, Pastor. You make me think, and you challenge me. I need more of that." After a lengthy discussion, the Parish Council agreed to restructure their worship service. They retained the choir as an aid to singing, but deemphasized the entertainment factor. In the hour-long service, they agreed that fifty minutes would be given to the teaching and preaching of the Scriptures.

Morgan said nothing during this phase of the discussion. He yearned to spend more time instructing the people of God, enabling them to fortify themselves spiritually and showing them how to grow. Yet he had a nagging feeling in the pit of his stomach that somehow they were not going about this correctly; at the same time he had no alternative to offer.

"And finally, our pastor has been urging us to form study groups for over a year," Hiller said. "I think it's time we stop resisting and that each of us commit to leading such groups. Those of us who aren't teachers can find people who are gifted in that way. But most important, we want to prepare ourselves to withstand the enemies of God."

Morgan's eyes moistened as he listened, fully aware that the day would come when some of these men, these leaders who supported him so fully, would find the way too difficult and the pressures too severe. Surely some would turn away. But for the moment he couldn't concentrate on what lay in the future. Right now he needed to respond to the present needs. "Let the will of God be done," he said simply.

The following Sunday, Morgan announced a special service on Thursday evening, a time of intercession for Christian leaders. "They need our prayers. And not just leaders," he said. "We need each other."

Rev. David Morgan then stepped out of the chancel area and walked down among the people. "My heart is heavy now as I stand before you. I plead with you to be faithful. The fires of testing will come to all of us. Pray! Pray! Pray for me! For yourself! For the leaders of God's people!"

On Thursday evening three hundred people grathered at St. Luke's Lutheran Church to pray. Most of the people prayed silently; a few raised their voices and cried out to God.

After more than an hour, Morgan said, "I've had a heavy burden for almost a week. Many of you have heard of the British evangelist and preacher Neville Wheatley. I have been wrestling with the demons of darkness for this man. Please . . . please pray with me for him."

As the believers paused to raise the man to God, Morgan felt a greater heaviness in his heart than he had all week. He wondered if it was already too late.

T·E·N

One thing marred Neville Wheatley's peace on a Tuesday morning in January of 1998. He had just finished reading a letter from an American named David Morgan. Naturally he had heard of the man. Although Morgan had been catapulted into the public eye only within the past year, he already had a considerable following. Reluctantly, Wheatley admitted that Morgan had shown considerable insight into spiritual matters.

He handed the letter to his wife Joan. "Read this," he said simply.

Neville Wheatley, as one admirer said, spoke with the fire of John the Baptist tempered by the love of John the Apostle. In his early fifties, he looked younger, especially when he moved. His close-cropped fair hair had kept its color; his ruddy cheeks suggested good health. The flesh of his face and, for that matter, the rest of his body had remained remarkably firm. His mouth occasionally told another story because of its slight downturn; in repose, his lips clamped tightly together. His teeth were strong but blunt, worn by a constant grinding in his sleep, the only outward manifestation of a tension which stretched back to childhood. His eyes were large and open, their irises a deep brown. When in public, Neville Wheatley could throw all of himself into those eyes, conveying trust and inviting intimacy. At other times, caught unawares, the eyes showed that he was a deeply troubled man.

Although nominally a member of the Methodist Church, he had long received recognition from all evangelical faiths. To Wheatley's surprise, the previous November the Archbishop of Canterbury had extended an invitation for him to speak to all Anglicans throughout the world.

Such an offer flattered Wheatley, who had repeatedly attacked the state-controlled Church of England. The offer also left him slightly suspicious. After a private meeting with the Archbishop, being convinced of the sincerity of the prelate, Wheatley spoke at Canterbury and the following week at York Cathedral and then at Coventry. He now had the sanction of the entire British Christian community.

Over his wife's shoulder he read Morgan's letter again. The words contained a warning to Wheatley of spiritual testing "because the powers of darkness seek to control you." Morgan pleaded with Wheatley to go into temporary seclusion, to make certain of God's guidance in his life before it was too late. The letter concluded, "I have prayed that your faith fail not when Satan sifts you. And, my brother, forgive my impertinence, but I have a feeling I cannot shake that my letter is already too late."

Joan read the letter carefully, then looked up at her husband's disturbed features. "Another of those cheeky American upstarts. They always know how to tell others to live and to conduct their business." She tore the single page into four even pieces and dropped them into her husband's wastebasket. "Who does he think he is?"

"He seems like a fine man," Neville protested weakly.

"Oh, does he now? Is he the great living saint of the world? You've been preaching Christ for years, and this young man pops up from some crack in the kerb and advises you. Quite a jealous fellow."

"You think so?"

"Who made him a prophet of God?" she asked. "Aren't you even more of a man of God? Just consider your experience and age." Joan Wheatley, a thin, small-boned woman, was eleven years older than her husband. She dressed in subdued gray; with her dyed black hair, pale lips, and white skin, she stood out in a crowd. Her eyes were large, dark, and easily her most attractive feature. "Cheeky American, I'd say, dear."

"Thank you," he said. "You're so much better at sizing up people."

"That's because you're too kind, much too compassionate," she said.

Neville smiled in appreciation. His wife, far more ambitious than he, had guided him thus far in his career. She had always been right, and he had no reason for doubting her judgment. Yet in the deep recesses of his heart, a tiny part of Neville Wheatley wondered. As he thought of the question, "Who made him a prophet?" he recalled that he had read that somewhere. After Joan left the room, Neville found the verse in the Bible. Moses' sister Miriam had asked the same question, and as punishment God had turned her temporarily leprous. *Odd*, he thought, *that my wife would use a similar expression.*

A ninety-minute, prime-time program featured Levis Cothran as Annella Maxwell's only guest. For two weeks CBS had publicized the event. The head of the network did something he rarely found necessary: He called on those who owed him favors. He asked, occasionally begged, and twice threatened for everyone of importance he knew to get people watching "Annella Presents Levis."

Sixteen major corporations competed to sponsor the program. Columnists plugged the show; newspapers found ways to make it a news item. Prominent leaders in the arts, politics, industry, and the entertainment world arranged an array of parties in their homes or in public places, all of them built around their guests watching the ninety-minute program.

As the show started, Annella Maxwell came on stage wearing a beaded gown that emphasized her excellent features, yet was carefully subdued. She welcomed her listeners and then said, "I don't need to spend a lot of time introducing Levis Cothran. This man needs no one to introduce him!" She started to applaud, and Cothran walked on stage.

He wore a pair of tight-fitting jeans and an embroidered shirt that showed off his athletic build. He flashed his famous smile, and the audience applauded for four minutes.

Cothran acted embarrassed by the attention and kept gesturing for the people to stop. Once the applause died down, Annella said, "We are going to pause to show you the fine companies who are paying for this time. Once we pass this one-minute commercial, we will have no further breaks until 9:28 when the program ends!"

Again loud applause, and the two of them embraced while the cameras switched to an automobile advertisement.

Exactly sixty seconds later, Annella looked into the camera. "I asked Levis to tell us his story—as only he can tell it. This is a man who had everything in life that anyone could want, but it wasn't enough. Despite millions in the bank and enough investments to enable him to live in high style for a hundred years, he said life held no meaning for him. But I want him to tell you himself."

Levis Cothran leaned back in his chair, then crossed one leg over the other at the knee, exposing his rhinestone-studded cowboy boots. "I don't need to tell you much about my career. It seemed like I couldn't make a picture that failed at the box office. Maybe that's what made me aware of the emptiness inside."

Levis Cothran's name on a film, whether drama or comedy, had ensured high profits. Against his better judgment he made a western, and it became the highest-grossing picture of its genre. A science fiction film followed, and it more than doubled the intake of *Two Thousand Forty*, the previous all-time winner.

The public knew some things about Cothran's private life. He had married young, before he came to Hollywood. That marriage lasted four years, ending in a divorce that charged him with adultery, which he never denied and which, in fact, added to his mystique. Over the next twenty years, Cothran married and divorced four more times. He wed yet again, and wife number six, the queen of Hollywood melodrama, Margaret Alexa, seemed the perfect marriage partner. They both won Academy Awards the same year.

That marriage, too, ended in divorce. Oddly enough Margaret Alexa never made a popular film after the divorce, while nothing hindered Cothran's continued popularity. Yet behind the public smile lay private pain the public didn't know about. Levis had undergone psychiatric treatment under a variety of doctors, but nothing helped. One therapist after another advised him to adjust to his inability to remain faithful to one woman and to accept this as part of who he was. They encouraged him to accept the idea that some people aren't good marriage partners, that living with women might be a better solution and easier to cope with than going into additional marriages. His rigid upbringing, they all agreed, had marred his psyche, causing him to feel guilty.

Levis Cothran, raised by strict parents and members of a small Holiness denomination, finally sought the help of ministers. A Holiness pastor tried to force him to locate his first wife (who had long ago remarried and had five children by her present husband), and to beg her to leave her "present, adulterous relationship" and be reconciled to him. When the film star spoke with her, she laughed at him and accused him of being on peyote.

An independent church pastor told him that God would forgive him, but he could never marry again. "After all, God gave you six chances." The clergyman advised him to learn to live in celibacy.

Willing to give the church one final try, Levis Cothran contacted a bishop of the Episcopal Church. One of his friends said, "This man is so understanding, and he never condemns anyone for anything."

Bishop Singer lived up to his reputation. He listened quietly to Levis Cothran's pitiful tale of broken marriages, his yearning for a loving relationship and his inability to find one that lasted. When Levis, overwhelmed by pain, allowed himself to weep, the bishop touched his shoulder in sympathy. And for the first time Levis sensed there might be hope because he felt that this man of the cloth understood.

"My son," the kindly bishop said, "yours is a sad history. I suggest that you continue your search. You must live by the best guidance you have."

"But, you see, I've violated the Law of God by adultery, by . . . well, a hundred different things. And the Bible pronounces judgment on such acts."

"My son, don't allow yourself to be unduly wrought."

"But God and the Bible—"

"Remember that the Bible is an ancient book, written for people who lived in ancient times. Laws that bound them are not always binding on us."

"They're not?" he asked. Although Levis Cothran had not been inside a church building in nineteen years, he had never questioned the consequences of his lifestyle.

The bishop met with Levis Cothran on nine different occasions. He threw out theological terms like "redaction criticism" and "historical accuracy," and pointed out that "We must not blindly follow the rules of the Bible simply because we read them in print."

"What should I do then?"

"Live by the best insight you have. Trust your inner guidance. If you find another woman—and I'm sure you will—and you want to share your lives together, then pledge your faithfulness to each other and live together in peace as long as you can."

"You make it sound simple . . . easy."

"Perhaps not easy, but quite simple," the bishop said and smiled. "My responsibility is to help people face themselves and to find peace. They don't find peace by enslaving themselves to archaic laws."

On the television show, as Levis recounted the meetings with Bishop Singer (whom he did not mention by name), he said, "I rejected what he said initially. But that message became the first of many liberating thoughts for me."

"In what way?" Annella Maxwell asked. "It seems to me that he confused you more."

"On the contrary," he answered, "through the words of that bishop, I realized I had been made to feel guilty by my religious beliefs in childhood. My parents' outdated insistence on calling the Bible the Word of God had confused and led me astray."

Levis Cothran then began his search. He didn't retire from films; he simply didn't make any more. No one knew of his whereabouts. Occasionally rumors circulated of his death from a drug overdose or that he had been murdered by the Mafia. Cothran traveled first to India, then to Japan and Sri Lanka. He visited every guru, teacher, instructor of religion he heard of—carefully avoiding the Christian faith, which he knew now had nothing to offer him.

"Slowly the truth came home to me," Cothran said. "I then had to find others who understood. At the time I felt as if I were an alien on this planet, as if I alone had opened the door of understanding. Yet, instinctively I knew there must be others somewhere, seeking, yearning for truth. And then I found them, and in finding the others, the ultimate answers also came."

"Levis," Annella said as she moved closer, "this is what the audience wants to hear. What did you find and how?"

"Believe it or not, my ex-wife, Margaret Alexa, was the one who showed me the way."

Cothran had returned to Southern California, to his isolated home outside Los Angeles. He had heard of a group called The Master Plan that met twice weekly in San Bernadino. He visited one evening, carefully disguised with a beard and with his hair long and dyed gray.

His first surprise was in seeing his former wife, Margaret Alexa, sitting on a chair in front of forty people. Levis positioned himself in the shadows of an alcove where Margaret could not see him. It amazed Cothran for her to be present. Even more astounding, she was apparently the leader. Of all the women he had known, Margaret had been the least spiritual.

Margaret rang a small bell, and all talking immediately ceased. From one corner of the room, a young man started to play a music tape. Cothran, who had a fine musical ear, recognized the sitar as the primary instrument. All the music was on an atonal scale, and soon he found himself listening instead of analyzing the strange, haunting melody that began to sound to him like a waterfall.

"I now contact my spirit guide, whose name is Misama," Margaret began. "If everyone will sit quietly while I vacate my body and personality, Misama will come to me and speak. If any of you have come here tonight with questions or needs, Misama will guide you." Sitting in the lotus position, Margaret Alexa chanted her mantra for several seconds until her head dropped as if she had fallen into a deep sleep.

"I am Misama," said a strange voice coming out of Margaret's mouth, a high-pitched nasal quality so different from her carefully trained and modulated voice. "I have come from far away to be near you. I have come to bring you comfort. If you will but open yourselves to me, I shall speak to your innermost needs."

A quietness fell upon the people. Levis Cothran looked around, and everyone seemed caught up in the spirit of the meeting. Two women in front of him began swaying as they chanted softly.

"One man is here tonight," said Misama. "He is troubled, and he has sought answers in many places around the world. He has returned to this country, still uncertain, still seeking. I have an answer for him tonight."

Levis Cothran realized Misama was speaking to him, but how could such a thing be? As he puzzled over this, Misama spoke again. "You are uncertain. At Sri Lanka, did not the old man say to you, 'The final answer is within'?"

Levis's body shot upward, and he shouted, "That's exactly what he said!"

"But you did not listen," Misama said. "You thought he meant you had to sift through the pieces of a puzzle."

"Yes, that's right—"

"But the answer *is* within you. *You* are your own answer. You can answer your own prayers. You determine your own destiny!"

For several minutes Misama spoke, her voice rising and falling as if spoken to a musical scale. The volume continued to increase until the voice filled the room. The spirit guide told him that he held the secrets of the universe within himself. "You are vitally linked to the great cosmos; a portion of the cosmos resides within you. As you open yourself, as you merge into the great cosmic consciousness, you will begin to fulfill your destiny."

Levis Cothran, in his sonorous voice, told this tale to the television audience. "I know," he said as he ended, "this sounds strange to you. Can you imagine how it sounded to me? I walked out of that house confused—more confused than ever before in my entire life. For a week I refused to see anybody or talk with anyone."

Each day he walked alone among the scrub trees on his property, wandering for hours through his vast estate, until finally he slowly began to piece together what Misama had said to him.

"The answer is in me because I am god," Levis Cothran heard himself say one late afternoon. "That is it! I am part of god. I am the creation, but I am the creator as well." The words flowed from deep within, and Levis Cothran knew he had found the answer for which he had been seeking. "I am god!" he screamed. "I am my own god, and I need to worship no one else!"

To the audience, Levis said, "And now I am ready to tell you—all of you who are listening to me—the secrets of living with this knowledge."

He got out of his chair and walked to the edge of the stage. "What I'm going to say to you now will seem incredulous. And I won't blame you for being skeptical, perhaps even thinking I need institutionalizing."

"I believe you," one woman said. "I hear such utter sincerity in your voice."

"Thank you," he said. "I have since become part of The Master Plan—the group that has taught me my truth and enabled me to live a life of freedom at last." He leaned forward and called a man and woman from the front row to come to him.

"I'm not wearing any makeup for this television special, and I want you to touch my face, feel whatever part you want, do anything you want until you're convinced."

Shyly they touched him and remarked that he wore no makeup.

"One more thing . . . Look at my skin, at my features. Do I look any different now than I did ten years ago when I left the screen?"

"I wouldn't think so," the woman said. "You don't have a wrinkle on your face."

"Now be careful," he said. "I want both of you to examine me closely. Whenever anyone has plastic surgery done—a facelift if you will—the surgeon has to leave telltale scars somewhere, small though they might be . . . Usually behind the ears, but always there."

He paused and allowed them to go carefully over his face. From the ninth row a woman stood. "I'm a licensed plastic surgeon in the state of Michigan. May I come forward? I can easily tell."

"Come ahead!"

The attractive woman walked to the front. She called for one of the klieg lights to be brought closer. She moved his face into several positions, carefully scrutinizing him. "Thank you," she said to the man who held the light.

She turned to the audience. "It's true. He has never had plastic surgery." She sat down.

"Thank you for verifying that." He jumped off the platform and walked down one aisle. "Look as close as you like," he said, "because you'll find no indication of surgery. I've never had any kind of surgery. Ever."

Levis Cothran smiled at his audience. Now he was ready to reveal the secret—the secret of eternal life.

E·L·E·V·E·N

The camera zoomed down for closeups of several members of the audience. Many were unconsciously actually holding their breath, waiting for the end of Levis Cothran's dramatic pause.

"I have come to offer you eternal life," he said quietly, "to inform you of its possibility by my own physical presence. I have not aged for some time, and I shall not age—at least not for the next fifty years."

Annella Maxwell stepped up beside her guest. "I've known Levis for a dozen years and, believe me," she paused and winked, "I've known him well."

"I like *intimately* better," he said and kissed her cheek.

Annella playfully pushed Cothran away. "I can tell you that Levis is as youthful-appearing today as he was when we first met in the 1980s. He is forty-seven, but anyone can see he looks twenty years younger. Right?"

"Right!" cheered the audience.

"Do you believe me?" Cothran asked, a look of innocence on his features. "That's important for me to know before I proceed any further."

"We believe you," shouted a young woman. "Tell us the secret! Tell us!"

"Yes, tell us!" chorused another.

"Tell us! Tell us!" A chant started from the rear of the building, and soon everyone in the audience was caught up in repeating the two words.

Cothran held up his hands. "Hey, I'm convinced!" He laughed. "Now to the serious matter . . . I have unlocked the keys of life. I can tell you how to reach and to remain the exact body size and weight you want. A fellow named Jesus said that by worrying, a person could not get any taller. You can't by worrying, but I can tell you short folks how to increase your height—permanently."

Drowned by cheering and clapping, Cothran waited until the audience quieted. "But there's far more. I can show you how to succeed financially—and I'm not teaching you to say a lot of positive things about yourself, learning tricks to make yourself seem important. I can teach you how to have a healthy self-love, to like yourself as your own very best friend."

The famous movie star stepped forward to the edge of the platform. "Think of that for a minute. I can promise easily enough, but I can also deliver on these promises!"

Levis Cothran came down the three steps and walked over to the side. "I have brought a few guests with me today. Instead of my telling you what you can do with your life, I'd like these people to stand up and speak for themselves."

Grabbing the first man by the arm, Cothran said, "Here is the one you want to hear first. Six months ago he was heavily in debt; today he is worth at least a million."

"Nearly three," the man said.

"Speak up. Tell us your story."

"They won't believe me, Levis," he said. "Like I said to you before the show, they won't believe me."

"Try them." Cothran patted the man's shoulder. "You might be surprised."

"My name's Charles Stanford—Chuck Stanford—and for nine years I worked as a gardener for Levis Cothran. My wife and I used to think that he looked so unhappy all the time. Then I saw this big change come over him, and I began to ask him questions. Levis took me to—to a strange kind of meeting. I'd never been to any kind of religious thing since I was a kid in the Catholic Church. Anyway, the wife and I went and listened. Then the wife said, 'Sure, why not? Look what it did for the boss.'"

Stanford told of his going to that meeting, where they introduced him to a spirit guide named Achzib. A stillness came over the large audience as he spoke. Stanford was a small, light-boned man wearing an expensively tailored gray suit. He smiled often, and his dark eyes exuded a sense of wonder. He was middle-aged, of sallow complexion with black hair and a mustache, making him look Greek or Italian.

Achzib had said, "Ask and it shall be given to you, whatever you want."

"If you're for real," Stanford answered him, "you can make me a millionaire."

"Only a millionaire? I can do more."

"OK, then, two or three million. That ought to be enough for a start," Stanford said in his laughing way that often disguised his nervousness.

"You must buy lottery number 1344238. It is worth one million dollars after taxes."

"You're putting me on."

"You will see."

As Chuck continued to relate the incident, he said, "So I figured I had nothing to lose but one buck. The next morning I went out and bought a one-dollar lottery ticket and asked for that number. You know, with the computers and all that and other people being in the meeting, I didn't know if 1344238 was still available, but it was." He smiled and sat down.

"Wait a minute, Chuck," Annella said. "Don't keep us in suspense. What happened next?"

"Oh, I won, of course."

"Just like that?"

"Well, the lottery drawing was three days off, so I had to wait until then. But, yeah, I got the money and then I did a really smart thing."

"What?" Cothran asked.

"I figured if I did that well with listening to the voice of Achzib, I'd ask him again what to do. So I did, and he told me to invest five hundred thousand dollars in Chromo-Dynamics. I did, and do you all know what happened three weeks later?"

"Three weeks later," said Levis Cothran, "the stock doubled in value because Chromo-Dynamics announced they had developed the first mass-produced solar-powered automobile for General Motors."

Stanford explained that he had sold his stock just a few days before appearing on the show. He figured his net worth as nearly three million dollars. "And my spirit guide told me only this morning that I can double that amount this year." He sat down.

After lengthy applause, Cothran motioned for his next guest to stand. Jan Johnson wore a simple dress of blue linen that whispered of its Christian Dior design; its color perfectly matched her eyes. In her middle forties, she brushed her graying-dark hair so that it fell to one side of her forehead. Her lips, parted in a spontaneous smile, were a soft pink.

"I'm not sure I need to introduce Levis Cothran's next guest to you," Annella said, "because she is already a celebrity. So tell us about it, Jan Johnson."

The radiance in her face developed an instant rapport with the audience. Jan Johnson explained that she had started to write when she was seventeen. "For twenty-six years I wrote and sent my manuscripts to publishers, only to get them back rejected. Then, in the fall of 1995, I started to attend the Master Plan meetings in Davenport, Iowa. I was so discouraged about my writing, I was ready to give up. After fifteen full-length novels and not a single sale, wouldn't you be discouraged too?"

The audience immediately sympathized with Jan, primarily through the expressions on their faces. "I didn't have a spirit guide like Chuck here. But I did grasp reality—the truth of truths that I am god and that I can create my own universe, my own destiny. So I decided to go to New York the next day and personally take my manuscript to an agent's office. I would demand that he read the manuscript on the spot. After all, if I am living in convergence with the great cosmos, why couldn't this be?"

Jan Johnson said that she flew to New York, where she arrived unannounced at the office of Adams and Grider, one of the top literary agencies in the nation. "Edgar Grider happened to be in, the secretary said, only because of a rescheduled luncheon. Without waiting for her to ask him, I walked right into his office and said, 'I have a book manuscript, and while I know you don't do it this way, I want you to read it right now.' And you know what? He blinked a couple of times, took the three hundred pages, and sat down. For quite a while I watched him read without seeing any reaction from him."

Jan told them that the literary agent read seventy or eighty pages, dropped the manuscript, and looked up at her. "I think this is the best manuscript I've read in a decade."

Jan Johnson left Grider's office with a contract in her hand for Adams and Grider to represent her, and a verbal agreement to mail him her other fourteen unpublished manuscripts. "He loved every one of them. On two of them—two of my early ones—he said I'd have to do some moderate revising. Mr. Grider sent copies of my novel *Forever Is* to the top six publishers in New York, asking them to bid on it, with only two weeks to make their choice. William Morrow purchased *Forever Is* with an advance of eight hundred and fifty thousand dollars."

Clapping broke out, and cheers reverberated throughout the room.

"Wait a minute, folks," Cothran said. "She's too modest. Actress Jodie Foster has purchased the book for filming by her own production company, and *Forever Is* has now been Number One on the *New York Times* best-seller list for twelve weeks."

"Oh, and we have already sold three other of my novels," she said. "Morrow is bringing out one every six months in hardback, and Dell is doing the paperbacks."

"And," Cothran said, "she is in the middle of finishing book number sixteen, which Simon and Schuster has already optioned with one million plus dollars for the hardback rights!"

"I owe it all to my understanding of myself and my destiny. I hope you won't think that Chuck and I are flukes—you know, just strange people who've been picked out. I personally know at least another forty people who have stories every bit as dramatic as ours."

"It's true," Cothran said. "By learning the secrets of the Master Plan, you can have anything you want in this life! The world belongs to you and to me—it's out there waiting for us."

Cothran then introduced Nancy Bechtel, head of Cravings, the fastest-growing chain of family clothing stores in North America. In just four years Cravings had bypassed Wal-Mart, Sears, Penneys, and K-Mart as the Number One department store chain in America.

"I want everyone to know the secret of my success." As she spoke, Nancy Bechtel resembled a fashion model more than an entrepreneur. She was tall with dark hair, even features, and large deep-brown eyes; she wore a black dress with a white scarf at the throat. "Here is the promise given to me by my guide. He said to me, 'Whatever you ask for, believing, you shall receive.' He has also told me that I can live as long as I choose, that I need never die until I grow tired of living. If we are converging into the cosmos, why not?"

"Why not?" shouted Cothran. "Why not?"

The crowd reacted as a hysterical mob chanting, "Why not? Why not?"

A wave of nausea overcame David Morgan as he watched Annella Maxwell's show. "I've never seen anything so demonic in my life," he said aloud. "Every sentence reeks with the Devil's handprint . . . Constantly quoting the Bible in the context of evil."

That night on his own program David Morgan said those very words. "The most disgusting part to me was to hear the words taken directly from the Bible, the holy Word of God, and used by Satan and his wicked spirits to corrupt the hearts of people."

Morgan quoted the same Bible verses, explaining their meaning and context from the New Testament. "This is one of the most Satanic devices of all—stealing the Word of God to turn people toward a worship of the Devil."

Near the end of his program, Morgan said, "Never before have I spoken so harshly, or needed to, against anyone or anything. I do so now because of the utter travesty of God's honor! Please don't be taken in. The Devil promises so much—and perhaps in the beginning a few get something. But the Devil originated the confidence game, and he wants to suck everyone into his evil schemes.

"The Devil began his career on earth with a lie—he lied to Adam and Eve, telling them that they would be as wise as God. Jesus said in John 8:44 that the Devil is a liar and the father of lies—by that He meant that our enemy is the originator of everything false and evil. The Devil's past is clear—lies, lies, lies. The Devil's present work is just as clear—lies, lies, lies!"

After the taping, David walked to the parking lot, heavyhearted, wondering if anyone really listened to what he was saying during his program. *Quite a lot of competition to fight against. On that show Annella Maxwell had carefully orchestrated testimonies and an enthusiastic audience; the entire script had all come from the seat of Hell itself.* Aloud he said, "I wonder how many will believe me?"

"Hey, you . . . Morgan!" shouted a voice from the center of the parking lot.

"Yes—"

"You did a lot of preaching in there," the man said, "and some of it sounded pretty good. But, well . . . I've got a question."

Morgan walked over to the shadows where the man stood. "What's the question?"

"How do we know *you're* telling the truth? I mean, you get paid to yell and sling mud at people."

"And everyone loves Levis Cothran," said a woman standing next to him. "Why, that man is so sincere!"

"Sincerity isn't everything," Morgan said.

"But we've already profited," the man said. "Why, just today I got a new car and yesterday I had an old clunker."

"I'm happy for your prosperity," Morgan said, "but I wouldn't count on it lasting."

"Listen, you!" The man grabbed Morgan by the lapel and struck him across the face with his free hand. "Just shut up about Cothran, and you won't have any more trouble."

The woman came around behind him and gave him a karate chop, just barely missing his neck.

Only the lights of a car coming into the parking lot made the couple drop Morgan and rush off. As they left, Morgan fell to his knees and waited until his head stopped reeling. The blows hurt, but fortunately the chop had done no real damage. Slowly he rose to his feet and stumbled toward his car. Once inside, he sat a long while, waiting for his strength to return.

"God, I guess this is the time to praise You," he said. "I know that when You warn people, the Devil fights back. But I guess we've won this time."

David Morgan had no realization that the battle had only begun.

T·W·E·L·V·E

The *London Times* called him "Britain's most influential citizen," and whenever they featured an article on the man, they sold out each edition. Without their giving out this information, other newspapers in Great Britain also discovered their circulation increased whenever they featured an item—of any length—on Neville Wheatley.

One enterprising magazine, *Hot Stuff,* which had long been an underground-type periodical, began to rake in enormous revenues by featuring a testimony by one of Neville Wheatley's converts in each issue. It didn't seem incongruous to the readers that the rest of the magazine devoted itself to semi-pornographic material.

On Maunday Thursday, 1998, Wheatley had just finished reading the *Times* article when his secretary came into his office, announcing that two gentlemen had come to see him. They had stated that their purpose was urgent and extremely important for Mr. Wheatley. "They said they would not take more than five minutes of your time—unless you asked them to stay longer."

"Who are they?" Wheatley asked. "Did they give their names?"

"A Mr. James Burton with the Assemblies of God Church and a Mr. Gerrard Coker who represents one hundred and thirty-five independent churches in Britain."

"More meetings, I suppose," Wheatley said. "I wonder how thin I can spread myself."

"You do work terribly hard, sir," his secretary replied.

"Show them in," he said.

When they entered his office, Wheatley offered them tea, but both refused, so Wheatley dismissed his secretary. A minute later he regretted his decision because he liked his mid-morning tea better than at any time during the day.

They introduced themselves and then Burton, the smaller of the two men, said in a surprisingly husky voice, "We don't wish to impose on your time."

"So we shall say our piece quickly," added Coker. "We are here as the official representatives of more than two hundred evangelical churches."

"Mostly in Britain, you understand," said Burton, "but a few in Canada."

"And Australia," said Coker. "We are also only the first ones to come to you."

"Yes, you see we have consulted twelve other evangelical leaders in the Western nations—without even going elsewhere."

"And so we have come to ask you—"

"To beg if necessary," said Burton.

"You see, we believe it is time to unite all of God's people into an evangelical association."

"A *fellowship* is the term we have come up with," said Burton.

"We want to make everyone see that we are united in our desire to serve the world," Coker said. "Mr. Burton and I, along with a dozen key members, have been quietly working behind the scenes for eight months."

"And we have concluded that only one man in the world today could unite us."

"And you," said Coker, "are that man."

"I?" Wheatley replied. "I have no desire to join a denomination or—"

"Not a denomination," Burton said. "A coalition if you like."

"Or a communion of churches," said Coker. "We believe it is time for God's people to stand up to the world with one, united, unequivocal voice. And we are convinced—"

"That you are the only man who could do this," interrupted Burton.

"Surely not!" Wheatley said, surprised but, to his surprise, delighted at the offer.

"Oh yes, absolutely," Coker said. "The Americans have had their try at uniting behind one evangelist or evangelical leader after another and have failed at every point. We require a young man."

"That is, a mature man of your age," corrected Burton.

"A man of reliable character, of great ability—"

"Behind whom we can unite," finished Burton.

They wanted Neville Wheatley to accept the title of bishop of what they would call the Fellowship of Love. If Wheatley accepted, he would continue his evangelistic endeavors and this new role might, in fact, enhance his popularity and his recognition. Already they had made contacts with church leaders around the world, and without exception these leaders had seemed joyfully receptive of such a fellowship. As Burton said, "You are the only name upon whom all of us could agree!"

"It is the right time," said Coker. "The World Council of Churches had a splendid idea once, but they put the wrong emphasis on their organization. We would have one leader—one bishop."

"You!" said Burton. "You would become the spiritual head of a communion of believers dedicated to proclaiming the message of Jesus Christ all over the world."

"Naturally that's quite flattering, but I hardly know what to say. I don't really think—" Wheatley paused, already aware that he would accept. "We should have to work out details, such as what you would expect of me, of my time, before I could think seriously—"

"Oh, we already have that worked out," Burton said. He unzipped his briefcase and extracted a computer-printed booklet called *Proposed Plan of Organization: The Fellowship of Love.*

"You understand," Coker said, "that you will be in a spiritual position similar to that of the Pope. That is—"

"You will be the spiritual head," Burton said. "You will be the one to unite us theologically, declaring God's will for us and—"

"Enabling us to unite in bringing in God's Kingdom here on Earth," said Coker.

"It may be premature to tell you this," Burton said, his voice in a conspiratorial hush, "but we have church organizations in Europe, Africa, and Southeast Asia eager to unite. Those in Central and South America expressed their willingness a fortnight ago."

"Our American friends have grown so discontented with the disorganized religion of their country, they are ready for any kind of change," Coker said.

For forty-five minutes Wheatley asked questions, and the two men had answers ready for him. They discussed the inroads of Eastern religions, New Age movements, the Master Plan, and witchcraft. They assured him that as threatening as these movements might be, the right leader could unite Christians in overcoming such lures. Only Wheatley, they insisted, could lead them out of the quagmire and onto solid footing once again. They had decided that London would become the temporary spiritual capital of the world. Eventually they could set up headquarters in Jerusalem, Geneva, New York—wherever Bishop Wheatley wanted—just one of the many things to work out in the future.

In terms of compensation, all financial arrangements would come under the auspices of the Fellowship of Love, including the family's food, clothing, and personal items. In addition, they offered him one hundred thousand pounds sterling per annum as salary, to do with as he chose. They had already engaged lawyers to arrange for every cent of the salary to come to him tax-exempt.

"You are worth such an amount," said Coker.

"And you are the only man who can unite Christians around the world to face this great hour of darkness and opposition from Satan."

Wheatley stood up and faced the two men. "I am deeply humbled and unworthy of this offer . . ."

"And you will agree?" Burton asked, automatically leaning forward.

"I cannot believe you want me. But, yes . . . I accept."

"We are pleased," Coker said.

"Totally," said Burton.

After the men left, Neville Wheatley again stared at his reflection in the window. "Bishop Wheatley," he said softly. "Bishop Wheatley."

He liked the sound of the words.

The following day, Reuters announced the formation of the Fellowship of Love, with Neville Wheatley as bishop. Comments from evangelical church leaders around the world spoke in favor, often echoing that Wheatley was the natural choice and the only man under whom the true church could unite.

From Atlanta, David Morgan said that evening, "This is the beginning of the end. The formation of the Fellowship of Love will hasten the decline of faith in the world."

Morgan predicted that within a short time other church and parachurch organizations would follow. "The Pied Piper is playing his enticing and enchanting song. Soon many evangelical churches will belong to this structure. Once that happens, they will begin to denounce the truths we live by."

That evening as David Morgan opened the door to his car, he spotted a small box on the seat. Opening it, he found only a single sheet of paper. "This is a warning. The next time it might be a bomb that will go off when you lift the lid. We don't need your kind who rail against good men!"

A sadness filled Morgan as he drove north on Peachtree Street. A light rain was falling, matching his mood. "O God," he said, "can't they see what's going to happen?"

People choose what they will see, the Inner Voice said.

As Morgan had predicted, the Fellowship of Love daily attracted new organizations to its ranks. A highly prominent conservative synod of the Lutheran Church announced it was "in discussions," and a Reformed Church wing stated that "we have started examining the feasibility of such a move."

The Episcopalians, Presbyterians, and Baptists listed their names as affiliates. Some Baptist churches held out. However, the popularity of the Fellowship of Love, commonly called FOL, was so powerful among average churchgoers that congregations voted their pastors out of office if they did not agree to participate in a special convention held in Chicago.

With an unparalleled unanimous vote at the Chicago convention, the dissident Baptist denominations joined the FOL. By then, smaller Christian church organizations had already declared their allegiance. A period of only fifteen weeks passed between the announcement of the formation of the FOL until the enlistment of a few remaining church groupings.

Despite theological differences, all members of FOL agreed to the following:

1. The Bible as the Word of God,
2. Jesus Christ the Savior of humanity,
3. Eternal life for all believers.

"We are now exhibiting the peace and power of God throughout the world," stated Neville Wheatley. "We have united true Christians under one banner. We have done what

Muslims and Hindus have never been able to do within their own faiths. We are God's people, commissioned to save the world for God!"

David Morgan made repeated attacks on FOL, urging people not to be blinded, not to fall for this latest deceit of the Devil. As before, Morgan stirred up controversy, which gave him higher ratings. Yet, in many circles he became a joke. "Let's tune in and see what Morgan's raving about tonight."

One listener wrote, "Is your name Morgan or Moses or maybe Malachi? Who gave you the right to sound like those holymen?"

Despite the taunts, and occasional threats to shut his mouth for him, David Morgan continued to relentlessly speak from his conviction.

On Sunday, July 14, 1998, a day Morgan would never forget, he had spoken for twenty minutes from Ezekiel 33. After he explained the context in which Ezekiel wrote and the purpose of the message, Morgan said, "And now I want to show you the relevance of that passage for us right here in Atlanta, Georgia.

"I want you to know and to mark this: Some of you will leave us. You will cite many reasons, but you will leave. Many of you will despise me, calling me an angry preacher, accusing me of being against everybody.

"I have a mandate from the living God. I didn't choose this role, but I must cry out to you, like the shepherd in Ezekiel's time. If you listen, you will save your own souls. If you depart, you'll perish in your sins. But my hands are clean. I warn you, I beg you, don't be deceived!"

"That's it!" shouted a man in the third row. "I can't take any more of this negative preaching!"

"Nor can I," said a woman two rows farther back. "We came here for edification and to hear God speak to us about love and compassion . . . not to hear this kind of rot!"

She grabbed her two children and pulled on her husband's arm. They filed out behind the man from the third row.

"I moved here from California because I thought you brought us a word of truth," said another member. "Now I realize that you really have nothing to offer. You're against everyone and everything. You want to enslave us with legalistic practices. No thank you. I want my freedom in Jesus Christ."

By the end of the day, St. Luke's Church had lost twenty families. The news did not disturb members of the Parish Council. "So we lost a few malcontents," said Tom Grundy.

"We took in an extra eight thousand dollars this week," said Bob Kilgore. "So we must be doing something right."

"Oh, we are doing something right," Morgan said half-aloud. "That's only too evident." And as he left the members of the Parish Council, he said, "The Lord gives and the Lord takes away. Blessed be the name of the Lord."

However, David Morgan spoke the words with deep sadness. St. Luke's Church was losing members. Although he knew that this would happen, he still found himself wondering what he could have done differently.

Mastermind met every two weeks in New York City. By the summer of 1998, they concentrated on raising the standard of living in the Western hemisphere. Yatawazy, working behind the scenes, devalued the Japanese yen by increasing the country's trade deficit. He manipulated currency until most of the Eastern nations underwent severe economic depression.

In the meantime, the United States' claims in Antarctica were paying off. The Antarctic Treaty, renegotiated in 1991 when seventeen nations made claims to the land at the bottom of the world, had resulted in the United States and seven European countries taking control. Because of an economic slump, Denmark sold their interest to the United

States; the Soviet Union, desperate for wheat and corn, made a similar arrangement.

By August 1998, the United States controlled two-thirds of the vast frozen land, but expressed their willingness to share resources with West Germany, England, and France. Although insisting on a double share of employment opportunities for themselves, the United States made jobs available to their allies and, with positions still available, opened the door to the rest of western Europe.

The discovery of diamonds, coal, and oil made Antarctica the most valuable spot in the world. U.S. production of oil not only exceeded that of the Middle East, but Americans offered the world market a superior quality of crude oil. Soon only Third-World nations imported from OPEC.

OPEC—The Organization of Petroleum Exporting Countries, created in 1960 at the urging of Venezuela—had attempted to set world oil prices by controlling oil production. Until 1973 they had succeeded. For the next twenty-five years, member nations constantly fought among themselves, few realizing the genius of Mastermind behind their squabbles.

By late 1998 Saudi Arabia, Algeria, Iran, United Arab Emirates, Iraq, Libya, Kuwait, and Qatar met to mourn the death knell of OPEC. Although they refused to formally admit its demise, they knew they had lost their economic power in the world.

On September 7, 1998, the United States and most of western Europe moved into the four-day workweek, followed by Canada and Mexico enacting similar legislation. As the senior senator from Vermont said at the time of the vote, "We have plenty of money. Now we need a chance to spend some of it."

Emil Wensela, the only person his father ever came close to loving, occasionally traveled with his parent when he made his twice-monthly trips to New York. Hanse Wensela told his son about Mastermind, through whom he enjoyed the pleasure of having his own aero-ship, a retinue of servants, and more wealth than he had dreamed possible.

Emil, at age twenty-six, envied his powerful, brilliant father. Yet, he found he couldn't despise his late mother whom his father consistently referred to as "the cow." Emil's highest ambition was to be as much like Hanse as possible.

He might have followed in his father's footsteps—except for Michelle Maxwell.

T·H·I·R·T·E·E·N

Michelle Maxwell, as beautiful as her mother Annella, heard her mother say often, "You're just like me, darling. Exactly like me." She always smiled at that remark, knowing her mother wanted her to grow up to be as ruthless and as hard as she was. Yet Michelle knew she was not like her mother in one key way—and that factor changed everything.

She had absorbed or inherited one characteristic from her father, a man she scarcely remembered. He had a conscience, and so did his daughter.

Although Ted Wilson had lived with Annella for eight years following the birth of their daughter, they were not happy times for Ted. He showered the young girl with affection, but he also taught her to make choices in life based on consideration of others, along with the joy of doing things just because they were right or avoiding them simply because they were wrong. He instilled in her that the way people went about achieving their goals was of greater value than attaining the goals themselves.

Slowly, over those formative years and without

Michelle or Annella being aware of it, the daughter developed a conscience. For the young girl growing up in a highly permissive atmosphere, this reality meant she often could not participate in the profligate lifestyle of her wealthy playmates. She had never known any surroundings except among families of wealth and fame and the catered-to American royalty of the entertainment industry.

Conscience—Ted's sense of right and wrong—finally split Michelle's parents apart. He, whom she remembered only as Ted, wanted to get married, had wanted to marry Annella when they first met, had insisted upon a wedding after the birth of Michelle, and demanded it by the child's third birthday.

A few years later her parents clashed, and Michelle overheard their voices.

"I don't need a husband," Annella said firmly. "I don't need another name attached to mine."

"Keep your name," Ted said softly. "You know that's not the issue. I want a home—a proper home—for our child."

"Because we have never had a piece of paper to show the world, we are terrible people, is that it?"

"I happen to believe in something called old-fashioned morality."

"I happen to believe that I'm tired of you," Annella said.

"That's your choice, but I'm begging you . . . For Michelle's sake, for whatever we've had between us—"

"Oh, spare me," Annella interrupted. "I don't need a husband. I don't need a man. Most of all, I don't need a sniveling, stupid man like you messing up my life."

The words between the couple continued for a long time while Michelle listened to every word, not sure she understood what they argued over. But she understood the anger and the sharpness of their voices. And before the night ended, Annella and Ted had settled the issue.

The following morning Ted took Michelle out to the stable, and they walked around for several minutes in silence. "I'm leaving, darling," he said.

"I know. Annella doesn't want you anymore."

"It's probably better this way," Ted answered. "We fight a lot . . . So I'm leaving. But hear me—I love you."

"Oh, Daddy," she said, "I love you too." She called him Daddy, but her mother never allowed anything but Annella.

"I don't know if your mother will let me see you again."

"Oh, she will," Michelle said. "Why, she must. You're my daddy."

"I'm your father, but she doesn't want me around here." He picked up the girl and held her tight. "If you never remember anything else about me, will you remember that I love you? That no matter where I am, you'll always be in my heart?"

"Oh, yes, Daddy," she said. "Then you can come back, and we can go for a ride on my pony."

Her father must have said more, but only that memory remained intact. After he had been gone for many months, her tears dried, but the sadness remained, perhaps hiding below the surface. From then on, Michelle had a long series of daddies, uncles, or Annella's boyfriends moving in and out. In time, the face of Ted receded and she couldn't remember what he looked like.

That would have been the end of Ted's influence in Michelle's life, except she never forgot his voice. She never forgot the gentle way in which he would stop her from being disobedient by saying, "No, dear, don't." She never forgot the importance of treating others with kindness and respect, no matter who they were. As the years progressed, the memory of her father receded from her consciousness; yet the voice never did. By the time Michelle was twelve, she had long forgotten where the voice had come from, but it never left her. She didn't think consciously about the voice, but was simply aware that there were some things she could do and some she could not. And she was miserable when she said no.

Michelle grew up with Annella Maxwell, learning her mother's value system which strongly departed from any kind of normal morality. Despite Annella's urging her daughter toward ruthlessness and teaching the motto, "Anything you want, don't give up until you get it," Michelle remained under the influence of that inner voice. That voice remained her great secret.

In early 1998, when the Mastermind was working effectively in thousands of places at the same time, Michelle Maxwell and Emil Wensela, along with Maison Quayle's twin sons, were already sitting in and listening to the plans that came from Mastermind. They were never allowed to speak, though they occasionally received reminders from Mastermind of their special privilege, as well as promises that they too would profit from the changes in the world.

None of them needed to be told to not talk about the channeling of Mastermind to anyone outside the ten people in that room. When Mastermind was in a particularly lengthy session, Emil Wensela and Michelle Maxwell occasionally grew restive and left the meeting. The twins, giving rapt attention to the proceedings, never noticed they were gone.

In the fall of 1998, during one of those interminable sessions, Emil had suggested that they stretch a few minutes, and Michelle agreed. Outside the meeting room, Emil said, "Whew, if I had to sit in there much longer I'd fall asleep."

"The room's a little stuffy," she answered. "I was starting to yawn."

The building, purchased for the exclusive use of Mastermind, had the bottom floors available for people called in for specific assignments. Aside from the six apartments, the four offspring also received permanent residences.

"I was thinking tonight," Emil said, "that you and I've never really gotten acquainted, have we?"

"We see each other regularly here—"

"That's not exactly what I mean."

"I'm not sure we have that much in common otherwise," Michelle said, feeling distinctively uncomfortable. Earlier she had noticed frequent glances at her from Emil when he thought she wasn't aware.

"Let's go to my place," Emil said, nodding toward the elevator.

"What for?" she asked.

"For a while." He laughed and took her hand. "I think that after all this time, you and I need to get to know each other a little better." That Emil resembled his father physically was particularly evident, as he walked with the same grace as Hanse. The son's sparse frame, however, would always reject the tendency toward flab that now clung so tenaciously to his father. Emil's golden hair, a little thicker and a shade darker, had the slightest bit of natural curl, one of the few physical inheritances from his mother. The real difference between them lay in the pale-blue eyes. Emil's eyes had not yet seen and experienced the world's corruption and the disillusionment of his father. The eyes had not yet hardened, though the young man was well on his way.

"All right. So long as it's only for a while," Michelle said. "A very short while."

"The choice is yours, how long you want to stay," he said. Michelle liked the huskiness of his voice with its deep undertones. And she had always thought of him as particularly handsome.

When Emil opened the apartment and turned on the lights, Michelle glanced around the large room. "Quite interesting. Everything's white. The furniture, the carpet, walls—"

"Like it?"

"I think so. Yes, I think so."

"I did it to impress. Everything in here is from the William and Mary period."

"I don't know much about period furniture."

"It's easy to distinguish William and Mary," he said as he pointed to the chair behind her. "The backs are high, rounded at the top, and upholstered. Then the legs are turned, and the feet are what we call Dutch ball-and-claw."

"Yes, I see."

"One way to identify this period," he said as he stroked the white upholstery, "is that the arms of the chairs are usually flared outward. The whole piece has a graceful curve to it, don't you think?"

Michelle sat in one of the chairs. "Quite comfortable." She turned toward the white-tiered window. "Lovely view."

"I didn't invite you here to study my furniture or the view," Emil said. He walked over to the wet bar, of modern construction but with the same lines as the rest of the furniture. He poured a glass of chablis for both of them.

"None for me," Michelle said.

"Then I won't either." He put both glasses on the bar.

"I have some top-grade hashish I think you'll like."

She shook her head.

"You sure?"

"Yes . . . Nothing, thanks."

"All right," Emil said. He came over toward Michelle and stared into her face. "Your eyes are different from your mother's, aren't they?"

"Hers are blue, or maybe blue-violet, depending on the light," she answered. "Mine are a yucky blue-green."

"Jade-green," he said. "Beautiful."

"You didn't invite me to see the view or admire the furniture. I didn't come for you to talk about my eyes."

"Michelle," he said "whenever I've thought about bringing you here before, I've always been totally involved with somebody else. Unlike my father," he laughed, "I'm a one-woman-at-a-time man." He leaned closer. "I think you're beautiful. More beautiful than any other woman I know."

She blushed and started to tell him that she thought him extremely good-looking, but that she had seen others as handsome. In her mother's circles, they saw nothing but beautiful and handsome people, even if it cost them a fortune to attain such physical attractiveness or another fortune to maintain their looks.

Before she could get the words out, Emil took her hand. "Are you ready?" He nodded toward a door.

"For what?"

"What else? The bedroom, of course."

"I'm not sure I understand—"

"Let's not play naive with each other, Michelle. Why else would I have invited you to my apartment? So, shall we go?" He nodded toward the bedroom door.

She shook her head.

"What does that mean?"

"It means," she said softly, "that I am saying no to you."

"But I thought you liked me."

"I don't dislike you. I mean, I didn't until just now."

"Was I too slow in leading up to this? Why, your mother would have—forget that. Tell me where I blundered."

Michelle pulled away from him. "I'm not my mother. I have never, never done anything like this with a man, and I'm not going to start now!"

Emil grabbed her arm, and the rasp in his voice shocked her. Emil's face, contorted in anger, didn't seem like him at all. "I don't like wasting time. I have had many beautiful women in my bed."

"That's your choice, Emil." She pulled her arm out of his grasp. "But it's not mine."

"You're afraid. That's what it is."

"No," she said, surprised at the firmness of her voice.

"You aren't one of those strange women who don't believe in sexual activity? Surely not. You know, my father taught me at a young age that sexual desires are part of our nature. I can think of no better way to satisfy my desires than with you. Simple, isn't it?"

"Not to me," she said. "I know how you live. I know how my mother lives, and that she probably doesn't have the same man in her bed three nights in a row. But I'm . . . I'm not my mother!"

Michelle turned and walked toward the door. She picked up her purse and paused to look at him. Emil dropped onto the sofa and stared sullenly at her.

"I'm sorry," Michelle said. "Really—"

"Sorry? Sorry?" After cursing her, he yelled, "Why did you lead me on?"

"Lead you on? How can you say that?"

"You came in here with me."

"I came with you, Emil, because I thought you were a nice person."

"Nice person?" He jumped from the sofa and advanced toward her. "I thought you were a nice person," he mimicked. "I'm not a nice person. I'm not a kind person. I'm not sweet either. I'm the son of one of the most powerful men in the world. When I know what I want, I take it! I'm ruthless, and I can have everything I want!"

"Not everything," Michelle said. Three strides and she reached the door. "Not everything." She slammed the door.

Wearily Michelle walked to the elevator and waited. She had been foolish not to have anticipated what Emil had in mind. She had liked him, and she would have yielded to him except for one thing. That voice in her head had said softly, "No, dear, don't."

All her friends went from one affair to another, often bragging on the number of different partners they had slept with. But Michelle had never given in. She didn't know why except for the voice inside her head. Like Emil, she hadn't been taught moral values or given religious training. Michelle hadn't even considered her reasons for refusing, except that her quiet voice whispered, "No, dear, don't."

As long as the voice spoke, Michelle knew she would always be an outsider among her own people. Tears filled her eyes and dripped slowly down her face. "I wish . . . oh, I wish I belonged to somebody . . . to some place . . . instead of always feeling alone and different."

As she rode the elevator up to her own floor, she contemplated silencing the voice and behaving like the others she knew. "But I can't," she said. "This voice—you're like a jailer to me. Won't you ever let me be happy?"

The hum of the elevator going up was the only sound she heard. "I wish—I wish . . ."

As miserable as Michelle felt, as much as she spoke

about her dislike of being different, another part of her knew she had done the right thing.

As she lay in bed, a peace came over her. She knew then that she had been right, no matter what Emil or Annella or anyone else could say to her.

F·O·U·R·T·E·E·N

In what they had called The Master Room, the six members listened as Annella Maxwell channeled the Mastermind's will to them. "You have done well," The Voice spoke. "I am rewarding each of you in your own way. By the time you return to your home, Yatawazy, you will have become the largest employer in the nation of Iran because you are singularly responsible for bringing modernization, productivity, pollution, greed, individualism, and all the other marks of Western decadence to the country." One by one he told the others of their increased possessions or power.

"And now," Mastermind said, "we are ready to make our next attack. The leader is Bryant McFarland."

"One of my countrymen," Maison Quayle said. "But I warn you, we shall have to be quite clever to catch him.".

"I am clever," Mastermind said, "and I am ready to tell you how to discredit and destroy him."

"That'll be the day," said Maison Quayle with a hearty laugh. "Oh, I can just see it happening. Old Goody Boy is what we call him."

"No one is incorruptible," Mastermind said. "No one.

And you must never forget that. All human beings have at least one weakness. Our task requires finding the areas where they are vulnerable. And because they are vulnerable, we can destroy them."

"How d' you propose—"

"Quayle, if you were not such an utterly corrupt and nonmoral being, I would no longer suffer your questions and disruptions."

"Aah, but you see, Mastermind, you selected me, and when you did, you knew all my weaknesses. And questioning authority is one of them."

"Be that as it may, you will sit in silence as I explain the plan of attack. I begin with one observation, and I believe I can leave it to your fertile minds—yours especially Maison Quayle—to formulate the step-by-step solution. Listen to his preaching. After you have heard him consistently, you will realize he has one overarching theme."

"Ah ha," said Quayle and then, remembering the recent admonition, lapsed into silence.

"And that," Mastermind continued, "is where you trip up McFarland. Good preachers preach about the topics where they themselves struggle, or wish to deny, or try to project on to other people. Forget his topic, ignore the passages of the horrid book he reads from, but listen carefully to his illustrations, his practical suggestions—"

"Oh, that's easy enough," blurted out Quayle. "It's sex."

"Now the rest of you can understand that, despite Quayle's repugnance, he is extremely perceptive—in some ways, the most perceptive among you. And therefore, Quayle, I put McFarland into your hands."

"We'll have a grand time with him, M.M.," Quayle answered.

"Never forget that I am always with you. You need only to call on me for whatever wisdom or resources you need."

"Ah, but I know that already," said Quayle. "And I think I've just now come up with a plan."

"And again, you have not disappointed me."

"I'll begin by pumping him up, making him a really big name. The higher they hop, the louder the plop!"

Bryant McFarland championed the cause of independent Christians throughout Australia. The Anglican Church, being not only the state church, but dominant and powerful, had long been a favorite target of the chapel-goers (those who didn't attend Anglican services). McFarland had built his reputation by appealing to the emerging middle class of Australia. He stood before them as a man who understood their temptations and problems and who offered them hope and victory.

Although McFarland had received offers to go abroad, he remained in his own country. "I'm content to be a big fish in a small lake," he often answered.

At age forty, a man of medium height who had always wished he were at least two inches taller, McFarland had plenty of firm muscle and no spare fat because he worked out for an hour every morning. He had a remarkably open, ingenuous face that not only made him look younger, but also made him appealing to his audiences. His neatly brushed hair was dark and his brown eyes cheerful. His slightly too-wide mouth easily relaxed into a broad smile, showing strong, even teeth. Only the decided jut of his jawline and the marked eyebrows gave any clue to the inner strength of the man.

McFarland remained unaware of the impact of his message, the influence of his preaching, his physical appeal to women, and his acceptance by men. His recorded sermons went by mail across the world. Soon his business manager started videotaping his preaching, and the hundreds of new requests soon threw McFarland into big business. By October of 1998, the evangelist had his own television show, which was well received by audiences, even non-Christians. McFarland allowed this commercial transaction, providing he receive no additional remuneration, insisting that his total income be made a matter of public record, and that all proceeds go toward wiping out hunger in the world.

On a Tuesday morning as McFarland ran over the notes for his address that evening, a feeling of confidence filled him. He was speaking to a newly formed but large society called The Legion for Decency and Morality, and they had particularly asked him to speak on the topic of sexual immorality.

McFarland had no way to know that the Legion had been formed through the finances and power of Maison Quayle. Yet even had he known, the evangelist would have consented to speak. "It's another opportunity to speak about Jesus Christ," McFarland said when speaking opportunities came to him from non-Christians. "I won't turn down any invitation where I can do some good."

He smiled as he penciled in a few words on the second sheet, an illustration that would make his point neatly. He had just reached the end of his notes when his secretary buzzed to inform him that his appointment had arrived.

McFarland knew only that her name was Betty-Anne Freeman and she had called three days earlier, saying that McFarland was the only minister she would be comfortable consulting.

When his secretary, Elizabeth Bodine, opened the door, McFarland blinked in spite of himself. The contrast between the two women was startling. He had never thought of Mrs. Bodine as anything but average-looking. Now he saw her as the plain and staid woman she really was. She was a middle-aged widow, thirty pounds overweight and all distributed in the wrong places, having mousy-brown hair that she seemed unable to manage. She wore only shoes with Cuban heels and square toes, which made her short stature appear dwarflike. She had only two qualities that kept her in her position: a high level of efficiency and an undisguised love for her employer.

Next to her stood Betty-Anne Freeman—tall, statuesque, with thick raven hair that curled lightly and naturally at her shoulders. Her expensive gray suit emphasized the slimness of her body without calling undue attention to her obvious beauty. She was smiling with perfect teeth and inviting black eyes.

"Do come in," he said as he walked forward and extended his hand.

"So good of you to see me," Betty-Anne Freeman said with an obvious accent that revealed her Southampton, England roots.

"Tea please, Mrs. Bodine," he said, not bothering to look at his secretary. "And, Miss Freeman—or is it Mrs. Freeman?"

"Mrs. Freeman. But everyone calls me Betty-Anne or just plain Anne. Would you call me either Betty-Anne or Anne, please?" she said and allowed him to take her hand.

Although Bryant did not say so, he thought to himself that he had never touched a hand so smooth. He particularly noted her long fingers and neatly manicured nails, surprisingly free from polish. Then he realized she wore only a slight trace of lipstick and no other makeup. *But then*, he thought, *this woman needs nothing more.*

Sitting down across from her, he asked, "Tell me what I can do for you."

"Just listen, that's all," she said. "I'm in terrible trouble. I don't know where to turn. I have faith in God, but sometimes that's not enough. Sometimes we need a human being, a person who is kind and caring . . ." She took a tissue from her purse and daubed her eyes. "I've watched your television show, and I feel you truly understand people's problems."

"I'll certainly do whatever I can."

The office door opened, and Elizabeth Bodine brought in the tea. She poured for both of them, stepped back, and watched like a sycophantic waiter.

"That's all, Mrs. Bodine," he said. "I shall call if I need anything."

"Yes, sir." Elizabeth's eyes narrowed as she turned toward the door.

His secretary already out of his mind, McFarland handed Betty-Anne Bodine a cup and picked up his own and sipped from it. "Please tell me."

"It's not easy . . . Most embarrassing as well."

"That's all right," he said. "As a minister of the gospel I've heard just about every kind of story known to the human race."

"I'm a model, a good model actually." She named four magazines in which she appeared regularly, including *Woman's Day.*

She accepted the tea and stirred it slowly. "Two years ago I moved to Australia because I tired of the glamor and shallowness of my profession. Mind you, I had already been paid a handsome packet of money, and invested it wisely so I could afford to retire. I haven't actually retired yet, of course. I still work three or four months a year, but I'm thirty-two, which is considered old in my business."

"Really?" he said as he stared at her features. "You hardly look twenty-five."

"I inherited good bone structure," she said. "And God gave me no other real talents except a good figure, so that's what I've capitalized on. You—you don't think I sound immoral, do you? I mean I've never exposed, well, you know, anything—"

"I'm sure you haven't done anything wrong," he said.

"Perhaps I'd better start from the beginning," she said. "About my childhood—if you have time—"

"Plenty of time, my dear."

Betty-Anne Freeman began her tale of her life as part of a titled family who, she stated, were actually in the royal line, "although something like three hundred and twenty people would have to die before it got down to us."

By age thirteen Betty-Anne had developed physically, so she looked much older although she made no effort to do so. During their August holiday from boarding school, Betty-Anne attended a birthday party for her best friend whom she called Widget. Afterward Widget's father took Betty-Anne outside to show her the grounds.

"Then he asked if I should like to see his vineyard. He

had imported grapes from the Rhine and would soon start his own winery. I agreed, and he pointed out the stages of growth of his cuttings. Then he wanted to show me the distillery, so I followed him and . . . and that's when . . . that's when he touched me."

With appropriate pauses for tears, Betty-Anne Freeman went through the whole scene, frequently saying "and then he" until she told her whole story of being degraded and ashamed.

"Afterwards when I cried, he called me beastly names and threatened to tell everyone that I was nothing but a guttersnipe and that I had invited him outside to trap him." She cried a long time.

In sympathy, Bryant McFarland reached over and lightly patted her hand. She looked up at him with her black eyes, and he read a word of thanks for his compassion.

For the next twenty minutes Betty-Anne told him of going from one sexual event to another because she really believed she was a guttersnipe. "But then, four years ago, I heard your message called 'A Second Chance,' and I left that wicked way of life. I turned to Jesus Christ and have been a faithful, churchgoing woman since."

"It sounds as if you've made a remarkable adjustment in your life," McFarland said, a feeling of sympathy for the attractive woman flowing over him. "You are a woman of great courage as well as beauty."

She smiled through her tears. "Then I met Skipper Wilborn. Actually his first name's Byron, but everyone calls him Skipper. And we met in church too, you see. So I quite naively assumed he was a good man."

"Quite natural to assume that."

"And he spoke kindly and treated me ever so nice, and we fell in love and somehow, in a moment of weakness, I allowed him to—you know, do things with me. Our wedding was already planned and all—oh, I feel so evil in telling you this."

"I do understand," the minister said. "I really do."

Betty-Anne told of her splendid wedding. Her family flew in from England, and everything went smoothly. "Then we learned that I—I—well, I can never have children . . . not ever, and this angered Skipper and . . . he . . . he hit me . . . hard . . . just about every place except the face. And now he's living openly with another woman. He doesn't want a divorce. He only wants to stay with her, he says, until he tires of her, and then he'll come back to me and we can then live together as if—as if—"

"Terrible! Terrible!"

"I'm afraid of him, Mr. McFarland. I—I don't know what to do."

"I'm not sure of everything," he said, "but I know we've got to get some help for you. Have you contacted your solicitor?"

"No." She dropped her head. "I'm too humiliated."

"Give me his name, and I shall contact him. We'll use all the legal means we can to see that he doesn't bother you again."

"Oh, thank you—"

"Do you still love Skipper?"

"I don't think so. How could I? And I don't know what to do about a divorce. I've heard you speak against divorce, and I want to follow God's will in all of this. Oh, what shall I do? Please, please tell me, because I have nowhere else to turn. I feel trapped."

"He's committed adultery—quite openly, you say?"

"Oh, yes. Why, he's even sent me pictures of them in—in . . . well, poses that make me blush."

"Then, according to my understanding of the Bible, you are free to divorce this beast. Adultery is the one legitimate cause for divorce that our blessed Lord gave us."

"Oh, you are so marvelous. I—I knew you would help me feel better." She clutched his hands in hers.

Betty-Anne Freeman stood. "I'm sorry for taking so much time. You have been so terribly, terribly kind. And . . . may I come back again? You are so easy to talk to. Your level of understanding is overwhelming."

"Why not tomorrow?" McFarland blurted out, and then wished he had not appeared so enthusiastic.

"Oh, could you make room for me again so soon?" She smiled. "You are ever so kind."

They were both standing at the opened office door, under the hawklike gaze of Elizabeth Bodine, who made no pretense of doing anything but observing.

"Mr. McFarland, it is easy for me to understand why you have made such an impact on this country. You are not only the finest minister I've ever heard, but you are without question the kindest, most considerate man I have ever known." She grabbed his shoulders and kissed his cheek quickly before pulling back. "Oh, I'm sorry I simply got carried away—"

"It's quite all right," he said and then, forcing himself to move away from her, turned to the brooding Mrs. Bodine. "Mrs. Freeman will be coming to see me again tomorrow. What time can we schedule her?"

"Tomorrow is quite full," Elizabeth said in a flat voice.

"Didn't Mr. Handley cancel our luncheon?" He turned to Betty-Anne. "Suppose you come at half past twelve. A little shop down the road has carryouts. Mrs. Bodine will have a light lunch for us, and we can continue our discussion . . . If that's satisfactory."

"Oh, yes," she said. "Thank you." She turned to Mrs. Bodine. "How much he must depend on you. My father always says that behind every successful man is a successful woman—his secretary!" She smiled at the plain woman. "I expect you are his right arm and that he could not possibly function without you."

Despite herself, Elizabeth Bodine smiled. "I try my best to please Mr. McFarland."

"Oh, I wouldn't quite know what to do without good old Elizabeth here. She steers me on a straight course all right."

"How wonderful to have a woman so devoted and so good at her work. You are a fortunate man—no, a blessed man, a remarkably blessed man."

As she walked out the door, Elizabeth Bodine beamed. *That woman*, she thought, *understands*.

F·I·F·T·E·E·N

Betty-Anne Freeman came to Bryant McFarland's office three more times, always behaving discreetly, always taking time to chat with Elizabeth Bodine and to point out the woman's superior qualities to McFarland in the secretary's hearing.

A week after her last appointment, Betty-Anne Freeman called and identified herself. When Elizabeth said Mr. McFarland was out of the city, Betty-Anne said, "I didn't call to speak with him. I wanted to talk to you . . . to invite you to a luncheon in my home. It's a small group, eight others and myself. So do say you'll come. I should like an intelligent woman among these ant-brained women."

"Well, I do have to eat . . ."

"Splendid. I'll have my car pick you up at 12 sharp."

Betty-Anne Freeman, aware of the influence of Elizabeth Bodine over Bryant McFarland, knew she could never ruin the man without the cooperation of his ox of a secretary. She also knew she would have little trouble winning this woman over. And in winning her over, Betty-Anne Freeman would learn more about the man than anyone else could tell her.

Later, when Betty-Ann Freeman reported to Maison Quayle, he asked, "What about his wife?"

"Oh that," Betty-Anne laughed. "You can handle her easily enough. Get her out of the way."

"Kill her?"

"Oh no, I shouldn't think so. Death takes longer to get over. Just make her ill—a lengthy illness—and not anything immediately terminal. You know, something that will throw the poor lady into bed, so she'll have three or four years to pine away."

"I can't wait three or four years for results—"

"You shan't have to," Betty-Anne said. "You get the wife bumped out of the picture, and I shall deliver McFarland to you within six weeks." She gave him her brightest smile as she added, "Maybe within a month. That can be my Christmas present to you. He's quite a weak man sexually and doesn't know it."

"Will that make it more difficult?"

"Not at all. When people don't know their weaknesses, they fall more quickly."

"So I know," Quayle said. "The weaker the man, the easier the plan."

Alma McFarland had contented herself with being in the background of her husband's life. She had long known his weakness toward women, but because she had always been a loving companion and had adequately provided for his sexual needs, Bryant McFarland had never strayed.

When the doctor gave Alma the results of her tests, immediately she thought of her husband. What would happen to him now? She shuddered, not because of her pain, not because of the negative prognosis, but because she was letting him down.

The phlebitis in her left leg was bad enough. But worse was the strange disease of the skin itself, a rare condition with many symptoms of lupus such as sensitivity to the sun and constant aching of the joints. Her specific ailment, called Carson's Lupus (after the man who isolated the illness, but had not as yet discovered the cure), meant that anything rubbing against her skin, with even the slightest pressure, brought ravages of agony. Painkillers, injected every hour, made it bearable for her to lie on an air-filled mattress at night. During the day she lay in a plastic tank-like container recently introduced to Australia. A watery substance kept her body feeling as if suspended in space and, more important, relatively free from suffering.

Alma sensed she would never walk again or be a normal wife to her husband. Often she wanted to burst into tears, but held herself in rigid control because even the touch of tears against her face tortured her delicate skin.

When Bryant came into the bedroom each night, he sat on the chair near her and told her everything that had gone on that day. She knew about Betty-Anne Freeman and perceived her husband's vulnerability. Alma wanted to warn him, to plead with him to stay away from the woman, but her advice would only separate them further. The gap was already there; she certainly didn't want to widen it.

"Betty-Anne has now provided me an excellent opportunity. Thursday next she has arranged a marvelous dinner at her home. She will have fifty guests. Can you imagine feeding fifty people at a sit-down dinner? I haven't seen the place, but she says she will require nine large tables and have them set up in the ballroom. Must be quite a mansion."

"Must be, dear," Alma said, fighting to stay awake. Her nurse had injected her minutes earlier, and her body was properly relaxing. She would soon drift into sleep if she didn't fight to stay awake. Alma moved her left thumb, each effort causing a jarring pain. But it worked, and she remained fully alert as long as her husband spoke to her.

Emil Wensela and Michelle Maxwell had avoided speaking to each other. Although they had seen each other from time to time, the two of them had never been alone since the night Michelle went to Emil's apartment. And then, when Maison Quayle asked each of them for their help, they consented and flew together to Australia to be guests of Betty-Anne Freeman. Quayle had prepped them to ask the right questions of McFarland.

Since Emil and Michelle stayed at the same hotel, it was natural that he call at her door to escort her downstairs to the chauffeured limo.

"Nice to see you again," Emil said. "Alone I mean."

"My first time in Australia," she said.

"I'm sorry . . . you know," Emil said, "about that other time."

"I understand," Michelle said, "I really do. You're used to having what you want whenever you want it."

"I just never had a woman refuse—I mean a woman that liked me as much as I thought you liked me. I hope you don't hate me."

"I don't even dislike you," she said. "It's just that—well, I don't—I can't do—some things. Like sleep around—"

"But it's perfectly safe with me."

"It's not the safety issue," she said.

"Then what is it? Your mother encourages it; my father taught me how. You said you like me well enough. I am using the latest techniques."

Michelle shook her head. "None of those reasons."

"Then what? I mean, you don't make much sense."

"I just don't want to . . . I mean I want to, but I—I—Oh, never mind."

"Please," he said. In the darkness of the limo, he reached over and took her hand lightly in his. "I would really like to know. And I promise I won't do more than hold your hand without your permission."

"You'll laugh at my reason."

"I promise I won't."

"Okay. I don't because it's wrong."

"Wrong? You mean like immoral?"

"Yes." She turned and looked at him. She could just see the outline of his features. "I knew you wouldn't understand."

"I don't. I mean, I've heard of people who have some sort of system of good and bad, predicated on religious superstition—"

"Not that. I have never had religious training. At least not any that I recall." Michelle pulled her hand away. "I didn't think you'd understand."

"Wait a minute," he said. "Don't brush me off like that. True, I've never heard of such a thing. It sounds like . . . well, like something I've read in a novel. I've never actually met anyone like you before. I'd like to understand. Really."

"I believe you," she said.

For the first time in her life, Michelle told someone about the voice in the back of her head, the voice that would tell her not to do something. It was a man's voice, a kind, warm voice. But she couldn't remember if she had actually heard that man or if the voice was merely something she imagined. But she had known since childhood that when the inner voice spoke to her, she must not disobey.

"Sounds frightfully dull to me," Emil says. "If you don't do drugs or have sex, what do you do for fun?"

"You'll laugh this time for sure."

"Promise I won't."

"And you won't tell my mother?"

"Again I promise."

"I'm a volunteer three days a week with the Red Cross at their blood center. Mother doesn't know it, but I'm also a graduate nurse—I sneaked that training in while she thought I was doing a Master's degree at the University of Michigan. And twice a week I do volunteer work at a thrift shop—a place where we sell clothes to the poor and needy for a few cents each item. I take castoffs from my friends—they don't know what I'm doing with them—and sometimes work to remake them so the poor people can use them."

"You're telling me the truth, aren't you?"

"Yes, of course. And you're the only person I've ever told."

"Why me?"

"Because I like you, Emil. I know we both come from families where wrong only means getting caught or diseased. But I'm not like that. Sometimes I wish I were, but I'm different from the rest of them. And . . . I think that deep, deep inside you are too. I don't know how I know that—"

"You're right," he said, "and I suspect you're the only person who has ever seen that element. It's what I used to tell myself was my fatal flaw—the thing that kept me from living up to my father's expectations. Not that I'm like you or anything, but sometimes . . . once in a while I feel—well, I don't have a word for it, but I ask myself why I'm living this way."

"And what kind of answers do you get?"

"I'm afraid I don't listen for an answer."

"But you *are* asking the question," she said. "That surely must count for something."

He laughed, and they fell silent. Emil's mind turned toward his father. He could easily envision the wrath of his father if the older man had heard their conversation. He wondered how his father would react if he knew of his earlier contact with David Morgan also. It had been an accidental meeting, but what happened afterward would surely set off Hanse Wensela's malevolence, even if Emil was his son.

And before he realized what he was doing, Emil told Michelle a story no one else knew. At one time Emil had thought of becoming a novelist. Since his father was going to be in the United States for six months, he decided he would enroll in a college. He had selected Emory University in Atlanta, and enrolled in a course called "Creative Writing — The Novel."

On the day of the first class, Emil had been suffering from a dreadful hangover, and when he parked in a no-parking zone, the campus policeman had refused to take a bribe and wouldn't allow the young man to leave his car. Emil ended up leaving his Jaguar a mile away and taking a taxi to the university. Being late and in a rush, Emil had gone to the right room number but the wrong building.

The teacher did not particularly impress Emil, but then

he hadn't been impressed with any authority figures since childhood. Although he did not realize it, he had walked into a class of fifty students being taught by the Rev. David Morgan.

"I know you've never sat in any of my classes before," Morgan was saying, "and I want to put you at ease. I've never been before a class of students before."

A feeble joke, but something about the man piqued Emil's interest. He sat down in the last row, prepared to listen.

"I think it's fair if I tell you about myself," Morgan said. "I made my first religious decision at the age of ten: I decided to leave the church because I thought it was a place for mental retards and senile adults. Until I was nineteen, I had no thoughts of God and didn't want any either . . ."

As Morgan described himself, Emil wondered what this had to do with writing a novel; but then, he had missed the first ten minutes of the class and assumed it would become clear. Perhaps that background was to set the stage to tell how the professor had ventured into writing.

Morgan then told about his brother Tommy, who had died of cancer. "He was the good kid in the family, the religious one, the one who deserved to live. On his deathbed, hours before he breathed his last, he smiled at me and said, 'Davey, you've got to take my place. You've got to tell the world about Jesus Christ. I'm going to leave and be with Jesus, and you've got to stay here and teach.'

"'No, Tommy, you can't go. I don't even believe this stuff.'

"'You will, Davey, you will.'"

Morgan told the audience that his brother died the following day, a smile on his face. "I was there, holding his hand when I felt it grow cold and knew he was gone. As I stared at him, I knew that no one could accept death like this unless he was ready for it. Yet how could this kid—thirteen years old—be at peace, be actually smiling when he died? At the funeral I kept thinking, *Maybe there is a God. Maybe there is something to this.*"

Morgan told of his finally talking to Tommy's pastor and, after nine months of weekly talks, arguments, readings, and debate, Morgan realized that he had begun to believe in Jesus Christ.

"And now, nearly twenty years later, I'm standing in front of you to tell you that God is alive and active in my life. And you have come here to learn how to present this message of love and peace to others."

"What's going on here?" Emil yelled as he stood. "Am I in a peanut factory? What kind of course is this?"

"It's called 'Pastoral Evangelism,'" David Morgan said. "Even if you're not signed up, I'd like to have you stay."

"You have fallen out of the sky," Emil said as he made his way toward the door, "and landed on your head."

Outside the building, Emil immediately saw where he had made his mistake. Seeing a stone bench, he sat down and thought of what he had heard. That man really believed what he was saying. It was utter, total nonsense, and yet the man was so genuine, so compelling.

In a husky voice Emil told Michelle, "The next day I waited until the class had started, cracked the door just an inch, and stood outside and listened. I couldn't believe what he was saying—I still don't believe all of that mumbo. But there was something about that man—he's different from anybody I had ever met before. There's an honesty about him that I find rare in people. He's a man at peace with himself, a man not afraid to talk about what he believes in."

"Did you do that every day?" she asked. "Listen outside the door, I mean?"

"I probably would have except that the third or fourth time he arrived late, and just as I was cracking the door he came up behind me."

Emil told Michelle that he heard the footsteps behind him, and as he turned he faced David Morgan. Embarrassed for having gotten caught, he nodded and started to walk on.

"You don't have to leave," Morgan said softly. "I thought that if I came out to meet you this morning, you might choose to come inside and sit down."

"You know I've been listening?"

"Sure. So why not come inside and be comfortable?"

Emil let loose a particularly violent string of invectives, calling the man every name he knew Morgan would find repugnant.

When Emil paused, Morgan laid his arm on the young man's shoulder. "You've got a rather extensive vocabulary." He smiled and said, "I'm not sure what a couple of the words mean. But I'd still like to have you come inside."

Emil brushed Morgan's arm away. "You don't know anything, do you? You know why I've been listening? I stand out here and laugh at your primitive philosophy. You sound like something that escaped from the last century."

"Probably I do," Morgan said. "I'm going into class now, but the invitation is always open."

"Did you get bounced on your head a lot when you were small?"

"Can't recall that I did," Morgan answered. "But I did get a lot of loving from my parents."

A string of scatological terms filled the atmosphere as Emil went away.

"I never went back to hear him," Emil told Michelle, "but that man did have some ongoing influence. Once in a while I'll start to do something—something some people outside our circles might term really bad. Like I fixed it all up to raid a corporation, pump up the stock value, and then dump them. I was all set to sign on the line and . . . you know what? I saw Morgan's face staring at me . . . right in front of a board room filled with the top men in the food industry. Like what some people might call an apparition."

"What did you do?"

"I was so unnerved, I dropped my pen and said, 'I've changed my mind.' I walked out. I also forfeited more than a million dollars in a contract pledge." He laughed. "My stupidity enabled the company to reorganize and resist any further takeovers."

"Just think, Emil, that's small money to you, but it may have meant everything to some of them."

"So what?"

"Right," she said. "Not our concern."

Emil played with Michelle's fingers. "Guess that's the only thing I ever encountered that sounded like a conscience. I sure hope it doesn't happen again."

"Oh, it will, Emil," she said. "I know it will."

He stared at her, his mouth open. Just then the car braked at Betty-Anne Freeman's house, and Emil said nothing more. But Michelle's words stayed with him all evening.

S·I·X·T·E·E·N

Bryant McFarland was pleased as he stared at himself in the bathroom mirror at Betty-Anne Freeman's house. He had talked three-quarters of an hour, far longer than he had anticipated, yet the questions kept coming. "How can I believe in Jesus?" "What do I have to do—really—to be a true Christian?"

As he dried his hands, he hummed a gospel hymn. These were obviously wealthy people, people of influence. They could open doors for him to preach elsewhere—to the unreached, to those who prided themselves on being above their need for Christ. And he owed it all to Betty-Anne Freeman.

Betty-Anne had proven to be the most spiritual, the most enthusiastic disciple he had ever worked with. Every word he spoke, she received as if God had spoken from Sinai.

Bryant McFarland also realized that he had stared at Betty-Anne differently tonight. He had tried not to, but he found himself constantly aware of what a beautiful creature she was.

It had now been five weeks since Alma's confinement to bed. Ordinarily the Rev. Bryant McFarland would have prayed for strength to overcome the temptation he felt as he gazed at the most desirable woman he had ever known. But tonight he did not pray. Worse, he didn't even think about prayer.

"Oh, there you are," Betty-Anne said as he came into the ballroom.

Servants had cleared away the tables, and at one end of the room they were setting up chairs. "No one wants to go home, Bryant," she said as she took his arm and led him forward.

"I'm sure Bryant will talk for a few more minutes," Betty-Anne told her friends. "I haven't asked, but I don't think he'll refuse."

"I'd like to be a Christian," an older woman said forthrightly. Her jeweled neck and expensive gown obviously set her apart from ordinary people. "But I don't believe in hocus-pocus, so you will have to help me."

Immediately Bryant launched into answering the woman and then replied to a second person. Michelle and Emil asked questions, and it surprised both of them how fully they listened to the answers.

Another twenty minutes and, although Bryant didn't notice, a bare nod of the head from Betty-Anne brought a comment from the woman who had first asked a question.

"My dear Mr. McFarland," she said, "I simply must give a party next week and invite you. The Prime Minister is one of our dear friends, and I'd like to invite all his cabinet members as well—that is, if you have no objections."

"I'd be honored to attend."

"But you must promise that you won't leave until you've explained to them about the Christian faith."

"You have my promise."

"Oh, thank you. You see, many of us grew up equating boredom, stupidity, and cold cathedrals with Christianity. I must say that you have truly opened my eyes. And I wish to thank you." She stood and walked forward to shake McFarland's hand.

As he took her hand, he felt her lay something in his palm. He stared down at a check made out for five thousand dollars. "I don't want money—"

"Of course . . . not for yourself," the woman answered. "But you are so aware of needy people in this world . . . I am entrusting you to use the funds as you see fit." She smiled and paused before moving on. "And I shall tell each of my guests that I expect a contribution of no less than one thousand dollars. You will hear from me within the next day or so, as quickly as I can make arrangements," she said and left him.

Four other guests also asked for the privilege of setting up dinner parties. McFarland knew two of them—by name only—and realized that with their backing, he would soon reach every upper-class family in Australia. God was indeed blessing him.

Betty-Anne Freeman kept him at the door shaking hands with guests. He met Emil Wensela and immediately guessed he was the son of western Europe's wealthiest man, an avowed atheist. *But through his son,* McFarland thought, *I might be able to speak with him.*

He had known immediately that Michelle was Annella Maxwell's daughter. *And even prettier,* he thought, again wishing he did not have to go home to face a bedridden wife.

The last car gone, the servants had cleaned up and turned off most of the lights. Bryant stood in the hallway with Betty-Anne.

"I know you must go," she said. "I've kept you terribly late and I apologize, dear Bryant."

"I enjoyed every minute."

"You behaved marvelously. You knew exactly how to speak to every single question. Bryant, you are a wonderful, wonderful man."

Bryant felt himself blushing as he said, "I've only used the gifts God has given me."

"Of course," Betty-Anne said. "And you're the pick of

the crop." She stepped forward until her body was only inches from his. "You are the finest man I've met in my entire life, Bryant, and . . . one more thing . . . I hope you won't be offended if I tell you this."

"I don't think you could ever do anything to offend me."

"I'm in love with you. Oh, I know it's forbidden. After all, I still have that monster of a husband. But worse, you have a wife and will have for a long time. So I know that nothing can ever be done about it. But I do want you to know that I love you. I can't help myself."

"Sometimes gratitude and love get mixed—"

"No, dear Bryant," she said, "it is love. I'm grateful to you, of course, but something deeper, purer, more wonderful is going on inside. And . . . I'm going to do something terribly bold and hope you'll forgive me."

"What could you do that—?"

Betty-Anne put her hands behind his head and pulled his face toward hers until his lips met hers. She held him tightly against her for a moment and then released him and stepped backward. "I'm sorry, Bryant, truly sorry. I couldn't help myself. But please don't remain angry. Please, please say that you'll forgive me."

"Nothing to forgive," he said.

And then, hardly aware of what he was doing, Bryant leaned forward and kissed her tightly on the lips. As he released her, he said, "We both know this cannot go any further. If the circumstances were different . . . but they aren't." He turned and opened the door. "Good night."

After he had gone, Betty-Anne smiled. Bryant McFarland had fallen.

He didn't know it yet, but he was already in the pit she had dug for him.

"And what did you think of tonight's affair?" Emil asked.

"A little sad," Michelle said. "I don't think I'll go back again. I'm not made for this kind of charade."

"Of course it's a charade, but it's so much fun. And the poor fellow hasn't a clue as to what we're doing."

"That's what bothers me. It's like everyone has a copy of the rule book except poor Mr. McFarland."

"Is that the inner voice speaking again?" Emil joked.

"I don't think so," she said. "In fact, I know it isn't. Strange as it may seem, it's a—a conclusion I've come to on my own."

"Watch it, lovely young lady. You'll soon be one of McFarland's genuine flock."

"I don't think so," she said as she reflected on his words. "I'm not good enough for that."

On December 20, 1998, Edmund Staats, who held degrees in theology, philosophy, and sociology, was not reflecting on the upcoming Christmas celebration. He was staring at his cuffs. They were worn, and he needed to replace the shirt. Another year or two, he told himself, the same thing he had been telling himself for weeks. He simply could not afford to purchase new shirts; finances had become that critical for him.

He sighed as he thought of the golden dreams of his early twenties. He had shown so much promise as a scholar who read widely, grasped intellectual arguments quickly, and could explain them in plain terminology.

He had been converted while a university student in Basel, Switzerland, and then went on to do his theological studies at Tubingen, West Germany, the place where great neo-orthodox scholars such as Bultmann and Barth had made such impact.

He accepted everything he heard or read. And then, just as he was completing his final year of studies in Tubingen, he realized how far his instructors had departed from the true faith. He made a full swing himself then, embracing the orthodox view of the Bible. In particular, he disagreed with his aged mentor, Rudolph Bultmann. The old man had made faith the primacy of theology and had said often, "It does not matter if the Resurrection literally happened. It is faith that counts, not historicity."

"You are wrong," he told Bultmann. "And you are leading people astray."

"Then it is up to you to set them straight," the old man said.

Edmund Staats accepted the challenge and wrote a small book, entitled *In God's Defense*. A German house published the book, and, to his surprise, the following year the then-prominent British publisher Monarch printed an English translation. America's Harper and Row bought the American rights.

Immediately Edmund Staats wrote a second volume, entitled *Defending True Faith as a Life of Faith*. His third in the series, *These Truths We Defend*, established Edmund Staats as the world's most renowned Christian apologist. He was the single most popular defender of Christian orthodoxy, fighting against neo-orthodoxy, the emptiness of existentialism, and the sometimes incomprehensible Tillich. He raised the cudgel against humanism and Altizer's God-is-dead craze in the 1960s. He made his stance against the inroads of Eastern religion in the following two decades.

The scholar had written thirty-eight books, and now, at age sixty-two, he feared to look at his future. His books, excellent sellers through the 1970s, had declined in the 1980s. As he faced the end of a productive life, he realized he had little to fall back on. He had taught part-time at a little-known university for fifteen years, just long enough to have a small pension provided, half enough to provide for his most elementary needs.

"What shall I do?" he asked himself as he looked out the window at the Christmas decorations that covered lamps and buildings. He had been asking himself the same basic question every morning for the past two months. Twenty years earlier, his wife, now dead, had urged him to invest heavily in Bolivian minerals. And they had done well, but with her lengthy illness and the extensive care she required, most of the retirement funds were gone. She had remained in a nursing home in Zurich for six years with Alzheimer's.

"I don't know what to do," he said. "God, I don't know what to do."

Hanse Wensela had painstakingly studied Edmund Staats over a period of four weeks. Everything confirmed what he had intuitively known in the beginning. "A hungry man is ruled by his stomach," Wensela said laughingly. It was an old saying of his late father, and he had always found it to be true. Some hungered for love, others for fame; but touch the area of hunger in a human being, and you knew how to rule him. He had no doubts about Edmund Staats.

Before leaving for Staats's home in Amsterdam, Wensela had informed Mastermind, "I shall deliver him into the palm of your hand within a year at the latest, six months if you insist."

"You have the time you require," Mastermind said. "I want total submission from him."

"You have nothing to fear," Wensela had answered.

And with that annoying self assurance that troubled his enemies—troubling because he deserved the assurance, Hanse Wensela arranged an appointment with Edmund Staats.

Upon arrival, Wensela noted the small house. The living quarters, comfortable enough, showed the creeping hand of penury upon it. The main room contained low, simple furniture. Books filled the three cases, and Staats had stacked the overflow several feet high along one wall. The place didn't offer much of a view. On a side street Wensela could see small cafes and shops topped by two or three stories of nineteenth-century facade, now converted from private homes into offices and dressmaking workrooms.

From where he sat, Wensela could see an efficiency

kitchen, a gleaming bathroom, and an inadequately stocked pantry. Nothing surprised him; it was exactly as he both hoped and expected. "You are perhaps wondering why I would make an appointment to visit you?" Wensela asked.

"The thought has puzzled me several times. You're an avowed atheist—"

"Was an avowed atheist," Wensela said. "Until three weeks ago."

The older man stared at Wensela, hardly able to believe what he was hearing. For years he had personally considered Wensela his archenemy, a man without scruples or feelings. He shook his head slowly. "Please forgive me, but I cannot but wonder if you are toying with me."

"You are perfectly correct in being skeptical," Wensela said. "I can only tell you my story and let you judge for yourself. And it's important that I come to you, because you are responsible for this change in me."

"Truly?"

"I'm aware that you have considered me totally profligate and have aimed a number of your writings at me. You were correct, because I exemplified everything with which you charged me. But then you probably didn't know that I read your books."

"No, I didn't expect you bothered."

"I have read every book you have written." Wensela cited titles, commenting on several of them. He had read them thoroughly as part of his preparation. He wanted to be certain how the man's mind worked, and now he knew. If he spoke convincingly enough, Staats would want to believe in his conversion. And wanting to believe was almost as good as having him convinced.

"All of this began when I read *A Final Judgment*. Not the kind of book I would normally consider reading. But a friend, a man I've known for years, handed it to me one day and said, 'Read this. Then refute it.' I laughed and took the book, which I began that night. The truth is, I could not put the book down. Or more accurately, four times I became so angry I threw it across the room. I hated you, Edmund

Staats. I hated your God, your logical mind, and most of all I despised your audacity at telling me that I would be eternally tormented."

The listening Staats, only slightly older than his visitor, had kept his body under careful regimentation. His disheveled white hair, falling over his high forehead, shadowed melancholy brown eyes. His high cheekbones added to the gauntness of his face, and his complexion seemed to have a grayness about it because of the inferior lighting of the room.

"I have come here for two purposes," Wensela was saying. "If you will hear me out, then you can decide on the truthfulness of my words."

"That seems fair enough," Staats answered. He leaned back, prepared to listen without comment.

"First, I have given my heart to Jesus Christ. I ought to have known how to do that, shouldn't I? After all, I've read it often enough in your books." He chuckled. "You nailed me in so many places that I finally knew that only in God could I ever find peace of mind."

"Nothing could please me more than to hear you speak this way."

"That's my first reason for coming here . . . to tell you what has happened to me. And my second reason is a corollary. Since you have been the human instrument to turn me from my sins, I have a proposition to offer you. I have already consulted with my lawyers and am ready to begin an organization called Truth International. It's purpose is to disseminate the truth—the only truth in Jesus Christ—and to combat all the forms of evil among which I have lived all my life.

"You see," Wensela leaned forward as he made his point, "you are the world's most able apologist for Christianity and my spiritual progenitor. I would like you to accept an appointment as the head of Truth International." He smiled and added as casually as possible, "With a suitable compensation, of course."

"I would need more details," Staats said noncommittally as he felt a pumping of adrenalin in his wearied body.

Not surprised at the man's hesitancy, Wensela had baited the trap and now he was ready. "Six of my friends and I will personally fund *Truth International* at the rate of two million pounds sterling each year—that's roughly 3.75 million American dollars."

"I am not just speaking of the money, of course," Staats said.

"Of course not. I have a six-storied office building in Paris for your use and shall remove the tenants within the month so that the entire building is yours to use. If you accept this appointment, you will receive compensation in the amount of . . ." He paused and pulled a folded sheet of paper from inside his pocket. ". . . of $50,000 per annum beginning the first of the month—in monthly payments, if you agree to head up this venture, and I am hoping you will feel so inclined. If you decline, I would like you to recommend the next best man. I wish to state again, I am hoping to persuade you to accept this offer."

"I'm immensely flattered."

"Flattered?" Wensela waved aside the scholar's objections. "This is not flattery. You know a great deal about me. I do not work with mediocrity. I accept only the best."

"Yes, I know."

"And you, Edmund Staats, are the best, the only one who could possibly fill this position."

As Staats stared into his eyes, Wensela knew the man was almost convinced; only the slightest doubt remained. Wensela was ready to destroy the last question.

"Please understand—you will have total autonomy. I am prepared to put in writing that I will never in any way interfere with your opinions, statements, or pronouncements. You will be solely in charge of a six-page magazine called *Truth International*, and you alone will decide the full content of this magazine. Further, you will aim this magazine at what we call the intellectuals, the unconverted, the agnostics and atheists."

Wensela paused and sat in silence. He had no doubts of the response; he knew this man too well.

"My dear brother in Christ," Staats said and offered his hand.

S·E·V·E·N·T·E·E·N

"I don't want to be involved with the Mastermind anymore," Michelle told her mother.

"But, darling, I've counted on you," Annella said. "And you promised to help."

"You also told me that when I was bored or wanted to do something else, I could. I'm ready to do something else."

"A man? Is that it?"

"If I said it was a man, you'd want to know all the details of how I seduced him or how he seduced me."

"You're right. I won't pry, but I do want to know. Is there a man involved?"

"Two men."

"In that case, I can see why you don't want to help me," Annella said, "although I am disappointed. You're missing out on such a great opportunity. But then . . . when it involves a man . . ." She came up behind her daughter and kissed her softly on the top of her head. "You know, my dear, I'm tough and I play rough and I can outwit any man around. You are the only weakness I have."

"Strange that you call me a weakness," Michelle said

with a mischievous wink. "If I didn't know you better, I'd think it was love."

"Whatever you call it," Annella said.

Later when Michelle left her mother's apartment, a lightness came over her. *I'm free,* she thought, as if she could not yet believe it. *I've left the stifling atmosphere that made me feel so ill at ease.* Michelle had no word as yet to express the repugnance of her former life, but she sensed she would soon.

Immediately she took a taxi to the Manhattan Public Library. She asked for microfilm of the *New York Times* issues during the year before her birth. She had decided it was now time to find her father. Michelle knew his first name was Ted, but she didn't remember his last. *If he is still alive,* she vowed, *I'm going to find him.*

Michelle smiled about her cryptic answer to her mother. She had played a game of deceit by withholding information. But then, she had learned from a world-class expert to play games of deceit.

Yes, she thought, *there is a man involved. There's also a second one. I know the first man's name, and he's the one I have to find. The second name I want to erase from my thoughts.* The one way to erase the second name was to leave Mastermind, for the second name was Emil Wensela.

The searing pain in David Morgan's chest made him wince. It appeared suddenly and disappeared just as quickly. The momentary agony took his breath away, but it was enough to make him remember. This had happened several times recently and, once assured medically it had no physical cause, he prayed. "God, if this is some kind of message for me, let me grasp it."

I told you that I do nothing without first revealing it to My prophets. The pains are to tell you of the fall of another leader. One by one they yield to the seduction of the enemy. More will fall, but you must remain faithful. You must continue to warn those who have ears to hear.

David Morgan had no way of knowing who had fallen, but he knew that evil was slowly encircling the earth, more blatant than ever, as if it had nothing to fear. He constantly saw more emphasis on pleasure and enjoying life, more shrugging off of responsibility, less awareness of spiritual poverty.

No offices stayed open on Friday in the United States; in western Europe, none of them remained open on Monday. More and more businesses were moving toward a three and a half day workweek. The governments of most Western nations provided an abundance of welfare programs, and America had at last turned to socialized medicine. Anyone needing medical assistance had only to go to the nearest hospital or clinic. Doctors, paid enormous salaries, were rapidly training assistants to do most of the routine work.

Morgan's concern weighed heavily on him as he read the newest resolutions passed by Congress. Two years earlier Congress had set up the Federal Euthanasia Committee (FEC), which had become grudgingly accepted and now was enthusiastically endorsed. The bill provided that whenever individuals were "no longer productive," through their next of kin filling out the proper forms, signed by two medical doctors, family members could arrange for the patients to be "mercifully put to sleep," "thereby avoiding the horrors of suffering and of draining their finances and those of their families," as one nationally-known doctor put it.

Abortion no longer caused a furor because the clinics had closed—they were unneeded. An abortion pill developed a decade earlier in France, and now manufactured and marketed in the United States by one of the Iranian companies owned by Sami Yatawazy, made abortion pills readily available to any woman anywhere, upon demand, at low cost. Of course, Yatawazy made vast sums of money from the governments who subsidized the pills.

A new pill, soon to be on the market, had special appeal for men. It was developed primarily for male birth control, but researchers discovered a side effect: its use increased energy and aided better muscle tone. No one knew that after five years users would become addicted.

Nations were changing, not only in name, but in control. Although the Soviet Union ostensibly had its Politburo, it was now commonly known that P. K. Sari controlled those who controlled that nation. He had also deposed the leadership in Japan, China, and India and had realigned the boundaries of all the Asian nations. He was starting to tighten his iron fist throughout the rest of the Orient as well. Rumors circulated that he would soon encroach on the Middle East.

"O God," Morgan prayed, "everything seems chaotic. People won't listen, no matter how hard I try. I feel as if I'm speaking to the air."

Those who have ears to hear will hear. Do not let your heart be troubled. Believe in Me.

Although attendance at St. Luke's Church remained high and the membership still showed growth, it disturbed Morgan that the people had become so lax in their attendance. By now it had become the custom in most American churches to attend worship services twice a month. "Enough to keep us on the right path," said one church leader, "but not so much as to make us fanatics." At times David Morgan felt as if he preached to rotating shifts.

When trying to explain this dilemma to the Board of Elders (formerly called the Parish Council), the Board members mentioned the overall rising attendance, and that giving had increased ten percent in the last year alone. "Where people put their money is where their heart is," stated Grayford Hart.

"But if their hearts are here," Morgan said, "why are they not physically present?"

"People do need to unwind," said Tom Grundy, the man who had pleaded two years earlier for a no-frills church. "We live in a stressful world. We need time to relax, have a change of pace, get away, to—"

"Three days at a time, two weekends a month?" asked

Morgan. "That's the pattern of at least one hundred families in our midst."

"Pastor," said Benjamin Gabbard, "we follow you because you're concerned about individuals. You do care— which is one reason why we're willing to pay you so much."

"Then cut my salary."

"Wait," Gabbard said. "We like you because you're not constantly dictating what we can do. You're not screaming at us that we're sinning by just about everything we do. So you don't need to worry. We have a solid group of Christians here."

"If you think attendance is bad here," said Bob Kilgore, "you ought to check out River Dell Presbyterian Church down the road a ways. Why, the pastor told me that he doesn't see his elders more than one Sunday a month."

"I'm not trying to compete or compare ourselves with Presbyterians or anyone else," Morgan said. "I'm concerned about our obedience to Jesus Christ."

"Pastor," Bob Kilgore answered, "I can assure you that you are the pastor of the most spiritual congregation in the City of Atlanta. Almost everyone knows your stance, your commitment."

"That's true," said Gabbard.

"That's why I come here," said Grundy.

Morgan was not convinced that all was well. He felt deeply troubled that his church's Board of Elders, a board which now consisted of twenty-four men and women who were supposed to be the most spiritually-minded in St. Luke's Church, saw dollar totals and filled pews as evidences of commitment.

And as he looked around the room, he counted only sixteen present. One-third of them were gone, probably out of town or involved in what Tom Grundy called "relaxation." And yet, as recently as a year earlier no one would have missed except for the most extreme reasons.

Things have changed, Morgan said to himself. *And people have changed. Yet the gospel is the same . . . so what's happening?*

The following Sunday, Morgan preached with all the conviction of his own soul. "I stand before you as a messenger. I stand here to warn you. I stand before you to plead with you to become aware of Satan's devices."

Morgan pointed out the seductive tools of greed, sex, power, pride. As he concluded with the benediction, he wondered if any of them had heard—really heard—anything he had said. And his wondering made him sad.

One person listened intently to the sermon of David Morgan that Sunday morning. Not everything made sense, and he had a lot of questions. For instance, he silently asked, *What's so wrong with greed? Anything wrong with that?* he pondered. *Isn't part of being human the desire to keep reaching out for bigger and better? And what about power? Why not have all the power available? If I don't grab the whip, someone else will. Strange, strange man with radical ideas,* he decided.

Emil Wensela allowed these questions to race through his mind as he once again considered that Morgan just might be mentally ill. He might have dismissed the sermon and the man except that David Morgan's earnestness intrigued him. From the time Emil had first seen the pastor on the Emory University campus, the preacher-scholar had held a fascination for him.

At the end of the service, Emil Wensela followed the crowd to the door. David Morgan stood at the end of the line, shaking hands and commenting to every person. Bending his head slightly downward, Emil Wensela decided at the last minute to go out a side door. He had taken only a few steps when he heard, "How nice to see you again."

His head bobbed up, and David Morgan was in front of him, a smile on his face. "I never did learn your name. And I missed your coming back to my class."

Emil straightened up and looked directly into Morgan's open face. "You are a fascinating man."

Morgan cocked his head. "I feel that's only the first part of a statement. As if you want to add *but* . . ."

"You're correct," Emil said. "I respect you as a man—a man of deep conviction and sincerity, but I detest the things you stand for."

"I'd really like to discuss that further with you," Morgan said. "How about my coming to see you this week?"

"Are you out of your mind?"

"Let's get together. That's one way you can find out. Or you might come to my office—"

Emil resorted to a string of swear words, having forgotten that they hadn't worked before. He turned and raced out of the building.

Who does he think he is? Emil asked himself as he drove away in his Jaguar. *Why doesn't he let people alone and allow them to be happy the way they are? His preaching only makes them feel guilty.*

"Guilty?" he repeated aloud as if he had suddenly realized what he had said. "Guilty?"

Emil Wensela stepped on the accelerator. For the first time in his adult life he felt condemned, as if he were the most evil man in the world, as if no other human being had been so wrong, so cruel, so misdirected and helpless. He could do nothing about his situation except to loathe himself. "What a contemptible man you are!" he screamed at the emptiness of his vehicle.

As Emil Wensela drove rapidly into Atlanta's Midtown, terrible thoughts came to him, such as ramming his car into a guardrail at a hundred and thirty kilometers per hour. Or perhaps he could jump off the bridge that spanned the Chattahoochie River. At least that would get rid of this horrible feeling inside. Right now he felt as if a large, pointed finger directed its attention toward him, as if no person in the world was as wicked and guilty as he.

Emil Wensela decided he wanted to die; he had no reason to live.

Seconds before he aimed his car for the guardrail, a strange thing happened to him: He heard a voice.

"Don't!"

"What?" Emil turned his head—he knew he had not imagined that sound. Yet, no one was in the Jaguar with him. "Who said that?"

"Don't!"

This must be a dream, Edmund Staats kept thinking. *I'm having so much good fortune now . . . more than I ever expected.*

Although he had believed Hanse Wensela, and accepted the position with Truth International, it remained a shadowy dream until he met Arno Hajford, a Norwegian who spoke eight languages fluently. Wensela had hired Hajford as the treasurer of Truth International, providing Staats approved. "This is only to help you get started, but you are not required to retain his services," Wensela added.

Staats's meeting with Hajford had taken place a week after his talk with Wensela. He had flown from Amsterdam to Rome's Fumigino Airport. A chauffeured limo took them both to the Excelsior Hotel, a place where the staff knew how to be helpful, polite, but not obsequious to their many wealthy guests.

In Staats's luxury suite, the younger man discussed how he envisioned the financial structure of Truth International, his role as the corporation treasurer, their various responsibilities. Staats agreed with Wensela's choice of treasurer and told the man.

Hajford, a compliant, quiet man, explained the financial working of the organization, showing how contributions would come in, how he paid expenses. Because of the high-powered computers Wensela was providing, Staats could have an accurate financial accounting at any time, needing approximately eight minutes from the time he punched in the code until a hard copy came off the printer.

"We are, of course, required to keep strict records,"

Hajford said. "And we need safeguards against theft, particularly embezzlement. You understand, of course."

"Certainly," Staats replied.

"The following point may be an inconvenience to you, but one which I personally believe is quite necessary: No checks will be negotiated without both your signature and mine. Each day I will bring you the checks we need to issue, so you can sign them. I shall be pleased to answer any questions. It is most important that we pay no bills without your approval." The small man with the thinning, blond hair paused and said, "I do hope this is satisfactory with you."

"Yes," Staats said. "I can't see how anything could go wrong this way . . . especially when it requires both our signatures."

"Exactly my thoughts," Hajford said.

As the treasurer left Staats's suite, he smiled. He had known Staats would be easy to convince. It surprised him how gullible and trusting the man was.

E·I·G·H·T·E·E·N

In February 1999, Neville Wheatley read a *New York Times* article for a second time, secretly pleased. A similar article had appeared the day before in the *Manchester Guardian*, which had been impressive enough. The *Washington Post*, although not giving as much space, also quoted him.

The headline of the *Times* blared at him: FOL NOW WORLD'S LARGEST CHURCH. Under the headlines the article produced statistics to prove that adherents of the Fellowship of Love far outnumbered the Roman Catholic Church. The article also stated that heavy defections were taking place within the Catholic and Orthodox Churches. More than ten million Catholics had converted within the past six months.

With few exceptions, across the world all denominations had rallied behind FOL. One paragraph in particular pleased Wheatley, and he read it until he could quote it perfectly:

> The Rev. Neville Wheatley is, by any kind
> of measure, the most powerful religious

leader in the world today. Although he has
seldom made *Proclamations* (similar to the
papal bulls that claim divine command and
adherence), he is now able to guide the
Christian faith in any direction he chooses.
He has the confidence and the support of
more than two hundred million people.

The article also pointed out mass conversions to the
Christian faith from other religions. For the last eleven
months, all other religions had shown a marked decrease.
The article concluded by quoting Bishop Joseph of Southern
Africa as saying that this phenomenon had come about for
two reasons: first, the grace of God at work in the world;
and second, the charisma of Wheatley, the only man who
"can lead the ark to safety in the midst of the storm around
us."

Neville Wheatley turned from newspaper to newspaper,
and without a dissenting statement all of them spoke of his
popularity, his charisma, and his leadership. He found it
slightly difficult to realize how far he had come. FOL had
been in existence only a year—what had taken place since
then was extraordinary.

In eighteen more minutes he would give a worldwide
television interview. He had prepared a short statement of his
surprise, his gratitude to God, and his desire to serve the
needs of the people of the world. He had read the statement
over several times and believed it had just the right note of
candor and modesty.

Neville Wheatley cleared his desk so everything would
appear neat for the cameras. Someone had opened his Bible,
and he started to close it and put it in a drawer. Then he
decided that a Bible would be a nice touch if placed on the
corner of his desk where it would not be intrusive. As he
moved the book, his eyes fell on a verse he himself had under-
lined years earlier: "Beware when all men speak well of you."

Neville Wheatley read the words, but his mind was not
on the verse. He was still thinking of his preparation for the
interview.

The interview lasted three-quarters of an hour, and when the reporters, cameras, and microphones emptied the room, Wheatley sank into his chair. It had been a good ses sion. He could feel the rapport with the media people, always a sure indication of how the public would respond. These cynics had heard it all, seen it all, and were far more difficult to convince. When he had concluded with his statement and finished with their questions, they broke into spontaneous applause.

One reporter yelled out, "I used to be a Jew. Because of you, I became a Christian!"

Yes, he reflected, it had been a good interview. Not a single time had there been any awkwardness, lengthy pauses, or questions for which he had no ready answer. Everything had gone so well, far better than he could possibly have anticipated.

His reverie was interrupted by his secretary reminding him that Ken Boyce had arrived for his appointment.

"Yes, send him in," Wheatley replied, quickly turning to his notes. Boyce represented a group called Mercy Research, of which he knew only that they had already made large financial contributions to FOL. He skimmed the page and saw that the amount had already exceeded two million dollars. Mercy Research claimed a constituency of eighteen million individuals.

Although pleased at their financial assistance, Wheatley wondered why they were coming to him.

Boyce, carefully instructed by Amwago Zolo, had been ready since early morning. His palms sweated, and he felt a slight nausea, the way he always did before he went into action. But once he started his presentation, all his nervousness and uneasiness would vanish and he would be fully in control.

The visitor wore a gray suit that would immediately make Wheatley know it was tailor-made and of the finest wool-and-silk blend. Complemented by his hand-painted tie and a diamond ring on his right hand, Boyce had no doubts that his appearance alone would win the man's confidence.

The men shook hands, and Boyce saw the appreciation and awe in Wheatley. Several times the church leader stared at the exquisite lines of the suit. Wheatley had always been clothes conscious, and he respected men who insisted on top quality in what they wore.

"I'll get to the point, Bishop Wheatley," Boyce said. "You're probably one of the busiest men in the world. But first I want to tell you how much I admire you. I don't want to embarrass you, but it is important to me to say this to you."

"I deeply appreciate your words."

"Mr. Wheatley, you're not only our spiritual leader, but you are a man of great kindness, of rare and extremely deep compassion for all people. You genuinely care about individuals, especially the oppressed and the underdogs."

"I like to think so."

"You've proven it in so many ways. For example, your stand for the rights of the mentally ill was brilliant, making us aware of the needs of the sick who cannot possibly speak for themselves."

"They are human beings, after all. And dare we ignore the plight of such people because they are different?"

Boyce leaned back, knowing that if he remained patient, he would have exactly what he wanted without pushing. *This man is really naive,* he thought. *He actually believes all this garbage about himself.* He only had to keep throwing out the word *compassion.*

"And what you've done for the homeless, especially in India and Pakistan . . . Such—such compassion. When no one else would speak up, you found people starving, unwanted, unloved, and you became their champion."

"That may be a bit thick—"

"Oh, no," Boyce interrupted. "Do you know that in Madras they have the Wheatley Home operating for those who need shelter? It's a complete program to rehabilitate and train individuals, even families, and get them into respectable places in society."

"I knew of its existence, of course—"

"Why, by the end of this year thirty-eight Wheatley Homes will operate in India. In Thailand, four such homes came into existence last month." Boyce handed Wheatley a two-page report showing a total of ninety-three homes within the Third World.

"I am pleased to be in a position to do some good."

"Your progam to help prostitutes in Manila is going to be the pilot for the rest of the world. Because of you—and it is your personal touch in this—over five thousand women of the night have turned to Jesus Christ, gone through counseling, and are now productive members of socicty."

"I am pleased that God has seen fit to allow me this opportunity to reach out to the world and to express the love of Christ. You see, Mr. Boyce, I believe that the gospel is concerned not only with saving the souls of humanity, but also with doing something for their bodies. We need compassion for all people and in all places."

"Exactly," Boyce said. "And by your example, your compassion, your courage, you have done wonderful things—the kind of things no other leader could . . . acts of mercy that few leaders would care about."

Neville Wheatley blushed then and, to cover up his embarrassment, hurriedly said, "Don't forget the financial support of organizations like yours. Everything has come about because of contributions. Not one farthing from a government source."

"You are so right," Boyce enthused. "And today I have one more needy group to bring to your compassionate attention . . . one more group toward which you may now bestow your loving concern."

"Another group?" A puzzled expression appeared on Wheatley's face. He could think of no one they had neglected.

"I'm talking, sir, about the world's homosexuals."

"Oh, yes—"

"Wait until you hear me, sir. Statistics tell us that approximately ten percent of the population in any country is homosexually oriented. Research now indicates quite clearly—just short of proof—that individuals are homosexual because of their genes—a genetic predisposition."

"Are you certain of that?" Wheatley asked.

As if he hadn't been interrupted, Boyce said softly, knowing that he had to keep the conversation in control until he reached his major point, "For instance, we know that most alcoholics are predisposed because of their genes."

"Is that so? I suppose I knew something like that—"

"Oh, yes," Boyce said. He extracted from his briefcase a pamphlet printed at Johns Hopkins Hospital in Baltimore. The hospital authorities didn't know, of course, that Amwago Zolo had arranged for two well-known researchers to come up with these desired results.

"And now we are aware that the same thing is true with homosexually oriented people. It is not their fault they are the way they are. And because they are victims, they live lifestyles not of their choosing. These people are condemned to live a lie because of societal hardness, and they need a champion. Because they have inherited the wrong genes—factors over which they have no control—these people need your voice to speak for them, to plead for understanding and compassion on their behalf."

Ken Boyce spoke with emotion in his voice, a slight tearing of his eyes as he leaned forward. "Please understand, I'm married with children and have no leanings that way myself. But that is quite beside the point actually. I am pleading for these people, born innocently into the world, condemned to follow a way of life not of their choosing, to be hated and despised by the Christians and by the heterosexual community at large. You understand, don't you, Mr. Wheatley?"

"Yes," Wheatley said, responding more to the emotional level than the evidence presented by Boyce. "I suppose I hadn't thought much about this issue before," he temporized.

"But if you, the most influential, the most godly man in the world today—if you would speak compassionately for those who cannot speak for themselves, we could go on with our research and begin to help them. Our hope is that eventually we will be able to determine those who will become homosexually oriented, inject the fetus with a corrective gene, and bring nothing but heterosexually oriented individuals into the world. Do you—do you grasp the situation? Oh, surely you do!"

"Yes, I quite see your concern."

"I knew you would," Boyce said. "And I am now ready to tell you that the eighteen million members of Mercy Research are homosexually oriented individuals. Excluding me, of course," Boyce said as he thought, *one more lie isn't going to hurt.* "And think of these eighteen million, sir. Don't they deserve to know loving acceptance by Jesus Christ? Didn't Jesus invite everyone to come as they are—right now—and be received with grace?"

"Of course we must exercise compassion," Wheatley said, feeling uncomfortable, and yet believing he could not consistently stand up for minorities and reject this group. "They . . . ah, they definitely need to know the love of God as well as any others."

"You are a good man," Boyce said. "I knew I could count on you." He handed Wheatley a check for five hundred thousand dollars, made out to him personally. "This is a gift of appreciation to you from Mercy Research. No strings attached. You notice it is a cashier's check and made out to Bearer. Sign any name you want if it's a problem."

"I shall endorse it over to the Fellowship of Love," Wheatley said. "I am so well provided for financially, I don't need anything."

"As you choose," Boyce said. "And just one final thing before I leave . . . Mercy Research has a request to make of you."

"And that request is?"

"That you declare that homosexually oriented persons may become members of the Fellowship of Love."

"Members? I don't see how I could take that stance. The Bible thoroughly condemns—"

"The Bible condemns women cutting their hair. The Bible condemns wearing cotton and wool together. And on ad infinitum. But," Boyce said, "we're not asking you to sanction or approve their lifestyle. We are asking of you, as the world leader of love and compassion, to reach out to this people who cannot help themselves. Accept them as members—certainly not as leaders—simply members—so that they can be full recipients of the sacraments."

While Bishop Wheatley struggled with his conscience, Boyce made another point. "I have personally talked with fifty-three leaders in private." He paused and took out a list of ministers around the globe, all of whom Wheatley either knew personally or by reputation. "They have already endorsed such a stance if you will be courageous enough to make this public. And as you can see, all are men of influence."

Boyce wanted to add, "Of course they are also leaders who have been corrupted." Instead he said, "These leaders agree with the position we're advocating. They have signed a statement . . ." He produced a copy, printed in four major languages. ". . . and have stated that if there is any fallout, they will take the brunt of it. However, they anticipate none."

"I'm not completely sure—"

"Not sure of compassion? Of the need to reach out lovingly toward this segment of society? We—that is, they ask only to become part of this universal church and not have to remain outside the pastoral care of God's ministers."

Wheatley then produced valid arguments, stronger than Boyce had expected. But in the end he capitulated, as Boyce knew he would.

The next day the announcement appeared on the front page of every major newspaper in the world and was equally well reported by radio and television.

Thelma Harris of NBC's affiliate in Chicago reported, "Today the ever-popular Bishop Neville Wheatley announced that church membership is now open to people who are homosexually oriented. This will entitle them to full privileges of the sacraments. The announcement raised little outcry. Most leaders agree with the bishop that the church has no right to exclude membership to anyone."

As Bishop Wheatley watched the announcement on BBC, he wondered, *Did I do right? Have I made a mistake?* Then he reminded himself that more than fifty leaders worldwide had endorsed his position. They had congratulated him on his courage and pledged their support.

If they all feel that way, he mused, *could I be wrong?* Yet something deep inside still disturbed the bishop.

N·I·N·E·T·E·E·N

When Thelma Harris read, "The announcement
raised little outcry," she obliquely referred to
one voice that publicly protested. David Morgan, after a
stormy meeting with his Board of Elders, announced that
the St. Luke's Church had, with deep regret, decided to sever
all connections with the Fellowship of Love and to
be an independent church. Ecclesiastical experts in Atlanta
estimated that the St. Luke's Church would probably
lose less than two percent of its members through this
decision.

"It is time to draw the line," Morgan said in his commentary. "Beyond this line we refuse to budge. We have been
dragged by Christian opinion a long way since the day our
denomination formally joined the Fellowship of Love. But
we cannot with conscience take this present step.

"The Bible condemns homosexual behavior, and anyone who practices this has flaunted his will against God's
laws. It is not on the same level as such regulations as not
cutting the hair, as Bishop Wheatley would like us to believe.
Homosexual behavior is an affront to God!"

The pundits in Atlanta were wrong: twelve percent withdrew their membership and their financial support.

When media people asked Morgan to comment on the defection, he said, "I cannot speak for them. I can only remain loyal to my conscience, to God, and to the infallible Word of God."

The next day a man raced into David Morgan's office waving a gun and firing. One bullet struck David in the arm, causing only a flesh wound. The assailant was quickly overpowered and led away. He screamed, "He hates me. He hates me because I'm different!"

Threats by phone became so frequent, David Morgan used an answering machine to screen his calls. Every day he received at least two letters threatening to kill him. Morgan didn't fear the threats on his life. He wished, however, that God would allow him to go back to a peaceful pastorate once again.

The Fellowship of Love also crusaded for prosperity for the whole world. A monetary reform swept over the Earth, taking any funds in excess of five million dollars from individuals and devising a sliding scale for corporations. By using the secret organizations of the various nations, carefully orchestrated behind the scenes by members of Mastermind, governments confiscated millions of dollars. These collected funds were put into public projects and new industry.

No one knew that the six members of Mastermind felt the effects of these changes only by the marked increase of their financial holdings, most of them in corporations, foundations, or accounts to which even the governments had no access.

At this time, Western nations cooperated in a new space exploration program. Colonization of the moon had begun in 1992, and Venus in 1996. The Office for World Space Exploration (OWSE) targeted Mars, with its two satellites, as its next goal and projected colonization by the year 2001.

Truth International succeeded far beyond Edmund Staats's expectations. People responded to his messages defending the faith and restoring scholarship to Biblical studies, despite their frequent scholarly flavor. Large sums of money poured in. Publishers begged Staats for permission to republish all of his books, some of them having been out of print for a quarter-century. He received more royalties for them in the reprints or in their slightly revised form than he had from the original editions.

No longer worried about retirement, Staats worked hard, producing new books, being careful to copyright them in his own name and to receive a personal share of the royalties. This was acceptable to the Board of Directors of Truth International.

Life had drastically improved for Edmund Staats. He had moved from a narrow, weatherworn house next to Amsterdam's North Sea Canal to an eight-bedroom house outside Paris. Truth International paid for a full-time chauffeur/handyman and two live-in maids.

Staats bought rare editions of scholarly treatises, books he had never hoped to have in his possession. He received many others as gifts and legacies because of his work in the field of apologetics. One expert estimated his library to be worth more than one million dollars.

Occasionally Staats explored the great city of Paris, admiring the Louvre, preferring the Saint-Chapelle to Notre Dame. He looked through Paris from all sides of the Eiffel Tower and loitered at the bookstalls, being pleasantly surprised at the amazing variety.

Yet one thing nagged at Edmund Staats from time to time—his first troubled self-questioning. *Is this right?* As quickly as the questions arose, he wondered why. After all, he was serving God, using his talents to evangelize the scholarly and the intellectual. Why did the question persist?

Staats had never before asked himself such a question. For the past year his life had moved smoothly forward. He seemed only to have to wish for a possession and it was his.

Now he found himself troubled as he thought of retirement approaching and leaving this invigorating life.

But worse, his mind filled with thoughts of acquiring. Staats frequently investigated property where he could have a larger library, more privacy, and perhaps a little higher lifestyle and added conveniences.

Having no direct inkling that he had been captured in the web of possessions, Staats satisfied his conscience by reminding himself of the years of hard work that had gone by unappreciated by the world. He had no idea that soon, very soon the spider would pounce upon the entangled victim.

Michelle Maxwell had spent weeks trying to locate her father. She could have done it more quickly, but that would have meant less discretion. Any direct action would have been noticed by someone who would have gossiped to someone else and eventually the information would have reached Annella Maxwell's ears. And her mother was the one person she did not want to know.

Her father's real name was Ted Wallace, a screenwriter and director at the time he met Annella at a Hollywood party. After the party, he had asked her to go out with him. She refused and then said, "But I'd like you to go with me."

"Sure . . . Where?"

"To my place." She kissed his lips lightly. "I don't waste time when I see something or someone I want. We don't need to play the wooing game, do we?"

Ted Wallace eagerly went with the woman with the almost-violet eyes. The next day Annella's staff cleared out Ted's apartment and brought everything he owned to her place. For the next nine years they lived together, the longest Annella had stayed with anyone.

Michelle, not knowing her father had changed his name after leaving Annella, went through a frustrating time trying to locate him. First she tried the various professional associations. None of them listed a Ted or Theo or Theodore Wallace.

Michelle started visiting people who had known her mother a long time. "It's still in the thinking stages," she said, "but I've been considering doing a book about my mother. You know, told by her daughter and people who knew her. That kind of thing."

They responded, often giving Michelle anecdotal material that would have been useful. One way or another, she asked about Ted Wallace. None of them knew.

Michelle, ready to admit defeat, decided to visit one more person—but only after warranted reluctance. Johnny Burbank had been her mother's first agent—the man who helped her climb to the top of the big heap, only to have her turn around and fire him. Burbank, long retired, proved fairly difficult to find because he no longer floated among the notables of the entertainment field. But again resorting to professional organizations, she discovered his name and address.

Burbank now lived outside Tucson, Arizona. So Michelle flew from Los Angeles, rented a car, and drove to his home unannounced. The Burbanks lived in a spacious, ranch-style home and were having a lawn party. Seeing all the parked vehicles, Michelle almost backed away.

Then, determined to continue after all the trouble and expense she had gone to, she rang the bell. The butler, once he learned she did not have an invitation, told her she would have to telephone for an appointment. "Otherwise you cannot possibly see Mr. Burbank."

His insistence made Michelle all the more determined. "I'm not going anywhere until Mr. Burbank knows I'm here. Just give him my name—that's all I'm asking. If he won't see me right now, I'll go away and I won't phone for an appointment."

"Mr. Burbank is entertaining—"

"My name is Michelle Maxwell. Please tell him."

Flashing an angry glare, the butler closed the door and left. Not more than a minute passed before the door opened and a smiling Johnny Burbank held out his right hand.

Johnny Burbank had lost his left arm in military service

during the Korean conflict in the 1950s. He had no difficulty in recognizing Michelle, although she had been a child when he last saw her.

"Come in! Come in!" he said, leading her by the arm. "What a pleasant surprise to see you again."

"I have to talk to you, in private," she said. "Please, I'll only stay five minutes—"

"Ah, forget the party out there. They can get by without me." He guided her down the long hallway to the last room on the right. The room was square, warmly lighted by a pink-shaded lamp. Heavyweight red curtains covered the narrow windows, blotting out the sun and silencing the indistinguishable voices of the guests.

The same butler came in quietly, laid a tray on the sideboard, and departed without a word.

Michelle glanced around her. A double bed covered with red silk took up most of the floor space. Johnny Burbank pointed to a round table and two chairs in the far corner. "A guest room. Don't imagine anyone will trouble us here."

Michelle declined refreshments and after the introductory chatting, she started with her normal line. "I'm considering writing a book about my mother—" She stopped and shook her head. "Johnny, that's not true. I've only been using that as a ruse to find out something else."

"Then suppose you tell me," he said as he walked over to the sideboard, his left sleeve flapping loosely, reminding Michelle of a bird's broken wing. Even at his age—and he must now be in his mid-seventies, Johnny Burbank moved with a lightness in his step, giving the impression he was still a man of enormous energy and strong will. Despite his pale brown eyes, small but restless, his receding hairline and small nose made Michelle realize Johnny Burbank must once have been an immensely handsome man.

"I don't want my mother to find out I've been here."

"From me? You think I'd tell her?" He laughed. "She dumped me, remember?"

"I know you hate her, and that's why I want to be honest—"

"I don't hate her, Michelle. Oh, I did for a time, but I got past that years ago." He took a long drink of lemonade. "I became a bit of what some call religious, and I learned that we have to forgive those who do us wrong or the grievance eats away like a cancer inside. No, my dear, I no longer hate your mother. I pity her—that I do." He took another drink and silently asked if she would change her mind.

"No," she said. "I've made . . . well, a break from Annella."

"Bully for you!" He laughed. "I can't tell you how pleased that makes me."

"And now I want to find someone . . . my father. Ted Wallace."

"You do, huh? And why, after all these years? How old are you, anyway?"

"I think I was eight when he left, and I'm twenty-seven now," she said.

"And why do you want to find him?"

"Personal. I—I can't explain it to you, Johnny, but it's important. I wouldn't have come otherwise."

"No, I suppose not," he said. Johnny Burbank returned to the sideboard and poured himself another glass of lemonade. "How hard have you looked?"

"I've tried everywhere. He's just evaporated. I realize he might be dead, and . . . I know this will sound silly, but something deep inside me says that he's alive and that . . . that he wants to see me, too."

Johnny Burbank sat down. He jiggled his right foot as he contemplated an answer. "He's alive. Very much so."

"Then you know where he is?"

"I like Ted . . . Always did. Despite what happened with Annella, he remained my friend. Still is, you know."

"Then tell me . . . please."

"Ted got hurt too, you see. Worse than I did. I only lost money. He loved her, and nothing really hurts worse, I suppose, than love rejected. Besides all that, he's a changed man. He's not the way he used to be."

"I don't care," Michelle said with determination in her voice. "He *is* my father. I need to see him. I have to. Please."

"His name is now Theo Wilson, or sometimes Ted Wilson, and he still writes screenplays, submitted through my old office under the name of Theo Wilson."

Johnny Burbank gave Michelle her father's address in Clayton County, on the southside of Metro Atlanta.

"Bryant . . . Bryant . . ." She got out only two words before she broke into sobs.

"Betty-Anne?" Bryant McFarland answered. "Is that you?"

"Yes . . ."

"You're crying. What's wrong?"

"I . . . needed desperately to hear your voice. I can bear anything if I know you care."

"What's going on? Are you sick?"

"He beat me . . . Really bad. Skipper—"

"Your husband?"

"He would have killed me," Betty-Anne said, her voice communicating her terror as the words told of her pain. "He would have except that the cook's husband was in the house. He heard my screams and burst into my bedroom. They fought and then he—the cook's husband—struck Skipper with a poker. He's dead, Bryant. Dead. I saw him dying before my eyes—"

"How dreadful for you—"

"I'm at the Mayfair Hotel, registered under the name of Diana Johnson. Room 504. Can you . . . can you come . . . for just a few minutes . . . Oh, Bryant, it was horrible." She burst into tears and finally said, "I—I can't talk." She hung up.

Betty-Anne lay back on the bed. She estimated it would take at last twenty minutes for Bryant to arrive, and she would be ready.

She did hurt. The brute had taken his job too seriously, but he was out of the way. She had attentively pulled Bryant along; now was the time to pull in that string. He would rush toward her. This part was so easy, she could have done it with half of the effort. But with the fees she received, she gave her employer full measure.

Bryant arrived in fifteen minutes and knocked. Betty-Anne stumbled to the door. "Who is it?"

"Bryant here."

Betty-Anne had left on only one light so that when she opened the door, Bryant would be able to see the outline of her body. He stared at the puffy eyes and the cuts across her forehead. Her torn nightgown exposed just enough to tantalize him. Betty-Anne had reasoned that Bryant would be in no condition to ask why she had changed clothes.

"Oh, Bryant . . . I thank God you came. Oh, you are so wonderful." She grabbed his arm and pulled him inside. After closing the door behind them, Betty-Anne turned and stared at the handsome man. She murmured, "Bryant, I—" before she collapsed into his arms. "Just hold me . . . for a moment. I'm so afraid . . . and weak . . . and I hurt . . ."

Bryant McFarland embraced her as she pressed herself against him. Genuine sobs fell from her lips. And, as she had expected, he picked her up and carried her to the bed—the only furniture in the room except a dresser and a straight chair.

As Bryant pulled away, Betty-Anne stopped him. "Don't . . . not yet . . . Just sit on the bed beside me. Hold my hand. Touch me. I need your closeness . . . I need your strength."

Bryant sat chastely on the corner of her bed, holding her hand. "You poor thing," he kept saying as he brushed her long hair off her face. "Such an ordeal."

It took little effort before she had him lying next to her, her head in his arm. "Oh, perhaps with you beside me I can sleep," she said. "Without your being here, protecting me, I wouldn't sleep for a minute."

They lay in the dark room for several minutes, and Betty-Anne allowed her body to relax. She said, "Bryant, I'm better . . . really."

"You sure?" He started to get up.

"Don't move yet. Let me . . . let me tell you something important. If I don't tell you now, I shall lose my nerve and never have the courage to say the words." As Betty-Anne spoke, she felt Bryant's body tense, knowing what she was going to say. She was just as certain he would respond as she had planned.

"Skipper came in, threatening me. He accused me of having an affair with you because we're often seen togeth-er. I tried . . . oh, I tried to tell him what a decent and kind man you are. That you would never, never take advan-tage of my vulnerability. Besides, I pointed out that you have a wife languishing in bed, that you're a man of strong moral fiber. He wouldn't listen. Oh, everything was terrible from then on. Skipper started yelling and laughing, calling me frightful names and then . . .then he beat me."

"I'm so sorry," Bryant said, acting as if he were oblivi-ous to the fact that he had pulled her closer.

"One thing he was right about. He accused me of lov-ing you . . . And I do, Bryant. Forgive me for that, but I do love you. I have never, never, never loved anyone as I love you. And since this love of ours can never be, I've decided that tomorrow I'm going away . . . far away."

"Away? Why?"

"Why? Because I can't have you . . . If I stay, I won't be able to control myself. I can hardly control my emotions now."

"Betty-Anne . . ."

"But you do care for me too? I mean, a little?"

"I love you," he said. "I've fought this desire toward you these weeks. Honestly, I haven't meant to love you, I didn't want to fall in love with you, but—"

"Oh, Bryant, what shall we do? What *can* we do?"

The words passed rapidly between them for several minutes, but Betty-Anne had prepared well. Bryant McFar-land was hers.

The man of strong moral fiber had finally yielded in his one vulnerable area. Mastermind had known, and now the real plan for Bryant McFarland was ready to begin.

She smiled in the dark. She hadn't been able to deliver McFarland as a Christmas present to Maison Quayle, but she was only a month late.

T·W·E·N·T·Y

The Master Plan which originated in Southern California embodied Westernized versions of Eastern religion and metaphysics. Ever since the 1997 television special with Levis Cothran, the Master Plan had spread widely, using literature, advertising heavily on television, promoting a lifestyle of "joy, peace, and the fulfillment of human potential."

As their major advocate, Levis Cothran, along with a bevy of popular entertainers, traveled from city to city recruiting those "who are hungry for reality and truth."

The Master Plan carefully avoided controversy and competition with the Fellowship of Love. When asked about FOL, the Master Plan devotees would say something like, "We stand for many of the same things, but with a different emphasis."

Alida, the famous composer-singer who introduced a type of music called "New Age Rock," said in a television interview, "In the Master Plan we put more emphasis on the spiritual in life, but we absolutely endorse everything the Fellowship of Love stands for. After all, isn't love the most important ingredient?"

When pressed, Alida admitted, "The Master Plan believes that love, the most important element, by itself isn't enough. We do believe that, being part of the divine cosmos, we are love, we are linked with the Earth and with our brothers and sisters in FOL. Our purpose isn't to divide and destroy. We want everyone to enjoy fulfillment and prosperity . . . right now . . . in this life. Most of the devotees of FOL seek their prosperity and fulfillment in the life ahead. I suppose that's the real difference between us . . . I mean, if you insist on pointing out a difference."

The *Detroit Free Press* estimated that more than nine hundred people in Chicago alone joined the Master Plan as a result of Alida's statements. They also pointed out another trend: people who were members of FOL were now also joining the Master Plan.

"Why not?" asked a Pentecostal pastor in San Antonio. "We are one in the Spirit!"

Members of the Master Plan did not divulge everything about themselves. Like good advertisers, they sold the sizzle of the product. Only after initiation did the leaders slowly lead their converts into their fifteen-step program of full living.

In the fourth step, initiates learned about channeling. Instructors showed them how to discover their own spirit guides. These guides then aided them through the rest of the program.

In step six initiates learned how to use tarot cards, were introduced to I Ching, and received instructions on crystal healing. Only after reaching step eleven did they learn about astral projection.

In astral projection, converts learned to put themselves into deep relaxation—delta two brain waves—where they fully yielded themselves to their spirit guides. They then left their physical bodies and traveled to other places on Planet Earth on missions of mercy. For instance, one man reported that his spirit took him to the oncology unit of the Kosair Children's Hospital in Louisville, Kentucky. At the bedside of a terminally ill child, he touched the boy's body and then left.

The next day Louisville's *Courier-Journal* reported a spontaneous remission of a nine-year-old boy dying of leukemia.

Master Plan astrologers designated February 17-24 as a World Convergence Celebration. They heralded the arrival of a new age of spiritual enlightenment. An African psychic named Ja-Neko made an announcement to the world via a new system of intercontinental television called tele-media:

> February 17 is the first day of the rest of the world! On World Convergence Day the spirit guides of all faithful believers will converge above the atmosphere and, for one week, in united action, will deploy their energies toward the enrichment and betterment of the human race.
>
> The spirit guides have waited thousands of years for this time to come. They will guide us into fulfillment, will lead us out of the wasteland of despair into the vastness of our potential as human beings. These same spirit guides will see that no follower ever goes hungry or is in need again.

Ja-Neko appealed to the people of the world to join with him in welcoming the World Convergence Celebration. He asked that on each continent followers hold hands, stretching a human chain from one coast to the next. Within hours after Ja-Neko's tele-media announcement, leaders called for "spontaneous excitement about these human chains."

The people of Los Angeles formed the first human chain, and within two days it stretched all the way to New York. Another reached from the Ivory Coast to Tanzania. People stood from France to Poland and across the width of the Soviet Union. Other human chains extended across India and Burma. The Master Plan had not yet attracted as much attention in the Far East and virtually none in the Middle East. When asked why, Master Plan leaders said, "Their time to join us will come soon."

Members of the Master Plan also had their own song, translated into every major world language, but sung predominantly in English.

> We are the world; we come to give.
> We come to love; we come to save.
> We now are God; we come to live.

In every major city in the western world, members of the Master Plan set up a World Convergence Celebration. They provided a carnival-like atmosphere with free food, rides, games, and first-class musical entertainment that extended from heavy metal to soft rock to bluegrass to pop to jazz. In fifteen cities, soloists sang arias of a newly written opera called "In Praise of Us."

As crowds went past the food, games, and entertainment, they began to see different kinds of booths. One advertised crystal healing, another presented the successor to the Ouija board (now named MasterBoard), which not only offered guidance, but enabled inquirers to experience their "energy field" as they operated the board. Many left with a sense of "peaceful presence." As one person said, "I felt loved and a part of the universe."

Other booths offered body-healing massage (where practitioners diagnosed and healed as they gently massaged each part of the body). Aural readings took place, and participants were taught how to recognize the auras around others.

No one charged for any services offered during World Convergence Celebration. "This is our gift to ourselves—our world!"

For a week the world media reported on the World Convergence Celebration. People, picked at random from the crowd, told of their experiences. One woman reported being healed from a congenital heart disease through using a crystal; another woman, advised by a tarot reader, quadrupled her lifetime savings on the stock market. On and on went the testimonies, and each time the cameras moved, someone was singing "We are the world; we come to give."

"It works," declared one Holiness preacher from Seattle, Washington. "I'd always been against this—this—" He pointed to a room with a closed door where the sign indicated that a channeling experience was in progress. "My denomination taught against it. I didn't believe any of what the Master Plan people said until I came to this celebration."

"What changed you? Something specific?" asked the reporter.

"Specific? Just let me tell you. I met this incredible man who said he had a gift from God to help people find their way. Without my asking him for anything, he laid his hands on me and blessed me and then said that all things in life are mine if I want them. I laughed and said, 'In that case, I'd like a Cadillac—a new one.' The next day—the very next day, mind you—someone knocked at my door. He said that he had decided to give away his store-new Cadillac that had been driven less than four hundred miles. He went to one of these World Convergence Celebration booths in Spokane, and the woman gave him my street address! Can you believe that? I went to Seattle, this man went to Spokane, and I received a new Cadillac!"

Others rushed to the microphone to tell of their experiences. One man said, "I am convinced now that I am God. That is, I am part of the divine consciousness. I have decided never to age and never to die. And why not? I am God."

David Morgan had left immediately after services on Sunday, having arranged to be alone in a private retreat during World Convergence Celebration. He was emotionally and physically drained. His church was losing membership—not in a flood, but in a steady trickle. Each week the attendance would drop, showing two or three people fewer than the week before. No one else seemed to notice.

Offerings, on the other hand, had increased. The church, contrary to Morgan's expressed conviction, erected a multipurpose recreation building that housed a basketball court, running track, six handball courts, a complete line of fitness equipment, and an Olympic-sized swimming pool. Tom Grundy was now insisting on constructing a golf course which he would personally pay for and maintain.

Against none of these things could Morgan stand up and cry out, "They're wrong." He did talk to the Board of Elders about diluting the gospel, about getting mixed up in things not spiritual. The Board voted him down, reminding him that it was better to have Christians on church property than out in the terrible environment that faced them in the world.

An old friend of Morgan's had a home in the north Georgia mountains, secluded and adjacent to land controlled by the federal government as a public reserve. There he could be alone and pray for divine strength.

Morgan drove slowly north from Atlanta, avoiding the expressways, taking side roads that wound uphill like a snake basking in the sunshine. He passed Helen, a tourist city built to resemble an alpine village. After passing through the town, he realized evening was drawing near. The cool breeze of the hillside gave way to the still air of a valley, and sounds were magnified. He heard the strains of music from Helen, and smiled at the clear tones of a trumpet and an accordion. The drum beat out the music in a happy four-four tune.

He arrived right at dusk. The level land where his friend's rustic house was located was cool now. The sun had less than an hour to travel before it slid behind the mountains. From the south, he observed the thickening gray-white mist. Morgan felt vastly better. Eating the fruit and sandwich Katherine had packed, he made himself tea, fell across the bed, and slept. It was the next morning before he awakened. Getting up, Morgan prepared himself a cup of herbal tea, ate a handful of grapes left from home, and lay down again. He slept until dark.

By then, Morgan was physically refreshed. He was ready to talk to God and to receive directions . . . and he needed guidance badly.

David Morgan had come to the Georgia mountains largely out of discouragement which was far worse than any he had experienced previously. People still listened to his preaching, but not with the attention he had observed before. The message had not changed, nor had his theology. But people seemed apathetic, as if they didn't want to bother to think about the things of God.

Saddest of all, David Morgan believed that the members of the Board should be people of the highest spiritual caliber—these people he talked to, counseled, and who counseled him. For years he had called them his support group. But that had changed in the past six months. Morgan could not count on one member of the Board of Elders to be at church four Sundays in a row. Fewer people wanted to serve, and yet they gave lavishly of their funds to hire workers. The church now had twelve, full-time staff members who did everything from ushering to locking and unlocking the doors.

"I'm so weary, God," he said. "I feel as if I'm fighting a losing battle. Is it time to take me home, God, to get me out of the way . . . or to send me to another area? Bring in someone who will cause them to hear Your word."

He prayed and, in silence, waited for the Inner Voice to speak. *Just a simple word. A Scripture verse. Anything.*

But again, only silence.

Until long after dawn, Morgan knelt by the bed. Sleep eluded him, and so did peace. He felt as if he had pleaded with an empty sky, and his heart grew heavier. He dozed toward morning, but he never got into the bed.

At full light, Morgan heard footsteps on the wooden porch, followed by a pounding at the door. When he opened the door he saw a young man named Mitch Hege, a boy he had known since his toddler days. Mitch was now seventeen.

"Sorry to bother you, Mr. Morgan, but I was praying last night and God gave me a Bible verse for you. Just the reference, and I didn't even look it up. Your wife didn't want me to bother you, but God wouldn't let me give up. I begged and begged and finally she told me where to find you." He handed Morgan a slip of paper, waved, and called out, "God bless you!" as he walked toward the road. "That's the only reason I came!" He waved a good-bye to his pastor.

After the young man left, Morgan read the reference: Ezekiel 3:17-21. He picked up his Bible and pored over the passage:

> "Mortal man," he said, "I am making you
> a watchman for the nation of Israel. You
> will pass on to them the warnings I give
> you. If I announce that an evil man is going
> to die but you do not warn him to change
> his ways so that he can save his life, he will
> die, still a sinner, but I will hold you respon-
> sible for his death. If you do warn an evil
> man and he doesn't stop sinning, he will
> die, still a sinner, but your life will be
> spared.
>
> "If a truly good man starts doing evil
> and I put him in a dangerous situation, he
> will die if you do not warn him. He will die
> because of his sins—I will not remember the
> good he did—and I will hold you responsi-
> ble for his death. If you do warn a good
> man not to sin and he listens to you and
> doesn't sin, he will stay alive, and your life
> will also be spared." (TEV)

Two hours after receiving Mitch Hege's message, Morgan started walking through the trails that ran from the secluded house. He wasn't used to physical inactivity, and he walked until the sun was overhead before he turned back.

Just before he reached the house again, he saw a man sitting on the front porch, his head bent forward. As he got closer, Morgan recognized the visitor.

"Hello," Morgan said, extending his hand. "Now I really am surprised. You turn up in strange places."

"I followed you from Atlanta Sunday," Emil Wensela said. "I've been wanting to talk to you for two days, but I was afraid that you'd kick me out."

"Sit down. Let's talk."

"My name is Emil Wensela." He paused. "Does that mean anything to you?"

"No," Morgan said, "unless you're trying to tell me that you're related to Hanse Wensela."

"My father," the young man said. "And until the day I accidentally went into your class at Emory University, I wanted to be exactly like him."

"And now?"

"Now I'm confused; I don't know what I want."

Morgan, not a trained counselor, intuitively knew, however, that listening was the simplest and the hardest part of counseling.

"I mean, my father is a man without scruples. Not just a man who's incredibly wealthy through questionable and sometimes illegal doings . . . He's an atheist, too."

"Didn't I hear of his conversion some time back?"

"Just a trick to take in some dummy in Europe." The young man got up and paced the porch before he was ready to talk again. "I have never had feelings—I mean tender feelings—the kind you read about. My father taught me how to pretend that I had them, how to say the right things and to express the proper facial expressions and gestures, but I've never experienced real emotions . . . Until now, I mean. I guess I thought most people were like that."

"What changed your opinion?"

"Oh, a woman I met. She's not important except that she came out of the same kind of background—you know, morally corrupt, if-it-feels-good-do-it-as-long-as-you-don't-get-caught concept. Things like that. Only she . . . well, she has a conscience. She couldn't do some things. For instance, when I meet a woman that I find attractive, I take her to bed. It's quite simple—we both enjoy it, and that's that. But then this woman—a very attractive woman—didn't want to do that. She says she's never slept with a man. I tell you, I couldn't believe that . . . except I knew she was telling the truth."

Hardly aware of what he was doing, Emil Wensela told of his experiences with Michelle Maxwell. "Now she's gone, I haven't any idea where. Her mother just said she had something going with two different men. I don't believe that, but I don't know where she is.

"And you know what's crazy about all of this? I—I feel something toward her—something I've never experienced before in my life. I mean, I think about her. I even dream about her. Do you think I need to be examined by a shrink?"

"Not at all. I suspect you've developed emotions whether you want them or not."

"Yeah, and that's not the worse part. You're responsible for the other thing that's happening." Emil cursed the preacher again. "You did this to me! And I hate you for it!"

T·W·E·N·T·Y O·N·E

Although David Morgan had heard many experiences of personal journeys to Jesus Christ, each sounded unique, reminding him of the myriad ways the Holy Spirit works. Listening intently to Emil's recounting of his own experience made the pastor aware of the obstacles God overcame in reaching needy people. When the young man finished, Morgan asked, "What now?"

"You ask *me* that?" replied a surprised Emil. "That's what I came to ask you."

"What do you want, Emil? You went to a lot of trouble to follow me, staying out in the woods all night—"

"I want to get rid of this feeling. I've never hurt like this before. It drains my energy, keeps my mind off everything else. I've never been so miserable. Just—just show me how to throw off this—this terrible guilt."

"Sorry, but what I can tell you doesn't work quite so easily." Morgan leaned forward, placing his hands on Emil's shoulders and gazing into his blue eyes. "For the first time you can remember you're experiencing true emotion, and you want to get rid of it, run away from it."

"But it hurts . . . diverts my thinking. It claws at me all the time."

"That's what guilt is supposed to do."

"And I just have to live with it? Is that what your religion does? Makes us feel bad?" He started to move away.

The older man pressed his hands tightly against Emil's shoulder blades. "Listen carefully," he said softly. "Sometimes you have to feel bad before you can feel good. You have to know how bad you are before you can know how good God is and—"

"I didn't come here for a lecture in religion."

"But you did," Morgan said, his voice remaining calm. "You don't like the form it takes, but Jesus Christ is the answer, my young friend, the only answer."

Emil backed off and swore at Morgan, then caught himself. "Sorry. I did that in anger."

"Or frustration," Morgan said. "Frustration because I won't be bullied into giving you a simplistic answer. I can help you though . . . if you really want help."

"I do," he said. "Anything to take away this—this feeling."

"Let's go inside and talk some more," Morgan said. "I believe you're ready." As they went inside, Morgan silently thanked God for sending Emil, a hungry soul, and for restoring his own faith by giving him hope again.

Emil Wensela stayed at the rustic cabin for the rest of Morgan's planned retreat. They ate nothing, drank nothing but water. Mostly they prayed, sometimes together, often separating and walking around the building in silence. Each evening they sat next to the lamplight and alternated reading lengthy Bible portions. Occasionally Emil would ask Morgan to explain a verse, but mostly they just read, both eager for more understanding.

"If we're going to fight the battle against evil," Morgan said, "we must fortify ourselves. Prayer and reading the Bible are the two major weapons I know that won't fail us."

"I wish I knew that," Emil said. "I'm so new to all of this, and I'm not sure—just not sure if I can stand up against my father and Mastermind."

"I want to tell you one thing, Emil, and don't ever forget this: God is always strongest in our lives when we're the weakest."

"I promise you, I'll never forget that."

Morgan would later recall those very words and wonder why he had not heeded his own words.

Edmund Staats stared at the letter on his desk. *If I had known in advance . . . If I had prepared myself.* There had been no warning, not the slightest hint. Two days earlier he had checked the receipts, and they were at that time receiving the most contributions since the founding of Truth International.

He stared at the letter again, consisting of six brief paragraphs, but this time he read only part of the fourth:

. . . no more contributions after this month
. . . the terminus of Truth International.

Logically everything presented in the letter made sense. The generous contributors had decided to move their contributions to the Fellowship of Love, which already had a firmly established division that specialized in defend-ing the faith. Staats hadn't always liked what their material had to say, but he admitted they did their work well.

Immediately his mind came back to his own dilemma. With the closing of Truth International, there would be no place for him.

"Jobless," he said and allowed his eyes to take in his luxurious office. As his fingers brushed down the lapel of his new suit, he realized how high a standard of living he had set for himself. And now, in only a few days he would have nothing but an inadequate pension waiting for him—a pension that paid in one month what he spent in three days on personal expenses.

"O God, how did I get into this mess? How did I get caught like this? Why didn't You warn me? Why weren't You here to help me?"

Staats walked over to his credenza, where he had been preparing a study booklet based on the Old Testament story of Joshua and the Gibeonites. Attempting to divert himself, he picked up the pages and skimmed through them. He had worked hard on this article, "Blind to Truth," perhaps harder than he did on most. The point of his article was that had Joshua prayed for guidance when the Gibeonites first came, he would have known what to do and would have made the right decision. Instead, the spiritual leader had allowed the strangers' dusty, old clothes and moldy bread to confuse and lead him astray.

In the Biblical account, the people of Gibeah feared the approaching Israelites in the new land. They knew they would be completely wiped out, so they deceived Joshua and the elders by pretending to be people from a far-off country who wanted to make a peace pact. Too late, Joshua realized his mistake.

Staats, had he been a man with a sense of humor, would have laughed at the irony. Instead he tore up the pages of the hard copy of his booklet. He kept tearing and tearing until the entire thirty pages lay in a heap of postage-stamp-sized pieces. He pounded his fist.

"God, why did You do this to me? Why did You allow this to happen? Why don't You care about me? Why would You play tricks on me like that?"

Unaware of his action, Staats's fingers curled around the pages of his Bible, the very pages that contained the story of the Gibeonites. Angrily the old man ripped them from the binding. "You don't care about me. You never did. You've always made me a second-class Christian! And now You do this to me. Are You satisfied? Are You happy at the mess You've thrown me into?" Staats wadded the paper into a tight ball.

"How could a loving God do this to me?"

Michelle Maxwell rang the bell and waited. She tried to breathe normally, but she was too nervous. Her weight shifted from one foot to the other. She punched the bell a second time.

"Coming!" she heard a voice from far-off yell. Seconds later a tall, broad-shouldered man opened the door. He smiled and said, "Sorry . . . I was in the backyard and just walked inside. Hope you haven't waited long."

"No, only a couple of seconds," she said, afraid her voice sounded tiny and high. He was still handsome, with rugged features and deep-set gray eyes. "I—I, well . . . first, are you Ted Wilson? Or Theo Wilson?"

"I am. I have been for a long time," he said smiling at her. "I probably will be until I die."

"You—you used to—to live with Annella Maxwell? Like twenty years ago or so ago?"

He nodded. "Not one of the nice parts of my life, but yes, I did."

His voice, like a punch in the stomach, was so real she keeled forward. He caught her and held her a second. "You all right?"

She straightened. "Oh, yes . . . yes . . . yes . . . You see . . . my name . . . my name is Michelle."

"Yes, I know."

"You do? I mean, how?"

"You're my daughter, aren't you?"

"I think so. I mean, I've been searching for you for . . . for a long time."

"I changed my name, so I guess that made it difficult."

"Almost impossible to find you. That's why I didn't come sooner."

Ted stared down at the young woman, hardly able to believe she was so mature. "I did a lot of rotten, ugly things in my life, Michelle, but being your father wasn't one of them. I loved you from the minute I first saw you. I've found ways to get pictures of you, to sneak up in public gatherings and peek at you. Oh, yes, I know you."

"Then I have just one question for you. If you're my

father, and you know that, and you say you love me, why did you go away? Why did you leave me? Why did you make me stay with . . . with that woman?"

"I think you'd better come inside so we can talk," Ted said.

"We had good years together, Annella and I, at least in some ways," Ted Wilson told Michelle. "Your mother decided she wanted what she called a love child; so you came into the world."

"But she didn't really want me after I was born," Michelle said. "I'm not angry about that, just a little sad. I've known for a long time that my mother doesn't know how to love or to care for anyone. It just isn't in her."

"Yeah," he said. "I think I knew early on, but the woman is so dazzling, so talented . . . It was as if she could read my thoughts before I had a chance to think them. And then she did everything to make me happy. Or I guess I thought she did."

"Why did she do it? You know, cater to you like that?"

"I guess it was a stage in her career when she wanted the world to see her playing the ideal-mother-and-wife bit. She was just beginning to be noticed, and she wanted nothing but good reports of her domesticity."

"And then she threw you out, didn't she?"

"I would have left earlier, Michelle, if it hadn't been for you. Believe me, I'd have stayed on, regardless of how bad things got, if it had meant being able, to stay with you."

"I sort of know that. Maybe it's because I know her so well."

"Nobody really knows Annella Maxwell, do they?"

"I know most of her tricks and habits and behavior—"

"Michelle, as much as this might upset you to hear, I think she is the most evil individual I've ever met in my life."

"Perhaps," Michelle said. "Except that right now she's

mixed up with five powerful men, and it's a toss-up as to who's the most evil."

Knowing they now understood each other, Ted Wilson told his daughter the rest of his story. His parents had been Christians and raised him in the church, but he rebelled when he was a teenager. "They were against everything that seemed like fun, and they couldn't make me understand why it was wrong."

After college he went to New York, where he got a chance to write for a local talk show; then, because they liked his work, he got more jobs. Finally a New York playwright asked him to adapt his script for the screen. It was an immense success, and Ted Wallace ended up in Hollywood. He directed an occasional film, but mostly he wrote screenplays.

Then, deciding television was more lucrative, he formed his own organization along with three other writers. The four men became highly successful, soon known as Hollywood's top writers, with a variety of projects offered. Wallace developed a special talent: He knew how to patch up bad scripts, even bad films after they were made. They called him The Writing Doctor, and still more opportunities to write came his way. Tiring of the Hollywood scene and the sleaze around him, Ted dropped out of the partnership and moved to New York.

"There I met your mother, and I devoted myself to writing exclusively for her. When she kicked me out, I couldn't find a studio or production company open to me."

"Courtesy of Annella blackballing you?"

"Yes, although no one would actually say that in words. I changed my professional name to Ron Ryan and started again. She found out and cut me off. So I began working with Johnny Burbank by changing my name to Theo Wilson, and he agreed to represent me as a new writer. He took me with one stipulation: under no circumstances would I return to Hollywood or New York. I was delighted to agree. So, Michelle, I've now made myself fairly successful for the third time, doing mostly comedy for television. I don't like a lot of slop on the tube, but I manage to make a living at my trade. And a living is enough."

"I'm happy for you."

"Something better happened in my life. I returned to my roots. After returning to Atlanta where my parents lived—they're both dead now—they helped me to get on the right path again."

"Dad, do you know the pastor here named David Morgan?"

"Know him? Why, he's the pastor of the church my parents attended. He's the man who got me straightened out."

"Then help him. He's in real danger from my mother and her friends. They call themselves The Master Plan." Michelle explained how the six of them sat in a circle and opened themselves to a spirit called Mastermind, who then spoke exclusively through Annella. "Mastermind's overall plan is to get rid of all Christians by destroying their leaders first. They're taking away and discrediting the leaders through all kinds of things—mainly finding their human weaknesses. And, Dad, Mastermind will soon control the world. He says that only Christians are hindering his complete dominion. They're especially after David Morgan. Mastermind says he's the strongest, but he's also the weakest."

"What does that mean?"

"I don't know, except that they're going to ruin others as well. But David Morgan will eventually be their primary target. Mastermind says that Morgan is the one to fear the most and that they must destroy him slowly and carefully."

"Then we ought to warn him."

"Can we do it together?" she asked.

Edmund Staats did not leave his office all morning. He wanted to talk with the treasurer, Arno Hajford. Perhaps because he too would be out of a job, he might have an idea what to do. He asked his secretary to notify him when Arno came in.

At one o'clock his secretary buzzed. "Mr. Hajford came in, and I told him you wanted to see him, but he said he was in a hurry. He will get back with you later today."

"Thank you," Staats said as he switched off the intercom. That response didn't sound like Arno. The man, if anything, had been too obsequious. Why this change? Could he have known in advance? Surely not.

Or could he?

A narrow passageway connected his office with Arno's, a convenience that allowed the two men to move from one office to the other without visitors in the reception area seeing them.

Using the passageway, Staats walked into Hajford's office and appraised the usual neatness of the room. He sat down at the computer and called up the financial records. Truth International had liquid assets of more than four million dollars.

He got up from the computer and started back toward his own office when he noticed a suitcase under Arno's desk. That puzzled him. Not only would the man never leave anything out of place, but Arno hated to travel and avoided it whenever possible.

Again, Staats had a feeling that Arno Hajford had had some kind of advance warning. He wondered how. *No,* he thought, *I'm jumping to a conclusion and condemning a man against whom I have no evidence.*

He stared at the brown leather suitcase several seconds before picking it up and placing it on the desk. He opened the case and stared at numerous stacks of money, most of it in thousand dollar bills . . . all bound bills, all in American dollars. And below that, he found stacks of bearer bonds. Flipping through the currency and bonds, Staats quickly estimated their value—at least three million dollars, possibly more.

"What can he be doing with that kind of money? Where would he get that amount? Embezzlement?" he asked aloud, then started to dismiss it. "Surely not. Not that sycophant."

Staats took the suitcase into his own office, where he placed it in the back of his closet. "I'll find out when he returns," he said, "and he'd better have a good explanation."

He flipped the intercom button. "When Mr. Hajford returns, please buzz me."

As he leaned back in his chair, he wondered what kind of legal action he would have to take against Hajford if he had stolen the money.

As Staats contemplated the matter, he found himself drawn back to the suitcase. He opened it a second time and painstakingly counted the money. The cash and the bearer bonds added up to four million, one hundred thousand dollars. It could only have come from one place.

"If only it were mine now," Staats said wistfully.

T·W·E·N·T·Y T·W·O

A discouraged preacher looked down at the empty pews, the half-bored stares. No, he decided, it wasn't going to be easy today. Michelle Maxwell and her father had warned him about Mastermind, adding details that Emil Wensela hadn't told him. He had no illusions now: they were after him. But then, he reminded himself, Satan had always tried to destroy him and any other Christian who wanted to follow Jesus Christ.

"The love of many will grow cold," Morgan preached to the congregation. "Some of you who are listening to me will turn from your love of God. I wish it would not happen." He paused momentarily and stared again at the crowd before him, realizing that at one point in his career, six hundred at a single service would have seemed like a significant number. "Yet this will happen. It is already happening. I don't mean only that many will stop attending—that's already taking place. But something more insidious, more evil is taking form. Hearts are growing cold, losing their fervent love for Jesus Christ. And saddest of all, I know that many of you will turn on me and on your brothers and sisters in Jesus Christ."

The congregational attendance had continued to dwindle, and Morgan watched it happen week by week. He'd observe a family quite heavily involved in the church, and then the wife or the husband would say something such as, "It's so far to bring the kids over here for the youth programs," or "We never have any time at home just for ourselves. One family member or the other always seems to be running here for something."

He had gotten so good at observing the trend, he had worked out a formula. From the time of their first complaints, it took six weeks before the family missed one activity, usually something during the week. Another month and they wouldn't attend a Sunday service. At first they would stay away only a week or two, then they'd extend their absences for longer periods. Within three months the family became occasional attenders, and after six months they would return only for Christmas and Easter—if then.

Morgan had known this falling away from God would come—the Bible made that clear. Yet it grieved him to see it happening before his eyes. He knew they all were entering the foray against the final onslaught of the Devil and his workers. Despite all this knowledge, and the speaking of the Holy Spirit to him, Morgan still tended to take defections as personal rejection. No matter how hard he tried to talk himself out of feeling that he might have done more or worked harder, in the pit of his stomach the feeling refused to leave that they had turned against David Morgan as much (or even more) than they had turned against God.

"O God, I've failed," he often wept. "If I had been more sensitive to Your Spirit, more open to You, I could have kept them from being snatched away. Forgive me."

One day as he prayed in great agony of spirit, a member of the Board of Elders, Joe Strenk, came to his office. He was resigning, and he wanted to tell Morgan personally.

"I have no quarrel with you personally," Joe Strenk said, "and Lisa and I want you to know that. Why, Mr. Morgan, if it hadn't been for you, I'd have left a lot sooner. I've tried to hold on, but I've got to resign. If I don't, it'll cost me my marriage and my family."

Pushing aside his own pain, Morgan said, "Perhaps you'd better tell me the whole story, Joe." The pastor gazed at the man in front of him. In their late forties or early fifties, the Strenks didn't have their first child until they were in their mid-thirties. They now had three handsome sons, all bright, all involved in the children's activities.

"I don't want to lie to you and tell you anything except the truth. Both Lisa and I came from really poor homes. Our folks sacrificed to help us get through college. I took a lot of low-paying jobs until I found exactly what I wanted."

As he talked, Morgan nodded occasionally. He had known this part of the Strenks' story. They were poor folks who had wanted so much to live among the wealthy. In the past year Joe had finally made it to the top of his profession and was earning more money than he had ever dreamed possible. Lisa, who had gone back to work two years earlier, had become vice-president of a small company which manufactured an inexpensive but good-quality nail polish. Lisa had pushed and planned, and the company had done so well that the Max Factor group was vying to buy them out, with the proviso that Lisa remain for five years as Chief Executive Officer.

"Now we've got all the money we've ever wanted and all of the things we never thought possible. In case anything happens to us, we've had ample funds set aside for the education of our kids. Right now, we're confronted with the one thing we both want, that we both need—a social life—a life not limited to being involved in the church five days and four nights a week."

Morgan understood. *Acceptance.* The moneyed people, the affluent, had begun to recognize Joe and Lisa. They were receiving invitations for weekend parties, balls, and gala occasions. They asked Lisa to plan their entertainments and benefit programs for the underprivileged.

"And frankly, David," Joe said, "it means a choice. We're finally able to get everything we've ever wanted . . . more than we ever asked for."

"And where is God in all of this?"

"God's there. Here. With us. Didn't Jesus promise to be with us always? God knows where we are, and we're not doing anything immoral."

"Do you really believe what you've just said to me?" Morgan asked.

Joe dropped his gaze. "Don't try to talk me out of this, David. I've made up my mind."

"I won't stop you. How can I? It's your choice. But I wonder if you've ever thought of the question Jesus asked people in just your situation."

"What question is that?"

"'What shall it profit a man if he gain the whole world and lose his soul?'"

"I'm not losing anything," Joe said, a tone of defiance in his voice. "While we're no longer going to be active here at your church, we're not leaving God behind. Can't I be a good Christian out in the world? Or do you think you have to go to church six days a week to be a true Christian?"

"Joe," David said, "I'm sorry you've made this decision—"

"It's my life!"

"I thought it was God's."

"You twist around everything I say. Lisa warned me you'd do that. I guess I should have just written a letter."

"No, you did the right thing," David Morgan said. "But at the moment, I'm thinking about a young man mentioned in the Bible. He traveled with the Apostle Paul for a long time, endured persecution, and suffered hardship until one day he left. The Apostle Paul writes of him only a simple statement: 'Demas has forsaken me, having loved this present evil world.' And, Joe, although it hurts me to say this to you, because I love you I'm saying it: You are a Demas!"

"Who are you to judge me?"

"I'm not a judge. Your own words convict you."

"You think you have the answer for everything! You act as if you're the only real Christian left in the world."

"Maybe you're right," Morgan said. "I admit that sometimes I feel like I am the only one left!"

Joe Strenk stared at the sad face in front of him and then dropped into a chair. "Maybe I'm wrong, David, but I don't have strength like you. I'm too weak to hold out, and I can't keep fighting Lisa and the kids. And—and I want what these people have to offer me." He laughed and said, "Strange, I wanted to get angry at you—to have a real verbal blowout. Then I could leave justified."

"Joe, do what you've decided to do. But I intend to pray for you every day. I'm going to pray that God will snatch your soul from the grasping hand of Satan." Morgan said the words so softly that it took several seconds for them to impact on Joe.

"I don't want your prayers."

"Prayer is all I can do for you once you leave here," Morgan said. "It is the only weapon I have to fight with."

"Don't fight over me. I'm not worth it."

"But you are, Joe. You . . . Lisa . . . the kids. Each of you was worth the death of Jesus Christ. Each of you is worth fighting for."

Joe Strenk stood and shoved his chair against the desk. "You're getting me all mixed up again. I know what I want, and I've made my choice. Now shut up and don't ever talk to me about these things again!"

"You're not the one I intend to talk to," Morgan said, a slight smile on his face.

Joe Strenk spat out a curse as he left the pastor's office. Once outside the building and in his car, he sat quietly for several seconds. He had never talked to anyone that way before. He had certainly never dared to speak to David Morgan or any other Christian leader with such vehemence. He felt as if someone else had taken hold of him, leaving him with no will of his own.

Joe Strenk sat in his car and, for the first time since boyhood, wept.

Edmund Staats pondered the mystery of the cash and bonds in the suitcase. Where would Arno Hajford come up with such an amount? It had to have come from Truth International. But how could he have obtained them from the corporation? The bylaws of the corporation had stated that both the president and the treasurer had to sign all checks. Staats had scrupulously watched everything he signed. He hadn't suspected Arno—or anyone else; it was merely his nature to check on details.

Then an idea occurred to him. He went back into Arno's office and called up the bank records on the computer. As he suspected, the money had come from more than one check. Eight of them in all. Eight of them made payable to individuals, names he had never heard of before.

Turning to his chex-fax, he pulled up a copy of all checks drawn for the past two months. Then he realized how Arno had done it. He had forged Staats's signature—and done a bad job of it at that. Banking people never bothered to match signatures with the signature cards on file.

A quick figuring showed that Arno had embezzled just short of five million dollars, all of the funds in cash, all of it cashed by Arno himself. Being well-known at the bank, he had made the checks out to bogus individuals, then signed his own name underneath.

So, somehow Arno had received advance notice and was preparing to loot the company. Anger filled Edmund Staats as he thought of what the man he had trusted had done. How dare he do such a criminal thing! And Arno was a Christian!

Staats went back to his own office and tried to occupy himself with proofreading his final editorial for *Truth International* magazine. But his mind refused to remain on his work. With a start, Staats realized that while he worked with his pen and paper, his left hand had not ceased to stroke the soft leather of the suitcase under the desk.

"Mr. Staats," his secretary said, "there is an emergency telephone call for you from M. Claude Dijon, police prefect of Paris."

When Staats picked up the telephone, the man identified himself and said, "I am sorry, *M'sieu,* to trouble you. I am an avid reader of your publication, and it is because of this fact and my admiration for your work that I have called you personally."

"Thank you," Staats said, his voice unusually shaky as he wondered why a policeman would call him. "You told my secretary this was an emergency call?"

"Yes. I regret to inform you that one of your employees, M. Arno Hajford, has been badly injured in an accident."

"How badly? What happened?"

"Perhaps you could come here and talk with us?"

"How badly injured?" he pressed.

"He is dead, *M'sieu.* My records say that M. Hajford had just purchased an Alfa Romeo and was driving from the showroom down the Rue Faubourg St. Honore where a van was making a left turn. The van clearly had the right of way, and M. Hajford—well, M. Hajford's vehicle crashed into the van. His broken speedometer indicates he was driving at an excessive speed of one hundred and fifty kilometers."

"Yes, yes," Staats said, "I'll come right away and identify him."

"We called because he has nothing in his possession to indicate a family, *M'sieu.* Only papers that showed your organization employed him."

"He has no family. He is an only child, and his parents are dead. He never married," he said, adding, "I shall come at once."

Staats left hurriedly and an hour later returned to his office. There was no question whatsoever: Arno Hajford was dead. Staats sat down at his own desk, knowing he ought to mourn the man with whom he had worked so closely for months. He tried to coax emotions of regret or sadness to the surface, but he felt absolutely nothing. Sighing deeply, Staats opened the suitcase, and this time he also noticed a small compartment in the top of the case. He unzipped it to discover a one-way aero-ship ticket to Washington, D.C. and a second ticket made out to Manuel Montes from Washington to

Rio. He found one other item—a passport for Montes, but the picture was that of Arno Hajford with hair dyed black.

I've saved the company's money, he thought. *Why, had it not been for the accident and my finding the suitcase, he could have absconded with millions.* Edmund Staats continued to stare at the bills in front of him. How ironic. He was soon going to lose his position and high standard of living, and yet in front of him was a suitcase with more than four million dollars.

And only I know about the money.

The money would have disappeared completely, he reminded himself, if Hajford hadn't died. And the evidence incriminated Hajford beyond doubt. Because the forged signatures were so badly done, no one would consider that Staats himself had countersigned. And, he recalled, Hajford had actually cashed the checks himself.

Without admitting to himself that he had already made a decision, Edmunds Staats ran his hand through his disheveled mane as his mind segued logically from point to point, reviewing every facet of the situation: *First, the organization is going out of business; second, I'm going to be shoved out the front door with no pension benefits, no severance pay from Truth International; third, I shall have only my insulting pension; fourth, before me lies this money, and only I know of its existence; fifth, the benefactors of Truth International certainly owe me something for my loyalty and my commitment. After all, I did leave my university post and forfeited additional pension benefits, meager as they might have been.*

The old man stared at the money before him for a long while before his hand clutched the first stack of bills. Then quietly, methodically Edmund Staats stuffed his own briefcase with bills in the amount of seven hundred thousand dollars. He left the rest of the money in the suitcase. After more thought he took out the remaining bills and, using a box that had previously contained copies of his own works, taped the lid tight and placed the funds in the back of his closet.

Waiting until the office staff left, Staats went down the

back staircase to the parking lot. He dumped the now-empty suitcase in a trash barrel. Returning to his office, Staats placed the tickets and false passport inside the top middle drawer of Hajford's desk.

When Edmund Staats went home for dinner, he could not slow down his peppy steps. He had not felt so alive or so young for a very long time. A longing to celebrate filled his thoughts, but not daring to show positive emotion after the death of his coworker, he resisted the temptation. Staats worked to feign mourning and determined that he would live cautiously for the next few weeks. In the meantime he would transfer the cash and bonds into his safe-deposit box. That would be the best way, and no one could ever trace anything to him.

As Edmund Staats opened the door to his opulently furnished house on Place Beauvau, one word flashed into his mind and he quickly banished it.

It was a simple English word: *thief.*

T·W·E·N·T·Y T·H·R·E·E

"You know you can't ever go back to your mother," Ted Wilson said. "If you take the next step with me, you've made the final split with Annella."

"When I decided to find you," Michelle Maxwell said, "that's when I made the final break. I can't go back, Dad, but I want you to understand—*I don't want to go back.*"

"I just want you to be sure," he said as he took her hands in his. "She's powerful . . . ruthless."

"She's evil." Michelle said the words without emotion, yet she knew she had described her mother accurately. "I don't know much about God and being a Christian, but if there is such a thing as a person being too wicked for God, that describes mother and the other five members of the Mastermind."

"I wouldn't know about that," Ted said. "because I like to think all of us have the potential for being God's people. We choose to go astray or turn our backs on God or whatever we call it. Maybe some people deliberately go so far astray, they place themselves out of God's reach. If that's true, Michelle, remember that it's their choice to do that . . . Not God's choice, but their own."

"I still feel sorry for her," Michelle said. "I wish . . . oh, I do wish it were different. But you're right; she chose this way." Michelle was unaware that tears slipped down her cheeks as she said, "I lived in the same house with her. For years I watched her play with drugs and witchcraft . . . the constant parade of men . . . drugs to get to sleep, drugs to wake up. You know what's funny? Back then I wished I could be like her. I didn't know any better, and I kept thinking that something must be wrong with me."

"I don't know how you survived all of that," he said, "except for the grace of God."

"Some of her boyfriends came after me," she said. "One named Fred almost overpowered me, and he would have if Annella hadn't walked in."

"What did she do?"

"She laughed and told him to pick on a woman he could handle. She took his hand and led him up to her room. The next day Fred's maid found him dead in his own apartment. The police said it was the result of a drug overdose, but I think she killed him for trying to molest me, or maybe for trying to get to me instead of lusting after her. That's the kind of woman my mother—" Michelle sobbed, unable to finish her sentence.

Ted wrapped his daughter in his arms, holding her tightly as she cried. "There, there," he said, "let all the pain and heartache from all those years drain away from you."

And as his daughter wept, Ted silently thanked God for protecting her from all the evil influences that had constantly surrounded her.

"We have proceeded according to my plan," Mastermind said. "Each of you has done remarkably well, and I shall reward you accordingly. I am preparing greater spheres of power for each of you."

Mastermind spoke through Annella, telling them of vast amounts of money, larger portions of land, and added, "Whatever desires you have as yet unfulfilled, you have only to ask for . . . Believe me, I shall give you dominion over all of this earth. Only to me shall you be obedient."

"We are your servants," they said, again pledging faithfulness.

"Now is the time to broaden the scope of our activity. We have most of the Christian leaders within our control."

"We do?" asked Maison Quayle. "I still see a lot of churches lying about and people going to them. Those sitting in a pew are not so few."

"Ah, but they cause us no problem. If we were at this stage to outlaw Christianity, or should openly begin to annihilate the Christians, many former adherents would return. You know how it is: they have this desire to show their courage, to be heroes and martyrs, and we will not give t hem the opportunity. No, we will allow the churches to continue . . . for now. With diminishing influence, of course. We need pay little attention to the Christians who sit in pews. We can ridicule them, and we'll certainly publicize the affairs of those who fail."

"I'm there with you," Maison Quayle said. "I've got a squad of people who make sure that every time a church leader goes astray it makes the news."

"Precisely!" Mastermind said. "You have learned well and quickly."

"I've had a master teacher!" Quayle laughed.

"We are now in control of the great Christian leaders in the world," Mastermind said. One by one, he told them of the status of the leaders. He had brought clouds of doubt upon the church leaders in such diverse places as Korea, China, Argentina, Brazil, and South Africa.

"I should like to give you a further report on one Edmund Staats," Hanse Wenscla said.

"Yes . . . another silenced voice," said Mastermind.

"This scholarly man, to whom we gave the position of president of Truth International, is an embezzler. Everything has worked as we planned." He turned to Amwago Zolo. "I must confess the false passport was an excellent touch you added."

"It is a method I have used myself many times," Zolo said, pleased to have his contribution recognized.

Hanse Wensela reported that he had waited five weeks after Staats's embezzlement, giving the thief a false sense of security. Wensela then arranged for Amwago Zolo to telephone Staats's house, to make an appointment to see the man by saying he had a business matter that concerned the late Arno Hajford.

Amwago Zolo took up the report. When he entered the lavishly furnished home, a butler ushered him into the study. Although Staats made a pretense of being deeply involved in working on a paper, he didn't fool Zolo.

"I have come to speak to you about an important event," Zolo said. "It actually concerns Mr. Hajford only indirectly."

"Yes, then, what is it?"

From his case Zolo extracted six photographs, eight by ten glossies, and laid them out on the table in front of Staats. They showed Staats in various stages of handling the four million dollars, including stuffing some of the funds into his own pockets.

"You understand, Mr. Staats, these are only still photographs. A series of hidden cameras has given us a total play-by-play of everything you did on the day of Arno Hajford's death."

"So you know everything and you have come to take back the money?"

"Yes and no." Zolo leaned forward. "Yes, we know everything. No, we do not want the money."

"Then why are you here?"

"We want your silence," Zolo said.

"Now I see," Staats said as he stared into the empty eyes of the African. "You set this up, didn't you? You and Hanse Wensela? From the first you had this rigged. My receiving the high-paying position, the funds being cut off—"

"Everything."

"All in exchange for my silence? My silence about what?"

"About anything we ask."

"And who is we?"

"Does that matter? We are your benefactors, Mr. Staats . . . Think of us that way. You have more than enough money to live comfortably the rest of your life. You will shortly receive a message from Neville Wheatley asking you to accept his appointment as theological advisor of the Fellowship of Love—which you will accept. This new position will provide you with an adequate income on top of what you have already, shall we say, managed to save."

"You seem to have gone to a lot of trouble over me."

"That is our decision, Mr. Staats. Remember only this: at any time, we could reveal these pictures to prove that you are a thief and an embezzler. The world that respects you and reveres your scholarship could turn on you just as quickly and hate you for your evil ways."

"No more than I already hate myself." Yet as Staats said the words, he knew they were mere words. He felt no self-hatred, no self-anger, and momentarily wondered why.

"Be that as it may," Zolo said. "You have made your choice. You have received your reward on earth—and a splendid reward too, is it not? Now you must pay for it by your obedient service."

The old man nodded. And as he did so, he wondered why he felt no sense of guilt over his crimes. Why couldn't he at least experience remorse? *Strange,* he thought, *how four million dollars can destroy a man's conscience.*

In the Mastermind meeting, Zolo continued, "At this point, it is like catching a fish in the net. The fish is ours, even if the poor creature does not yet know it."

"Oh, but he does know it," Maison Quayle said. "He can only wriggle so far. But, of course, when a poor man suddenly has millions with more to come, it's amazing how contented he can be."

"And cooperative," added Sari.

"In the matter of Neville Wheatley," spoke Mastermind, "we have made splendid progress. Today he will offer Edmund Staats a post of prominence in his church hierarchy. But more important, Maison Quayle has accomplished a major victory with Mr. Wheatley.

"First he convinced Wheatley to admit gays and lesbians into church membership. Now, within a week Wheatley will make the announcement that will open the door for them to have *limited leadership*—to use his phrase—in the church. He has also opened the way for them to become officers in local congregations."

"And, of course," Yatawazy said, "the greatly respected Edmund Staats will add credence to the position by citing historical evidence along with his personal plea for compassion and mercy."

"You know," Quayle said, "what we're doing reminds me of an old story my father used to tell me. It's about an Arab and a camel."

Without waiting for anyone to ask, Quayle told the story. "It seems that an Arab stopped in the desert one night, put up his small tent, and the camel knelt beside the tent. As you know, when the sun goes down, the desert becomes particularly cold. So the camel moved around until he had his nose inside the tent. 'Oh, master,' he said, 'it's so cold out there. Just let me keep my nose within your warm tent.'

"The Arab agreed. A little later the camel put his front paws inside—"

"Until the camel had taken over the tent and the Arab had to sleep out in the cold? Is that not the story?" Zolo asked.

"Yes, except I'd have enjoyed telling it in detail."

"I think we are clever enough to grasp the point," Sari said.

"Also," Hanse Wensela said, "on the business at hand,

we're preparing the way for sexual perversion—as the Christians call it—to become acceptable to the world."

"You please me greatly," said Mastermind.

"Soon we shall be able to wipe away terms such as sexual perversity," Wensela added.

"As Quayle has made clear through his little story," Mastermind said, "we are operating exactly like the camel. First the nose, then the head, then the neck, and we slowly move forward until we have total control."

"But what if the Christians become aroused?" asked Quayle. "That's the one thing that bothers me."

"You have no need to be concerned there," Mastermind said. "I am using a method of the ancient Romans by making the masses happy with money, prosperity, and activity. Such affluence dulls their minds and warps their consciences. We do it slowly, ever so slowly."

"I hope it continues to work," Quayle said. "One of these days, somebody might stir the sleeping giant."

"Ah, but you see, the people who might ordinarily stir giants are themselves asleep," said Yatawazy.

"We haven't silenced Morgan," Quayle said. "He's the only bloke I've feared all along."

"And we cannot destroy him in the same manner as we did the others," said Mastermind. "He is different. Our methods must be especially resourceful."

"You're the boss," Maison Quayle said.

"And you, Maison Quayle, must never, never forget that fact!" Mastermind said. "Nor must the rest of you. I am preparing for the grand finale, the ultimate victory. And all of you will be rewarded beyond measure only as long as you remain loyal."

As Annella's voice spoke the words of Mastermind, she felt an inner chill. A moment of fear touched her as she wondered what Mastermind would do to her if she strayed ever so slightly.

"And, Mr. Quayle," Mastermind said, "we await your report of Bryant McFarland."

"Oh, going extremely well, I can tell you." He grinned

and leaned back. "That man is lustier than I would have imagined. Scratch beneath his messages and he's like a man without sexual restraint."

Quayle told them of his recent visit to McFarland. "I went to a house in the suburbs of Perth that McFarland purchased for his daily rendezvous with Betty-Anne Freeman. Since no one knew of this house, McFarland was immensely surprised at my appearance."

"Excellent," Mastermind said.

Quayle smiled as he told the details, knowing he had done a particularly good job.

"We have been aware of your activities for a long time," Quayle said to McFarland.

A wave of suspicion swept over McFarland as he asked, "Is Betty-Anne in on this?"

"Of course not," Maison lied convincingly. He needed McFarland to continue his obsession with the young woman, for that would guarantee their control over him until he had no will of his own. "We watched until the occasion presented itself, and you took a deviant path, m' lad."

"But you must understand, my wife Alma—my wife is physically ill and—"

"But adultery is still called by the same name, isn't it?" Maison Quayle asked. "Or have you figured out a way to call it something else? Perhaps Betty-Anne is a concubine. Isn't that the way they talked about women like that in the Bible? Or you might want to move to Africa or the Middle East where polygamy is legal—"

"All right," McFarland said, "I've sinned against God. Now what do you want? For me to give up Betty-Anne?"

"That's a decision of indifference to us," Maison Quayle said. "I don't give a kangaroo's hind foot about your love life."

"What do you want then?"

"Your cooperation. It's that simple," the Australian said as he tossed five photographs on the table of McFarland in bed with Betty-Anne, all in different beds and without clothes. "We'd have no problem exposing you to the world if that was what we wanted, y' understand?"

"What do you want then?"

"Your unqualified support of Neville Wheatley, no matter what position he takes."

"Is Neville in on this?"

"That is none of your concern," Quayle said, deciding to let McFarland bite on that idea for a while. "You continue to preach—you'll find many new doors open to you as you move among the wealthy and the socially prominent."

"And all you want is for me to support anything Wheatley says? I don't believe I quite understand."

"Oh, you will," Maison said. "And, of course, your own preaching will, of necessity, reflect this. Clear?"

Although puzzled, McFarland nodded.

"Here's a little something to help with your already heavy expenses," Quayle said as he dropped a large envelope containing fifty thousand dollars on the desk. "It must cost a real packet to operate two households."

As Quayle finished his accounting to Mastermind, Zolo laughed. "You are clever. I must tell you that I never perceived *how* clever until now."

"I don't know about clever," Quayle said, "but I'm as much of a reprobate—to use a common term of McFarland's—as you. Don't underestimate my ambition either. I'm equally as ambitious as you, Zolo, despite my casual manner and lighthearted ways."

"So I have learned," Zolo said. "And I promise I shall never let you see my back in the dark."

"You learn fast," said Quayle.

"And now, my servants," said Mastermind, "since we have effectively muted the voice of the church, we are ready to move forward."

"But have we?" Quayle asked. "You haven't given us any instructions about that bloke David Morgan. Every plan has fizzled on that one. Or perhaps you used the wrong people."

"He has held up more remarkably that I had anticipated," admitted Mastermind. "I have brought him to the point of total discouragement, making him feel utterly abandoned by his spiritual protector, and yet he manages to be revived. But, no matter . . . he will not remain a serious threat to us."

"The more noise he makes," Wensela said, "the more people will turn from him." He laughed. "We can assure you of that."

"People in his congregation are also becoming quite wealthy, being encumbered with higher standards of living, more free time, greater freedom . . . They will do anything," said Sari, "to hold on to their wealth."

"Yes, as long as they have a great abundance," Zolo said, "they are like chickens who follow whoever feeds them."

Quayle listened and said aloud, "I wonder."

"You have doubts?" asked Wensela.

"If we don't wonder, we're apt to blunder," he said.

T·W·E·N·T·Y F·O·U·R

Michelle Maxwell and her father felt like fugitives as they made their way around Atlanta. Although they had nothing in the way of evidence to convince them that Annella was having Michelle watched, they operated on the principle that she might. They were well aware that she constantly had a network of co-ags working for her.

"She's done it before," Michelle said. "In fact, looking back, I realize mother hired someone to lurk in dark corners most of my life. She said it was to protect me. Now I wonder."

"I imagine she's keeping you under her eyes. Especially because she'd like to know the identity of the two men." He laughed. "Can't you picture her reaction when she finds out about me?"

She began to protest, but immediately knew her father was right. If Annella didn't find out today, she would eventually. She wanted to postpone the confrontation as long as possible.

Michelle had been extremely careful in visiting Johnny

Burbank, using a false name at the airport and paying cash for the rental car. She had moved more cautiously in traveling to Atlanta, going by way of Denver to St. Paul to Orlando and then to Atlanta, changing carriers and giving a different name each time.

She made only one mistake. One of Annella Maxwell's spies—or at least a man who would pass on information to her mother—spotted her and Ted when they were leaving the Ritz Carlton in Atlanta's Midtown. They had gone there to meet a business associate of Ted's before they made their way to David Morgan's office.

Michelle was holding Ted's arm, and they ducked back inside and mingled with a crowd of conventioneers until they managed to slip out a side entrance. Although they had eluded the man, Michelle wasn't sure whether he snapped a picture or not. He did have a camera with him. If he got a good shot, she was sure that the man didn't get a good look at Ted's face.

"Or at least I hope they didn't," she said.

While Michelle and Ted zipped across the expressway, moving to an exit without warning, making quick right turns, and doubling back, Annella Maxwell was speaking on the telephone to a man named Melvin Doyle.

"Handsome, was he?" Annella Maxwell asked.

"I didn't get a good look, but I think so," the man said. "I had the impression he was a lot older."

"That's all right," Annella said. "Don't do anything. I only want to know his name."

"I'm not sure I can locate her again. It was an accident, you know—"

"For two thousand dollars' bonus, you'll locate them," Annella said and hung up. She was smiling.

Apparently her prudish daughter had finally come to her senses and taken a lover. "For a long time I wondered if she'd ever want to go out with men," she said to herself.

Curiosity kept her wondering about the man's identity. She smiled again, knowing her co-ag would have the name eventually. In the meantime she was comforted. "Late-bloomer," she said, thinking of her daughter.

She had often wondered why her daughter had not turned out right and had been standoffish, almost puritanical at times. The child had never had anything to influence her differently. There had been Ted, of course, but he had left so many years ago. What a drag that man had been. It was a good thing she had gotten him out of her life when she did. She had liked him—more than she had intended. If he hadn't started pressing her to get married and live in what he called a respectful manner, she would have kept on with him . . . for a while anyway. But none of the men in her life had been able to hold her permanently, and Annella liked it that way.

Except now and then a wave of loneliness swept over her. And oddly enough, when that happened her thoughts went back to Ted Wallace. One of these days she'd have to find out whatever happened to him . . . or if he was still alive.

In late February 1999, just after sunset on the night before the month-long Arab feast of Ramadan, an explosion lit up the skies for miles outside of Jerusalem. By morning the whole world knew the basic facts, and they were reported with a fair degree of uniformity.

England's BBC pictured Rosaltha Murphy-Smythe in front of a wailing crowd of people. In the background soldiers picked through the rubble. In her distinctive west-country accent, she said:

> At approximately nine o'clock last evening, the entire city of Jerusalem was shocked with a series of blasts and fires that filled the sky for hours. The famous Mosque of Al Aksa, also known as the Dome of the Rock, was destroyed by time-set bombs in at least five places.

Most unfortunate in the situation is the
recovery of ninety-six bodies and another
twenty-three persons unaccounted for.
These were pilgrims, preparing themselves
for the beginning of Ramadan this morning.
From sunrise until sunset no orthodox
Muslim touches food, and they all remain
in a spirit of prayer. From sunset until sunrise, they feast.

But there will be no feasting this year,
Muslims say. They are vowing vengeance
on the murderers who executed this cow-
ardly deed. No evidence has surfaced as yet,
although the sentiment is that Israeli agents
are to blame.

The BBC will continue to update as we
have more information.

For the next six hours conflicting reports spread
throughout the Middle East. As far away as Northwest
Africa, Muslims were vowing to throw Israel into the sea
once and for always. Libya and Turkey called on their armies
to prepare to avenge the deaths of the pilgrims. Yemen, Saudi
Arabia, and Pakistan vowed to join them and began to
recruit for their special armed forces.

Later the same day came a story that shocked the
world. One recovered body was that of a former Israeli citizen—a man who had, only weeks before, cut himself off
from Jewish ties and openly converted to the Christian faith.
Under a pile of rubble, searchers uncovered an unexploded
plastic bomb in the man's hand.

Intensive investigations began while the Muslim world
continued to amass troops. The Knesset in Jerusalem
appointed a committee to get to the truth of this matter
immediately.

Less than an hour before sunset, Israel's Prime Minister
spoke from his office on tele-media:

> We have uncovered the facts in one of the
> most vile deeds of this century. A mere
> twenty-four hours ago the destruction of
> Mosque Al Aksa took place, and the world
> pointed its fingers to the Jewish nation.
> We now have irrefutable evidence
> which I am sending to the heads of Arab
> states to show the innocence of all Jews.
> This crime was planned and perpetuated by
> a group of *Christians*—called fundamental-
> ists—from the United States.

The Prime Minister explained that a radical group of
Christians believed that Jesus Christ would return to the
exact spot where the mosque stood. As long as the mosque
remained, they contended that Christ could not come back.
The destruction was intended to "hasten Christ's return."

The Prime Minister closed the newscast with these
statements:

> These vile murderers did not care about the
> ninety-six innocent Muslims who were
> praying in the mosque, nor the fact that the
> world would rise in shock and outrage over
> their evil. We have proof that they have
> been planning this action for five months. It
> would have been a perfect crime, with all
> blame to fall upon the state of Israel had
> one of their own not been brought to justice
> by the falling rubble.

As the Prime Minister explained in his communique to
the Arabs, on the young man's body they also discovered a
pouch which contained a half-page of written instructions.
Investigation of the man's friends led them to others who
were members of a sect known as the Evangelical and Fundamental Churches with headquarters in upstate New York.

At her next report, Rosaltha Murphy-Smythe stated
that through the combined efforts of the American FBI and
CIA, they had brought about the arrest of members of the

Evangelical and Fundamental Churches in America. Israel's Mossad had already jailed six members in Israel. Of the six, two of them had already confessed to their involvement in the bombing.

One of them, a woman named Evelyn Harper, wearing prison clothes, appeared on Israeli television to make public confession of her crime. The woman's features were finely molded, and some would have called her attractive. Her sullen face belied the normally sparkling countenance. She looked tired, and she stumbled when she entered the room where she had agreed to give a statement.

Harper reiterated what the Prime Minister had said and added significant details. She concluded, "The authorities keep asking me why we have done this. I am pleased to tell you. The world has become a place of total wickedness and depravity. We live in the world's darkest hour. For us, God's true and faithful believers left in this world, the only answer, the only solution is to bring back Jesus Christ to save us. This is what we are doing. We have destroyed the hated mosque, and now we have prepared the way for the blessed return of Jesus Christ! To God be the victory!"

During the month of Ramadan, each morning, some-where in the world, reporters told of one or more mosques being destroyed. By the end of the month, nine hundred mosques and eight thousand deaths were known. Muslim armies, fully aroused, pledged to torture and kill every member of the Evangelical and Fundamental Churches.

Leaders of the Evangelical and Fundamental Churches, speaking on behalf of their membership of approximately seven hundred thousand, denied involvement in any of the incidents.

"We know of the confession of Evelyn Harper," said Carl Ivor Spencer, elected head of the denomination. "Although she calls herself one of us, she is not a member of any of our congregations. Although she claims to be a missionary, she is not working, nor has she ever worked under our auspices. Evelyn Harper and those with her have done this dastardly deed to discredit our churches and our members. We are not warmongers. As Christians, we don't believe in doing evil to bring about good. With sad hearts, we regret the evil done, the lives lost, the chaos that has ensued. As the leader of the Evangelical and Fundamental Churches, I personally pledge that we will do whatever we can to rectify this mistake."

David Morgan was interviewed several times on television, and on each occasion he urged restraint. "Please do nothing precipitously. Be certain of the evidence. Then, and only then, can we learn the truth in this matter."

Documents from the files of the Evangelical and Fundamental Churches began coming to the attention of the public. Although forged, no one could prove otherwise. They had letters in which Carl Ivor Spencer spoke against "the menace of the Muslim horde." One letter read, "I pray to God that they'll be wiped off the face of the earth."

A careful checking of their financial accounts showed large sums of money being designated for "Muslim missions."

Evelyn Harper gave a public interview to Western reporters from her prison in Jerusalem. She stated that she had received money from the Evangelical and Fundamental Churches. (Later Carl Ivor Spencer showed that these were sums of money given through six of their key churches as offerings for her, but that she was not, nor had she ever been recognized by them.)

In a second interview with international correspondents and carried live on tele-media, Evelyn Harper spoke with courage and openness, telling everything about the denomination, a clever mixture of half-truths and total lies which no one could satisfactorily refute. Evelyn Harper, whose real name was Kathleen Trainer, a woman who had completed many unsavory missions for P. K. Sari, had no worries about her future. In exchange for going through this ordeal, Sari assured her of a last-minute rescue, plastic surgery to change her face, and two million American dollars already deposited for her in a Zurich bank.

"I operated as the leader in the bombing of the mosque," she said, her eyes blazing. "And I would do it again!" her shrill voice screamed. "Muslims are lice that crawl upon people. If we exterminate them, we do the world a favor, and we glorify the name of our God!"

When Evelyn Harper returned to her cell, she was peacefully planning her new life, having already decided that Wales would be a lovely place for her to live. Unfortunately, Evelyn Harper never received her freedom. Two bribed guards killed her during the night and made it appear as a suicide.

Voices of anger erupted throughout the world. Finally Pope Viktor stood before the crowds in Rome, pleading with them for restraint and peace. Ten thousand people gathered below in the open square. He had spoken less than three sentences when the first voice shouted in English, "Don't listen to the senile idiot!"

Another voice cried in Italian, "Kill the Pope!"

Pandemonium took over, and the entire crowd was shaking its fists at Pope Viktor, as if they all had acted with the singular purpose of not allowing him to finish his message. The police found themselves helplessly outnumbered and blocked off by protesters. As soon as they attempted to silence anyone, another group surrounded the armed men, pinning them in place with their bodies so they couldn't move.

In frustration, Pope Viktor turned and walked back inside. He sat down on his velvet-covered chair and wept, hardly able to believe that anyone would do this to a modern-day Pope.

The next day Roman Catholic Bishop Tutoma from South Africa called for a special interview on tele-media. He urged all Roman Catholics to defy the Church, which, he said, was attempting to cover up for the Evangelical and Fundamental Churches. He raised his fist and said, "I too defy the senility of the Papacy. I spit in the face of Pope Viktor!"

Tutoma further announced that he, "in concert with all of the bishops on the continent of Africa," had chosen to withdraw from the Roman Catholic Church. Their churches would now be called the African Catholic Church. He announced a list of reforms, including:

    * mandatory marriage for clergy,

    * sanctioning of marriage to persons of the same gender,

    * divorce for any "humanitarian reason,"

    * seeking closer ties with the Fellowship of Love.

A similar message came from the Asian subcontinent through the Bishop of South India. Each day new Roman Catholic Church leaders voiced their denunciation of Pope Viktor, criticizing papal infallibility while announcing their "desire for closer ties" with the Fellowship of Love.

Two days later, the *Manchester Guardian* and the *Cleveland Plain Dealer* broke the story that Pope Viktor had had a mistress for twenty-nine years. He called her his "housekeeper," the publications charged.

For a handsome sum of money, the middle-aged woman appeared on tele-media and said simply, "He is a good man. He was always gentle and kind to me."

"But you were his mistress, were you not?" asked a reporter.

"I was his friend."

"But did you ever go to bed with him?"

"Isn't that what friends do for one another?" she said simply, having carefully memorized her answers to the pre-planned questions.

Six days after Pope Viktor's public humiliation, his aides found him in his own bed. He had been dead for at least four hours. Some claimed it was murder; others said he died of a broken heart; a few whispered suicide. Only three people who worked under Sami Yatawazy knew the real story—an undetected poison in the cocoa the Pope drank each night before going to sleep had killed him.

Pressure from telegrams, telephone calls, lobbyists, and most of the members of Capitol Hill forced the President of the United States to appear on public television to denounce the Evangelical and Fundamentalist Churches. Speaking with the support of both houses, he declared that every member of the "sect" must go on trial before the Muslim world. In joyous response, Muslim leaders selected Baghdad, Iraq as the place of venue, declaring that all who did not travel there within the next ten days would be presumed guilty and condemned to death by firing squad.

Less than half the members of the EFC Churches went to Iraq, and mass murders occurred across the United States. In the Christian Fundamental Church, located on Highway 173 in Zion, Illinois, a small city north of Chicago, a blaze broke out at 11:12 on a Sunday morning. Forty-seven adults and twelve children were inside praying. None of them survived.

Those who went to Iraq, recognizing the possibility of death, but hoping for fair treatment, were thrown into prison upon their arrival. The mass trial, using forged documents and the recorded confession of Evelyn Harper, was corroborated by four others who claimed to be under the pay of the EFC and had receipts to prove it.

Two days later, the court, composed of twelve judges (five Muslims, two Israelis, and five Westerners) unanimously sentenced all members of the EFC to death. In groups of fifty, the members of EFC who had been tried were driven to the desert outside Baghdad and shot. It took fifteen hours to complete the mass execution.

The following day, the President of the United States spoke from the White House and said, "At last the world will be free from fear and the tyranny of religion. At last we can live as human beings who care about one another." He also asked "Americans and compassionate people of the world" to stand with him in urging a commutation of life in prison instead of death for the surviving members of the sect.

The President's listening audience was one of the smallest ever reported. Most Americans were too involved with their own lives to worry about such issues as commutation of sentences. Congress immediately called for the the confiscation of properties owned by members of the EFC. Through governmental agencies, they distributed to the poor all personal effects such as clothing and food. EFC real estate and money became parts of giant lotteries now held in every state in the Union.

As one woman said who won the Kentucky lottery, worth thirty-five million dollars and including fourteen pieces of ELC real estate valued at another 1.7 million dollars, "It is an ill wind indeed that blows no good for someone."

Technology around the world expanded rapidly toward the end of the twentieth century. Only the poorest homes lacked robots. In late 1998, a survey of American homes showed an average of 2.7 robots per home.

Robot manufacturing had become the most profitable venture in the western hemisphere. Several companies, especially in West Germany, programmed their products for domestic duties, calling them DomRobs. Finland developed Tufrobs for heavy, industrial work. By mid-1999, Americans could purchase as many as nineteen specialized robots. IBM was the first to announce a programmed robot who could prepare up to one hundred and twelve different food dishes for one to eight people at a time. By the time other companies had cloned this breakthrough, IBM models could provide eight hundred different foods with four specialized models that did only desserts or salads or coffee and mixed drinks or appetizers.

"I plead with Americans," cried out the solitary voice of David Morgan each day on television, "don't be lulled to sleep. You are allowing the Third World to starve while we enjoy the best of this life."

But fewer and fewer people bothered to listen to him.

Not only did the attendance continue to shrink at his church, but Morgan's television audience hit the lowest level on record. Among those who sat in front of the sets, few cared what Morgan said. Most of them had tuned in early to watch "Million Dollar Lottery," which followed his program.

"Now that program's really something to watch," said Joe Strenk one evening as his family gathered around their wall-sized television set to view "Million Dollar Lottery." They had purchased their daily tickets and were waiting eagerly for the announcement of the winning numbers. Winners were always given a chance to win a second time. In fact, once a month the lottery officials selected only from those who had won during the previous twelve months.

"Dad! Dad! That's my number! That's my number!" squealed Nick, his just-turned fourteen-year-old son. "I get a million bucks! I win! I win!"

"Ah, yes," Joe said as he dialed the number that flashed across the screen. Life was great. They would soon be a million dollars richer.

T·W·E·N·T·Y F·I·V·E

"**W**hy is it," the orator Bani Barakan asked, "that *they* have so much and we have so little? I give you the answer to that question. It is because they have joined together in a conspiracy. It is the Christian conspiracy. They plot together. Oh, you will not see it openly, but it is true."

"Bah!" replied one of the eighty Muslim leaders. "You will soon have us believing that the Christians also plan to wipe us off the Earth!"

"That is exactly what they are planning!" Bani Barakan said. "The evidence shouts to our dull ears. You have only to open your minds—that is, if you are willing to open your eyes and look around you. Where is the money of the world today? In America and western Europe. And what is their religion? Christianity! Who controls Antarctica? The same people. And where do we find the highest standards of living in the world?" He paused, his black eyes flashing, beads of perspiration now covering his face. "It is time to change all of that!"

"You are grasping at nothing. Did we not have control

of the world's currency because we controlled the output of oil? Did we not control the greatest amounts of capital right here in the Middle East?" asked Yakubali Sidik.

"Exactly my point! Bani Barakan said. "Then it passed through our fingers like this . . ." He picked up a handful of sand and let the grains slowly fall to the ground.

"We had it once. It was ours!"

"Are you blaming us—the Muslims—for this misfortune?" asked Bani Barakan as he stood next to Sidik Kassam. "You are blaming us for losing our prosperity? You are wrong. You are stupid. You have eaten the sweet lies they mix with our food. We have nothing left! Nothing left because of them—" He pointed westward. "No, my brothers . . . the Westerners conspired to make the price of oil drop so that we produced more, exhausting our supplies; they made a profit from our situation. Now as our wells are drying up, hunger gnaws at the bellies of our babies."

The arguments went on until sunset when they paused for prayer to Allah, followed by food, rest, and eventually sleep. At sunrise, immediately after prayers, the Arab leaders met again. For three days the words flowed back and forth. In the end, the persuasive words of Bani Barakan prevailed.

"And now, my brothers, I tell you something else. We followers of Allah are not the only ones the Westerners have raped. They have determined to wipe out all Hindus."

"And Buddhists!" screamed a chief. "By the truth of Allah, I know it is so. And the Shintoists and—"

"And everyone who does not embrace their easy, useless faith!" Bani Barakan said.

"But what can we do? They have power, technology—" said Yakubali Sidik.

At last the question Bani Barakan waited for had arived. Now was the time to lay before them the plan, though it wouldn't be easy. Because of their inbred distrust of their own blood brothers, it was never easy to deal with other Muslims. But, being carefully trained and filled with extraordinary patience despite his seeming impetuosity, Bani

Barakan was prepared to stay with them, to wear them out, to brainwash them if necessary.

Bani Barakan walked to the center of the vast circle and waited until everyone gave him their full attention. "There is only one way for us to win over the infidels!"

"What is that? *Jihad*—a holy war?" Yakubali Sidik asked, the adrenalin already surging in anticipation of revenge.

"No! A better way . . . A way that sometimes seems strange to us, but it is the way of the wise!"

"Then tell us," said Yakubali Sidik.

Everyone fell silent. Eyes turned immediately to Kassam Ishmael. Although of no higher rank that the rest, he had earned the respect of the others because of his sagacity and his careful, unemotional deliberations in negotiating with Westerners. He had warned the people as early as 1992 that Westerners were preparing to cheat them out of their oil. No one had listened then; now they knew he had been right.

Bani Barakan bowed his head in submission to the old man, who stepped forward.

He said, "I have been traveling from one end of the world to the other. I have spoken with men of every faith except that of the Christians—and, of course, I also would not tolerate speaking with Jews.

"The other faiths of the world, although inferior to the religion of Allah, are, even as I speak, preparing to join with us. We are determined to overthrow the power of the Western nations. We have more people, we have greater wisdom and are men of slier cunning, and most of all, we have Allah to lead us."

"Join with infidels against the Christian infidels?" an elderly leader asked, shaking his head slowly. "I do not think that Allah would be pleased—"

"Ah, my brother from Yemen, you have not heard it all," Bani Barakan said. "Is it not profitable for us to join with these others—these inferiors—until we have clutched victory?"

"Ah," Kassam Ishmael said to Bani Barakan, "you, though young, speak with the wisdom of hoary heads."

One more day of talking remained, but Bani Barakan knew they would all agree. These were desert leaders who loved intrigue, men who would willingly do anything to wipe out Jews and Christians.

"We shall call ourselves One Faith," said Kassam Ishmael. "We will practice what we believe as always, but we line up beside the others. We make a show of our strength. And then—then we call for the deaths of every Christian!"

"And the Jews as well!"

"Once we have destroyed the Christians, who can stop us from wiping out the Jews?" Kassam Ishmael said as he smiled. "Yes, it is a good plan."

In the West, people heard of a growing sentiment toward the joining of religious faith, but most of them paid little attention. They were too busy finding fulfillment and joy in life to involve themselves in anything but their own pursuits.

The Master Plan had encouraged people to find greater fulfillment in life through a thorough self-knowledge. Much of this self-understanding, they taught, came through faithfully working with channelers and spirit guides who helped them grasp why they behaved as they did and what they really wanted out of life. People no longer underwent psychoanalysis to change themselves or to become more authentic (as the jargon had put it for two decades). Now they sought to discover who they were at the core of their being. Once they learned the essential self-truths, they were ready for self-acceptance. However, they could not get to their core without the help of the channelers. These spiritual mystics had learned to penetrate the veil that shut people off from their past lives.

Spiritual Enablers (as they now defined themselves) taught their devotees to go backward in time, to learn their pain and failures in past lives. These unresolved conflicts of past lives, taught the Spiritual Enablers, prevented their reaching nirvana-harmony (the stage of total fulfillment and peace).

Other Westerners, following a different path, began to testify by the millions about physical and mental rejuvenation, many claiming that they were not aging. Others spoke in terms of "enjoying cosmic health," which meant that they had accepted their role as part of the cosmos and the physical benefits derived from that commitment.

"Be happy" marked the trend of the times and was the goal of healthy, well-adjusted individuals. Citizens of the West, encouraged to expand their consciousness and to seek total happiness, moved into new spiritual practices. In what had formerly been known as Costa Rica (and since 1995 the fifty fourth state in the American Union), rumors surfaced that the wealthy had been luring Third-World people to their shore and enslaving them.

The news met with apathy. "Those are not issues that concern us," most people said. Or, "I'll ask my Spiritual Enabler if I should get involved."

What the media failed to report, and few paid attention to, was the suicide rate in the West, now the highest in recorded history. Young people from the ages of fourteen to twenty were in the highest category because they found themselves unable to adjust, to be happy. Statistics indicated that thirty-one percent of those in that age span had already taken their own lives. Not understood by their parents, scorned by their peers, many young people chose death rather than living in sadness in a world of happy, cheerful, carefree people.

Nick Strenk, now in the ninth grade, was one of the outsiders because he wasn't happy. Although the youngest boy in his class, he didn't consider that a cause. He simply didn't know why he wasn't happy. Joe and Lisa Strenk, though having resigned from the church board and having stopped going to church altogether, nevertheless gave their children everything they needed and wanted, and more. Nick already had won a a million-dollar lottery jackpot, had a prepaid college education waiting for him, had previously been one of the most popular kids in his class at the other school. He was incredibly bright, which teachers assumed caused his problem. He thought too much and too deeply, they said. As his confusion increased, Nick started standing back and watching his classmates.

"It seems so unreal, all this smiling and saying nice things to people. I feel like nobody is real," he told his father.

"Nick, my boy," his father said, "you're just too sensitive. Lighten up. Enjoy life. You're young. You've got no problems."

Nick smiled obediently, but inwardly he was more confused than ever. If he had no problems, if everyone around him was genuine, why did he keep feeling they weren't? What was wrong with him? Why wasn't he happy?—he had all the reasons to be. "I'm a misfit," he said. "I'm no good."

One Tuesday afternoon Nick opened the medicine cabinet in his parents' bathroom, where he found five rows of bottles, segregated into two types. Those with green labels, although of several different brands, were anti-depressants. The others, with black labels, were stimulants. Since 1997, all mood-altering drugs in America could be purchased by written statement not to abuse them; no one needed prescriptions anymore.

Nick counted out ten pills from each of the bottles and hid them in a box in his room. The next day he visited with friends and, in their bathrooms, found similar supplies of anti-depressants and stimulants. More cautious this time, he took only two from each bottle. For the next two weeks, Nick visited in the home of many classmates until he had accumulated two hundred pills.

"This ought to do it," he said. "Now my parents can be happy without my dragging them down all the time. They don't need any bummers like me."

He wrote a note and left it on his parents' bed: "I'm sorry I couldn't be happy and that I made everyone else so miserable."

Nick returned to his own room and, after opening a
bottle of burgundy from his father's wine cellar, played a
game with himself. He put two pills in his mouth, took a
swig of wine to wash them down, then added two more pills,
followed by more wine. He wondered which would give out
first, the wine or the pills.

David Morgan felt a gnawing inside him that he
couldn't shake. All morning he had been troubled, but
couldn't put his finger on the cause. It was a kind of uneasiness, a sense of foreboding, but nothing specific.

At noon he came home to study, but he couldn't keep
his mind on his book. He tried to prepare for his broadcast
for that evening, but nothing came to him. Kneeling to pray,
the pastor battled for half an hour, but he felt as if his words
hit the walls and bounced back at him. His appetite van-
ished; he felt tired and yet had no desire to sleep. Nothing
seemed right.

"Katherine," he called out, "I'm going for a walk,"
hoping the fresh air would clear his mind.

He ambled down the street that led toward his church,
but decided to turn left so he wouldn't end up there. Then a
strange thing happened to David Morgan. A new wave of
energy flowed through him, an aliveness he hadn't felt for
days, and his pace picked up. Soon he was running, and he
didn't seem to be able or to want to stop himself. His breath
came in frenzied puffs, but he didn't slow down. Three
blocks, four blocks and his heart raced, causing him to feel
the pulse in his head; he wondered if he was going to have a
heart attack. Yet he didn't stop, couldn't stop, and his body
carried him forward as if he had a destination and he
couldn't pause until he reached it.

On and on David Morgan raced, his feet exercising a
will of their own. At one corner he made a right turn, then
went another block and stopped. Morgan had no more
explanation for his stopping than he did for starting.

The pastor stood in the middle of a block of expensive homes, shaking his head. "What came over me?" he asked aloud. "Am I going crazy or something?"

As Morgan turned, he recognized the house he stood in front of: Joe and Lisa Strenk's new twenty-room mansion. He had been praying for them every day since they dropped out of the church. Every time the family came to his mind, a heaviness pounded at him, forcing him to cry out to God for mercy for the Strenk family. "O God," he prayed often, "use some way, any way, to get through to the Strenk family."

The Strenks had become involved in the pursuit of happiness, acquiring not only a new home but four new cars, wearing only designer-label clothing and personalized jewelry.

Oh, well, the pastor reminded himself, he had talked with them on several occasions, but nothing had helped. On the last occasion Joe said, "Don't call us; we'll call you . . . maybe."

David Morgan started to turn around and head homeward, but realized he he couldn't lift his foot. He tried the other foot, but it too felt glued to the sidewalk. Momentarily he gazed at the Strenk home, and he heard a soft inner voice whispering, "Help me . . . Please . . . Nobody cares."

The voice was different from any he had ever heard. It sounded like that of a child in desperate need. David Morgan tried to shake off the feeling. "All of this is bizarre," he said aloud. Yet he couldn't move.

"God, is this You? Are You trying to lead me?" When no answer came, David said, "If You brought me here, then—"

He burst out laughing. "You make me miserable all day until I finally go for a walk. Then You make me run a couple of miles before stopping me in front of the Strenks' house." Suddenly the circumstances seemed to bring understanding to Morgan's inquiring mind. "I hear this child crying, and I'm standing here asking if You're trying to communicate! God, I'm sorry. I yield myself to You, no more questions."

David Morgan turned and walked down the lengthy

driveway and across the small wooden bridge, then followed the upward path for another fifty yards. They had built a beautiful brick home; the lot had a stream lazily running across the property, giving it a pastoral atmosphere.

But today Morgan didn't care about the pleasant view. He pushed the bell and waited. No one answered. He rang again for a long time. He cocked his head, listening for sounds from within but hearing nothing. Glancing at his watch, he saw that it was only a few minutes before 2 in the afternoon. Obviously no one was home anyway. Ordinarily Morgan would have retraced his steps, but he didn't; he couldn't force himself to leave. Morgan stood at the door and waited until he knew what he had to do.

"Okay, God," Morgan said, "I don't have the first clue as to what You're going to bring out of all this, but I know I can't get away until I get inside this house."

He turned the handle, and the door opened. He stepped into the parquet hallway. "Hello! Anybody home?" His own words echoed back at him. "Okay, God, You'll have to keep leading me."

As soon as he said those words, David stepped forward and up the winding staircase. On the landing he turned left and walked down the hallway to the second door on the left. Morgan didn't hesitate before opening the door.

A surprised and glassy-eyed Nick Strenk stared back at him. He was just taking his fifteenth swig of wine, and had decided that the pills were going to win if he didn't take smaller drinks.

Seeing the pile of pills next to the boy and the bottle in his hand, David Morgan realized what the boy was doing. He knocked the bottle from the boy's hand, which also sent the pills flying across the room. Grabbing Nick with both hands, he picked up the inert form and raced into the bathroom with him.

Nick, drunk and drowsy, smiled at his former pastor. "I don't think anybody's home today."

"This is going to be uncomfortable, but it's the only thing I know to do right now." He forced the boy to lean over the tub. Holding an unresisting Nick with one arm, David stuck the boy's fingers into his own throat, causing him to gag. The boy tried to pull away, but David pushed harder.

Finally the boy vomited. When Nick finished, Morgan made him go through the process again. After the fifth attempt and nothing came up, satisfied that the boy had nothing left in his stomach, the pastor washed the boy's face with a damp cloth and carried him back to bed.

By now the boy was crying. He stared up at Morgan. When he could finally gain control of himself, he asked in a weak voice, "Why did you do that?"

"God loves you, Nick. And God sent me to you. God doesn't want you to die."

"But I'm not happy like everybody else."

David Morgan stroked the boy's wet hair. "God wants to make you happy, son. That's why He wouldn't let you die."

The two of them carefully cleaned the bedroom and bathroom. Then, before he left, David Morgan promised Nick he would not tell the boy's parents if Nick would promise not to try to kill himself again.

After the pastor left, Nick smiled and closed his eyes. He was too sick to figure out everything, but he knew he wasn't going to die. Even better, he didn't need to die. If God loved him, then maybe he wasn't such a strange, bad person after all. Maybe there was hope.

T·W·E·N·T·Y S·I·X

David Morgan had unbuttoned his shirt in preparation for bed when the telephone rang. He grabbed it on the second ring, so it wouldn't disturb Katherine.

"This is Joe Strenk," the voice said. "Nick and I have been having a long, long talk. He told me . . ." Joe's voice broke, and he started to cry.

David Morgan waited patiently for the man to regain his composure.

"Anyway, thanks, David," he said. "And . . . and more than that, Nick's experience has opened our eyes. Can we come and see you right now? Or could you come here? Please, please talk to us. Help us get back on the right path again, will you? We've been wrong . . . so wrong." Joe burst into tears again.

"I'll be right over," Morgan said. As he put down the receiver, he thanked God for saving the child and for using that sad incident to open the minds of his parents.

At the moment David Morgan was rushing to the Strenk home, in Paris Edmund Staats was putting the finishing touches on a most important document. After months of labor on this paper, he decided not only to release the entire text, but a shortened, popularized version for the media.

He paused in reflection, wondering how he could ever have believed in Jesus Christ. All those wasted years of defending the faith he could no longer support. Trust in God? What had God ever done for him? He reflected on his years of penury, having given up everything to serve Jesus Christ, and what good did it do? What was it all for? To serve a God who didn't answer his prayers? A God who was the figment of dreams and fancy? A God who was a fraud? Staats despised those years of privation, of going without, of watching others accumulate and move up the economic ladder. He was getting old now, but he still had his health; at last he had gotten his mind straightened out, and he had money—plenty of it—and more to come.

The manuscript he held in his hands would shake up the world, he knew that. He expected a glowing sense of pleasure to come over him as he thought of the repercussions, but none did.

He had phoned Neville Wheatley minutes earlier and confirmed that he was ready. The press associate with the Fellowship of Love had already promised the media an announcement of immense proportions.

Not long later, Staats smiled genially at the cameras, shaking off his nervousness. "I am holding in my hands a complete manuscript showing the results of relentless study done over the past few months. You see, in an archaeological dig in Northern Galilee scholars unearthed a storage of manuscripts, most of them perfectly preserved. We know—and the experts have all verified—that these are the earliest known manuscripts of the New Testament. One of them, a Gospel of Mark, is written in Aramaic, the language of Jesus and the Jews of the first century. It may actually be the original document because it closes with these words: 'This ends the words of Peter as written by his servant, John Mark.'"

"Unbelievable," a reporter said. "And you're sure?"

"You understand that this will take years to fully authenticate, using carbon dating and all the scientific equipment available to us. However, after all the preliminary investigation, without the slightest bit of contradictory evidence, everything implies that we have the original manuscript."

"Now do we know more about Jesus than before?" asked one reporter.

"A great deal more," said Staats, "many pieces of information not found within the four Gospels."

"Exactly what happens next?" the reporter persisted. "Revise the Bible?"

"Yes," Staats said. "And that is precisely why I have delayed this newscast. I have taken every measure I know to determine the authenticity of these documents before telling the world of my findings."

Edmund Staats cleared his throat and said, "I can tell you without the slightest doubt in my mind, and borne out by the first-century records, that Jesus Christ did indeed live. He was tried by the Romans and crucified on a cross, and he died." He took a deep breath before he added, "*And he stayed dead.*"

"You're saying that Jesus wasn't resurrected?"

"That's exactly what I am saying. Jesus Christ died, and on the third day he stayed dead. On the fourth day he remained dead. And two thousand years later, Jesus Christ is still dead!"

On May 7, Associated Press writer Grantland Light sent the following information across the wires:

> "The Gospel of Mark" in the *New Testament*, long accepted by scholars as dictated by the Apostle Peter to young John Mark, has been verified from scrolls dating back to the first century. These scrolls, still under

investigation, have been unananimously accepted as authentic.

These scrolls of "The Gospel of Mark" end with the death of Jesus Christ, and with Peter's lamenting the loss of his leader and hoping for a resurrection. He wrote that believers had waited outside Jesus' tomb for three days, but nothing happened. That is, no return from the dead of Jesus. Because no resurrection occurred during that period, on the third day Peter, James, and John broke the seal of the tomb and stole the body.

Their purpose, according to Peter's account, was out of fear that zealous Jews might want to descecrate the body. They buried Jesus' remains in an unmarked field. Before their return to the grave, however, five women, including Mary Magdalene, had come to the tomb, and discovered the stone rolled away and the body gone. They declared that Jesus Christ had risen from the dead.

Peter states that he saw how the news of Jesus' resurrection changed the women and others who heard their report. The view of the empty tomb made them believe, and they began performing miracles such as healing sick bodies and casting out evil spirits. Consequently, Peter, James, and John promised not to tell the true story.

As the new Gospel account closes, Peter is now quite old, and the Romans have imprisoned him and will crucify him shortly. He does not wish to die with an unclear conscience. He declares that it is now time to tell the full story.

Muslims around the world, who had always doubted the death and resurrection of Jesus, applauded the courage and honesty of Edmund Staats and of the Fellowship of Love.

"Now we know that at last a few of you seek truth," stated Bani Barakan. "We Muslims have always declared that the Resurrection is a fabrication. You have now told the world the true facts, and we embrace you Christians for being a church of honor."

"We are not Christians," Edmund Staats responded. "Making this document known to the world shows that we are not going to perpetuate the falsehood of a resurrection that did not occur. We do believe in God! We worship the Creator of the universe . . . the God of the cosmos. If we must be called a church, let it be one that speaks for truth and embraces the world with love!"

When Edmund Staats completed his interview, and after hundreds of questions and dozens of photographs were taken of him holding a copy of the Mark scroll, he sighed. He was tired. It had been an invigorating time, and he loved laying aside the the deception of the church. More than once his personal bitterness started to erupt, but he held himself in check.

He sat at his desk and stared at the window, barely seeing the spire of the venerable Notre Dame. "I hate You, God," he said quietly. He shook his fist into the air. "You deceived me for so many years, causing me to believe a lie!"

As he stared out the window, Edmund Staats faced a terrible reality. He had cast God out of his life, and he had nothing with which to replace the resulting emptiness. Despite his immense wealth, the respect of his peers and those of One Faith, he knew himself as a man alone in the world.

This announcement had brought him worldwide fame and popularity. Bishop Wheatley had hinted that he might even win the Nobel Peace Prize for his work, because he had brought FOL and One Faith closer than anyone else had, and he was therefore promoting peace within the world. Yet, Staats cared nothing for the Nobel Prize. He had taken his stand for truth because the scroll convinced him of the church's deception. But nothing in life could replace what he had lost through embracing the truth. He sighed, wishing the story of the Resurrection had been real. It would have given him something to believe in. Now he had nothing. Even if they awarded him the Nobel Prize and hundreds of other honors, he would still have nothing to believe in. As he continued to stare at the world beyond his window, he wished he had something—anything—to believe in.

Yet he had nothing. Only emptiness.

The Soviet Union, a major power that dominated the world for decades, had slowly lost its iron grip on the throat of the people. They had admitted in 1988 that their national government was nearly sixty billion dollars in debt. By 1992, they were forced to face the reality that they could not feed their own people because of inefficient farming methods, droughts, and natural disasters. Slowly the Hammer and Sickle slipped as the adherents of One Faith moved in, grasping power and ousting Communist leaders.

By mid-1999, One Faith controlled the entire continent of Asia, all of the island nations except Australia and New Zealand, most of the Middle East, and the entire African continent. They executed those who refused to bow to One Faith or, as an act of humanitarianism, occasionally deported them to the West.

In the West, politicians first aligned themselves with FOL and, seeing the trend in the world, officially joined with them. By the close of the last decade in the twentieth century, Planet Earth had evenly divided itself between two powers, both fighting to overpower the other. Neither of the two powers, nor their leaders, realized that behind the scenes, Mastermind was coordinating each move.

A new order issued by Neville Wheatley and bearing the endorsement of all leaders of the Fellowship of Love ostracized all adherents of One Faith, except those who were willing to serve in subservient positions. Most of these latter were deportees from One Faith who, along with political and religious refugees, held steadfastly to a faith other than that of the FOL and received the lowest status in the economy of the West. While never called slaves, these adherents, many of them kidnapped from their homelands, worked at the menial tasks in industry not done by robots. The government referred to them as Franchised Workers.

One Faith pumped new resources into the Soviet economy as they also opened the frozen tundra for settlement by the overcrowded peoples of China and India. Researchers, working on environmental control for over a decade, had learned how to lessen the Arctic temperatures on the great landmasses of Siberia and Mongolia. The new inhabitants planted trees with a prospect of developing hardwood forests. Through a procedure called neo-budding, scientists could now grow trees as high as forty meters within three years. They had begun by grafting the fast-growing eucalyptus to the slower-growing Russian oaks.

Scientists, many of them defectors from the FOL, worked to reclaim the deserts of the Middle East and Africa. In the Gobi Desert, Arabs, for the first time in their lives, saw small cooperative farms springing up. Citrus trees bore fruit. Oases soon merged into small cities that pulled the nomadic population toward permanent settlement.

By a careful manipulation of air masses, the same scientists now knew how to bring rainfall to the Arabian peninsula. They had already developed a grass that would grow in the Sahara. Once the grass took hold, they would bring in permanent irrigation from the Mediterranean Ocean.

While few of these achievements made news in the West, which normally devalued any progress in the East, One Faith was slowly emerging into a period of unprecedented wealth and prosperity.

Another group of researchers, mostly headed by Soviet-trained experts, worked slowly at the problem of nutrition. Their goal was to develop grains and vegetables that contained all the necessary vitamins and minerals. They had set for themselves the goal of putting on the market five such products that could sustain life and enhance health. They had begun with cross-pollinating legumes. As secondary goals, these must be crops that grew in abundance, required little care, and produced two harvests a year. Further, these products had to be able to grow in small areas.

One American-trained Iraqi scientist made the initial breakthrough by discovering the genetic code to the date. From that, he had developed a small tree much like the date palm, with a sweet-tasting fruit with high nutritional value. His product lacked one essential ingredient: Vitamin A. He projected that he would have this solved by 2001.

Western powers held full control of the moon and Mars. While they prepared for colonization of Jupiter, scientists in Japan and China had already landed their first humans on Jupiter. They had not as yet determined any economic value they would derive from colonization—or if colonization would be feasible. However, they were preparing to ship habitual criminals not eligible for the death sentence, along with political recalcitrants and social misfits, to the new planet.

"This way," Kassam Ishmael announced, "we rid ourselves of pesky flies and use their productive skills at the same time."

"We have our modern Siberian Gulag," laughed Bani Barakan.

"That we do," Kassam Ishmael said with a smile. He was already plotting how to discredit Bani Barakan and "allow" him to spend the rest of his days on Jupiter.

Westerners, content to enjoy their prosperity, cared little about conditions under the domain of One Faith. In a few instances, one group's needs impinged on the other, which aroused resentment, sometimes anger, and occasionally retaliation. Bishop Neville Wheatley met regularly with Kassam

Ishmael and Bani Barakan as they settled disputes between the two faiths.

Word had reached Wheatley that One Faith nations were enslaving Westerners, especially those on the borders of Poland and Bulgaria. Wheatley raised the question, prepared to offer irrefutable proof.

"Quite right," Kassam Ishmael said, waving away the Englishman's charge. "A few we have taken now and then, but nowhere near the numbers you have stolen from us."

"I know nothing of our taking any of your people—"

"Ah, but you do," Kassam Ishmael said. "In your own private grounds at Balmoral as well as the former American White House, you use what you call Franchised Workers."

"Is that so?" asked Wheatley.

"Yes," Kassam Ishmael said. "So, you will report in your media that our talks are making progress."

"Agreed," said the bishop. "And I have a proposal to show our progress. It is a convenient way for you to rid yourself of undesirables, and we can do the same."

"Speak on," Kassam Ishmael said, already prepared by his people to agree to what he knew was coming.

"I propose that any criminal sentenced for a crime of more than one year be immediately shipped to the other side of the world where he or she becomes Franchised Labor."

"I shall consider this suggestion," Kassam Ishmael said, "because it may have merit."

"A great deal of merit," Wheatley replied. His underlings, prepared and prompted by Mastermind, had informed him that One Faith would agree.

After six hours of discussion, the two leaders agreed and announced their joint decision on tele-media. The practice pleased the people of the world. Crime rates dropped (or so it appeared on the statistics), and the Franchised Labor force of both faiths increased.

"Yes," Bishop Wheatley said, "it is an arrangement that satisfies both of us."

"But of course," Kassam Ishmael said. "We can coexist, can we not?"

As both men smiled at each other, they were also aware that given the least opportunity, they would step in and overpower the other.

T·W·E·N·T·Y S·E·V·E·N

Kai Jong was one of the few internationals who traveled as widely among the Westerners as he did among One Faith nations. One day, standing in Central Park in New York, a local television reporter interviewed him.

"The world is moving toward greater enlightenment," he said. "We are learning the secrets of the cosmos which generations before us called God. We shall see more clearly in the days ahead that is what we call those things we do not understand or cannot control. As we master more of life, the word will become increasingly meaningless."

"You don't believe in God?"

"I believe in me. I am god. I have all power at my disposal. This is not new to you, surely."

"I don't think we've ever heard it quite so succinctly before," said one reporter.

"We make our own world, we create our own reality. As I move into greater frontiers of enlightenment, why do I need some vague, undefined force out there somewhere?"

At the end of his interview, Kai Jong concluded, "The

emerald is, in my opinion, the most beautiful and precious gem of all. So I like to say that we are moving now into the Emerald Age. It is time to change our clothes, to become new people, and to walk in the light."

The next morning the *Washington Post*'s headlines blared out in four-inch print: EMERALD AGE ARRIVES.

All over the world, adherents of One Faith and FOL picked up the term. This was a time for everyone to prosper, for everyone to move into greater knowledge and to leave behind the superstitions of the past.

Kai Jong, a renowned Buddhist monk before converting to One Faith, would never have attained notice by the world except he claimed to have learned the secret of astral projection. Long known and claimed by its adherents as possible, Kai Jong proved it real.

Astral projectionists stated that those of the highest spiritual order, when in the deepest form of meditation and with their brain waves slowed down to the delta level, could project themselves to any place in the world. Kai Jong demonstrated that he could send his spirit from one geographic location to another by asking Edmund Staats to select any Spiritual Enabler he wished and to have this person in Staats's office at exactly midnight.

Staats picked a female Spiritual Enabler, but told her nothing of what she was to do. At exactly midnight she went into a trance and said, "I am Kai Jong. You did not believe, but now you can believe it, Edmund Staats."

Edmund Staats saw nothing but a vague outline around him, a soft glow of off-white and pale blue. Staats had irrefutable proof that at that moment Kai Jong was in deep meditation on Mount Kobe in Japan.

"Yes, I hear your voice," Staats said. "Yet I need something more as proof."

"I am wearing a green robe with two red dragons on the back. You have only to ask your two men who are with me here. That will prove that I have come directly to you, disregarding space and time limitations."

Hours later, Staats's two trusted men who were with Kai Jong at the time of the astral projection reported what the man wore. The description matched exactly.

Edmund Staats now had a faith: he believed in astral projection. That truth led him into exploring his own former lives. Yet, he seldom had a night in which he slept more than an hour at a time. He suffered from terrible nightmares, and his Spiritual Enabler explained that as soon as they got back into all his past lives, they would discover the source of the nightmares and he would be healed.

One dream appeared at least weekly, a dream that gave him the most torment. He was standing in a large hall with dozens of other people when someone screamed. Staats often was the first to notice, sometimes another person. But they always looked up to a high wall.

Each time he witnessed words appearing on the wall. But no one could read them because they were written in a language no one had ever seen before.

People would cry out in terror, and Staats felt a fear overcome him as each time he cried, "Who can explain this to us?"

And each time the dream ended the same way: David Morgan was suddenly standing in front of him. "The message is clear, although written in the language of Heaven and not of humans. This is to show you that it is a message from God. The words say, 'Tested and Failed' and 'Hollow Heart,' and they are a message for you."

"But what does it mean?" Staats would cry out. "Especially 'hollow heart'? What does it mean?"

And each time he awakened and could not sleep the rest of the night.

For six weeks Edmund Staats submitted to a Spiritual Enabler who helped him regress to former lives. In none of them did he find answers. Each time he left his SE depressed. And one day Edmund Staats realized he was no longer depressed. He felt no anger, no resentment.

That night he did not dream, and he slept until morning. But when he awakened, he felt no joy or peace. He found nothing to arouse his interest or to excite him.

As he sat down to breakfast, he remembered the part of his dream that said "Hollow Heart." Now he understood. He was no longer a man. He experienced no negative emotions, but no positive feelings either. He was, as the dream said, a hollow shell.

Edmund Staats wished he could cry or feel sadness, but he felt nothing.

David Morgan continued to speak out, urging people to hear the truth. He had argued against the Galilee Scrolls (as they were called) and insisted they were forgeries. "Despite the words of the most eminent scholars and the results of technology, I contend that they are forged documents! I know Jesus Christ is alive!"

People ridiculed him; they laughed at his antiquated ideas. ABC kept his program going because during the Galilee Scrolls issue Morgan received more mail than any other personality—almost all of the letters negative—and strong threats of hate and death too. Morgan hired a woman who read through the letters for him. When she felt there was a chance of helping or talking with anyone who wrote, Morgan made contact himself. Occasionally he discovered hungry hearts, people open to hear the Word of God. But they were few.

On Pentecost Sunday, 1999, David Morgan prepared to close the service with the benediction. He paused to look at the faces of the faithful, less than two hundred people in a building that had been erected to seat eight thousand. He didn't want to be troubled; he had known this would happen. Morgan forced himself not to ask, *Where am I failing?*

"My friends, my brothers and sisters in Christ, I have decided to go on a fast. My heart is heavy with grief about the evil and the wickedness on this earth. I announce this because I invite you to join me. After the benediction I shall return to the chancel and pray."

Morgan had no idea how they would respond, and it didn't matter. He could not go on without spiritual fortification, and he told them so. "I do not intend to leave this building until something happens. Either God will speak or do a miracle or Jesus Christ will return or—" He paused to smile. ". . . or I die of starvation. But I shall be here."

As a dutiful pastor, David Morgan stood at the door to speak with those who left. To his delight, approximately half of the members were already in the chancel area praying.

The Strenk family, now attending for their fifth straight Sunday, remained to join him in prayer and fasting. Their renewed commitment warmed his heart. No one had been as supportive and as encouraging as Joe Strenk.

Just then Joe looked and winked. He held out his hand and pumped David's. "You gave yourself to us when we needed you. This is the least we can do for you."

"Thank you," David said as he knelt next to his friend.

In recent months strange things had been happening at the church. Just as in the days of the Book of Acts, several people began to speak to the congregation, but they spoke with a boldness, an authority that none of them normally possessed. Each would speak, without explaining or apologizing, and deliver a specific word of guidance from God.

At first it had startled the members of Morgan's church, but soon they grew used to hearing a member stand up and say, "I have something to say to you from God."

Then, Easter Sunday, the voices stopped speaking as abruptly as they had begun. By Pentecost Sunday, the voice of God had been silent for the entire seven weeks. Not one person, including David, had received any word from God.

"Have we failed You, God?" David asked. "Have we let You down? Gone astray? Show us."

All afternoon the members prayed with periods of oral prayer followed by lengthy silences. They prayed for themselves, but mostly they prayed for God to intervene in the world. Several pleaded for victory for themselves over all the evil around them.

At sunset, a ray of light sifted through the stained-glass windows and David Morgan stared, hardly believing what he was seeing. He turned his head away and then looked again. One particular ray of light rested on the head of young Nick Strenk. Was it a natural phenomenon? A sign from Heaven? Morgan tried to pray, but his attention kept returning to the light that kept growing stronger and brighter.

While Morgan was concentrating on the light, Nick Strenk got off his knees and knelt beside his pastor.

"How do you know if God wants you to say something?"

The stream of light from the window followed the young man, and as he knelt beside the minister, the light remained on Nick's head. Instinctively David glanced back to where the boy had been; it was now dark.

"You think God is speaking to you? Is that it?"

"I guess . . ." the teenager said. "I've never done anything like this before. But I keep hearing this voice inside my head telling me that I'm supposed to talk to everyone."

"Then do it, Nick. If it's not right, we'll know. But, son, I believe you really have something to say, something we need to hear from God."

"But you won't like it."

David Morgan put his arm around the boy. "Son, being faithful to God sometimes means we have to say or do things that other people won't like. Our first responsibility is to God. Regardless of what anyone thinks or doesn't like, you need to speak."

"I'm kinda scared."

"I'll make it easier for you." David Morgan stood and said, "Little flock, . . . and by the way, in case you didn't know, that's a term Jesus used . . . something strange happened a few minutes ago, and I want to tell you about it." He told them about the ray of light around Nick.

"So stand up, Nick, and speak to us," Morgan said.

Nick stood and walked forward.

His mother gasped. "The light! The ray of light is moving with you!"

"The shekinah glory of Israel! Oh, it is!" said an elderly woman. "It must be what the Israelites saw and followed."

Joe Strenk closed his eyes and gave thanks to God as he said, "A little child shall lead them."

Nick cleared his throat and began to speak.

"God keeps whispering to me that I have to tell you something," Nick said. "And I'm scared that maybe it's something I made up or—"

"Speak," an older man said. "I've been watching you for about half an hour, waiting for you to talk to us. Nick, God speaks to me. You know that, don't you?"

"Oh, yes," Nick said. Mr. Michalski was one of the people they called prophets.

"God told me He had given you a message for us . . . So speak."

"God says . . ." Nick swallowed, closed his eyes, and, despite the nervousness and physical trembling, opened his mouth. ". . . God says, 'I have hidden My face from you, but I did not leave you. I will never leave you. It pleases Me that you pray. It pleases Me that you fast. You are Mine and you belong to Me. No one will ever pluck you out of My hand. There are yet others—a few—who will join you, and you must receive them. But now is a time of falling away. Your number has greatly diminished, and still others will depart, denying they ever knew Me.'"

The light that had shone on Nick's head intensified in brilliance, bathing his whole body in a warm glow. Believers had to look away because the brightness hurt their eyes.

"'Stop praying for the world and its leaders. For too long I have pleaded, for too long I have waited with outstretched arms and with tender mercies. And for too long they have rejected Me. The whole world has now heard, and they must now make their final choice. But for you, expend your efforts in praying for each other. Pray that your faith will sustain you as you face the final hours.'"

Slowly the light around Nick diminished as the people pondered those words.

"God has spoken," David Morgan said softly. "Now we know what we must do: concentrate our prayers on each other. Let's remind ourselves that we are united in Jesus Christ, and let us uphold each other."

"The times are perilous," said Michalski. "I speak to you as a spokesman for God. The hardships will worsen. In the days ahead, darkness will cover the moon and the stars will flee. A great and terrible time is coming and you, little flock, must be ready."

Michelle Maxwell and Emil Wensela were among the hundred who stayed at Morgan's church to pray and fast. They had knelt in a corner, keeping aloof from the others because they felt they knew too little about the Christian faith and weren't as spiritual as the others.

Rikard Michalski walked over to Michelle and Emil and held out his hands, indicating that he wanted them to stand. "And I have a message for you that comes from God." He stared into their faces. "Does this make sense to you? Speaking from God?"

"Oh, yes," Michelle said. "You know my mother is involved in this—in a Satanic way—"

"And so is my father," blurted Emil.

"My mother's an SE for someone called Mastermind. Of course, now I know that he is Satan himself. Many times Emil and I sat in their meetings and heard his instructions as he plotted to destroy Christians and church leaders."

"We believe all right," Emil said. "And I'm glad that we now know the True Voice!"

"Then come, both of you," Michalski said. "God has spoken to me to pray for you. Both of you." He beckoned those nearby, and asked them to gather closer. "We are to begin to pray for each other right here, right now." Michalski looked at Morgan. "I'm not trying to usurp—"

"My brother, you are speaking from God. I am willing to listen and to obey God, no matter who the messenger may be," Morgan said. "And remember, I'm not more holy than the rest of you. God has called me to lead, to teach and preach, but I'm a human like the rest of you." He patted Michalski on the shoulder and said, "Carry on."

"You don't think you're as good as the rest of us," the old man said to Michelle, "do you?"

"I know I'm not."

"That's exactly what God told me. Michelle, do you believe God speaks to me and gives me messages for the people?"

"I do . . . oh, I really do."

"Then listen to this. You are greatly loved by God for your purity of heart and your openness of spirit."

"Me?" she asked, breaking into sobs. "Oh, I want to believe that, I really do."

"And you shall!" Michalski said. "God promised me that you would soon experience this truth."

"I've felt that I could never be good enough for God, good enough to bear the name Christian."

"Do you love Jesus Christ?"

"I do."

"That's why Jesus Christ died, Michelle," he said. "He has removed all your guilt, taken away your failures, forgotten your wrongdoings. In God's sight you are pure and forgiven."

Michelle stared at the speaker, her lips trembling; and in those moments, faith and doubt fought for dominance. "I want to believe," she said, one word at a time. As she finished the sentence, a peace swept over her and she smiled. Faith had won.

Michalski turned to Emil. "You also have come a long way. You have come from the doorway of Hell itself." He laid his hand on the young man's shoulder. "You have persevered, but the real tests for you are yet to come. We're going to pray for you, that you won't fail in the crucial moments."

"Thank you," Emil said. And as he knelt for prayer, he shuddered, sensing he would face a time when he would stand totally alone. He feared he would not have the courage he needed.

T·W·E·N·T·Y E·I·G·H·T

The co-ag didn't know what to do with his coat and hat. They were completely soaked and were dripping on the carpet. He had stood for three hours in continuous rain because he didn't want to fail Annella Maxwell, and because he didn't want to lose the promised bonus.

Annella was pacing the floor, hurling swear words at the ceiling, striking the walls with her fists. "So he came back again! He dared to defy me!"

"Excuse me," the man said, "Everything we know indicates that your daughter sought him out. He changed his name to Wilson a few years ago . . . Theo Wilson is his professional name."

"He was the worst experience of my life," she said, not talking to the man in drenched clothes. "He was the only man I couldn't manipulate or control. He'd listen to my anger and then walk away as if I had given him the weather report. In all my life I've never hated anyone as intensely as I've hated Ted Wallace!"

Minutes earlier the co-ag had handed Annella Maxwell a Polaroid photograph and was waiting for her to calm down so he could give her the rest of the information. If she was this upset now, he wondered how she would take the rest of the news.

She went to the wet bar and grabbed a bottle of bourbon. Not bothering with a glass, she took a long drink from the bottle. She then slammed the bottle so hard on the counter, it broke with a spray of glass, and liquid covered the countertop. Annella Maxwell didn't notice.

She suddenly stopped, turned, and said, "There must be more. What do they do together? How often do they meet?"

"Mr. Wallace—or Wilson—travels some—always to San Franciso where he meets with an agent from Los Angeles. Theo Wilson has become a top writer for—"

"I know about that. I didn't know he was Ted, but I know of his work!" She swore again. It had not occurred to her that Ted would change his name a second time and stay in the business.

"Okay, Ted has won that one," she said, "but the war isn't over until the final battle. Okay, what else?"

"They meet twice, sometimes three times a week when he's in Atlanta. That's where he lives."

"I assumed that. With those idiot parents of his."

He didn't bother to tell Annella that Ted's parents were both dead. "Wilson and your daughter talk a lot. We've had his place bugged—"

"What kind of talk? I mean they can't just sit and talk about nothing?"

"About religion."

"Religion?" she echoed, and then the little bits of information began to come together. Things Michelle had said that didn't quite add up. "They're mixed up with that stupid, loud-mouthed preacher—the one on ABC—"

"Morgan."

"I might have known!"

"Michelle goes there—to the church—twice a week. She usually goes with the other man whose picture I have given you."

"Emil Wensela! Huh . . . He's a nothing . . . a weak-willed wimp of—" She stopped, lost in thought. Annella stopped pacing, and a smile appeared on her face. "I warned him years ago. I warned Ted that if he ever—"

Annella Maxwell smiled. "I have a plan to take care of Ted Wilson and my daughter at the same time. A simple plan."

Neville Wheatley had received every kind of human award possible. For the fourth year in a row, the Gallup Poll showed him the most admired man in the West. And the bishop loved being the head of the largest church in the world. His only quarrel was that here and there a few individual congregations had held out. Some stayed to themselves, saying nothing to attract attention; he didn't mind them. But a few of them, like this church in Atlanta, were a constant irritant to him.

The bishop had long since stopped praying, except in the most formal sense of public prayers and blessings. "Who needs God?" he asked his wife Agatha.

"You are God," she said. "Or the closest thing mortals will ever discover."

That remark pleased him.

The spiritual head of the West seldom talked with his wife, but when he did, she rallied behind him, feeding him with constant encouragement. She knew her husband better than anyone else. Had he chosen, he might have known about the many lovers she had taken in recent years, but she handled her life with discretion. His devotion to FOL was mistress enough for him, demanding his utmost loyalty and energy, giving him time for little else.

On Christmas Day, 1999, Neville Wheatley, standing in front of Westminster Cathedral, announced, "From this year on, we shall continue to celebrate December 25. However, we have decided that since we have already taken Christ out of our liturgy, it is time to take Christ out of Christmas. It thus appears consistent to change the name of the day."

Wheatley and his spiritual staff, whom he termed underbishops, had agreed upon a number of changes. They had unanimously decided that it was time to announce them, one being that after this, December 25 would be All Births Day.

"Let history record this as a day when we celebrate ourselves and each other. Let this be the day when we openly celebrate our past lives and use December 25 and the rest of the calendar year to prepare ourselves for our next lives."

The crowd cheered, as he knew they would. Neville Wheatley had reached the pinnacle of success, where he could do no wrong and make no mistakes. He smiled at the people who had gathered to hear his address.

"The underbishops have agreed with true unanimity that I shall no longer be your bishop."

"No! No!" voices protested.

"Wait!" He held up his hands. "I am still with you, and I won't leave you. They have selected a name which they feel is more fitting to my office. From now on I shall be called Great Parent Neville. They have insisted, and after days of arguing with them, I have consented to abide by their decision. I am your spiritual father!"

For nine minutes the crowd cheered. Several people had brought balloons which they released. Soon red, blue, gold, and green filled the air.

"And our underbishops and I have completed a study of the Fellowship of Love and have considered that it is time to reexamine the initial points of theology that brought us together. There were three of them, as you may recall: the Bible as the Word of God, Jesus Christ as the only Savior, and eternal life for all believers.

"We have met in meeting after meeting for months, rethinking these foundations. It is our conviction that in light of the Galilee Scrolls, we must bring our church into line. After all, we are not only the Fellowship of Love, but we are the fellowship and safeguards of truth."

Cheering broke out, this time lasting a mere three minutes.

"Here are the three historic points upon which we base the Fellowship of Love. First, we believe that the original Bible is the Word of God. We recognize that well-intentioned but overzealous disciples in the first century added several passages to the Bible not originally there, and unfortunately they also deleted sections. Our fine scholars are working as rapidly as possible to produce an authentic, true, and accurate Bible, the Word of God. We anticipate that by January 31, 2000, we will have an authentic translation of the true and inspired Word of God."

The second point, Great Parent Neville explained, meant changing "the" to "a," so that the statement would read that Jesus Christ is *a* Savior. "After all, he was a man zealous to do God's will. We can admire his commitment and emulate his devotion. He truly believed that his death would count for the liberation of all humanity."

Third, they would shorten the statement to read, "Eternal life is for everyone."

Six months earlier, a committee under Great Parent Neville had distributed literature for all study classes. Another group had prepared sermons and meditations for clergy. Inherent in the material was a belief in reincarnation, encouragement to consult with wizards and SEs, and an urging to openness to concepts kept from God's people for many centuries, such as astral projection.

In one session during the first quarter of lessons, they had dealt with the issue of witches and wizards. Some had raised the question of prohibitions in the Old Testament against visiting such personages.

As the *Authoritative Lessons* pointed out, God did forbid going to these people, but that simply showed that such powers were available and that people could find help. God had forbidden this to Jews because they were a nomadic people, and few could read and none of them were able to plummet the understanding of the modern age.

"It is only now, at the end of the twentieth century, that the people of the world are wise enough, mature enough, and educated enough to seek the counsel of such spiritual advisors."

When Great Parent Neville concluded his message, he pleaded for tolerance. "Some disagree with us. We must not exhibit harshness toward them. We know we walk in the light. We know that we are merging more fully into God each day. Can we not afford a little tolerance for others in their backwardness? I beg of you, do them no harm. Treat them as you would a retarded adult—with love, with patience, and with superior understanding."

A new line of attack had begun against the Christians: humiliation and degradation . . . no overt persecution . . . no martyrdom.

Mastermind said, "Killing only perpetuates what they stand for. Ridicule is a better weapon. Teach people to treat them as mental defectives. It is our best weapon."

Annella had called Michelle repeatedly, leaving messages on her daughter's answering machine. Michelle returned none of them. As she confessed to Emil, "I don't want to speak to her, because I can't be sure I'm strong enough to stand against her. She's so evil, and her wickedness makes her strong."

"One day you'll have to face her," he said. "God will help you when you do."

They were sitting on the sofa in her living room, his arm around her shoulder. They had finished a home Bible study with their group of six neighbors only minutes earlier and were now relaxing.

"I'm happy, Emil," she said. "I didn't know—I didn't believe—I could be so happy. Not in a million years."

"I know," he said. "I feel the same way. And for me, only one thing holds me back from being totally happy."

"What's that?" she asked, surprise in her voice.

"You," he said.

"What do I have to do with it?"

"I love you, Michelle. I suppose I've loved you a long time. I know I have. I'm not good at standing up and saying what I feel or think—"

"You're doing fine," she said softly.

"I love you and I want to marry you."

"That's all that keeps you from being really happy?"

"That's all."

"We can fix that easily enough." She leaned forward, and their lips met. They held each other tightly, their embrace communicating the depth of their feelings.

At that second the doorbell rang. Assuming someone in the study group had forgotten something, Emil jumped up and hurried to the door. His face fell when he saw who stood there.

"I've come to see my daughter."

"I'll ask her if she wants—"

Annella brushed past him. "She is my daughter," she said.

Michelle heard her mother's voice and came out of the den. "I wish you hadn't come here, Mother . . . uninvited."

"I wish you had answered my telephone messages."

"Funny," Michelle said, "but I thought you were smart enough to figure out that my refusal to answer was my answer."

"Very good," Annella said, smiling broadly. "You learned repartee from me quite nicely!" She turned toward Emil and said, "Unless you've moved in here and are sleeping with my daughter, I'd suggest you go home."

Refusing to take the bait, Emil looked at Michelle. "I don't mind staying."

"Maybe you'd better go," Michelle said. "You might not like some of the language my mother uses."

"Oh, he has used all the words himself," she said.

"I used to do a lot of things I don't do any more."

"Then good night, Emil," Annella said. "My daughter and I have some big-girl talk to do."

"I'll be fine," Michelle said.

Emil paused to kiss Michelle and again asked if she wanted him to stay. He half-whispered when she declined, "I'll be home praying for you. Call me when she leaves."

As soon as he had gone, Annella took off her chiffon cape and draped it across a chair. She paused, as if posing for Michelle. She wore an azure-blue crepe with a low-cut back, tight at the bust, waist, and hips, its trim line broken only by a slit in the left side. "How do I look?"

"Beautiful. Always beautiful. And at ninety, you'll still be beautiful—for your age."

"Ah, you do know how to add the stinger," Annella said. "Nice looking *little* house you have."

"Nothing opulent, Mother," she said, "but I like it. Very much."

"By the way," Annella said, "has your boy Emil ever told you about us? About our times in bed together?"

"Mother, I am sure he never went to bed with you, but your words don't shock me. Actually, you're probably one of the ten women he missed. But even if you two had had a torrid affair, it wouldn't make any difference to me. Emil's different now. He's changed—"

"Spare me the rest of the scenario. You have both had this wonderful change of heart because you have found true religion and each other. You love him. You plan to marry him and raise a household of little Emils."

"Something like that."

"He's really not much in bed, and you'll be disappointed."

"Mother!"

"Sorry," Annella said. "I forgot how sensitive you always were about things like that."

"Don't spar with me, Mother. I didn't invite you here, and I don't want you here. Spew out all of your poison now, and then you can be on your way."

"Oh, you should have told me to hop onto my broomstick—"

"If that's your mode of travel."

"Very good, dear!" Annella laughed. "Michelle, I didn't come here to fight with you. Truly I didn't." Annella walked toward her daughter, her arms stretched out.

Michelle folded her arms in front of herself and cocked her head. "That approach won't work either. Not any more. Mother, I lived with you most of my life. I know your tricks and just about every approach you've ever tried. You're now ready to tell me that you're getting older and you need me."

"Okay, Michelle," Annella said and smiled. "Actually, I was going to make it a little better. I'd invented a malignancy. So, I'll drop that line—"

"That's better."

"I'll say it straight. You've been in contact with that weasel Ted Wilson."

"I've been in contact with my father, and I see him regularly."

"I don't want you to see him again . . . Not ever again."

"You can't dictate terms to me like that," Michelle answered calmly.

Annella sat down and lifted her feet to the coffee table. "Then I'll say it one last time. If you ever see that toad again, I will have him killed. And you know I can . . . and that I will. Oh, it'll be reported and believed as an accident. I'll even provide ten witnesses to say so. But you'll know what really happened. And, even with this new faith you have, could your conscience bear your being responsible for the death of your father?"

"You will be the murderer. My conscience won't be troubled."

"Really? Then tell me," Annella said, "do you truly believe in this Jesus tripe? After all I taught you?"

"I not only believe in Jesus Christ, Mother, but I'm willing to die for Him if necessary. If Mastermind carries out his plan through you and those contemptible people, I may have to."

"We can worry about that later." Annella stood up and said, "I don't think I'll stay after all. But I do mean what I say about Ted. I hate that man, and I will wrest every pleasure and every joy out of his life, just as he tried to do with mine."

"You really will have him murdered, won't you?"

"Don't ever doubt me!"

Michelle felt herself shaking and finally said, "All right . . . you win."

"Never again?"

"He's coming by tonight. He's been on the West Coast. I'll tell him then."

"No!" Annella said and then added in a softer but colder tone, "Wait a minute. Yes, do tell him. Then he'll have no doubts about the reason. Yes . . . I think I'd enjoy knowing that you told him. And then, you'll not see him again."

"All right," Michelle said. "Now leave me alone or I'll probably vomit all over your chiffon dress."

T·W·E·N·T·Y N·I·N·E

Something had happened to his daughter. Ted Wilson sensed the change even before she spoke. As he entered her apartment, he paused, his eyes scrutinizing her dull features. As Michelle came toward him, she seemed to have to think about every physical gesture before she moved.

"Tell me what it is," Ted said. He embraced her and added with a lighter tone, "Little girls can tell everything to their daddies."

"I can't see you again," Michelle said. "Not ever."

"Annella's decision or yours?"

"It was a compromise."

"Compromises when it comes to decisions of the heart are the worst way to solve a problem," Ted said.

"This time it's the only way."

Ted released his daughter, took off his coat, and handed it to her. He sat on the sofa and waited until she sat down beside him.

Instead Michelle chose to sit in a chair across from him. "Dad, I love you, and I'm sorry it took me so long to . . . to get you back into my life, but I can't see you again. I don't dare have any contact with you. And, Dad, I'll always love you."

"Listen, you might as well tell me the total truth. Nothing Annella does would surprise me."

"It's the price I have to pay for your life."

"She's a smart one, all right," he said, leaning back, feigning a relaxed mood. "She hit your weak spot. Annella's good at that. Very good. I never told you, Michelle, but there was one other reason I left you . . . She threatened to kill you."

"My mother threatened—?"

"She would have too. With no regrets about it."

"That hurts, and I wonder why. Nothing about my mother ought to surprise me."

"She would have killed you. No idle threats from her."

"This time she's playing the game a little differently," Michelle said. She moved and sat next to him on the sofa. Taking his hand in hers, she said, "This time it's *your* life."

"I ought to be shocked. Or should I be flattered? At least surprised, but I'm not. It's typical of the way she works. When Annella stakes out her claim for or against anything—whether personal, business gain—it doesn't matter—she will go as far as she has to to get what she wants."

"That's why I can't see you anymore."

"What if I don't agree?"

"I'll run away if I have to," Michelle said. "Please, Dad, accept my decision—"

"I don't know," he said.

Ted Wilson leaned his head back against the sofa, closed his eyes, and prayed for wisdom. He particularly asked God to help him hear the voice of the Holy Spirit and to not allow his own desire to continue seeing his daughter obscure divine guidance. Finally Ted opened his eyes and said, "I'm going to abide by your decision, Michelle, but—and you have to hear the rest of this—I want you to be able to change your mind after you've thought this through. Agreed?"

She nodded. "Yes, but I won't."

"Later, okay?"

"If that's what you want."

"You know, honey . . . Jesus said that our enemies can only kill our bodies. Annella can't do anything more than that to me. I'm going to die, either by Annella's demonic hand, by natural causes, or by the terrible ordeals that God says are coming, but I am going to die and I'm not afraid. I've made my peace with God, and I'm ready."

"I know you are, but—"

"I don't think you quite understand," Ted said.

The father talked to his daughter slowly, in whispered tones as if they wanted no one to overhear. He had been reunited with her, and they had enjoyed each other. For her to compromise was giving in to Annella. Before she could protest, he reminded her that if Annella killed him, she was the one who would commit murder and have to answer to God. "You don't have to take responsibility for what your mother does or does not do to me. It won't be your fault."

"Didn't someone say that the heart has reasons that the head doesn't know about? Anyway, I grasp the logic, but my emotions don't want to cooperate."

"Whatever happens," he said, "I don't want you to accept blame. That would only increase her hold over you."

"I'm so mixed up. If I follow what I want, you'll die."

"Michelle, I want you to approach the matter differently. For now, accept her demands. Do what she says, but keep praying for God to guide you. You know I'll run back to you if you call me."

"Oh, Daddy," she said and started sobbing in his arms.

Just before dawn, with no more words to be spoken between them, they held each other as their tears mingled with their prayers.

And then Ted Wilson left.

"Our special guest today," Annella Maxwell said, "is making her first public appearance on television, but I assure you this is far from her last. Rather than telling you about her, let her tell you herself. Please welcome Yolanda!"

The orchestra played the final measure of "We Are the World," ending in a crescendo as the silvery curtain parted. From the back of the stage came a girl with light blonde hair, pale skin, and brilliant green eyes. With the poise of a professional, she curtsied to the audience before turning to Annella.

"Since no one knows anything about you—and your presence has been kept a complete secret even from my staff," Annella said as she led the child to a chair, "I want you to tell the audience about yourself. First, your name and your age."

"I am Yolanda. I have no other name."

"Why not?"

"Because my father and mother, who weren't married, couldn't agree on a surname. And . . ." She faced Annella. "Should I tell them about my parents?"

"I can do that," Annella said as she displayed her brightest smile. "Ladies and gentlemen, this is my daughter!"

The audience burst into applause. Cameras zoomed in for headshots of both. Their similar complexions and bone structures left little doubt of their relationship.

"Until a month ago she lived with her father—Levis Cothran!"

Again applause interrupted the show.

"From the beginning, Levis and I saw that we had brought an unusual child into the world. She was sitting up at two months, crawling at three, and walking—can you believe this?—at five months. By then she was already talking in complete sentences."

"I'm sure," Yolanda said, "that many of you are skeptical, and your attitude doesn't bother me. It is true, however . . . I am only six years old!"

"You sound twenty," said a voice from the front row.

"If you listen long enough, you'll discover I sound much older than twenty!" she replied and laughed.

"Yolanda speaks six languages without accent and has a vocabulary that astounds even me. Among her accomplishments, and they are many, she paints beautifully. In fact, her art goes on display next month here in New York. And it's not just that she paints extraordinarily well . . . there's something else about her work. Suppose you tell us, Yolanda."

"I am the reincarnation of Grant Wood," she said matter-of-factly. "My name as Grant Wood isn't well-known to some of you, but I was an American painter; I was born in Iowa in 1892, and I died in 1942. I have known and remembered everything about my past lives from infancy."

"Aw, give us a break," cried out the same voice in the front row.

Yolanda stepped forward, the camera following. "I don't blame you for being skeptical, but suppose you tell me what troubles you most about my statement."

"Look, I don't have any trouble with reincarnation, or as we now call it, pre-living. But how do you know you were Wood?"

"I can't explain in a way that will sound completely reasonable," Yolanda answered. "But I can tell you that from my earliest memories I have known that I am Grant Wood. And to help you understand that, I've asked Annella to display several of my paintings."

Annella Maxwell stepped forward. "For the benefit of you non-art types, and I'm one of them, Grant Wood is best known for a picture entitled *American Gothic,* which is typical of the work of Wood, who painted farm and rural life. The Midwestern artist became the first of a style of painters known as American regionalists—those who focused on capturing the style of rural America. Now, let me show you *American Gothic* and you'll recognize it immediately."

Two attendants brought in a covered picture and put it on a stand. When they pulled off the cloth cover, the audience saw a stern couple staring straight at the viewer, the man with a pitchfork in one hand.

"Oh, that one," the heckler said. "Yeah, I've seen that before."

"Oddly enough, it has always been my most popular work," Yolanda said, "although I've never figured out why people have found such fascination with it."

Yolanda then explained that when she died as Grant Wood on February 12, 1942, she was absorbed into the cosmos, where all souls go upon the termination of a life cycle. She would have returned immediately to Earth, but, she pointed out, the year was 1942. "The entire planet was immersed in a worldwide war. Millions died between 1939 and 1945, and the cosmos involves a fairly democratic process. You know, the first who arrives, goes first."

"You mean you waited more than fifty years to come back to this life?"

"No, I actually returned in 1971 as Corporal Robert Edwards of Brookline, Massachusetts. I was killed in Vietnam. But since I didn't accomplish anything extraordinary during those twenty years, I have chosen to ignore that phase of my life. However, if you wish to ask me any questions about my life then, I'll be pleased to answer."

"Wait a minute," a woman said, "you died in 1971—"

"April 14, in a midnight Tet offensive."

"And now you return as Yolanda—or did six years ago?"

"Right."

"But why take on the characteristics of Grant Wood?"

"I was going to explain that," Yolanda said and blew the woman a kiss. "Thank you."

Yolanda sat down again and described the painting techniques of Grant Wood. His one problem was that he painted slowly. In 1930 when he exhibited *American Gothic,* he became famous and his pictures sold well. But because he worked so slowly, he never used up his creative capabilities.

"I wonder if you understand CC—creative capabilities?"

The audience shook their heads.

"It's a term we use in the cosmos and probably hasn't reached you here on Earth. You see, the birth process is so traumatic that we forget everything of our pre-living experience—the trauma blocks out our past, and it's lost from us. You know, like a dream. When we dream, it's quite vivid, but as soon as we awaken, the images begin to leave us. Unless we find a way to keep that dream memory intact, within minutes it's gone forever. Now in the case of my birth, something happened that was different. Before being born to Annella, *I* decided that I would have an easy birth and that I would remember my pre-living experiences."

"Oh, yeah," a man said, "I remember when your father—when Levis Cothran—came on the program the first time, he said that we choose when to be born. I heard it, but it didn't make sense."

"Because we don't understand something doesn't make it untrue," Yolanda said. "For the moment, however, I hope you will take my statements about my birth and previous lives on faith. If after I've finished, you still disbelieve, all right. But please give me a chance."

"Hey, we're with you, Yolanda!" said a studio voice, which was echoed by others and then followed by enthusiastic applause.

"About our births, we can choose the timing . . . within reason. I mean, I could have delayed by a few days or arrived a month sooner. However, in the cosmos we know where we're going, and we are endowed with a limited amount of choice."

Yolanda explained that when a soul's number came up and the new life would send that soul into a situation similar to one he or she had lived before, one could turn it down, providing someone else would fill in. "That's no problem. Thousands are waiting to be born."

"Wait a minute," the woman said again. "You mention the cosmos, and I'm wondering if there is a God—a Supreme Being—who designed all of this?"

"But of course. Unfortunately, most of you don't even know its name. I say *its* because the Creator of the cosmos is Shining One, who is brilliant, iridescent, with a brightness no human words could express."

"That's His—I mean, the Creator's name? Shining One?"

"Yes," Yolanda answered. "And Shining One sent me to teach you and to let you know that you may use that name. Shining One has no gender, but you may say 'he' or 'she' because here on earth we have such limited ways of speaking."

"Yolanda," interrupted Annella, "I'd like you to explain your current purpose here on Earth."

"Shining One told me that I could return as Grant Wood—not precisely as Grant—but that I could take on his talents while I developed my own personality."

"Why?" asked a voice.

"Darling, I thought you'd never ask," quipped Yolanda. "You must understand one of the principles of the cosmos. Nothing gets wasted. Grant Wood had not used all of his CC—creative capabilities. That is, Grant Wood had many more pictures to paint, but died before completing his pre-destined lifework; so Shining One sent me to paint the rest of them. Quite simple."

"Can we see your work?"

"I thought no one would ask," Annella said as she signaled an assistant and another curtain opened. On a wall they had mounted nine paintings of rural America. Each painting showed the stark simplicity of Wood's work.

"Art experts have already authenticated that these nine paintings were done by the same person who did *American Gothic*, and a panel will interview three of these experts tonight here on CBS. These are the foremost art experts in the world," Annella told the audience.

"One of them," said Yolanda, "is employed by the Solomon Guggenheim Museum here in New York City, and he specializes in catching art forgeries."

"You see," Annella continued, "the experts claim that painting is like a fingerprint. No two artists make their strokes exactly alike. No matter how careful, forgers can never quite make their work the same."

"But I suspect you're not really interested in this phase of my life," said Yolanda.

"Tell us about life in the cosmos," said an old man in the rear. "I'm nearly eighty, and it looks like I'll be going there soon. What will it be like?"

"A wonderful place, filled with light and joy. You forget every problem you ever had. You never feel pain. No guilt. Shining One never punishes anyone."

"Not even me? I mean, I've done a lot of things . . . you know, things not so good."

"Shining One never holds past mistakes against anyone. Shining One says we are not yet perfect, and so we make mistakes."

The questions poured from the guests. When they asked about her pre-living, Yolanda told them she had been Queen Isabella of Spain who launched Columbus into the New World—but she had not been thinking of discovery as much as extending the boundaries of Spain and increasing trade.

"And that Christopher Columbus—as you call him in English—was a strange man. A staunch Christian, he wanted to convert the people of India—where he expected to end up. Yes, quite a strange man he was, but as capable as any when it came to the seas."

No matter what the question, Yolanda answered easily, whether it involved trivia, opinion, or world conditions.

"What about races? If I'm white, will I ever return as a black?"

"Not likely. Shining One seldom mixes races. I have never been anything but a Caucasian-type. Orientals remain oriental and so on. Shining One says we stir up problems when we attempt to merge different bloodstreams. Scientists are now bringing out evidence to show that there are differences in the blood of each race. To mix the bloods causes impurities and viruses."

As the program concluded, Annella said that Yolanda was already undergoing tests regarding her alleged knowledge of her past existences or pre-living.

"One final question," Annella asked Yolanda. "Why

did Shining One allow you to come to Earth with all this past knowledge?"

"To bring comfort," she said. "Shining One says wars will arise. Many—even some of you here—will die, but you are not to be afraid or to worry. Shining One has a place for you, reserved in the cosmos."

Annella said, "Yolanda tells me that once you reach the cosmos and are absorbed into it, you often prefer to stay there."

"And why not?" Yolanda said. "Life with the Shining One is pleasant and filled with great joy."

Annella winked and grinned as she added, "She also tells me that our glow bodies (as they call them) are perfected in the cosmos, and we can indulge in every kind of sensual pleasure we want. In fact, my next guests are sexologists. These two experts have studied sexual pleasure in the world's history. They have come to explain to us how to enjoy our sexual appetites more fully . . . here and now—on Earth!"

T·H·I·R·T·Y

David Morgan took off the lapel microphone as he prepared to leave the studio. He knew his words had fallen on empty ears. During his commentary, the camerawoman and the technical director thinly disguised their disgust, making it harder for him to speak. Yet, he had said what he believed God wanted him to tell the audience.

"Truth is still truth," he had said in closing, "no matter who speaks it and no matter how unpopular. The Devil is a liar—a very knowledgeable one! And I believe one thing Yolanda said. There is a Shining One—the Devil. He comes to us with promises and pleasant lies, and we fall into his trap."

As he walked down the hallway, he overheard the camerawoman say, "Why do they keep that clown speaking every night?"

"I don't know," another woman said. "He's a real joke."

By now Morgan was used to hearing such sarcastic cracks. Even so, they still hurt. As he continued on his way, David Morgan prayed, *O God, make me insensitive to these insults.*

If you become insensitive to harshness, you will become insensitive to other emotions. You will become unable to feel the pain of others. Is that what you want?

No, God, he said, *I'm sorry for asking.*

Within a week, art experts universally agreed that Yolanda was Grant Wood. She painted in the same style, without the slightest variation, but produced her work at a faster pace. She explained in one interview, "Considering my CC, I shall paint a total of ninety-four and then I shall stop. Grand Wood's CC will then be completed."

Immediately art collectors started bidding for her work. Sotheby, England's most prestigious art dealer, began to take bids on the unfinished paintings, assigning them numbers. She was currently receiving, as a minimum, one million dollars for each picture.

"Father," Emil Wensela said, "I would like to speak with you for a few minutes."

Hanse grunted as he glanced at his son. He had never particularly liked the boy, who cried too much as a baby, had sided with his mother too often during childhood, and had grown up, in Hanse's opinion, as weak and lacking the ability to trample upon his enemies.

"I know you never loved me, Father," Emil said as he sat down across from his father. "But I wanted to be like you, I really did. I admired the way you let nothing stand in the way of whatever you wanted."

Hanse smiled now and relaxed. "I wasn't aware of your interest."

"To be ruthless and hard like you was the only thing I wanted. You were a great teacher, but I wasn't a very apt pupil."

"No, no you weren't," Hanse said, "though I tried hard enough."

"I know," the young man answered. He vividly recalled a number of business coups his father had pulled off. He particularly remembered how Hanse had cheated—legally —Arabs out of millions of dollars worth of oil. He had everything set up, and it was a feasible operation. However, the Arabs had not studied the clause that allowed Hanse to win. "If either party . . ." the section began, and it gave the Arabs total opportunity to withdraw their funds at any point. They didn't realize it gave Hanse the same opportunity.

"I never quite figured out how you pulled it all off."

"Simple. Their comptroller ran off with the money, so I declared the company bankrupt."

"But he didn't, did he? Run off with the money?"

"Oh, I took care of him, so he might as well have.."

The enigmatic answer implied that Hanse Wensela had eliminated the man, and Emil guessed that meant having him killed. Such actions never seemed to bother his father.

"Father," Emil said, "do you ever think about people you've cheated? People whose land or money or possessions you've taken?"

"Think about them? In what way?" The expression on the man's face gave his son the answer.

"You know, do you ever feel troubled? Lose sleep over any of your transactions?"

Hanse dropped his stack of papers. "A troubled conscience? Something like that?"

"Yes . . . remorse . . . guilt . . ."

"Those emotions are for the weak. For people like your stupid mother, for ordinary people who haven't the courage to reach for what they truly want."

Emil retreated into silence, remembering the angry words his father had often shouted at his mother, regardless of whether the boy or anyone else heard. Her name was Clara, but he called her a cow and insulted her at every opportunity. He encouraged the boy to do the same. One time, Hanse commanded Emil to strike his mother because she had corrected her husband earlier that day in front of guests.

"I can't," the boy had insisted.

"You can, and you shall!" thundered Hanse. "She is nothing but a cow, a stupid woman who has no rights except what I give her! She is to be treated like an animal. Strike her!"

Emil had been fourteen then, a foot shorter than his father, an indication that he would never be as tall as Hanse. He had fine bones and the fragile look of Clara's aristocratic forebears. "Please don't make me," the boy protested.

"Strike her. This old cow deserves nothing better."

After several minutes of repeated commands, Emil struck his mother, his fist landing on her face, bloodying her nose and knocking her backward.

"Good lad," Hanse said. As a reward, he allowed Emil to ride with him in his chauffeured limousine when he went to his office that day. Hanse discussed with the boy his new venture in uncut diamonds. "And for obeying me, you shall go to Antwerp and Amsterdam with me tomorrow," he said.

True to his word, Hanse took the boy along as he visited the two cities, allowing the young man to view sights he had never known before because it was his first trip out of Germany. At restaurants, his father allowed him to order whatever delights he wanted from the menu.

That evening his father called him into his own room. "In a few minutes you will have a visitor—a beautiful woman."

"Who is she, Father?"

"Her name is unimportant, but you may call her Lilli. She is the proprietor of the best gaming house in Europe. Do you know what I mean by *gaming house?*

The boy blushed.

"She will be here to instruct you, son. Remember this always: every woman is like your mother. Some are more intelligent, others have better bodies, but they all have limited uses, and their purpose is in serving the men of the world."

Emil blinked, hardly believing what he had heard. Being an only child, he was an extremely well-read boy, quite bright, and alone much of the time. Opening his mouth, Emil started to blurt out that his father held antiquated ideas, but he knew his words would only sabotage the rest of the trip. Then he'd likely be sent back alone, in disgrace, and wouldn't be able to see his father for some time.

Hanse had never hit the boy. His severest punishment was to deprive his son of seeing him for days or weeks, often as long as two months. At one point when the boy refused to cheat on his secondary school finals (Hanse had the answers ready for him), the father's displeasure was so strong, he stayed away from Emil for seventy-three days. The fact that Emil made the highest score of anyone in his private school made no difference to Hanse. The boy had spurned using the advantage his father had given him.

"It is time for you to learn the lessons of life," the father had said that night in Amsterdam. "This woman I am sending to you will teach you everything you need to know. Do you understand?"

"Yes, Father."

"And one more thing," Hanse said. "Aside from the needs of a healthy appetite—and we all have this—never forget that power is involved . . . A struggle to dominate, to make women submit as they ought! Never forget that! You let up for one second, and they will attempt to usurp your authority."

"I understand, Father," Emil said.

As he waited in his room for the woman to appear, Emil found it difficult to accept these words of his father. For the first time in his fourteen years, Emil Wensela began to question his father's rightness in everything.

Four days earlier a boy of fourteen had boarded a private jet with his god; at the end of their business, the boy of fourteen returned on the same jet, sitting next to an idol with clay feet.

"Father," Emil said, breaking the silence, "I want to tell you something. It's important for me to say. I would really like you to listen."

"If it's important . . ." Hanse said absently.

"Until I was fourteen, you were like a god to me—I would never have considered doing anything to disappoint you."

"Yes, yes, I know that," Hanse said. "And then you went through a rebellious period. That rebellion pleased me, by the way. It showed me that you do have some guts—maybe not much, but some."

Ignoring the usual taunt, Emil leaned forward. "I had one ambition in life, and that was to be like you . . . Exactly like you."

"Too bad you failed," Hanse said. "But there's still hope for you. Some hope." He lifted the brandy snifter on the table next to him and sipped. "It isn't too late, you know."

Instead of responding to the last statement, Emil said, "Recently I figured out a few things. I know now that I wanted only one thing from you, Father. And it was the one thing you couldn't give, the one thing you're incapable of giving."

"Oh, and what's that? Some kind of pscyho-babel you've picked up?"

"An old word, Father. I just wanted you to love me."

"Love you? I suppose it depends on how you define the word. I can tell you that I did everything I knew to do to make you be like me. Besides giving you the best of everything, I taught you secrets that other men would kill to know. If that's not love—"

"No, Father, that wasn't love. You were only trying to re-create yourself. You wanted a son created in your own image, and I'm not like that."

Hanse leaned forward, thrusting his fist at his son. "Of course, I know that. You're too much like the cow! You don't have the backbone to be like me."

"No, it's not that at all," Emil said and he grabbed his father's fist and held it until the older man winced from the pain and relaxed his hand.

"You're physically stronger than I thought," Hanse said. "I always thought you were weak in everything!"

"I'm not like you, Father, because I've never hated myself that much."

"What kind of rubbish—"

"I asked you to listen to me because this is important. For once in your life, for the first time in my twenty-nine years, I want you to sit and listen to what I have to say."

"Hmm," Hanse said, "perhaps some of my lessons have paid off."

"I've changed . . . Not that you'd have noticed because you didn't know me before. I don't want to be like you, Father. I know now that you are heartless, inhuman, evil."

"You aren't trying to insult me with those words? Come now . . . For people like us—people above the ordinary—those words have no meaning."

Emil shook his head. "I don't think there is the slightest chance you could possibly understand what I'm going to tell you, but I want you to listen and if you try to move from your chair, I'll—"

"You'll do what?" Hanse said. "Hold me in it?"

"Maybe I'll strike you across the face, just the way you made me strike Mother once."

The older man blanched. He put down his glass, straightened his posture, and glared at his son.

Hanse Wensela had learned early in his life that by controlling his anger, by allowing his opponent to speak everything he had to say, to show no visible disagreement, he would win in the long run. "Let them talk all they want," he often said, "and when they've said everything, I'm ready to tear them apart."

It was no different as he listened to his son. True, he was shocked, having had no idea of his son's involvement with David Morgan's church. He had suspected the boy was just living with Annella's daughter, and that had pleased him. After all, Hanse considered, Emil might marry the little thing and so double his inheritance.

The older man had not been prepared to hear statements like, "I believe in Jesus Christ" and "I am a disciple, a follower, of Jesus Christ." Nevertheless, his son now told his entire conversion story and added how his attitude toward life had changed. "Now I have something that makes living worthwhile," Emil said. "And I finally know what it feels like to have peace with myself."

"You have finished?" Hanse asked when his son stopped.

"Yes, except that I wish you'd turn to Jesus Christ too. I pray for you—"

"I do not wish your prayers," Hanse said quickly. "Now is there anything else you wanted to say before I ask you to leave me alone?"

"Is that all you can say?"

"Oh, I can say many things," the father answered, "but I don't think they would benefit either of us."

"I want to hear your response."

Hanse nodded slowly, then pulled a cigar from his breast pocket, taking time to clip the end, light it, and puff. "It is all nonsense—everything you have said—and I don't wish to hear you speak about it again."

"You don't understand. I knew . . . You have no feelings, do you?"

"Feelings?" Using the cigar as a pointer Hanse said, "No wonder you are in this mess. You must learn to master your emotions, to overcome them."

"Why, Father?" Emil said. "Is it because your feelings remind you of weakness? Your weakness? Isn't that why you despised my mother? And me? Because we know how to bend, to feel, to love, and you can't, and you hate whatever is in us that you can never have?"

Hanse carefully laid his cigar in the ashtray and stared blankly at his son.

"Oh, you do have feelings . . . You know how to feel anger, hatred, greed." Emil rose and walked toward the door, and then paused. He debated with himself in silence before he turned and said, "That's all you can allow yourself, isn't it,

Father? To feel more than that would make you human. And being human would make you know just how weak, how truly impotent you are!" Emil turned the knob on the door.

With an agility uncommon to him, Hanse Wensela sprinted from his chair and grabbed his son from behind, swung him around, and placed his large hands around his son's neck.

"No one has ever spoken to me like that! I have killed many people for lesser things!"

"Killing me? Is that going to change anything?" Emil said. He did not flinch or attempt to release his father's hands.

"I hate you, Emil," Hanse said as his fingers tightened. "You are weak and worthless. You never did have any gumption. See! . . . You can't protect yourself even now."

As the man's fingers tightened, Emil struggled to breathe, but made no effort to resist his father. The fingers continued to tighten, and Hanse smiled. "I have another emotion right now. Pleasure . . . exquisite pleasure as your life drains from your miserable body."

A tap at the door momentarily distracted Hanse, and he released his grip. "Yes . . ."

"You are being summoned for an emergency meeting, sir," said the male voice. "In New York."

Not bothering to answer the servant, the back of Hanse's hand struck his son's face, and Emil stumbled backward. Hanse's fist hit him in the stomach, and he fell. Hanse kicked his son's body twice before stepping over him and opening the door.

"I choose never to see you again," Hanse Wensela said. "If you ever speak to me or attempt to communicate with me in any way, I shall kill you."

He slammed the door.

Emil lay on the floor a long time, his eyes filled with tears. "I tried," he mumbled, "Lord Jesus, I tried. Please, please forgive him. Please, make him human—"

Then Emil stopped. He recalled the evening at David Morgan's church when God had spoken through young Nick Strenk and told them not to pray for the people again.

"O God," he said, "I know he made his choice a long time ago, and I guess he's been dead most of his life." He stood up and held on to the door knob to get his full balance.

"The worst part, God, is that I love him. I don't know why, but I still love him."

T·H·I·R·T·Y O·N·E

Emil didn't have to worry about money, because his father had made him financially independent years earlier. But he didn't care about that money now and had no desire to use any of those funds. His sizable inheritance through his mother would adequately provide for his needs, certainly enough to survive for a few years—and in his heart Emil knew that would be adequate time.

He boarded a commericial aero-ship to New York. Michelle, thinking it would be easier to stay away from her father, had returned to her own apartment on the lower east side.

I have to see her, Emil's thoughts kept saying. *I want to marry her. Now. Together we can work for Jesus Christ.* He would phone her from the aero-ship.

Emil's call came at exactly the right time for Michelle. She had wandered around in her apartment, not eating, not wanting to talk to anyone, not knowing what to do.

After making the decision about her father and commiting herself to hold to it, Michelle had gone into a depressed mood. Nothing enabled her to shake it off.

The night before, she couldn't sleep and lay in the dark for a long time. Michelle was convinced she had not slept for an instant; yet she kept hearing a voice, a quiet voice, repeating the same words again and again. At first Michelle thought she was imagining this voice that sounded so real and insistent.

"God, is—is that the way You speak to people?" she asked. The same words came to her again.

When Emil called, Michelle almost blurted out what had happened, but she decided to wait. She'd tell Emil, and he'd know what to do. If he didn't, they could fly to Atlanta to see David Morgan. He would guide them.

Michelle met Emil at Rockefeller Plaza, and they decided to walk. They bought a sandwich from a street vendor and went up the Avenue of the Americas.

Emil told her about the rage of his father.

"You knew before you went," Michelle said.

"I know, and you warned me, but I had to speak to him at least one time about Jesus Christ."

"I'm glad you did," Michelle said. "Now he knows—"

"Oh, he knows." He showed her the finger marks on his neck.

"Darling, I'm sorry—"

"That's over," he said. "Let's make it the past."

"You're back," she said. "That's what counts now."

"And nothing will separate us again. Not ever," Emil said. "And I think it's time we made our wedding plans."

"Before we talk about getting married," Michelle said, "I must tell you about something that happened in the middle of the night."

Michelle told Emil about her depressed mood since she had agreed not to see her father. She related how she could not sleep, but lay in the room, hearing nothing but the frequent blowing of warm air and the silence when it shut off. "Then came the voice," she said, "like a sound from inside me, but I knew it wasn't me thinking the words."

"Sounds to me like the Holy Spirit at work," he answered.

"I just kept hearing one sentence over and over. The voice said, very softly, 'Read John 21:15-22.' So I got up and read the words. I guess I must have read them twenty times."

Not being familiar with the passage, Emil asked her what the verses said. Instead, she pulled from her purse a New Testament and read the account of Jesus' last appearance to His disciples. Jesus asked Peter three times if he loved Him. Then the passage told about Peter's death and the matter of whether John lived or died in relation to Peter's question.

"Here are the parts that seemed to stand out," Michelle said as she read aloud:

> "I am telling you the truth: when you were young, you used to get ready and go anywhere you wanted to; but when you are old, you will stretch out your hands and someone else will tie you up and take you where you don't want to go." (In saying this, Jesus was indicating the way in which Peter would die and bring glory to God.) Then Jesus said to him, "Follow me." Peter turned around and saw behind him that other disciple, whom Jesus loved—the one who had leaned close to Jesus at the meal and had asked, "Lord, who is going to betray you?" When he saw him, he asked Jesus, "Lord, what about this man?"
>
> Jesus answered him, "If I want him to live until I come, what is this to you? Follow me." (John 21:18-22)

"What do these words mean?" Michelle asked.

"I think you know," Emil said softly. "And it must be hard for you to accept."

"I suppose I do know," Michelle said. "All morning I kept hearing those words of Jesus in my ears, 'What is that to you? Follow me.' Could this—is this really God speaking to me?"

"Michelle, you have to be able to hear God speak for yourself. So I'll ask you, is this God speaking?"

"Yes."

"Now what?"

"I know what I have to do," Michelle said. "I suppose I should have known all along."

"Are you strong enough to make this choice?"

"No," she said. "but I'm learning something from David Morgan. If we do what's right, strength comes."

He kissed her cheek. "Are you going to call your dad?"

"Yes," she said "and then I'm going to Atlanta."

Emil was leaving for a business meeting in Queens, and then he would take his own aero-ship to Atlanta. "I expect to be there before 5:00."

After they separated, Michelle returned to her apartment and called her father's number. He wasn't in, so she left a message on his answering machine: "Daddy, I love you. I'm coming to Atlanta today. I'll call when I arrive. You were right: I have to put God first."

Michelle had several things to do to close up her apartment. As soon as she finished, she phoned Delta Airlines and learned she could just make their 4:25 flight if she hurried. It would arrive in Atlanta at 4:58. Michelle selected one small suitcase, taking only enough clothes to last her through the next day. She didn't want anything that belonged to her mother or had come from her mother.

As Michelle left the apartment, she knew that somewhere at least one spy was lurking, watching her movements. It didn't matter anymore. She had made her choice—the choice that set her free.

Upon her arrival at Atlanta's Hartsfield Airport, Michelle raced to a phone and dialed her father's number. The answering machine responded again, so she said: "Hi, Dad, I'm at the airport. I'm going to meet Emil and then I'll call you again."

She had carried her small case on the plane with her and headed toward the baggage claim and airport exit when she saw Emil running toward her.

She raced up to him and threw her arms around him, hugging him and laughing. "I made it! I made it and I'm free!"

"I was afraid I'd miss you," Emil said as he released her. "Did you talk with your dad?"

"I haven't been able to get in touch with him. I've left two messages on his answering machine. Do you suppose we can drive to his place?"

He shook his head. "I need to tell you something." He led her to an empty waiting area, and they sat down. "Ted got your call from New York. I know that because he immediately telephoned David Morgan. He was planning to come to the airport and meet every New York flight that came in today."

"Then what happened?" she asked and suddenly didn't want to know the answer. "Oh, Emil—"

"A hit-and-run accident at Peachtree and North Avenue," Emil said. "He had come from his office and had an errand to do before driving out to meet you—"

"And, of course, the police don't know who did it . . ."

"They do. A woman driver. Four or five eyewitnesses say that your dad had a clear view of the street and then ran out in front of the car."

"You mean like a suicide?"

"I'm afraid so," Emil said.

As the tears spilled down her cheeks, Michelle said, "She told me she'd make it look like an accident. She's good at everything she does."

"I'm sorry, Michelle, I—"

"Just hold me a few minutes," she said in a tiny voice. "Let me cry it out. When I leave the airport, I want to walk with my head high and a song of victory in my heart. I owe that much to Dad."

Emil arranged for the funeral to occur two days later at Patterson's at Peachtree and Fourteenth. Since Michelle was Ted's only relative, he didn't know whom else to contact. Michelle called Johnny Burbank, but he was too ill to fly to Atlanta. Emil did telephone the Los Angeles office through whom Ted worked.

Michelle and Emil went to see the Morgans and talked with the pastor and his wife, and then Emil took her to Ted's apartment in the Dunwoody section of Atlanta.

Michelle had liked his second-floor apartment overlooking a small lake. Despite the lateness of the season, ducks were still paddling around.

She wanted to spend the night there in her father's house, and she wanted to be alone. She asked Emil to leave her there and to call her in the morning.

"I need a little time by myself," she said. "I can feel close to him here."

Michelle turned on the lights and walked through the five rooms. Ted wasn't a particularly tidy man, but he had hired a cleaning woman who kept the apartment looking reasonably neat. Michelle walked from room to room touching his possessions, especially the ones that meant the most to him. She sat down at his desk and stared at the IBM-PC30 on which he worked at home. Tears spilled from her eyes and she thought of his sitting in the chair, punching away at the keyboard.

Then, quite unaware of her reason, Michelle turned on the machine. She idly looked at the projects on which he had worked. Then she saw one called *Michelle*. She pressed the key, and the entire file appeared in a form so reduced she couldn't read it. Michelle commanded the computer to give it to her one line at a time. He had dated it the day before:

> If you're reading this letter, then you know
> I'm dead and you'll know that your mother
> kept her word.
>   Michelle, I remind you of the promises
> of God and the true peace which only God's
> people can experience. I'm grateful to God

for bringing you into the eternal Kingdom,
and I know that we'll meet again at the feet
of Jesus Christ. And I sense it will be soon.

Forgive Annella. She is under the Devil's total control. Forgive her so you can live
with love and peace.

Until we meet again, my lovely daughter, remember always that I love you and
want your happiness.

Michelle brushed the tears from her eyes and read the
short message a second time. "Oh, Dad," she said.

The telephone rang. Michelle jumped and looked
around. She had fallen asleep on Ted's sofa. The lamps were
still on, though daylight was streaming through the room.
Groggily she picked up the receiver and answered.

"I'm so glad I finally found you," Annella said. "I've
just heard about—about your father."

"Just heard? I hardly believe that."

"Michelle, regardless of what I said to you and despite
the threat I made, I had nothing to do with your father's
death. Please believe me."

Michelle cradled the phone, trying to sort out her
thoughts, trying to decide what to believe. She finally said,
"I'd like to believe you. I'd like to believe that you wouldn't
do this to him."

"I didn't, Michelle," she said, her voice ringing with sincerity. "I heard about it on the news this morning, and then I
discovered you'd left—so I began calling and . . . Well, anyway, I want you to come back, dear."

"Very good, Mother. Excellent performance," Michelle
said without rancor in her voice. As she spoke the words, her
calmness surprised her. "You are quite convincing."

"I wouldn't do a thing like that, Michelle. I've done a
lot of rotten things in my life—"

"Oh, don't," Michelle said. "I can't recall the film, but

you sound exactly like Bette Davis. In fact, you actually do the role a little better. I'll bet if I were there with you, I'd see those deep blue eyes dripping with sadness."

"Don't, don't—"

"Don't what?"

"Please believe me—"

"Mother, I believe you. Remember, I'm your daughter. I believe you are capable of anything, and that includes murder. I believe you are so evil that you would stop at nothing to get anything you want."

"How can you talk to your own mother that way?"

"Isn't that from an Ethel Barrymore film? It's where the daughter finally realizes how wicked Barrymore had been and is leaving. Are you surprised I know all those old films? I had a lot of time alone, Mother. When you were changing men as often as you changed your hairstyle, I used to go into your film library and run those old flicks again and again."

"Michelle, don't do this to me—"

"And you know my favorite scene, Mother? You can play it if you want. It's where you say, 'I'm dirt, rotten to the core, and you're the only decent thing that ever happened in my life.' Then you're supposed to cry, really cry, Mother, and tell me that I'm the only person you love, the only person you've ever truly, totally loved."

"All right, Michelle," Annella said. "I won't play any more roles for you. But that last part—that you're the only person I've ever truly loved, is right. You are."

"I wish I could believe you."

"It's true. No matter what you think of me—"

"Mother," she said quietly, "please hear this out. I believe you. That is, I believe you believe you are telling the truth. I am probably the closest you have ever come to loving anyone. But you don't love me. You tried to mold me to be Annella Maxwell the Second, but I'm not like you. I never want to be like you. And the worse part is, I still love you. At least, I don't hate you, even though I know you plotted my father's death and did it without the slightest remorse. Goodbye, Mother . . . I'm going to hang up."

"Michelle, please, come back! Come back to me!"

"No, Mother, I can't. I may go to be with Dad soon, but I'll never be with you again."

"What is it you want?" Annella asked. "Just tell me. Anything. I can give you whatever—"

"Can you give me inner peace? Joy?"

Annella launched into a string of curses, and Michelle calmly hung up. She had heard those words of rage before. In childhood they had terrified her. Now she wondered if her mother might be terrified.

David Morgan stayed after the Bible study ended. It had lasted two hours. The handful of people present had listened eagerly, their faces showing their interest and commitment.

After they had gone, Morgan stared at the huge sanctuary, and the silence echoed in his ears. He had known it was coming to this. God had told him in many ways. Now that it had come, however, he felt crushed, wiped out.

He fell before the altar and pleaded with God for strength. He thought of the people who had once been part of the fellowship and who had slipped away, a few at a time. And David Morgan remembered that God had told him not to pray for the wicked any more, especially not for those who led them.

"I can't help it," he said. "I care for them. I know the danger they're in, and I want to rescue them."

If they won't listen to My word, if they won't listen to My Spirit speaking to their consciences, if they won't listen to your teaching, how do you think you can reach them? The Inner Voice had spoken, and he knew it.

"I don't know . . ." Although God had spoken, a heavy weight had descended upon Morgan's heart and refused to leave. "I feel so alone . . ."

You are never alone.

"I know, but I feel that way. And, God, I'm weak. I

don't think I ever realized before how weak I am and how much I want the approval of other people. I tell myself that You're the only one I have to please. But something inside me, something in my own human, fallen nature, makes me want others to like me. And I know I'm hated, laughed at, despised. Help me, God."

At last.

David Morgan sat up. "What do You mean?"

I told the Apostle Paul that My strength was perfected in his weakness. I can only give you strength when you know your weakness, My son. Now I can empower you. Now you are ready to fight the good fight. You can conquer all the forces of the enemy because you know you are weak and recognize the source of your strength.

As Morgan heard the words, he prostrated himself before the altar, too humbled to speak, too overwhelmed to think. He had no idea how long he had lain there or if he fell asleep or had dreamed, but when he stirred, he knew something had happened to him, something no human words could express.

He stared up at the stained-glass window, and he saw no light, but he heard a word—just one word—whispered, and an echo of that single word reverberated throughout the building, around and around, growing louder and louder.

Peace!

And God's peace filled his heart. David Morgan then knew that he might experience low moments in the days ahead, but he would one day kneel before Christ's throne to receive his own crown of glory.

T·H·I·R·T·Y T·W·O

R andy Rose, the youngest entrant ever, entered the Boston Marathon of 1999. Despite the unusually cold May morning, the youngster passed all the other runners by the time they hit the eighth mile. At Heartbreak Hill, the four favorites moved into their twentieth mile, aware that Rose was more than a mile ahead of them.

Randy Rose finished the Boston Marathon with an official time of one hour, fifty-nine minutes, and twenty-eight seconds. Not only a world's record—no one had ever come in under two hours—but a feat that utterly amazed everyone when they realized a young boy, only eight years old, had won the marathon.

Accusations and rumors filled the observing crowd. Is he a midget? Did they give him megamals—the refined steroids? Someone argued that Randy Rose was thirty years old, but scientists had retarded his growth to make him look young.

At the finish line Randy Rose, actually Randolph Rose, Jr., his parents in front of him, was giving interviews. His father produced a birth certificate that showed the boy had turned eight on March 13.

"How do you explain what you just did?" asked a newscaster as she thrust the microphone at the boy.

"I used to be Jim Thorpe, who you probably have heard of. Before that, I was a field and track man in England in the last century. In fact, in all my previous lives I've always been a runner or an athlete."

"You're like Yolanda?" another voice asked. "You recall your pre-living experiences?"

"Quite accurately," he said. "You see my parents have been followers of the Master Plan for twenty years. They fully surrendered themselves to the cosmos and, because they were ready, Shining One sent me."

The interview continued for nearly an hour, with question after question about his past. Then Wanda-Lynn Rose, the boy's mother, asked for a chance to say something.

She told of her involvement in a traditional church, how she had been bored and indifferent until she heard about the Master Plan and found answers to everything.

"But that's not what I wanted to say," the tall, attractive redhead said as she pushed back her lengthy mane. "I have already made contact with my next life, as well as the next life for my entire family."

"You mean—?" a member of the media said. "You don't mean that you know when you'll be born, what you'll do and—"

"I don't know all the details. Shining One says life would be terribly boring if I knew everything. But Shining One tells me that I will be a successful neurosurgeon at the end of the twenty-first century." She smiled. "Actually I don't know if I should have said that much."

"Are you the only ones who can do this?"

Randolph Rose, Sr. stepped forward, a robust man, six feet, seven inches tall, and said, "It is for those who sincerely give themselves to serve Shining One."

"Yes," Randy Rose said, "Shining One promised that I would have all the good things of this life and that in each rebirth I shall be stronger, healthier, happier, and wiser. I wouldn't want anything more than this, would you?"

"How—how do people—do we—do I—get into this?" asked another reporter.

"Tonight on the Boston Commons we are going to explain the secrets of unending life."

"Just one question," asked a young woman. "What do you think of the Christian faith—I mean, faith in Jesus Christ? Jesus is the only Savior—"

Randolph Rose's fist hammered against the woman's face, and she slumped forward. "That's what we think of a fraudulent religion that has ruined millions of people for centuries!"

"When I grow up," young Randy Rose said as he kicked at the fallen body and moved in front of her, "if there are still any of those people around, Shining One has told me that I can kill them. They are worse than cockroaches and rats. Those vermin poison minds and lead people astray."

The Rose family walked away amid heavy applause. Five other people trampled over the woman who had asked about Christ. She was bleeding internally with three cracked ribs and a ruptured spleen. Not having the strength to move, she lay on the ground, knowing that no one would come to her aid.

"Lord Jesus, receive my spirit," she said.

And the young woman heard music—more beautiful than anything she had ever heard before—and she smiled. Opening her eyes, she watched the clouds open. A voice filled her ears: "Come, blessed of My Father. Come to your rest and reward. Well done, good and faithful servant."

Bani Barakan had waited with patience for his reward in aligning the religious faiths of the East. Obsessed with power, it did not take him long to realize that Kassam Ishmael planned to push him into obscurity. This fact neither surprised nor disappointed him. He would have expected nothing less. Bani Barakan had only been waiting for the best moment to assert his rightful place as the head of One Faith.

Until Kassam Ishmael had concluded treaty talks with Great Parent Neville and FOL on the Canary Islands, to the west of the African continent, Bani Barakan waited patiently. These vital talks set world boundaries, and removed the pressure from both East and West so they could build up their forces for the eventual military encounter. Among other things, they agreed to the following:

* The two divisions of Earth would now be officially called Eastworld and Westworld.
* Neither power would admit or recognize franchised people from the opposite half of the globe.
* All Franchised Labor would come from within their own hemisphere.
* Arabic and English were the only official world languages.
* Eastworld and Westworld would erect a Temple of Faith in Jerusalem on the former site of the Mosque of the Dome. This site would also be the imaginary line that separated the two nations.

Upon successful negotiation of the treaty, Kassam Ishmael and his four top advisors were scheduled to fly to Baghdad for the One Faith Summit. This conference would set non-aggression policies with Westworld.

"I am deeply sad to announce," Bani Barakan said as he stood to address the One Faith delegates, "that a tragedy has taken place. The aerospace transport—a successor to the aero-ship and the first of its type—was transporting our beloved leader Kassam Ishmael from the Canary Islands to Baghdad. His craft exploded one hour ago over the Red Sea. No one survived."

Wailing began immediately and after a suitable time, to show respect, Bani Barakan released the few details he had received. The aerospace, a new scientific development, had departed the Canary Islands at 12:07 Eastworld time, and the flight should have taken fourteen minutes to Baghdad. Six minutes after takeoff, after crossing the African continent and flying above the Red Sea, the pilot reported a fuel leak one minute and twelve seconds prior to the explosion. "We do not suspect foul play," said Barakan as his final word.

After thirty days of mourning for the death of their leader, the presidium of One Faith unanimously elected Bani Barakan as their spiritual leader, bestowing on him the title *Al Baba*, Arabic for father.

The following day, Baba Bani spoke to the world, announcing that November 27 would be an international day of mourning, called the Day of Kassam, during which all true believers would be excused from work and would mourn the loss of their loved ones.

He further announced, "I have been in a period of spiritual retreat during these past thirty days. During those days, the Maker of the cosmos, Allah himself, spoke to me. He told me that he now is beginning to make our world the paradise promised in the days of his prophet Mohammed. I have further learned that our Allah has a name by which we may call him, and that now is the time to worship him with that name. He is *Al Moazam* (Exalted)."

The people of One Faith immediately took up the chant: "Allah is most great. I testify there is no other God but Allah, and his name is Exalted. Mohammed is his prophet, Bani is his Savior."

Great Parent Neville appeared on worldwide simul-cast, a device perfected in the late 1990s that superseded tele-media. He could speak from any place on Earth and be heard and seen at that moment in the remotest nations. Simul-cast's range also encompassed the moon, Mars, and Jupiter. When the Western prelate spoke, his voice caused non-activated sets to switch on. The colony on Saturn had not yet developed these capabilities, but Westworld technology enabled them to receive the transmission via Mars with a six-hour delay.

"My beloved children, my spiritual offspring," Great Parent said, "I have come to offer you great news. News that will enrich you now and comfort you all your days."

He spoke from the newly erected Temple of Faith in Jerusalem. The gigantic structure was actually two buildings, one facing east and belonging to One Faith. Great Parent Wheatley spoke from the side facing the west. Made of nineteen different types of marble, imported from around the world, its gold dome measured five kilometers in all four directions. The mantel and doorposts of both entrances contained rows of rubies, green emeralds, and white diamonds. Both doors opened to immense amphitheaters.

"I shall speak to you first," said Great Parent Neville, "and when I have finished, Baba Bani will address you from the east side of this magnificent edifice." He spoke in English, which was simultaneously translated into Arabic.

After Great Parent Neville concluded, Baba Bani said, "We have truly entered The Emerald Age—the age when all mysteries are being made known to us. It is the time when we, the present generation, are as wise as the gods. Are we not gods? Are we not merging into the cosmos?"

Great Parent Neville spoke a second time, sounding like an old-fashioned orator as he thundered on about The Emerald Age and what yet lay ahead of those who totally followed the Shining One.

"You have perhaps heard of a young girl named Yolanda or a boy named Randy. And today I am able to tell you that each of us is offered this same opportunity. We have the power to live as we are, to stay at our present age, or we can choose *Voluntary Liberation.*

"I use the word *liberation* instead of death because leaving Planet Earth involves a throwing off of the aches and pains, the problems, the hardships of this present life. To those who select VL—Voluntary Liberation, I as your spiritual leader am authorized to give the full assurance that you can select your role in your next life. For a limited time, those who elect VL will have the right to choose their next lives, beginning in the year 2025. Furthermore, VLs will have full memory of every pre-living experience, as well as the accumulation of all knowledge and wisdom you have acquired through the ages of your births."

Great Parent Neville pleaded for the infirm, the sick, the mentally and physically weak to consider Voluntary Liberation. He also urged families of such people to use their persuasive ability to help these candidates to understand their unparalleled opportunity.

"I have prayed for you," he said. "I have earnestly entreated for you with Shining One, who assures me that all is ready for you and that the outstretched arms of love and acceptance are open to you. Those who have the courage, who dare to believe in our benevolent Shining One, may express their wishes for their next life, and within reason they will receive exactly what they dare to ask for. And as a final incentive, Shining One assures me that after the year 2025, the world life will be better, fuller, more joyous than it is at present."

Minutes later, Great Parent Neville turned the media event over to Baba Bani. He called the members of One Faith to heed this same call and to give themselves to Exalted. Citizens of Eastworld would also have the glorious option of VL open to them.

"We are at the crossroads of all knowledge. Exalted tells me that those who choose Voluntary Liberation will step forward in their progress toward perfection. Some of you will merge into a life that is unending and unaging."

Baba Bani held up a poster with the three-meters-high letters VL written in red in both Arabic and English. "These posters will appear in all public places in Eastworld. Great Parent Neville is preparing to place them everywhere in Westworld."

When Great Parent Neville had another chance to speak, he said, "Shining One tells me that this offer is not for always. You must choose within one month." He chuckled and smiled. "After that, no promises like those offered today. From then on, it involves a series of spiritual exercises to prepare yourself for merging into the cosmos."

Thunderous clapping, chanting, and singing filled the amphitheaters on the East and the West.

Over the next thirty days, One Faith made daily reports of VL, and so did FOL. Most newscasts and newspapers showed them side by side, one day One Faith having more than FOL, only to be reversed by the following report. At the conclusion of the thirtieth day, One Faith boasted of having eighteen million who had performed VL, although Baba Bani knew the figures were slightly inflated and that the true count was closer to fifteen million.

A wave of anger swept over Baba Bani when he saw that FOL had twenty-four million VLs. He met with his advisors, asking if they should demand a recount.

"Let them win this one," they counseled him. "When we conquer them, there will be just that fewer left to eliminate."

Baba Bani smiled. "You advise me well. And I shall tell you the promise of Exalted. When the day comes for us to oppose the infidels, all of those we destroy will not receive life again. Their souls will go into oblivion!"

A quiet nod or a smile from each of his advisors convinced Baba Bani that Exalted had given him great wisdom.

T·H·I·R·T·Y T·H·R·E·E

"**U**nderstand," ABC's Sam Lesser said to David Morgan with his economical use of words, "we did best for you. Gave you opportunity. ABC put you on television screens across Westworld. Some in Eastworld."

"I know," Morgan answered. "You did your best. I did my best. We have nothing to regret."

"Troubles me," Lesser said. He had flown to Atlanta to meet with David Morgan.

As the pastor wondered why the executive had bothered to come in person, the older man started pacing Morgan's office. "I believe you." He continued walking.

"My message, you mean?" Morgan asked.

"Yes."

"Then those years of speaking weren't wasted."

He shrugged. "I don't disbelieve."

"Maybe, Sam, you'd better tell me what you're really trying to say."

"I'm troubled. Conscience?" He laughed. "Think I have a conscience?"

"Why not? God created all of us capable of responding." Morgan sat quietly, watching the agitated features of the man. Sam's florid complexion, his two hundred pounds of weight that had been accumulating over the years, made him seem to stoop slightly from the load.

"You—think—God could—would—might—?"

Tempted to jump in, Morgan waited, sensing the importance of Lesser saying it himself.

"Possible God forgive me?"

"Yes."

"You don't know me. Bad things in the past—"

"I don't need to know. I'm willing to listen if you feel the need to get it off your chest. God knows, and God's the one who forgives."

Sam fell on his knees in front of David. For the first time in more than twenty years, he broke his lifetime habit of holding back with words. "I've been fighting God for months, and I don't know what to do." In the longest monologue Sam Lesser had ever made in his life, he confessed his fears and his present quandary. "If I give in, if I surrender to Jesus Christ, I'll lose my job. That's quite clear, David. Whether you're aware of it or not, FOL has been slowly ingratiating itself, and now dictates policy to the entire media. We must be a member in good standing with FOL to hold any position—any job, even in the mailroom—"

"I knew that was happening," Morgan said. "Which is one reason I've been surprised you've allowed me to keep on."

"Only because I demanded that they leave you alone and let you become the butt of everybody's jokes. But you were no joke to me, David. You were—well, you were—you *are* a messenger of God."

David laid his hands on the balding head of Sam Lesser and started to pray. "God, thank You for bringing Sam to this point in his life . . .

" As Morgan continued to pray, he also thanked God for giving him fruit in his dark hour.

Morgan faced new problems. The remaining seventy faithful members of his church could no longer afford the upkeep of the building. He had urged them to sell the property years earlier. Now they had no choice. They put the property on the market, but despite its prime location, they could find no one to buy. Morgan knew why.

"Perhaps we could just give the building away," he said. "We could meet in a school—"

"No," Joe Strenk said, "the word is out. We won't find any building, any school, any place that will allow us to meet."

"Then perhaps it is time that we move back into the method of the first-century disciples," Morgan said. "We could meet in homes."

"You're welcome at our home," Joe said, "but you also ought to know that Atlanta will soon pass a zoning law that forbids meetings of more than six people unless they are related."

Lisa Strenk put her arm around her husband. "Of course, they won't enforce these rulings," she said, "except when it comes to people like us."

"Let's decide right now what to do," young Nick Strenk said. "I'm not afraid."

"I know you're not," Morgan answered and ruffled the boy's hair. "Right now we pray. God will guide us."

After the faithful members of the church prayed, a measure of peace filled them. They soon departed from the building.

After they had gone, David Morgan walked the length of the property. He had never wanted this building, never been interested in bigness. "Or maybe," he said to God, "maybe I really did, but I knew it wouldn't last."

As he walked, his spirit downcast, he recalled the words of Jeremiah and said aloud, "The heart is deceitful above all things and desperately wicked. And I know that doesn't eliminate *me*."

Morgan wondered if he ought to stop trying to teach. He knew that the forces of FOL were gearing up to persecute those who still held to true faith in Jesus Christ. He wondered if his stubbornness endangered the lives of other believers.

David hadn't noticed the car that pulled up or the couple who got out. They watched him as he completed the swing around the property. When Morgan saw them, they waved and came toward him.

"Michelle! Emil!" he said. He had not seen them since he had performed their marriage a month earlier. They had flown to Europe, then to California, and finally to New York. They both had business ends to tie up so they could live in Atlanta.

The three embraced and chatted, and then the couple joined him as he continued to walk around the property. They had heard of the church's inability to sell.

"You know why, don't you?" Michelle said. "Mastermind is trying to force you out of business. If you can't sell, you can't keep up the bills, so you file bankruptcy and are disgraced."

"I don't mind the personal disgrace," Morgan said.

"Yes, yes, you do," Emil said, his eyes fixed on him. "You did a lot of wonderful things, David. You reached many people—"

"And where are those many people now?"

"That's not the point," Emil said. "And I'm a little reluctant to do this, but I have something I need to say to you."

"Don't hold back."

"It's not easy," he said. "You're my spiritual father. You brought me to faith in Christ."

"Oh, oh, this sounds like something I'm not going to like." Morgan forced a laugh. "But if you have a word from God for me, say on."

"David, God told me to tell you something: some pride still lurks in your heart. A part of you won't accept failure. Until you do, you're going to keep on with your up-and-down moods."

David said nothing, walking slowly onward for several

minutes, and then he stopped, clutching both their hands. "You're right. And oddly enough I had been thinking of Jeremiah 17:9 just before you came. That's the verse that says the heart is deceitful above everything else and that none of us really knows our true self. That includes me."

"Then you do understand?" Michelle asked. "We didn't want to bring you harsh words. It seems like you've been beaten down enough."

"Not quite enough," David said. "I realize now that my kingdom has fallen, and my reputation is on the line. That's one of the things that troubles me. I'm worried about me and what people will think instead of being concerned only about God's glory. I wish it weren't true."

"But it is," Michelle said. "That's why we came today. God knows your weaknesses, and God loves you."

"And God is the one who gives us light, who instructs us," Emil said.

David laughed. "You know, when God warned us of hard times to come, dwindling numbers and all that, I felt so strong, so capable. I can handle it, I remember thinking. You've just dashed me into the ground and stepped all over me."

Michelle clasped his hand. "I'm so sorry—"

"Don't be," David said. He draped his free arm around Emil's shoulder. "I've tried to say for a long time that we are all ministers of God, that we—"

"We love you, David," Michelle said. "And it wasn't easy for Emil to speak those words to you."

"It's because I know you love me that I could hear them," David said. "But they still hurt. They hurt because they're true." Morgan's eyes moistened, and he looked heavenward and said softly, "God, forgive me for my pride, for my self-blindness."

"I have a further word for you, David," Emil said and he smiled. "God also sent me to tell you that because much has been required of you, much will be given. Don't ask me to interpret that—I'm only the messenger."

David pulled the couple closer into an embrace. "I need

you. I need your strength. I have God on my side, but for the first time in my life, I know I need people too." The words didn't come easily to David, but he knew he had to say them. "I've always believed that with Jesus Christ on my side I could handle anything. Until now I never grasped—just now—that God never intended me to survive and grow alone."

"You've always been available when we needed you," Michelle said. "I'm glad we could be here for you."

"I wonder if I'll ever learn."

"I think you just did." Emil, in European fashion, kissed David's left cheek, while Michelle kissed the other.

Mastermind's voice spewed out anger all afternoon. "He has escaped my clutches! He has eluded me once again!"

"Who?" asked Maison Quayle, already knowing the answer.

"Do not mock me," Mastermind said. "I made you and I can destroy you, just as I intend to destroy that preacher!"

The others then realized that Mastermind referred to David Morgan.

"I almost had him. He was ready to quit, ready to yield, and now he's stronger than ever."

"But he's got a mere forty, maybe sixty people on his side," Maison Quayle said. "Not many left."

"You are sometimes a fool! He has thousands in Atlanta and pockets of them around the world. But worse, it is that one group—that self-willed, strong group—that thwarts me!"

"I could rig a bomb—"

"You fool! Marytrdom is what we cannot have! Some of those who have come into our clutches would use just that fact to slip away from us. No, we shall find another way. And we shall find it soon."

Silence reigned in the room until Mastermind, speaking

calmly, said, "I have a plan that will work, and we shall be able to kill them—those who refuse to bow their knees to me. We will convince the world that these people are criminals, deceivers, frauds. We'll make the people of the world scream for their blood!"

Maison Quayle cocked an eye, but had the sense to say nothing. Yet, for the first time doubt filled his mind, as if he knew that Morgan and those like him had something even Mastermind could not conquer. He wondered what it was.

Clara Wensela, Emil's mother, had wisely invested her personal capital, most of it in places her husband had not known about. She knew her husband despised her—she had known ever since the night after their wedding when he told her it was a marriage of convenience. "*My* convenience," he had said. "I saved you from spinsterhood, and you have fortified my investment capital."

Fortunately Clara had income he did not know about, and, working through a prudent and closed-lipped broker, she had sunk her money into American investments. At that time, all of it was far away from her husband's knowledge and reach.

By the time he discovered her duplicity, he smiled to himself, never allowing her to have the pleasure of being told that he knew. In the end it would make no difference, he decided. Clara loved her son, and she would leave everything to Emil—which was exactly what Hanse Wensela wanted.

There was only one thing about the mother's and son's relationship Hanse had not known. At age fourteen, when the boy struck his mother at the command of Hanse, that night Emil waited until his father had gone to sleep, then sneaked into his mother's bedroom, laid his face against hers, and whispered, "I'm sorry" before scurrying from the room.

It had been a moment of weakness for young Emil, and it would have humiliated him had his mother ever mentioned it. Clara said nothing, keeping it her secret. Each day she prayed for her son, pleading that God would intervene and change the boy.

Clara had been a nominal Lutheran before her marriage, a faith she had inherited from her people, who had been Lutherans for at least six generations. But imprisonment in her own home, along with the utter degradation and repeated insults by her husband, forced her to find solace for herself. She had found it in Jesus Christ.

Before Clara died at age forty, an emotionally battered woman, she was at peace. She had suspected (correctly) that her husband had been slowly poisoning her over a period of months. Clara could have refused the morning cup of tea her husband personally brought to her. But if she did not allow him to triumph in this way, he would easily find another. Her one sadness was that Emil, to all accounts, was working at becoming like his father.

Clara, however, knew one thing about her son: he worked hard at being immoral and underhanded. Cruelty did not come naturally to the boy. And in that truth lay her hope. And her prayers. On the day she died, she prayed, "God, let me die in peace. And I shall have that peace only if You give me some kind of sign that You will change my son." Clara knew the sign she wanted from God.

She called Emil to her room, scarcely able to talk. "I am dying," Clara Wensela said. "I have something to tell you, and you must listen to my words carefully." She told him of her investments in America, mostly real estate in Southern California. And she had, on a whim, made smaller investments in the Southeast which had quadrupled in value. "I ask only that you not sell the property in the East. You must wait until someone needs the land, and then I want you to give it to them."

"Give it away?" Emil said. "Free?"

"This is part of my final wish," Clara said. "Will you?"

"Father won't like such an agreement."

"Don't tell him," she said. "All my holdings will become yours to do with as you please. My son, I have never begged you for anything before. I beg you to promise you will carry out this one request."

"Seems stupid!" Emil said, and his voice sounded like his father's. Then his tone softened, and he said, "I'll hold on to the land until I find someone who needs it and then give it away."

Clara smiled, despite the excruciating pain around her heart. She was losing strength and knew she had one more thing to do before she could rest. "I have only this." She opened her hand, which had clutched a gold chain with a cross. "Wear this for me."

"Wear that stupid relic?" he asked and pulled back.

"As a favor to a dying woman, as a last request of the woman who has loved you all your life." She held the chain up to him.

Emil took the object from her hand and put it around his neck. She could read his eyes and knew he planned to take it off after her death. His intention did not concern her, because she had asked God to make Emil accept the chain and, regardless of his intentions, never take it off.

She smiled and kissed his hands. Clara closed her eyes and, yielding to the pain at last, died with a smile on her face despite the intensification of pain that gripped her feeble heart.

Clara did not see the tears in her son's eyes, and he dried them quickly before he called a servant to notify his father.

And now, thirteen years later, Emil Wensela still wore the cross. For years he had hated the chain, despised the cross, and cursed himself for being so weak. When he was with women who teased him about wearing a cross, he had learned to laugh and say, "It is my good luck charm."

As the couple drove away from the church property, Emil Wensela, wearing a white shirt and hand-painted tie, felt the familiar chain under his shirt. He was thankful he had kept his promise. Now he had one important thing to do.

T·H·I·R·T·Y F·O·U·R

David and Katherine Morgan met Emil for lunch at a small cafe on Pharr Road in the Buckhead area. Emil wanted the meeting in a public place and yet with some privacy. Although his father's spies no longer trailed him, out of years of habit he didn't want anyone close enough to hear.

He handed David Morgan an envelope.

"What's this?"

"It's a deed to a piece of property with a modern building already erected on it. As a matter of fact, it's less than two kilometers from the church."

"And you give it to me because—?"

"Because it's property given to me by mother before she died. The bottom floor has two large showrooms, not currently being used. The other ten floors are all businesses with leases that will not expire for another ten years. Actually, I just renewed the leases for them at lower rates than they would have expected. And should they decide to move, they must still pay the rental or they will sublease. So your church has a place to meet. The income from the occupants will more than pay for the upkeep and provide a reasonable salary for you."

"That's wonderful," Katherine said.

Emil explained that this had been given to him by his dying mother and that part of the stipulation was that it must never be sold, only given away.

"Another bit of news for you, my friend. Yesterday Michelle and I paid all bills owed by the church. We gave the utility companies notice you were leaving the property and have paid them handsomely. They will have some rebate to send to you when you finally move out."

"Emil, thanks."

"On this one, my dad is the provider—without his knowing. Years ago he established accounts for me in a dozen banks around the world. I decided I'd use a little of that money for the church. When he learns what I've done—and he will—he'll find ways to cut off all those accounts. But in the meantime he's done something decent. At least once."

After Katherine and David expressed their thanks, Emil stood and said, "I have to meet Michelle right away. But one more thing . . . I have a buyer for the property. You're getting cheated by today's prices, but he'll take it off your hands and give you five hundred thousand dollars. He plans to knock down all the buildings and erect condo co-ops, the big thing now coming into Atlanta."

"Where do we sign?"

"He'll be at your office today. According to your bylaws you and four members of your Board of Elders must sign. Any problem there?"

"None at all!"

Before Mastermind laid out his plan, he said, "Hanse Wensela, for this plan to work, you must know what I propose. And it involves the death of your son."

"Emil? What has he to do with this?"

"Do not turn naive now," Mastermind said. "He has embraced that religion of Morgan."

"I am well aware of the stupidity of my son."

"And you aren't aware of what he has done this very week for that man?"

The mute man stared at Mastermind. He had purposefully not pried into his son's activities for months. He no longer cared what happened to Emil, but the words of his son tormented him when he thought of them. If only he could exorcise them from his mind, but they seemed determined to stay, to torment him virtually every day.

Hanse Wensela had been drinking more heavily and relied more than ever upon tranquilizers to sleep. Whenever his son came to mind, so did his son's words. Despite all Hanse's resolve and hardness, one man had penetrated to his core, and he despised his son for what he had done.

"I am going to destroy him!" Mastermind said.

"I am willing to do whatever you want," Hanse Wensela answered. "He is my son because I helped to give him life. He is not my son in either behavior or attitude. I hate Emil! I hate everything he stands for!"

"Ah," Mastermind said, "then we are ready to proceed."

One Faith and FOL had begun to cooperate in international legislation, and by the beginning of the year 2000 they had jointly enacted a criminal code, so that no fugitive could go from one domain to the other to escape prosecution.

And now, six weeks before what many had once celebrated as Easter, both powers brought charges against a group they referred to as "Friends of Jesus."

Great Parent Neville announced, as he stood on the East dais in Jerusalem with a smiling Baba Bani at his side, "We are here together to show you our mutual cooperation. I, the leader of the religion of Westworld, have come to speak on the religion of the East side. We are standing together—"

He paused to raise one of Baba Bani's hands and one of his own in triumph. "We are united to make known to the world the deceitful practices of one religious group . . . A group that has paraded itself as being moral has now been shown to have been attempting to overthrow both our legal governments."

"They call themselves Friends of Jesus," spat Baba Bani. "Had they been His friends, they would have been at peace and embraced us lovingly."

"They are deceptive people. Friends of Jesus is the name they use among themselves. They have pledged to deny their affiliation with any such organization. But we have painstakingly gathered proof over a period of two years."

The two men turned to Kurt Legait, Supreme World Judge, appointed jointly by the two groups. Crimes involving both Eastworld and Westworld came before the World Court. After reading the charges against the Friends of Jesus, Supreme World Judge Legait explained them.

Although involving forty-nine charges, he reduced them to three categories: first, actively plotting to overthrow the legitimate leadership of One Faith and FOL (if convicted, the mandatory sentence was death); second, attempting to proselytize from the two faiths (this action had been declared illegal since August 1998); third, insisting on a religion that elevated a single deity above that of either One Faith or FOL. The joint law of 1999 declared that both faiths, which included a multiplicity of minor deities, were of equal stature. To insist upon the prominence of one was to denounce others. The Friends of Jesus, stated the charges, had constantly and repeatedly, despite ample warning, continued their outrageous activities of saying that Jesus was not merely superior to other deities, but that He alone was supreme and without equal.

Judge Legait declared a six-day amnesty. "This period should be sufficient for such accused rogues to put their affairs in order and to appear before my court. Because the law wishes to demonstrate compassion, those who renounce their illegal practices and present themselves to my court will receive a full pardon."

Kurt Legait, the son of an American father but a Palestinian Arab mother, had built up a reputation of being humane and caring. Few knew the hardness within the core of the man, and he seldom expressed it. As he made his pronouncements, he secretly hoped that the choice of his words would enrage all friends of Jesus.

No actual group, organization, or fellowship existed with the name Friends of Jesus. In a secret meeting two weeks earlier, Legait, in concert with Baba Bani and Great Parent Neville, had come up with the term. By presenting charges with doctored evidence, they anticipated they could arouse the ire of the world's population.

"Remember," Mastermind had instructed his six servants, "you are now powerful enough to do whatever you choose. No one is strong enough to stand against you. However, it is wiser if you have popular support behind you. In time all denizens of Westworld and Eastworld will agree to anything you do. Such an attitude will make your work considerably easier."

As Hanse Wensela listened to the instructions of Mastermind, his mind frequently returned to Emil. How could he ever have sired such a son? How could this young man, who had shown some promise—limited as it was—while a child, have gone into such confusion and waywardness? Flawed child. Hanse had known, of course, that the boy did not inherit an innate hardness, but he had blithely assumed he could enable Emil to compensate for his handicap. How wrong he had been.

Next to Wensela sat Maison Quayle, smiling to himself. His twin sons had proven to be men after his own heart. They had continued in the way their father had taught them. Compliant chaps, both of them. He could foresee the day when they would replace members of the Mastermind. After all, men like Wensela and Sari were growing older and clearly had begun to lose their grip.

Patience is the key, he reminded himself. Because Maison Quayle was not by nature a patient man, he had to remind himself regularly. His Spiritual Enabler comforted him during this period, reminding him often that he was destined for great things.

"And your offspring," said the Spiritual Enabler, "will have even greater honor than you because you have made it possible. When you return in the next life, Shining One will place you above the power of your sons and your sons' sons."

These days Maison Quayle felt more confident, more satisfied than he ever had in his life. Only one thing troubled him. They still had one enemy who must be destroyed. They had to rid the world of David Morgan and his followers.

He had never met Morgan, although he had seen many hours of film, had heard his videos and listened to taped sermons. He had hated Morgan from the beginning with a special, deep hatred reserved only for the most pious in the world. But with Morgan he experienced one other thing; he felt fear.

David Morgan had met Katherine Miller in high school and had loved her from the first time he saw her. She had grown up in a home where her parents had loved Jesus Christ and diligently taught their daughter and son about their faith.

Katherine was one of those fortunate individuals who had never questioned her faith in Jesus Christ, who never doubted the God who loved her and could not recall a time when she did not know she belonged to God.

David Morgan, a bright, questioning newcomer to the tenth-grade class, sat directly behind her because teachers routinely seated their students alphabetically. He spoke to her at the end of the first class session in English Literature and again that afternoon in Sociology.

On the third day he invited Katherine to go to a party with him. "Just a few people. You know, a little boozing, a little dancing . . ."

"I don't think so," Katherine said.

Her words, direct as they were, didn't come across as harsh or make David feel rejected. He rightly picked up her message: she wasn't interested in that kind of party.

The next day he asked, "What do you do for fun?"

"Lots of things."

"For example?" he pushed.

"Oh, I'm involved with a youth group at Trinity Church," she said. "We go skating, hiking . . . we play soccer, volleyball. Sometimes we have a game night. Or we see a film together and then, over chili at somebody's house, we discuss what we saw."

"You sound like you do a lot of things," he said, trying to make conversation and decide how to approach her for another date.

"Would you like to visit our youth group?" she asked. "We're having a backwards party Saturday."

David Morgan arched his brow and stared at her. "Backwards party? What's that?"

"Oh, we just do everything backward. You know, we leave the party at the beginning by moving in backward and saying 'Good night.' We play games, but we start from the end of the game and go back to the start. We eat dessert first. Why, we even wear our clothes backward—those we can."

"Sounds different."

"You mean it sounds boring?"

"A little."

"Then maybe another time—"

"Not so fast, Katherine," he said. "If I can go there with you, I don't mind the party being boring."

They continued talking as they walked down the hallway, until David left her in front of the biology room and he went on to chemistry. He decided no party would be boring if he had Katherine beside him.

To David's surprise, he had fun. He saw other students from school, a group he had never paid much attention to before. Because he expected the youth group to be filled with nerds and DPs—displaced persons, a term his friends used to describe social misfits—the whole evening turned out great. Instead of only quiet kids, DPs, and nerds, David saw three of the football jocks. David, a field-and-track enthusiast, chatted with Phil Barnhart, one of his competitors.

For the next six weeks, David didn't know if he continued with the Trinity Youth Fellowship because of Katherine or because of the fun and newfound friends. But by the end of tenth grade, David was one of them.

By the time he entered eleventh grade, David had professed faith in Jesus Christ. Yet his faith had not come easy. He had laughingly called himself a semi-atheist, but he meant what he said. Until then he hadn't decided if God existed. Then, through Katherine's influence, David went to church, Sunday school, and youth rallies and read all the literature his Christian friends gave him. He read the Bible every day. Finally David Morgan could acknowledge that the material made sense.

One day David said, "I've never had a slam-bang kind of emotional experience that turned me to Christ, the way some of the others have, but I know I believe it. I'm ready to stake my life on it."

"Maybe someday you'll have to," laughed Phil Barnhart. "You know, it may not always be easy for Christians in this country. One day all of us might have to take a stand for what we believe."

"You may be right."

"And some of us may have to die for what we believe," Phil said.

David forgot the conversation and never thought of it again until the day he heard of the charges against the Friends of Jesus. Even then, he would have paid little attention except that Kurt Legait singled out both Barnhart and

Morgan in particular, referring to them as ringleaders and co-conspirators.

"What happens now?" Katherine asked.

"Only God knows," David answered.

"And He's the one who counts," she said as she kissed his cheek.

David pulled Katherine close and held her. "I don't know what I'd do if I didn't have you," he said. "You helped push me into the faith. You've always been at my side—"

"And I love you."

"Without you, Katherine, I'm not sure if I could make it."

Katherine placed her slender fingers against his lips. "Don't say that," she said softly. "You have God. If I'm not here, you'll always have God's comforting love."

"You're right, of course, but—"

"You know I'm right," she said. Katherine snuggled close, and the two of them sat quietly together, no need for words, both of them aware that time was running out in the world as they silently prayed for each other.

On Tuesday, the third day of the six-day amnesty, Katherine left the house a few minutes after eleven. On Tuesdays she visited patients in a nursing home in the Shallowford area of Atlanta. Her trips had begun years earlier when her elderly uncle, Robert Miller, diagnosed as having Alzheimer's, went to live in the nursing home. She visited him every Tuesday, and sometimes on other days of the week also. During those times, Katherine took time to greet and help other patients—some suffering from Alzheimer's, most of them from other debilitating diseases. Long after Robert died, she continued to visit every Tuesday.

Since Voluntary Liberation had become popular, few patients remained in the nursing home. Many of them forced the medical staff to overdose them so they could leave their pain-filled lives. Doctors, concerned for the well-being of their patients, complied, saying, "It is the best we can do for them."

On this Tuesday she parked her car and started up the

ramp to the nursing home. Four women were emerging, and one of them stared at her and said, "You're that preacher's wife, aren't you? That Morgan fellow?"

"Yes, I am."

Katherine Morgan never had the chance to say another word. The woman accurately plunged a knife into her heart.

An hour later, the police telephoned David Morgan with the news. The speaker barely concealed the hostility in his voice. "We have the woman in custody, and she's temporarily sedated. Apparently her sister once belonged to your church before she became involved with the Friends of Jesus and is now one of those facing trial in Jerusalem. She blames you and your wife for making the sister a fanatic."

"I see," David said, then asked about the body of his wife. She was at the Shallowford Community Hospital, which was awaiting instructions from the next of kin.

"I'd advise you to get the body out of there right away," the policeman said. "A lot of people are pretty angry about . . . well, you know."

"And have convicted us without trial."

David thanked the policeman and hung up. He called Michelle and Emil and told them what happened. They met him at the hospital, and the three of them walked inside together. Katherine's body was in a locked room on the second floor. An aide, barely in her twenties, Beth Lapsley, took them to her.

"She has thirty stab wounds," Beth said. "The first one was all it took."

"Thank you—"

"No one else was willing to talk to you," she said. "That's why I brought you. Look, I may get in trouble if they know I said this, but . . . please get her body out of here. If you leave without her, I promise you that you'll never see her in this condition again. I don't know what they'll do, but it'll be something—terrible—"

"We'll make arrangements right away."

David went in search of a telephone and found one in the lobby. He called every funeral home and every ambulance service, but as soon as they learned his name, they explained they were unable to help him. At first David was shocked, but by the time he had telephoned the fourth place, he realized all of them would give him the same answer.

He finally tried a black funeral home in Jonesboro on Atlanta's south side. The owner, who answered the phone, said, "Look, Mr. Morgan, we've already gotten the word not to respond to you. But I'll come anyway."

"Who put out the word?"

"Dunno," he said, "but it came yesterday afternoon from a high official in the FBI. If you called today, we were to refuse to help. That's all I can tell you."

"Yesterday?"

"Yessir," he said. "Does that mean anything?"

"Never mind," Morgan said. "Thank you for telling me. Don't come. You'll only have trouble for yourself."

"I'm a Christian—"

"Then stay alive and live for Jesus," David said, buoying his voice. "I'll take care of my wife."

After David told Michelle and Emil about the situation, he said, "We have to do this ourselves."

After a few minutes of quiet whispering in the hallway outside the telephone both, they decided that Emil would go out to the parking lot and drive the car around to the side entrance. "I think that's the least noticeable way to get out," David said.

"If we try to go through the channels here, I'm sure they'll find ways not to release her," Michelle said, voicing all their thoughts.

David's heart was breaking as he thought of what had happened. They—Mastermind's followers—had planned Katherine's murder. The word had been passed out a day earlier. And, he suspected, they wanted him to find this out so it would add to his despair.

Michelle and David located Beth Lapsley at the nurses' desk and asked her to take them back to the room.

"Awful busy right now," she said, not looking up at them.

"Then would you give me the key and I'll go by myself?"

"Can't do that," she said, her voice cold and efficient. "Against orders."

"What do you propose we do then? Stand here and wait until you're not busy?"

"I'm going to be busy a long time."

Michelle and David looked at each other, uncertain about their next step. Emil came down the hallway from the side entrance.

"She's gone!" he hissed. "The room's empty. Somebody is in there cleaning up."

David turned to the nurses' station again. "Where is my wife's body?"

The pain on the woman's face made David blanch.

"I don't know what you're talking about," Beth Lapsley said. "Who do you mean?"

"You know who I mean! Katherine Morgan."

"I'd have to check the records and see if we have anyone here by that name. I'll call Admissions!"

"She was here five minutes ago," David said, already sensing the uselessness of his words. As Beth Lapsley turned to the telephone, she inconspicuously pushed a sheet of paper his way.

David stared at what he read: THEY HAVE STOLEN THE BODY AND YOU WON'T GET IT BACK. GET OUT OF HERE. A GANG WILL BE HERE IN A FEW MINUTES TO CAUSE A RIOT AND TO KILL YOU.

David stared at the camera that scanned that section of the hospital. He knew the woman was telling the truth.

"Come here a minute," he said to Michelle and Emil as he took them both by the arm and led them back down the hallway. "We have to get out of here . . . right now," he whispered. "They're after us. Just move normally, and we'll walk on out through the door. Let's all get into your car, Emil. I don't think we can trust going around to the front and getting mine."

A minute later, they hustled into the car, Emil and Michelle in front. As Emil started the engine, he said, "Drop down to the floor. I have a feeling there might be people waiting for you in front."

Emil turned the radio on to a music station, the volume up loud, and drove through the parking lot. Near the front door of the hospital, he saw a band of seven men going inside. At the sound of his car they stopped and stared. One of them took a step forward, but another grabbed his arm and shook his head.

Once away from the hospital, Emil turned off the radio. "Well, we made it this time," he said.

In the silence that filled the vehicle, all three of them sensed what lay ahead and wondered how long before the Mastermind closed in on them.

T·H·I·R·T·Y F·I·V·E

David Morgan had to think, and he had to be alone to do that kind of thinking. Not able to sit at home, he didn't dare visit any of his friends. He drove Emil's other car through Midtown. Assuming safety lay in moderately traveled streets, Morgan avoided side streets. At Fourteenth he turned and drove down to Piedmont Park. Leaving the car in a shady spot, he started walking.

It was midafternoon, a warm but breezy day, and people were beginning to fill up the park. A soccer team had started to practice in one spot, and across from them he spotted a softball team of teenagers readying themselves for a game.

David walked, always keeping in sight of people, not wanting to be caught alone. He realized that Mastermind could use crowds and stir them up; yet he felt safer with people milling around.

Until now David Morgan had refused to let his thoughts dwell on Katherine's death, afraid he would emotionally cave in. Long aware of how much his wife meant to him, David Morgan struggled with his inability to keep going alone. "She was more than a crutch," he said softly. "She was a part of me. We were truly one in our thinking, in our aims, in our commitment. O God, it's like losing part of my body. I just don't know if I can keep going."

Tears filled his eyes, but he walked on, oblivious to anyone near him. Finally the loss of Katherine became so heavy, he lay facedown, feeling the coolness of the afternoon grass against his face. Silently he wept, giving way to his pain.

Later David got up and strolled through the park, his mind on God all the time. He kept silently asking, *Why did You pick me? I'm so weak. I'm not strong in faith like Katherine or so many others. Doubts intrude. I didn't ask to be put in this spot, and I keep wondering why You didn't pick someone a little stronger.*

Strength does not mean never having doubts. True strength comes from facing doubts while you still march forward.

Hearing those words encouraged David Morgan. He wasn't going to give up. He had remained committed to his destiny, and yet he had wondered how he could continue with Katherine out of his life.

Katherine is safe. She is with Me. Always.

David sat down cross-legged on the grass and stared at the azure softness above him. Low cumulus clouds sneaked slowly across the horizon. And peace descended on him. He became so absorbed in his reverie, he did not hear the woman come up behind him.

"Mr. Morgan?"

David turned and saw her, a beautiful woman, standing two yards in front of him. "I've just heard about your wife. I came to comfort you . . . in any way you need comforting." She added softly, "Any way at all."

He laughed. "You have nothing to offer me. I'm surprised that they'd put you up to something as stupid as this!"

She shrugged. "You never know a man's low point," she said. "And I like you." She bent forward and tousled his hair. "Wouldn't you at least like to have me stay? We could talk. Just talk."

"I'm fine," David said. "Katherine's gone to a far better place, a place of peace. I expect I'll join her soon. I don't need anything else in the meantime. Be sure to tell your employers that, will you?"

"As you like," she said. "But you can't escape us, Morgan. We're too strong for you. Don't you know that yet?"

He laughed again. "If your bosses are so sure, then why did they send you? They must be having doubts themselves right now. But there is one thing you can do for me."

"Yes?" she asked and stepped toward him. "Anything."

"Tell whoever sent you that Jesus Christ is Lord! He is the eternal victor!"

"Tell him yourself!" She stalked away.

"Who is *him*?" David Morgan yelled, but she didn't turn around. It didn't matter. Whether she referred to one of the six who made up Mastermind or to the Devil behind them, it now made little difference.

That evening Emil and Michelle met David as they had arranged. "I have another favor to ask you," the pastor said. "I'm ready to stand trial before the World Court. I don't know if it will do any good, but I have to appear."

"Have you considered that they might not want you to get there?" Emil asked.

"They might try to kill you before you get to Jerusalem," Michelle said. "Or on the way."

"I figured that we might call a press meeting and announce that I'll travel to Jerusalem on my own and that I'm willing to stand trial."

"We'll take you," Michelle said. "We do have an aeroship, you know, and it has a large enough fuel capacity that we won't have to make a stop. Four hours from Atlanta and we're there."

"We're going too. Both of us," Emil said.

"You're sure you want to go?"

"I'm sure we have to," Michelle said.

"And I'm sure we don't want to stay here," Emil said as he handed David a copy of the *Atlanta Journal*.

According to the lead article, Great Parent Neville and

any who were adherents of Jesus must appear in Jerusalem to face trial. They further declared that any of those who called themselves by terms such as Christians, Friends of Jesus, Followers of the Way, or any other name that espoused a faith in the false deity named Jesus must appear. Police in every state had received orders to kill on sight any Friends of Jesus not in Jerusalem by midday Friday.

"There is no escape," Emil said, "except by denying the faith."

"Why would we want to do that?" David Morgan said. "Our faith is what gives us a purpose in living."

"Then we go together," Michelle answered.

"Together," David said as they joined hands.

Mastermind raged. He had been irritated before, angry a few times. Yet the members of the Mastermind team had never witnessed this extremity. For more than nine hours the screams and charges flew against the six. None of them had been so humiliated and stripped so utterly naked since their first meeting when Mastermind revealed their inner secrets to each other.

"I have raised a pack of fools to sit on the thrones of the world! Idiots! One man—one weak man named David Morgan—and you can't trap him or trip him up! You useless, hopeless scum!"

At the end of another hour, Mastermind shifted abruptly. "Do not think you are the only ones to whom I can give these exalted places. I empowered you, and I can just as easily destroy any of you! All of you!"

Never had the six of them experienced fear so deeply before. Minutes of silence ticked away as Annella Maxwell fought to control the surge of blood that swept through her body and then was gone, leaving her limp. Terror, stark terror, paralyzed her. Despite the warmness of the room, she shivered. She knew she was but a second away from destruction by Mastermind.

"I have decided to give each of you a final chance," Mastermind said, once again taking over the body and voice of Annella. "I shall show you how to rid ourselves once and for all of these pests of humanity. And David Morgan will be in the midst of it all. We shall share in watching him die! This time we will rid the world of all conscience through the death of these remaining filth-dwellers!"

Slowly, painstakingly Mastermind instructed them. There would be no failures allowed at the great trial.

One hundred and twenty thousand people arrived in Jerusalem on Thursday and Friday. By midmorning all the accused stood bunched together as they faced the Temple of Faith, awaiting trial. They stood in such a way that the multitude stretched from the East side to the West.

They had received no food, no facilities to wash, and no toilet arrangements. When asked for such facilities, their guards only laughed. "What difference does it make? A few hours and you will be finished anyway."

While the Christians awaited the inevitable trial and decision, something else was happening outside of their knowledge. A rumor had started in Eastworld the day before and had spread until it came to the ears of Baba Bani's Behavior Force which policed Eastworld. After a full but hurried investigation, First General Geeta approached Baba Bani's palace and informed him.

"Great Parent plans to see that the Christians are released. He has instructed Supreme World Judge Legait to release them as an act of mercy. Great Parent will then arm them so they can aid him in fighting Eastworld."

"You are certain this is true?" Baba Bani asked.

"Not certain," replied the First General. "Did I not investigate this message that came through three different sources? I would say that our information ranges in the ninety-six percent accuracy range." The man smiled and asked, "Have I ever misled you with rumors before?"

"You have done well, always," the head of Eastworld said. "I shall accept your words as one more step in your ongoing efficiency."

"Thank you, sir," First General Geeta said. "I desire only to serve you because through you I serve Exalted."

Baba Bani stared into space as he said, "We shall thwart our enemy and be prepared to meet the intrigue of Westworld." Baba Bani gave orders to arm his soldiers, but quietly and without calling undue attention to this fact. If questioned, they were to say they suspected that the Friends of Jesus would try to fight for their lives and they were preparing themselves so that they could protect the public against them.

Within hours of Eastworld preparations, the superior spy network of FOL prepared to report to Great Parent Neville. They had also picked up rumors; combining this information with known facts, a delegation went to inform their leader.

Great Parent Neville faced a difficult decision and hesitated to make it by himself. He called Edmund Staats into his office. After explaining the rumors, the arming of Eastworld soldiers, and their deceptive arrangement, he said, "So it seems simple enough: Baba Bani and his toadying First General Geeta have conspired with Supreme World Judge Legait who will convict the Jesus followers and sentence them to immediate death. Once they have executed the Christians, Eastworld will declare that we pulled strings, influencing the court's decision when the evidence of their innocence was clear-cut. Baba Bani will remind the world of the closeness we have had in the past with this religious faction, since we all came out of the Christian tradition. They will say that we have wanted them killed to avoid any further competition. This news will enrage their armies to make them attack the forces of Westworld."

"So we have to match them, right? Force with force?" Staats asked.

"I don't know of any other way," Great Parent Neville answered. "I suppose it is useless to speak with Baba Bani."

"I can offer one option. It is what I would do if I were in your place."

"I am quite open to suggestions."

"I'd appeal to Mastermind."

"Who is that?"

"You don't know?" Staats asked in surprise.

"Should I?"

"I suppose the only answer I have to offer is, shouldn't you?" He walked away from Neville's desk, shaking his head. "I cannot believe . . . I can hardly fathom your not knowing."

"Apparently you know something, some kind of secret of which I'm quite ignorant."

"Neville, how do you think you were selected—originally, I mean—to head FOL?"

"I recall the event quite clearly. A coalition of Christian leaders came to me. Odd . . . in those days, *Christian* meant something, didn't it? At any rate, they believed I was the only minister of the gospel who could unite the various church factions."

"Utter rubbish!"

"What are you saying?"

"You were chosen all right," Staats said, "just as I was, but not with such high principles." The old man turned and faced the head of FOL. "You are a fool, Neville. A bigger fool than I. At least I know why they chose me!"

"How dare you speak that way to me!"

The old man waved Neville's remarks aside with a gesture of his hand. "You vain, egocentric fool! You've gotten so caught up in all of this, you actually believe you're this great holy leader of Westworld."

"I fail to appreciate your humor or whatever it is—"

"Shut up!" Staats said. "Listen, you idiot . . . we're both doomed men. Don't you know that? Don't you realize what we have done?"

Without waiting for an answer, Staats shook his fist in the other man's face. "We sold our souls for a mess of pottage. For thirty pieces of silver we betrayed our faith. *We have been seduced by the great deceiver.*" He spoke the last sentence so softly, Neville Wheatley had to strain to hear him.

"Just what are you saying?"

"You were a rather good evangelist, Neville. Unquestionably the best—or one of the best. And Mastermind knew your weak spot—an unbridled ambition that you never surrendered to God. Oh, the world has known many men like you—able, good men who sell out for power. And you went all the way. You went so far, you actually believe all this garbage."

"Edmund, do you realize what you're saying?"

"Of course I do. Allow me to retain some sense of integrity—not much, mind you, but some. At least I know how I fell and I know why." He shook his head slowly as he remembered the trap prepared for him. He told Neville how Mastermind had enslaved him.

"Money . . . prosperity . . . covetousness—my weakness. I never particularly wanted fame—just a better standard of living. Now I live as lavishly as any man could want. And you want to know something else? I find myself envying your possessions. Once a man allows the desire for things to enslave him, he never stops. He never arrives at the place where he sits back in contentment and says, 'At last I have enough.' No, Neville, we are alike, you and I. But the one difference is that I know what a wretched, evil man I am, with no desire to do anything to change it. You, on the other hand, deceive yourself—and you do, you know—by refusing to admit what I've just told you. But it doesn't matter much . . . We are both doomed."

"I resent everything you have said about and to me!"

Staats saluted Neville and said, "Hail, Caesar. Enjoy it now, because you will have an eternity to face reality!" He gave the prelate a mock salute as he walked across the carpeted floor.

"Come back here, you stupid old fool!" Neville said. "What is this Mastermind you were babbling about?"

"I can't tell you everything, but I am aware that Mastermind is not a person. Mastermind is the Devil's creation. Or should I say a creation of Shining One?"

"What tripe—"

"Listen . . . Years ago six totally corrupt individuals yielded themselves to his dictates, and through them he has set us up . . . every leader in the world." Staats named eight people, all outstanding evangelical leaders in the year 1990. "And now, a decade later, only one of them is an incorruptible man."

"What are you saying?"

"Isn't it obvious? David Morgan. He's the only one. And must I tell you why? Would you like to know?"

Neville Wheatley stared uncomprehendingly.

"The Devil couldn't corrupt Morgan because the man has one flaw—the single flaw that the rest of us didn't have. He knows he is weak. It's that simple. The rest of us, convinced of our invincibility, our unshakable faith and strength, were perched on a precipice, ready to be pushed off the mountain. Saddest of all, no one had to push us. We jumped off the escarpment all by ourselves."

"You have no idea what you are saying. I'll—I'll have you committed to a lunatic asylum!"

"Whatever you want," Staats said. "It no longer matters. And now, I salute you! Hail, Caesar, from those of us who are about to die."

Neville Wheatley, suddenly stripped of his self-delusion, sat in his luxurious chair. Despite his desire to shut out the words of Edmund Staats, he knew the man was right. In a way, he had always known, but had never wanted to face the painful reality: he was a pawn, a mere pawn in the Devil's chess game.

Then he recognized a second fact: the truth did not disturb him; he had no desire to change. As he fingered his own ring of office, a green emerald, he knew he wanted no other life. "Whatever must be, must be," he said. "And why should I allow it to trouble me now?"

Yet Neville Wheatley *was* troubled. He knew that he could be toppled as easily as he had been exalted . . . unless he took the initiative.

Neville Wheatley slept little that night. He knew that as long as he lived, he would never have another peaceful night. He was a man—a mere, weak human being—who didn't have the inner resources to change. And, like Edmund Staats, he had no desire to change.

Kurt Legait, Supreme World Judge, spent a sleepless night that Thursday. He could release the accused with no difficulty, but should he? All evidence showed them guilty and if guilty, deserving of death. Yet he received constant pressure—from both Eastworld and Westworld. Notes came to him every few hours from Baba Bani and from Great Parent Neville with a variety of suggestions and orders. Strangely enough, the two leaders had changed their minds.

Friday morning Legait had not decided which of the two prelates he should listen to. He knew what he personally wanted to do. Yet that might not be the wisest course of action.

The seventy-five pages of documented evidence had convinced Legait of the guilt of the accused. He could not with a clear conscience release them. Supreme World Judge Legait, if not particularly brilliant, had been a man hoodwinked and led astray by Mastermind for years. He had begun as a lower-level co-ag and was gradually elevated. Not once, over the period of his rise from obscurity as a minor legal official in Cyprus, did he ever doubt that he was totally correct in his decisions.

Now he examined the evidence again. These people were responsible for the spread of disease, earthquakes, the ecological imbalance now threatening Planet Earth. To allow them to go free would be to write a death warrant for the rest of the world.

Unknown to Legait, Annella Maxwell had actually

been the one sending the messages to the judge. They arrived in such a way that Legait never once suspected their origin.

Annella smiled nervously as she awaited Legait's decision. So much now depended on Legait behaving as Mastermind had insisted he would.

Annella Maxwell was the second member of the group of six who had begun to doubt.

T·H·I·R·T·Y S·I·X

"You know what today is?" David Morgan asked those standing near him.

"Friday," someone answered.

"Not just any Friday—"

"Good Friday! Of course!"

"And do you know what happened on the first Good Friday?" asked Morgan.

"Low in the grave he lay," began a soprano voice, and by the time she had finished the first bar, hundreds had joined her in singing a hymn to the Resurrection.

Following the hymn, words of praise broke out among the hearers. Others joined in, and within two minutes the entire one hundred and twenty thousand people were standing on the field giving praise to God.

From near the back, someone began to sing, "Now thank we all our God" in Spanish, an illegal tongue. Someone picked it up in another illegal dialect; a third group sang in Ukrainian. Voices rose as if they were all being directed by one leader, while their words resounded in ninety-one different languages and dialects.

"Stop singing!" the loudspeakers commanded in English and Arabic. The believers ended their hymn and began "Amazing Grace," all of them in their native tongue.

The announcer then screamed at them in Spanish, French, German, Urdu, Hebrew, and Swahili. The voices subsided.

"I, Kurt Legait, appointed Supreme World Judge of the Supreme World Court, have called you here today to charge you with crimes against Eastworld and Westworld. I want you to know that if convicted of these crimes, you will be punished by death.

"Sitting here as the assembled World Court are eminent people in the world—six from Westworld, six representing Eastworld." He introduced those from Eastworld and then the leaders from Westworld, including Great Parent Neville, Edmund Staats, and Bryant McFarland.

Legait read the list of charges, beginning with bombing places of worship, polluting the water supply, causing ecological disasters, propagating a faith that differed from that of One Faith or FOL. As he concluded the reading of charges, he said, "David Morgan, I appoint you to speak on behalf of the Friends of Jesus."

"Sir, that is not our name. We prefer to be called simply Christians. However, to be called a friend of Jesus is an honorable term, and we aren't ashamed of being called followers of the blessed Lord Jesus Christ."

"How do you plead to the charges?"

"If you will go over them again, I'll respond to each—"

"You do not have that choice. You must plead guilty to all or innocent of all."

"Then you leave us no choice," Morgan said. "But first I ask that you allow me to stand where the others who are charged can see and hear me."

"Granted." He motioned for a guard to escort Morgan to the far side of the platform. The guard handed him a microphone. David Morgan spoke more slowly than usual to allow for Arabic interpretation.

"Because we propagate our faith and shall always continue to do so, I am forced to plead guilty. If any of you out there do not agree with this decision, raise your hand, and I shall ask the court to consider you innocent and the rest of us will plead guilty."

David Morgan waited until he was certain everyone had understood and then, seeing no hands, asked again, "Is there anyone present who wishes to plead innocent?"

From somewhere in the middle of the crowd, a lyric soprano began to sing in Swedish, "I Surrender All," and soon all men, women, and children joined in, singing in their own language and repeating the chorus: "I surrender all . . . All to Jesus I surrender, I surrender all."

David Morgan turned and faced the jury and the judge. "I think the words of the music we sing gives you our answer. We are guilty of one charge—and one only—and for this one crime we are willing to pay the consequences. I have no doubts in your minds that we confess our faith in Jesus Christ and in a religion you have outlawed. Regardless of what you say, we cannot—we will not—depart from our faith or deny our allegiance to the only true God of this universe!"

"Thank you," Kurt Legait said calmly. He had hit upon his solution an hour before dawn. While he personally believed in their guilt, he would not allow himself to be the scapegoat.

"I have read the full charges. I have discussed them with my legal counsel. I am of a double mind in this matter. And acknowledging my lack of wisdom, I appeal to these twelve judges who sit here, allowing them to make their ruling on your guilt or innocence by secret ballot."

Five of the leaders from Westworld, thinking they had received instructions from Great Parent Neville, were prepared to vote for the acquittal of the Christians. Five members from Eastworld, thinking they had received instructions from Baba Bani, were told to convict the believers.

"The majority of Westworld," Legait announced, "have voted for acquittal. The majority of Eastworld have voted for conviction. I am prepared to hear arguments from the two sides."

For more than an hour, first one side and then the other argued. With tempers inflamed, accusations arose as the believers watched and listened in growing confusion.

After another lengthy debate, Great Parent Neville raised his arms and signaled Baba Bani. The two men crossed to the back of the large platform behind the Supreme World Judge and whispered together. Bani then announced to the crowd, "We have found ourselves evenly split. Now it is up to the wisdom of our Supreme Judge."

As Baba Bani spoke, he placed his left hand at his waist. Kurt Legait understood the silent threat. Baba Bani was saying, "Convict them or I'll kill you." Judge Legait knew his death wouldn't come right away, perhaps not for many months, but Baba Bani would carry out the threat. It was a sacred oath.

The judge sighed, accepting the failure of his ploy. He had tried to toss the decision to the two sides, but they had thrown it back to him. He gritted his teeth, convinced he was doing the right thing and pleased that the right decision coincided with Baba Bani's wish.

"In giving the evidence my fullest attention," Legait said to the crowd, "and after listening to the debate of these learned men, I have made my decision. The Friends of Jesus are guilty as charged."

Eastworld leaders smiled at each other as if to say, "We have won the day. We have succeeded and will now wipe out all of those from Westworld." The Westworld officials sat in silence, awaiting further orders. None felt any personal concern for the Christians; they simply had not been able to carry out their instructions for acquittal, and that troubled them.

"Execution will be carried out immediately," Kurt Legait proclaimed.

"Sir," David Morgan said, still standing at the edge of the platform on the lower level, "I would not attempt to argue with your sentence, but I do ask that you allow me to speak a final word on my own behalf and, since you appointed me as the speaker for all of the condemned, a word from the one hundred and twenty thousand here who have also been condemned to die."

"Why should we have to sit through all of this?" asked an Arab. "Kill them!"

"We've heard all we need to know," said Baba Bani.

This time Kurt looked squarely at Baba Bani and said, "I grant your final request, Mr. Morgan, but you must keep your statements brief."

"Thank you," he said and, holding the cordless microphone, he stepped up to the next level. "First, I'm ready to die. So are the rest of the people here," he said as he pointed to the believers. "I suppose I'm surprised at my own readiness, because I've always been afraid of death. But no longer, because I now understand how Christians of the past have reacted when the moment came for them to leave this life. God gives the strength and the grace needed for the occasion."

He turned so he could face the judges on the highest level. "I need say nothing more about my death or the death of my friends, but I do have something to say to you. While we don't beg for mercy and are prepared to embrace death, I want to tell you that you are also facing the end. Not the end of this life so you can pre-program yourself into a new existence. That promise is a lie, a deception that came from the originator of lies. Satan told the first lie in the Garden of Eden when he made promises to Adam and Eve, and he has never stopped his deceitful actions. You have fallen for the oldest lie in the world. This Shining One—this Exalted—is the Devil, God's adversary and the accuser of God's people.

"You'll die all right. Not with us, not for years perhaps, but you will die. And for this I am truly sad, because you'll suffer in torment forever afterward, and I wish it were not so.

"Death knocks at the door for all of us, and none can refuse entrance. There is no escape, just as there is no escape from our destiny after we die. And so, I beg you with my last breath, look at yourself . . . Think of what you are doing . . . Turn to Jesus Christ who is, even at this minute, willing to forgive you if—"

"Stop! Silence!" screamed Great Parent Neville. He rose from his throne and rushed down the steps to face Morgan. "You dare to speak to me—to all of us—in this manner?"

"I speak the truth, Mr. Neville. You know I'm speaking the truth."

"You may be speaking your truth, but not mine."

Morgan smiled. "There is only one truth—the truth you once knew."

Great Parent slapped Morgan across the face with the back of his hand. His ring left a deep, jagged cut on Morgan's left cheek, and blood oozed to the surface.

"You can silence my voice by taking my life; you can never silence the voice of God!"

Great Parent struck him again and then a third time. "Silence!"

"With my dying breath," Morgan said, his face streaming with blood, for the third slap had struck him in the eye and he felt the pain of the sting, "I remind you again that Jesus Christ loves you, Jesus Christ died for you, Jesus Christ—"

Great Parent Neville grabbed Morgan by the neck and shook his body as his fingers tightened. "Silence! Silence! Silence!"

Morgan made no effort to stop the prelate; yet Neville correctly read the mocking in Morgan's eyes and his fingers pressed more tightly. Long after life had drained from Morgan's body, he continued to tighten his grip.

When Neville released Morgan, the lifeless body fell. He stared at the form at his feet and then looked at his hands, hardly comprehending what he had done. He ignored Emil and Michelle as they raced onto the platform and lifted David Morgan's body. "We want to die by his side," Emil said.

"May God find some way to forgive you," Michelle

said. "May God's love somehow reach through your blind-
ness—"

Great Parent struck Michelle so hard, she stumbled and
fell from the platform, then lay moaning on the ground. Several Christians moved toward her and picked her up.

In the meantime, Emil Wensela, his arms under the legs
and head of his mentor, walked off the platform, singing
softly a hymn of praise to God.

Great Parent Neville watched them, and for a moment
he felt totally detached from everything, as though
he observed a scene in which he had no involvement. Then
he stared at his hands again. Bits of human flesh had
stuck to his ring, and he stared at the blood on his
hand. "What have I done?" he said aloud. "What have I
done?"

He lifted his eyes, and they met those of Edmund
Staats. A wave of bitter hatred filled his heart because he
now understood fully what Staats had meant, and he hated
the old man for telling him. Neville Wheatley no longer had
anything to hide behind, no ignorance, no illusions; there
was no longer a way to deceive himself.

Edmund Staats had watched the episode with Great
Parent Neville and Morgan. As he saw the life choked out of
the noble man, he felt nothing: no pity, no sympathy, no
revulsion. Edmund Staats again knew that he had not only
ceased to feel human emotions, but that he would never
experience them again. He might be alive in his body, but he
was already a dead man.

"I don't even hate anymore," he mumbled. "Even that
emotion has left me."

Bryant McFarland, seated at the end of the top row of
leaders, had positioned himself only meters away from the

rows of special guests. Betty-Anne Freeman, at the end, had smiled often at him during the proceedings.

Now he noticed that she no longer looked at him, as if she had no further interest in him or in anything he did. Her eyes focused on the scene below. Only once before in his life had he observed that kind of concentrated fascination. In his boyhood a man had started a fire in a warehouse and then stood across the street, watching it burn. Mesmerized by the flames, the criminal had an awareness of nothing else going on.

With revulsion, Bryant McFarland gasped. Betty-Anne's fascination made her eyes blaze and her cheeks glow. Bryant left his place and walked over to her. He touched her arm. Slowly and with reluctance she turned to him. Her dilated pupils and excited breathing met his gaze.

"I've never seen you like this before," he said.

"I've never seen such . . . such a sight before." She whirled around, once again concentrating on the scene below.

By now a company from the Supreme World Army had formed a circle around the Christians, their automatic weapons held at waist level, ready for the execution signal. Their modified automatic machine guns had come equipped with the newly developed heated bullets. These bullets, once lodged, continued to heat up to a temperature of two hundred degrees centigrade, burning anything that came into contact with the struck object.

"You!" Bryant McFarland said to Betty-Anne. "You're the Devil!"

"No, love," she said, not bothering to turn to him "I'm not that important." She burst into applause. "Kill! Kill! Kill!" she screamed.

Others around her took up the chant. The soldiers moved into position.

"Wait!" McFarland stumbled forward and grabbed the microphone from Kurt Legait. "Wait! Don't shoot them yet!"

He dropped the microphone and raced down the stairway and onto the ground. He pushed through the line of soldiers and stopped in front of Emil Wensela, who was holding Michelle.

"I'm not worthy to stand next to any of you," he said, "but I want to be here, to die with you." He burst into tears. "O God, please, please forgive me."

Michelle touched his arm. "Help me stand," she said and allowed him to drape her arm over his shoulder.

The three of them stood in front of the other Christians, and Bryant looked skyward. A cloud of darkness from the eastern horizon was moving toward them, growing rapidly in size and blackness.

"Onward, Christian soldiers," Bryant sang out, "marching as to war—"

The trio did not see Kurt Legait give the signal. They did not hear the blasts of the guns. The bullets struck the multitude, their force spinning the victims backward or upward. Within five minutes every body was aflame.

By then the cloud of darkness covered the entire horizon, and a clap of thunder roared; yet no rain yet fell. The eyes of all the living present stared into the heavens. Many of them trembled in fear.

Great Parent Neville stood alone, transfixed as a sudden downpour of rain now dropped from the sky and jury members ran to take cover. Yet he did not move, standing as if unaware of the torrential showers. Neville Wheatley saw nothing and heard only voices inside his head. He heard the words of David Morgan: "Temporarily you gain; but in the long run you get nothing free from Satan." He heard other comments Morgan had made over the years in his daily television commentary—words Wheatley had never consciously remembered and yet now came back to him as if the American TV preacher had spoken directly to him.

Neville Wheatley put his hands to his head, pushing inward, trying to shut out the voice. And for a moment he experienced a blessed silence. And then he heard a new voice, a voice like one he had never known before. *What if Morgan is right? What if Morgan is right?*

"No," he said, "I won't listen . . . I won't listen!"

What if Morgan is right?

"He can't be right," Wheatley said.

Baba Bani glared at Great Parent. The destruction of the one hundred and twenty thousand was only the beginning. Soon his own army would wipe out Westworld and then—he smiled as the thought filled his mind—One Faith would control the entire world.

As Great Parent Neville pulled his mind back to the events around him, he observed Baba Bani signal his captain. The war would now begin. Great Parent smiled because he was ready for the signal. His own general, watching every gesture of the Eastworld leader, had already signaled his captains to prepare for battle.

The soldiers of both armies had cleverly camouflaged themselves on different sides of the Negev and the plains of Jehoshophat. They were ready, and the decisive battle for world control would start soon.

T·H·I·R·T·Y S·E·V·E·N

Mastermind had assembled, and again the voice raged against the six. "You are thoroughly incompetent. And you, Annella . . . surely you could have controlled your own daughter. Look what you have done, you stupid woman! You turned her against you. You have made a martyr out of her."

"Martyr?" Annella asked. "Who cares now?"

"How stupid you are! Stupid! We have gotten rid of these religious followers—the strong, open ones. But you are so stupid . . . You don't understand, do you? When the strong fall, their martyrdom emboldens the weak. Ah, you need have no doubt about that."

Ferdinand Quayle, who had never addressed Mastermind before, said, "But all the Christians are now gone. What harm can there be at this point?"

"Are you as blind as the rest in this room? All Christians gone? Don't be naive. The secret Christians are out there still alive. Some will now discover boldness, a new surge of life. There is no one to lead them, but they will raise up new leaders . . . zealots . . . stupid men and women who will be anxious to die for their faith!"

Silence filled the large room until Mastermind spoke to Wensela. "And you are no more competent that the stupid woman, you imbecile. You cooperated with this moronic woman in forcing the decision to kill the Christians. And you—you weasel of a man who cannot even control his own son! You dared to make a martyr of him!

"Does any one of you have any sense? Can't I depend on any of the six of you? I chose you because you were cunning, immoral, and without conscience. And now look at you . . . We are within inches of total control and you sit like morons!"

"Listen, Mastermind," Quayle said, "I'm a bit tired of hearing all of this. If you want to kill off Annella and Wensela, then do it. Why take it out on the rest of us? Haven't we done our jobs properly?"

"You have," he said. "You completed an extraordinary assignment . . . except for Bryant McFarland. You failed as well . . . Don't you grasp that, you stupid mortal?"

"How was I to know he'd be a turncoat at the end? Anyway, I don't think most of the people knew who he was and—"

"Don't be as stupid as the other two! Of course people know! Live simul-cast! *Live.* The commentators, not prompted, clearly identified McFarland for the world to know."

"Okay," Quayle said, "so we didn't do a perfect job. But—" He paused and folded his hands across his chest.

"But what?"

"I'm a little tired, like I said," Quayle answered. "And I'm even more tired of hearing all your grumbling. You're the great spirit. Why blame us poor mortals?"

"Please, please," P. K. Sari said, jumping from his chair and standing in front of Quayle. "Oh, blessed Mastermind, do not destroy us along with him. Remember, he is a Westerner. He does not understand your vast power."

"He is a fool!" Mastermind said.

"As you say," P. K. Sari answered. "And as a fool, he does not realize his danger in speaking this way to you."

"Then treat them like world-class rulers," spoke up Ferdinand Quayle for the second time. "You give them instructions as if they are merely messengers. But you don't do much explaining about your overall plan."

"He is correct," said Woodrow Quayle. "I've often thought the same thing myself. If every one of us knew your plan, your ultimate plan, we'd be able to cooperate more fully and conquer our worlds a little better."

"I wonder if I might have done better if I had skipped a generation!" thundered Mastermind. "But never mind . . . So be it. I shall tell you the next phase of my plan and the reason for it. We shall encourage the armies of Eastworld and Westworld to fight until they kill half of the world's population. We shall have a New Earth for repopulation and a new world—the New World of Mastermind. I had planned for the six of you, along with your four offspring, to inherit the leadership of the world. But of course it is too late for Michelle Maxwell and for Emil Wensela."

"Surely you've got the resources to fill in the blanks for two more people," Quayle said. "You're the great Mastermind, and you own everything."

"Not everything. But I do have the power to strike you dead!"

Fear struck Quayle; his facial muscles twitched, and his body visibly stiffened. Attempting to smile, he looked grotesque.

"Silence, then, if you choose to live!" Mastermind said.

"We are quick to do your will, O Great One," said P. K. Sari. "We have fulfilled our roles imperfectly, but we vow to do our best in service to you."

"Ah, yes," Mastermind said, "you have the voice of a serpent, wily and slick. That is one of my tricks, but it does work!"

The six stared at each other, unsure of their next move, waiting now to hear the unfolding Plan of Mastermind.

"I have already selected two people to replace the defectors . . . and one additional person. They are waiting outside.

Sami Yatawazy, bring in the guests from Rooms 1, 2 and 3."
Quayle started to ask why three, but held his tongue.

Yatzawazy returned immediately, trailed by Baba Bani,
Great Parent Neville, and Edmund Staats. An audible sigh
went around the room. Everyone agreed that these men
would make excellent replacements.

Once the three were seated outside the circle, Mastermind unfolded his plan. He had already divided the world
into ten equal parts. With the changing weather patterns
because of increased pollution in the world, all lands in the
Arctic Circle would slowly moderate and within five years
would be suitable land for farming. The desert areas were
now already among the most fertile in the world. "No matter what part of the world you receive in reward from me, it
shall be a paradise for you."

"But there are eleven of us," Quayle said. "You said
ten—"

"You count accurately," Mastermind said, now speaking through Annella. "The plan is changing." He commanded the ten men to sit in a new circle, apart from Annella.
"She is my sacred Handmaiden," he said. "Despite her failure, I have chosen Annella for a different role. She is my
sacred prostitute-goddess."

"What does that mean?" Quayle asked.

"This Western mind knows so little," Sari said. He
turned to Quayle and said, "She is as Mastermind says: the
Handmaiden. She is the entrance to Shining One. To
approach the great power, you must go through Annella."

"Now, for the ten of you . . . Each of you will bear the
title of Ruler. You will act in concert with the others. At
future meetings, we shall be as we are here: the ten Rulers
and my Handmaiden through whom I speak."

Annella turned on a slide projector showing the division
of the planet; their lands were marked one through ten. "You
will receive your portion by a drawing."

"But, sir," said Baba Bani, "would it not be better to
assign us? I am from Eastworld and—"

"In a few days no Eastworld will exist. No Westworld

either. Your armies are prepared to clash at this very instant. They will fight, decimating a large portion of the people as well as military personnel. Then you are ready to rule your portion of the world.

"Forgive my ignorance," Baba Bani said, "but do you mean that you will transport the remaining population so that they will reside where you choose?"

"Exactly. And the lands will have new names. When we transport families, they will never again be united with relatives. We will teach each family to stand against all families. Parents will stand against their children and children against their parents. By keeping everyone suspicious of each other, we avoid their congregating and building up trust. You will rule by the power of fear! You will destroy those who disobey. I am giving you more power than you ever thought possible! By your power you will keep all people in total subjection at all times."

As Mastermind's Plan unfolded, each person present grasped the advantages of such a plan. They would only have to guard against those who attempted to unite with others. Mastermind explained his People-Watch program of rewarding spies and informants and punishing those who deviated in the slightest.

A tapping at the door interrupted Mastermind's unfolding Plan. Annella cracked the door and stared at Yakubali Sidik's flushed face.

"We cannot explain it . . . It—it does not make sense, but it has happened anyway."

"What are you talking about?"

"The Christians. They are not dead!"

"Bring him in!" Mastermind said.

Yakubali Sidik entered the room, bowed his head in reverence, and said, "A strange thing is taking place right now. Soldiers shot the Christians. Did we not all see this happen? . . . every one of them left for dead. That was three and a half days ago, was it not?"

"Yes . . . Go on . . ."

"The armies of Eastworld and Westworld have started

fighting, and thousands, perhaps millions of bodies lie stretched from the Negev to the Sea. But the Christians—the ones we killed—they are not dead. They are much alive. You can look at them and see bullet holes in their bodies, but they are alive!"

"This cannot be!" Mastermind screamed through Annella.

"But it is so," Yakubali Sidik answered. "Most of them are staying on the plain where they were killed. But two of them, wearing *gunia*—"

"Sackcloth, burlap material," interpreted Baba Bani.

"Yes, wearing burlap . . . They are walking through the streets of the city of Jerusalem. And while it is not possible, they are appearing at the same time in other cities around the world. These same two men and no one else . . . they are telling our soldiers to throw down their guns, to turn to—"

"To do what?" demanded Mastermind.

"To . . . you know, the religion of Jesus."

"You must be mistaken," said P. K. Sari.

"No, I am not. I have seen them with my own eyes. For three whole days and for all of this morning, they are going from person to person. They keep speaking of Jesus."

"And what is happening?" Mastermind said.

"Oh, it is sad, very sad," answered Yakubali Sidik. "Many are obeying. They are . . . they are worshiping this Jesus."

"Kill the two! Who are they?"

"The tall one we all know: he is David Morgan. The other we did not know because he is like a child . . . a young lad. We have found out that his name is Nick Strenk."

"Kill them both!" shrieked Mastermind. "If it takes one million bullets, kill them!"

"As you say . . ." Yakubali Sidik bowed and backed out of the room. At the door he stopped and said, "I must tell you, however, that all the soldiers are afraid of them. When our men try to touch either of the two, they fall backward as if Morgan and the boy breathed fire from their nostrils. At one point, an armed band of one thousand soldiers surrounded them, and Morgan called for rain to come down from Heaven. Immediately rain, as I have never seen in my life of forty-nine years, fell from a cloudless sky. It came so quickly and in such force that our men could see nothing, and they fled in panic. Now they are even more afraid of these two men. And . . . oh, it is quite sad, but everyone fears them. No one will touch them."

"Do you think I'm afraid?" Quayle said. "Just give me the word and I'll hop into my aero-ship and be in Jerusalem in less than two hours. I'll take care of them."

"Go," Mastermind said. "Go."

As soon as Quayle left, Mastermind said, "We shall wait until the return of Ruler Quayle."

In four and a half hours, Quayle returned to the room, a smile creasing his face. "Like Yakubali Sidik said, they were preaching away. I went up to Morgan first and held my gun on him."

"Did he back away?" Great Parent asked.

"Naw," he answered. "He continued to speak, and then begged me to ask God to cleanse my old soul. So I shot him four times in the head."

"And—?" asked Sari.

"He died. That's what he did. Then I turned to the younger fellow and shot him twice."

"You are positive they are dead?"

"No question," Quayle said. "I kicked their bodies, and I even checked their pulse. They're lying on the roadside, and the people are seeing that they are only human after all."

"You have done well," Mastermind declared. "Your heartlessness has redeemed you."

"I'm pleased to be of service," Quayle said and smiled at the others.

The following week Mastermind gave each of the ten Rulers a necklace of woven gold and platinum. It was lightweight but tightly fitted so that once put around the neck with the two ends firmly pressed together, the jewelry would not come off. "Only death will remove your necklace from you," said Mastermind.

"This is a symbol then?" asked Yatawazy. "Only death will take our Rulership from us?"

"Precisely," answered Mastermind. "The Ruler wears the necklace as a badge of office. It must remain visible at all times."

Three weeks after the Great Elimination weekend, the armies of Eastworld and Westworld turned on the civilian population, continuing to raze city after city, allowing no one to escape until word came from Mastermind. Once the population of the world was down to one billion people, repopulation and relocation would began.

Mastermind planned the move with remarkable efficiency. Since places such as the deserts and the Arctic regions had previously had little or no population, inhabitants went to those places first. Then the shift took place from continent to continent.

As people moved into their new homes, they automatically received an abundance of goods and money. Within weeks, the new nations were coming into being. Rulers appealed to their sense of nationality, of patriotism, of obedience to Shining One. No one went without the necessities of life and opportunities for improvement. At the same time, murder and robbery took place often, and nobody attempted to stop such activity. The commandment understood among the people was, "You shall not be caught in the act." Only crimes actually witnessed received punishment. No one paid attention to mere suspicions or accusations.

This arrangement also meant that terror became a part of all households, and each person—including the children—soon learned to use weapons to protect family property.

"It is a new world with grand opportunities for all of us to live in a utopia on this earth," the voice of Great Parent Neville declared on simul-cast. He made regular newscasts, keeping both his face and voice familiar to his own kingdom, but also to make himself familiar to the rest of the world.

Mastermind had not assigned the land that had once been known as Israel. He labeled that area Forbidden Zone.

Rejuvenated Christians remained alive. Even though Quayle had killed David Morgan and Nick Strenk, soldiers would make no attempts to kill the others. The Christians remained in Forbidden Zone, praying night and day, singing, worshiping, and crying out to God for the end to come.

The ten Rulers sent all undesirables to Forbidden Zone for either elimination or for transport as Franchised Workers to the newly explored Uranus. Trucks arrived each Monday with food and clothing at the one gate around the steel wall that sealed off Forbidden Zone. The trucks drove inside, dumped their loads, and left.

It constantly amazed the drivers and guards that none of the Christians jumped in and fought over the provisions. Instead, a crew of people counted and stacked all items, which were then taken to a storehouse. If and when anyone had needs, they could come to the storehouse and receive what they required.

Mastermind learned that drivers and soldiers often defected once they went inside the gates. He then ordered that the Christians must come outside the fence and collect all items themselves.

Despite this change, the defections did not stop. Anywhere from five to twenty people went through the steel gate to stay each day.

"Is this the end of the world?" asked Michelle. "Everything has changed so drastically—"

"I don't know," Emil said. "But I know that whatever happens, we are safe. We are with the Savior."

The ten Rulers, in preparation for their respective seats of power, called for a great celebration all over the earth.

They prepared to commemorate the elimination of Christians and other social misfits by observing Great Elimination Day. With improved airpower, an individual could fly completely around the globe in three hours. A few firms offered a two-hour trip.

The ten Rulers, in calling the world to celebrate, sent gifts to each other, feigning friendship and cooperation. Great quantities of precious stones and vast quantities of slave labor went from one domain to another.

Mastermind had erected a capital for the world in what had formerly been known as Singapore. This island nation, with a geographic size slightly smaller than what had formerly been New York City, provided the ideal location. At Mastermind's command, the International Army of Peace (the combination of the former Eastworld and Westworld armies) cordoned off the island, bombed every building, and killed every citizen. Once accomplished, construction crews came in to clean up the rubble and erect a palace that covered twenty square kilometers in the center of the island.

When the new capital, called Splendor, was finally completed and the ten kingdoms settled, Mastermind declared a week of celebration. It would begin that evening at the Splendor Ballroom. As soon as simul-cast projected the opening events on the screens around the world, each nation would begin their annual days of pleasure and celebration.

"From now on, the world's population can dwell in peace," announced the Rulers.

The people of the world listened, too fearful to argue.

T·H·I·R·T·Y E·I·G·H·T

Annella Maxwell arrived early at the Temple of Faith, fully dressed for the gala occasion. Levis Cothran had escorted her, along with Yolanda. While Levis and Yolanda stopped to drink and snack at the banquet table, Annella grabbed a glass of champagne and left them, going into the ballroom. From there she looked at video screens from around the world. The world was celebrating, and she was ecstatic.

She saw her picture being raised in New York's Times Square, in Athen's Constitution Square, in Bangkok and Spitzbergen. Now known as the "Queen of Heaven and Earth," she felt pleased. The world was now ready to recognize her as the Handmaiden of Mastermind.

Annella had not wanted to be one of the ten Rulers, and felt especially pleased that Mastermind had instructed them to pay tribute to her by bringing her fifteen percent of their gross income. She alone had direct access to Mastermind. They might not yet realize it, but she had become the supreme human power in the world.

The door of the ballroom opened, and Maison Quayle

and his two sons entered the room. They greeted Annella, but as they did so, she felt an apprehensive chill come over her. She raised her drink and said, "Hail to the new world!"

"To the new world," chorused the three.

Yatawazy and Sari entered together, and Zolo came in behind them, along with Hanse Wensela and Baba Bani.

"Looks as if the six of us are here!"

"Eight of us," corrected Quayle, nodding at his sons.

"Ten," said Great Parent as Annella saw Neville Wheatley and Edmund Staats coming in from yet another door.

"And for what better purpose to be here than to celebrate?" she asked. Annella sat on the gilded chair, the most luxurious in the room and raised on the highest step; below it were ten chairs, almost as ornate, arranged in a circle.

"Oh that, but something else . . ." said Maison Quayle. "We are here to make all things right."

"What do you mean by a statement like that?" she asked.

"Let me whisper to you," Quayle said. As he he put his mouth up to her left ear, his right hand grabbed her throat, choking her windpipe.

Like a flock of buzzards, all ten descended on her, tearing at her clothes, her hair, scratching her body, leaving deep marks as if wild beasts had clawed her.

"You think you are superior to us, do you now?" Quayle asked. "We are ten, and we don't need a queen over us, nor do we need to pay you any kind of money, do we?"

Annella never heard Quayle's words: she was already dead.

Great Parent Neville, who was now known simply as Ruler Neville, stared at the simul-cast. Earthquakes were becoming more common in the southern part of his kingdom. Only the previous week twenty thousand people had lost their lives, and this present quake seemed worse.

But at least, he thought to himself, his was an inland realm. The simul-cast had shown a series of tidal waves striking the coast of Realm Six, which had once been northern Europe. Most of Denmark was underwater. The entire Arctic ice mass had melted, and as the water flowed southward, the low areas of Greenland had been submerged. The coast of Realm Five, which once had been Scotland and England, were reporting water rising at the rate of half a meter a day.

Yet Ruler Neville felt secure. He controlled the vast heartland of the former United States and Canada. Despite the recent quakes, his geologists had assured him that another earthquake was unlikely for at least another fifty years. He hoped desperately they were right.

At last Neville Wheatley had everything he wanted. Yet as he stared at the row of simul-cast monitors, he felt an anger rising within. He had sensed a change in Realms Eight, Nine, and Ten, but he was not sure what it was.

Perhaps he ought to push his plans forward to invade Realm Four, under the domain of Ruler Edmund and undoubtedly the weakest of the ten. He had planned this to take place early in the spring. Perhaps he might do it sooner.

One Monday, three separate events took place at the same time in different parts of the world. None of the actors—Quayle, Sari, or Wensela—were aware of the plans of the others.

Quayle, known as Ruler Maison, had invited his twin sons to a banquet. "Just think, my lads, we control three-tenths of the world! Can you imagine what we can do together?"

"Why together?" asked Woodrow. "You gave us life, but you are an old man now."

"Yes," Ferdinand said, "and we don't need you, you know. We sat and licked your filthy boots for years, being exactly what you chose us to be. And now it is our time to make changes."

"You oppose me? You want to get rid of me? Take away my Realm?"

"Yes," said Woodrow as he sipped a glass of wine. "We have already divided it on paper."

"You feel the same way, Ferdinand?"

"Why, of course . . . Why not? We learned deviousness from you, and you were an excellent teacher." He lifted his own glass of wine and said to his brother, "Let us toast our late, great, departed father!"

The twins drank until they emptied the glass. Then they looked at each other. "Well," asked Ferdinand, "do I get the privilege of killing him or do you?"

"You hold him and I'll snap his neck," Woodrow said.

"Don't be too hasty," Ruler Maison said. "You won't make it anyway. I have a pleasant surprise for you—pleasant for me. In another forty-five seconds the poison in your wine will end your lives. You see, my beloved sons, I am even more greedy than you. I have watched you, hoping you would be content with what you had. I honestly had hoped that the three of us might control the rest of the world. But as I saw your covert glances and heard your treacherous plans—my spies bugged your houses—I learned of your intent. So, my boys, things have changed. Your father will control one-third of the world. For starts, that is."

Ferdinand started to move toward his father, clasped his throat, stumbled, and fell lifeless to the floor. Woodrow stared in horror for eight seconds before he too slumped forward, falling across the banquet table.

Ruler Maison rang a bell. "Dispose of them," he told the servants who came in. "And bring more food. I'm expecting other guests."

In Forbidden Zone, the Christians continued to pray for God's guidance. God gave them one message: "Fear not—I am with you. Remain here until I call you to Myself." Many of the believers asked God to allow them to take their witness to those in the outer world, but each time the Holy Spirit said, "It is too late."

P. K. Sari had lost more than anyone in land and people during the forty months of his reign in Realm One, the former continent of South America. The melting of Antarctica had seemed a blessing in the beginning. A solid mass of land under the ice with vast untapped resources gave him hope for greater riches.

But tidal waves wreaked immense destruction, and outbreaks of fire that seemed to come from nowhere burned forests and grasslands. The temperature changed from blazing heat to sub-zero within a thirty-hour period, and two days later became moderate again.

Sari brooded in the capital of Realm One, atop the Andes in what had formerly been Quito, but now was the sprawling metroplex known as City Sari. No matter when or how he died, Sari thought, he would at least leave this magnificent city for the world to admire. It was self-enclosed, so the weather did not affect it. No force of nature could destroy it. He was safe for as long as he lived.

P. K. Sari invited Rulers Edmund, Yatzawazy, Neville, and Zolo to feast with him in his magnificent city. He boasted the most perfectly designed and controlled metroplex in the world, and the others were eager to see it.

After their lengthy tour of City Sari, he ushered them into a vast room of mirrors. "This is my magic room. Within fifty-three seconds I can, simply by pressing the proper buttons, make the room into a swimming pool, a TV media center, a series of six bedrooms, or even a bowling alley."

"However could you make such vast changes in less than one minute?" asked Zolo. "I do not think that is possible."

"Oh, then I will show you." He walked to the door and opened a panel that contained rows of buttons. "I press one and the room changes. For instance, I shall press this one," he said, pointing to a red button on the bottom."

"What happens then?"

"Shall you not experience it for yourselves?" he asked. He held up his hand and said, "Observe." He pushed the button, and a hissing sound emerged from the sides of the room.

Amwago Zolo raced toward his host. "You are trying to kill us!"

Before Zolo could reach him, Sari deftly stepped out of the room, closing the door which immediately sealed the room pneumatically. Sari walked twenty paces down the corridor, then pressed another button that allowed him to watch the three men's bodies burn from the gaseous heat that was now destroying them. He sent in servants to remove the necklaces and bring them to him. He then pressed a second button that totally disintegrated the bodies, leaving only a small pile of black ashes.

Sari smiled as he walked toward his throne. He had been thought of as the weakest of the original six. Little did they know that behind the quietness and the obedience, he was the most ruthless of all.

Hanse Wensela, being a more direct man than either Quayle or Sari, paid an official visit on Ruler Bani of Realm Two. He had previously sent a message that he had plans for a joint venture he thought might interest Bani.

Wensela had often observed the greed on Bani's face, more transparent than on any of the others. This was the man to take out immediately because he was the most unpredictable, thereby making him the most dangerous.

Carrying with him a briefcase of papers, Wensela had no problem going through the body search by attendants of Ruler Bani. They checked him quite thoroughly, even having him walk through a modified X-ray machine that detected and identified any metal.

Wensela had planned this carefully after learning that the machine did not send out rays below the ankles of visitors. He had a special pair of shoes made that contained a small plastic gun, similar to the Derringer, in one shoe. Fired at close range, the deadly bullets would accomplish his purpose.

The two men greeted each other cordially and sat down at a large desk to work together. Wensela pulled out the papers, showing his plan for overthrowing the other eight Realms. The glee in Bani's eyes shone as Wensela explained his strategy.

"Mind if I take off my shoes," Wensela said as he bent down. "New ones . . . not really comfortable yet."

"Not at all," Bani said as he bent over the plans. His mind was working rapidly, trying to figure how he could also eliminate Ruler Hanse and become the world's Supreme Ruler.

At that moment, Ruler Bani felt the cold metal against the back of his head. He did not even have a chance to speak.

When Hanse Wensela left the grand palace, he wore a second gold-and-platinum necklace.

The following day simul-cast announced a restructuring of the Realms of the Earth into three. Ruler Maison controlled three portions, Sari five, and Hanse two.

The three men, agreeing to a truce, met at Splendor to discuss the future. "We must decide if we can live as three Rulers or if we will continue to plot against each other," Sari had said.

All three Rulers came with entourages that were prepared to protect them against any devices. Squads from each Realm inspected the temple before anyone entered. All agreed it was safe.

Three thrones, all of equal size, had been placed in the center of the room. Sari, controlling as much of the world as the combination of the other two, smiled benevolently. He sat in the middle spot. He was a patient man who could allow them to treat him as equal . . . for now.

"My Spiritual Enabler has told me that she wishes to communicate with me," Ruler Sari said. The other two men, less experienced in listening to their SEs, sat stiffly, waiting for Sari to surrender himself.

To their surprise, the other two men found themselves moving into a relaxed stage, so that within seconds all of them were operating from delta brainwaves.

"I have chosen to speak to all three of you at once," said the distinct voice of Mastermind. "You have played havoc with my plans. You have killed the very people you needed the most."

"Do we need them?" Ruler Maison said. "It seems to me that the three of us are doing all right for ourselves."

"Fools! You are fools!"

"We are only fulfilling our destiny," said Ruler Sari. "Did we not learn everything from you, Mastermind?"

"You killed my Handmaiden."

"We killed her because we don't need her," Ruler Hanse said. "What has she done for us besides costing us vast amounts of money?"

"You are speaking directly to us now," Ruler Maison said, "aren't you? We don't need an SE."

"You are cunning," he said. "Your actions have confirmed my original choosing of you."

"Right!" said Ruler Maison. "So, tell us what to do next."

"We have work to do before the world is totally ours," said Mastermind. "I am now ready to destroy—eliminate forever—the Christians. Once they are gone, the world is ours. We shall then populate the other planets in this galaxy, and I shall grant to each of you—and only to the three of you—the right to live in perpetual health, youth, and clear mental ability."

"Can you really, sir?" asked Ruler Sari. "I think not."

"What?" said Mastermind.

"We have learned much," Ruler Sari said. "You can take life, and you have done that often enough. But you cannot give life. That is not within your power."

"You dare to say—"

"I dare to say this," Ruler Sari answered boldy, "because I am your obedient servant. And as your obedient one, I now insist on no more lies from you. I am ready to do whatever you wish, but you must now speak to us with truth."

"Truth? Have I not always been truthful with you?"

Ruler Maison laughed. "Then let us say that a new day dawns when your truth becomes universal and not just your private treasure."

"If you are capable of such a thing," said Ruler Hanse.

"How dare you three . . .! I made you great! Now you speak this way!"

"We speak as we do," said Ruler Sari, "because we are now in human form what you are without our bodies. You have made us men who have no consciences, no compassion for others. Why should we then have concern for each other? . . . Or even for you?

"So we shall plot to destroy one another," said Ruler Hanse. "And we know that the most devious—or the most lucky—will win."

"But I can make all of you wealthy, powerful   "

"You have already, Shining One," said Ruler Sari. "But we are your creation, you must remember. You have so filled us that we cannot be content as long as we have rivals. Even though I am the most powerful of the three—I hold as much power as the other two combined—yet I am not content. My contentment can come only when I am supreme, with no rivals."

"If even then," said Ruler Maison quietly. "If even then."

"The end is almost upon us," said Joe Strenk to the group around him. They had been praying for strength to face that specific day, as they had been doing each morning. "Don't give up hope. We have a better world waiting for us!"

"We know," answered Phil Barnhart. "In the meantime, we are one in our love for each other and for Jesus Christ."

"Endure to the end!" one of them called out.

"We can make it until Jesus returns!"

"Hope . . . peace . . . Those are qualities the Devil can't destroy," said Lisa Strenk.

"And whatever happens, remember that God's Holy Spirit is always with us," said Phil.

Directly behind the Strenks stood a man in his late forties, though he resembled someone much older. Years of hard living showed in his lined face. As the man listened to the voices around him and to words of mutual encouragement, as he heard the Christians praying for one another, tears rolled down his cheeks.

His name was Steve Grubman, a man who had once served Jesus Christ in a worldwide ministry, only to fall prey to Mastermind's trap. For years Steve Grubman had live in guilt and shame, and just within the past few months had he straightened out his life. At last he had pushed the past behind him, because no sinful past existed for Steve Grubman. "I'm a Christian, a child of God," he said to himself. "God has wiped away my failures."

As he spoke these words, a woman next to him, seeing his tears, leaned over and wiped his face with her handkerchief. "One day," she whispered, "God Himself will wipe away your tears."

"He just did." Steve Grubman grabbed her hand and kissed it. "Through you." He smiled at her and then burst into singing "Amazing Grace." When he came to the line, "I once was lost but now am found," he experienced the truth of the words. *He had been found—again.*

Throughout the rest of the day, Christians raised their voices in praise. Multitudes began to sing:

"Lord God Almighty, how great and won-
    derful are your deeds.

King of the nations, how right and true are
    your ways.

You alone are holy. You alone are holy."

P·O·S·T·L·O·G·U·E

"Listen," says Jesus. "I am coming soon!
I will bring my rewards with me
to give to each one according to what he has done.
I am the Alpha and the Omega,
the first and the last,
the beginning and the end."

Happy are those who wash their robes clean,
and so have the right
to eat the fruit from the tree of life,
and to go through the gates into the city.

But outside the city are the perverts
and those who practice magic,
the immoral and the murderers,
those who worship idols,
and those who are liars, both in words and deeds."
(Revelation 22:12-15, TEV)

About the Author

Michael A. Youssef, a well-known author, lecturer, and academician, currently pastors The Church of the Apostles in Atlanta, Georgia, one of the fastest growing Episcopal churches in the country. He holds the Th.L. degree from Moore Theological College, Sydney, Australia, the Th.D. from Fuller Seminary, Pasadena, California, and the Ph.D. from Emory University, Atlanta, Georgia.

He has been a guest on the "700 Club" and the Moody Network and has published six books, including *Leading the Way, He-ism Versus Me-ism,* and *The Leadership Style of Jesus,* which has been translated into Korean, Spanish, Portuguese, and Chinese.

Dr. Youssef lives in Atlanta, Georgia, with his wife, Elizabeth, and their four children, Sarah, Natasha, Joshua, and Jonathan.